LEGEND OF CAEMERIS

VOLOC'S REIGN

BOOK TWO

CLARE L ROLFE

Cover artwork by Cathy Larsen Design
Text designed and typeset by Cathy Larsen Design

A catalogue record for this
book is available from the
National Library of Australia

Rolfe, Clare L.
Voloc's Reign / by Clare L Rolfe
Legend of Caemeris
Paperback ISBN 978-0-6450880-1-4
Ebook ISBN 978-0-6450880-2-1
Printed and distributed by Ingram Spark

Contents

The World of ARGLETHIUM

NORTHERN ICELANDS
VS OF WHITEFANG
Forest of Enan
NORTHERN RANGES
DOANDA RANGES
Doanda
Doanda Bush
OM OF DRAXUS
The Mighty Choasa R.
LANDS OF CHOASA
Ancrid City
Boabs
Kensai
MIDDLE OCEAN
of an
osiaan Citadel
MIDDLING ISLES
GREAT RED WASTELAND
SANDY SEAS
IRON COAST
Seraf's Altar
Land of Bluesmoke
Mountains
Forests
Rivers
Plateau
Free trade route/territory

Farag

Ange searched throughout the Keep of Lido peering into the columns of water. There were creatures still floating inside them but now they lay lifeless. She touched one of the columns.

'Not even a ripple Nekoda.' She spoke attempting to see deeper into the dark blue of the water.
Nekoda nudged her hand. His back was bare where the fire had scorched him. His hide was mottled pink and black flesh in contorted ropes. He sniffed the columns indifferently and meandered his way through the vast cavern. Ange stroked him as she let him lead her further into the maze only to become disheartened the more, she saw. They came across a series of pillars that stood in semi shade. They were so tall Ange could not see where they ended Suddenly a white tentacle appeared followed by huge translucent eyes. A thousand little crabs hjsuddenly appeared from behind the great creature. Ange's heart swelled with joy realising that not everything was dead in the water spirits' home. She placed her hand on the pillar and the crabs swam towards it but did not break the trembling barrier of water. Nekoda barked with excitement. Suddenly

they scattered as a black shadow engulfed the eyes snuffing out the two beacons of light. Pitch black met Ange and Nekoda on the other side. A strong sense of foreboding washed over her that one day she would find herself in a place such as this with nothing between her and that darkness. A sob of fear began to form in her throat as the blackness seemed to magnify more trying to push itself into her.

'Ange, Nekoda. Come' called Bensah.

Nekoda raced off hearing Bensah's voice. Ange roused as the trance of the darkness broke. She followed Nekoda with an even greater sense of doom weighing on her mind. Looking back into the watershed pillars she thought she saw a slight glint of red move away. She ran back towards the others wanting the comfort of their voices.

Gildas, Sa and Bensah were sitting around a fire. She joined them as Sa handed her something to eat. She refused it. Her heart pounded like the bush drums when danger was near. She placed her hand on her chest thinking she would feel her moving underneath the skin but instead she felt the prism. The same bubble of fear formed suddenly as she the thought that this thing would not save them from the beast that hunted for it but only bring them closer to its black heart.

Sa looked at her concerned.

'You must eat Ange. You will become sick if you do not take nourishment.' She thrust the leaf filled with some cooked fish and roasted roots. Ange tasted nothing as she swallowed the food reluctantly.

'What are we to do? We cannot lie in wait here for the beast to rise again and simply let it take what it wants. Girl show us this gift so much has been destroyed for' spoke Gildas.

Ange looked at Bensah not sure if she should show Gildas.

'We have no choice, Ange. We are here because of it.' Bensah urged her.

She pulled it out of the pouch. It sat on her hand. There was a slight warmth coming from crystal. Gildas went to touch it but she quickly pulled away.

'No, you mustn't.' Ange held the prism to a shaft of light. A rainbow formed on the opposite side to where the light penetrated it. The cave came to life with brilliant colours. Ange felt the heat move into her arm and towards her chest into her heart. She began to gasp. Suddenly an image vague and shadowy came to fill the cavern. Voices could be heard, cries of battle and a roar, deep and menacing grew in tenor eventually becoming a piercing scream. Ange put it away in the pouch as hers and the others' ears began to prick from the cacophony that was released. They all heard the voices and recognised them.

'It holds the key to the spirit realm and this battle that comes to our lands is who shall have dominion of it.' Spoke Ange.

Sa closed Ange's hand over the pouch.

'Take care child, you hold the key to our survival, and we must ensure that you keep it. Now I understand the destruction that will come if the wolf rises and takes it.' Sa spoke unsettled at the power the girl wielded.

'We cannot battle this beast. Once it grows strong again it will simply kill us and take it. Those gods fight amongst themselves and leave us to die at the hands of a demon they bought with them. You have been marked girl and our lives are forfeited to protect you.' Gildas growled.

As he looked at her his face rigid with agitation, he saw her eyes widen with fear. Ange pointed to something behind him. He turned towards the deep pool that lay to his back. Two snake eyes lay just above the surface. They were so large that the face would not fit inside the cavern. Gildas slowly moved to a crouch as did Sa. Both placed their hands on their weapons. Vipax tongue slithered out of the water and tipped them both over. Gildas hacked at the coiling tongue but it quickly shot away.

'Keeper of Caemeris and its custodians, you have called me.' spoke the serpent.

'I did not call you.' Ange squeaked as the tongue came near. She clung to Sa trying to get away from it as it slithered over her body toward the prism, but it pulled away before touching it.

'Ascendant's tears call to me. I am one of the first sentinels, Vipax. You lie here at your doom. The destroyer heals its wounds already. North you must go, the ice will be difficult for you to be found for the light of Belmaris is strong. The gift better hidden from the eyes of Voloc.'

'What are we to do ancient one for even in these lands under the protection of light and water will this shadow not grow strong enough to defeat all?' Sa had sheathed her dagger sensing the serpent did not mean them harm.

'The doom of Arglethium is not set like the stone it was forged out of. Even Vipax does not see or remember all things. Vipax time has come and now it is time for the clayborn to see beyond their own lands and understand the world which made them. See beyond the density of dirt and water and decide if they will defend it against the light and shadow of the Caemexa. Their power lies within you as well.'

'But how we have no armies of spirits or men strong enough to defeat it.' Gildas snarled.

'Ah I would like to fight you mighty warrior. Battle is in your blood. You have lead men before to their death.' Gildas tensed as he felt the serpent's eye bore into his mind and heart.

'This is different. No amount of muscle or sinew, battle hardened with the lust for victory will overcome the power of these spirits or the demon wolf.' He snapped back diverting his eyes to break the hold of Vipax inside him.

'The tears are a gift and a curse made by the same things which made the Caemexa. It is only that we are blind to these things and their power.' Ange could feel the gaze of Vipax pierce her mind. The prism burned into her flesh the more the serpent's gaze lingered.

'Go north. The ice is the demon's enemy for now. Gather the strength of the clay born and ready the clayborn to battle fiercely. The tears of Ascendant are what Voloc seeks. Only the Keeper and Voloc may have dominion over the tears in this world and no others. Remember if the gift calls me then it calls the demon.' As Vipax spoke its eyes slid under the water barely leaving a ripple. The others watched it slowly disappear, each slightly relaxing as the leviathan left. Ange remembered the serpent's words that only she and Voloc may lay claim to the prism. The heaviness of the burden that had been given to her swelled even more. A deep longing to lie down next to her mother back at her village and let the sand take her engulfed her. At least then she could rest and be with her family again.

'The Graan are all mighty warriors, the myths of their strength and fierceness are told across many lands. Are you not

Gildas Gol the Lord of the Graan? Would your people not help us?' Bensah looked at the northerner warily.

'Ay but imprisoned and disowned by my clansmen. It is twenty cycles since I have set foot on my tribe's lands. None will know me and if they do, the Gol name is a curse.'

'What choice do we have Gildas?' spoke Sa.

Gildas wandered off into the deeper recesses of the cavern. He looked at the columns of stilled water and the creatures they contained. Would Jarrod still be alive? He thought of Jesse and his brother. They had been his only true allies but, in the end, he had destroyed them. He felt the pricking burn of Voloc and the god Ascendant staring at him from inside. He turned and saw Sa standing behind him looking at the column. Her hand rested on it.

'We need to go north. Ange will be safer in your ice lands than here. What price was placed on your head warrior by your clansmen?'

'Death.'

'Are any of your clan alive?'

'I left my brother, but he may be dead by now or banished. Even if I can convince the Graan of uniting how would we defeat the demon? Its strength is beyond any here.'

'The Orynth told us of allies. Ko's people will not live in bondage to Ranik. I will seek Kado the heir to the throne. The people may unite under him or at least the last vestiges of the Draxus dynasty. Their superstitions of the ancients are still strong amongst the lower classes. They would still believe the favour of the dragon lay with the Drax. Even if we keep the girl safe until the gods' destinies are decided.'

'I would rather my death be in battle then to live like a caged rat rotting in silence with no hope or use' snarled Gildas.

The memory of the cell from Banrock came back to him as looked into the eye of a massive blue whale frozen in the pillar of water.

'We will fight Graanar, but I fear silence and patience to learn what we have become ensnared in, is where our hope lies' cautioned Sa.

Ange, Bensah and Nekoda had joined them. Ange moved to one of the columns and looked at her reflection. She was tall like Tessi. As she stood near the column the pouch around her neck touched the water. Instantly the water sprang to life. A school of rainbow fish began to swim.

'I will show your people. They will believe you and you will lead them against the shadow.' She looked directly at Gildas. He looked away nodding reluctantly. Her form annoyed him. Anything weak he wanted to strike down.

'We walk by day. Once we reach the northern ranges it will be hard. We will need furs once we pass over the mountains for the ice and the winds of Raajn will pierce your flesh and bones.' Nekoda barked and nuzzled Gildas hand. He looked at the mangy dog 'You especially hairless mongrel.'

The next dawn rose, and the group readied themselves with their satchels to carry food and water.

'Remember this place for it will serve as a refuge for the times ahead.' Spoke Sa as she joined Ange and Nekoda. Bensah and Gildas rolled a stone across the entrance and pulled vines across to conceal the door to the Keep. The canopy of the forest blocked the morning sun plunging them into a dark tunnel of vines and towering kapok trees.

'Let Nekoda go, girl, he will be our warning if there is any danger.' Ange did so reluctantly. Her heart ached for the dog almost as much as it did for Tessi as it bounded ahead of her.

The climb up from the floor of forest soon became so steep that they used the thick vines as ropes to heave up toward the edge of the forest. By the mid-morning they suddenly emerged into full sunlight.

'Where are we?' asked Bensah as they stood looking across a huge plateau of sand and eroded rock.

'I am not sure. The sun rises in the east over the desert ranges. We must be in the land of Matavia' replied Sa.

'If we follow the sun until it reaches its zenith then we can walk straight towards the north. Is there a path across the great mountains warrior?' asked Bensah.

'Ay but it is dangerous. Our road will be through the passage of Blackspike and Redblade to the east. We will need to be wary for the thieves and brigands that make their home there. They will be watching. We can buy furs and skins at the markets at the city of Shadaraq. I have nothing to barter with. Trader, assassin?'

'I have gold ducks but are worthless now but for the gold in them' replied Sa.

'I have some beads and goat skin that can be sold.' added Bensah.

Ange fingered her beads which Bensah had given her and Tessi so long ago. Bensah saw her and smiled. 'Maybe but we will use ours first.'

After seven days of walking the group reached the outskirts

of the village called Farag. They had gone un-noticed but the people and traffic on the road thickened the closer they came to the trader route. The pace had been fast to the point that Gildas and Bensah had to carry Ange. Gildas' strong back had been reassuring as he effortlessly carried her. The gentle way he had placed her back on the road when they had decided to stop belied the outward aggression of the warrior she had thought at the time. Standing looking down the main track leading into the township they saw smoke rising in lazy tendrils from a few huts. There were no people to be seen walking in the streets. Gildas pointed to the shadow of the northern ranges spanning the horizon.

'We will need to reach the base of the mountains by another cycle of the moon otherwise the road to my homeland becomes impassable. While the sun never sets in north the winds of Raajn are twice as lethal than in the summer. The great storms scream their revenge on the Ice Mother herself.'

Sa had turned towards the east. She could see the high peak of Sadom and thought about Kado.

'Gildas, I will meet you at the base of the mountains before the next full moon. I will bring furs and supplies for the journey.'

'Assassin we will not wait for you. You can purchase what we need on the way.'

'Nay I will go to the sisters of Sadom for coinage and the temple. There will be scrolls from ancient times that may help us fight the demon. I also seek Kado, heir to the throne of Ko.'

Sa gathered her pack. 'I will meet you at the gates of Shadaraq three dawns before the next moon.'

Ange grew frightened and grabbed Sa's arm to stop her. Sa was more their protector than Gildas.

'You cannot leave.' Ange pleaded with the assassin.

'Let go Ange. You will be safe with the warrior and trader. I must do this for we will need many allies for the days ahead. I will return. Remember what Gildas said. Our lives are forfeited because of this jewel the gods bring here. You must endure and be strong now and learn to fight. Let your childish ways go and stand now to your destiny, freely chosen or not. Sa Tuc has always been a bonded slave with no ointment for the wounds I have endured because of those chains. I protect you only until the day you are my equal so that you will not seek an arm to lean on but rather to stand with me as a friend or against me. I am not your mother Ange. Rise up. Meet this fate whether the victory will be life or death.'

Ange did not answer but she knew Sa spoke a truth.

'I can't bear to lose anymore ...' Ange saw that Sa would not understand as she peered into her unreadable eyes.

Sa pulled Ange's hand off her arm and turned to Gildas 'By the next full moon at Shadaraq.'

'We will not wait for you assassin.'

Gildas eyed the easterner and realised what a formidable weapon they had as their ally. Sa Tuc only knew how to fight. Her whole being was honed to kill and her purpose to meet the perfect opponent. A faint glimmer of hope rose in his chest. If she and this heir could rally the Draxus territories along with the Graanar, then perhaps there was a chance to defeat this demon spirit.

Nekoda barked at Sa's petite black figure in the distance as she turned to leave. She did not look at Ange again. Ange's heart was confused; it was like Sa did not care about them or anyone. How would she ever be her equal to fight, her body alone was lame making her a burden. Why did she stay with them if she did not care about them?

'Come warrior, I grow more wary every moment we linger in the open of the demon returning' urged Bensah.

He scooped Ange up and hoisted her onto this back. 'Nekoda' called Ange.

'We will make camp on the other side, but we will need to replenish food and water here.'

The travellers were not met by anyone as they walked past the main market. A rotten smell began to drift towards them as they neared the huts on the outskirts. Gildas recognised what made that sort of stench when burnt.

'Trader cover the girl's eyes and put a cloth over your faces. We cannot stop here.'

Bensah gave Ange a sash to cover her face. The smoke and odour began to thicken around them. A woman came to the door of a hut and threw some water out onto the street. She saw the three of them and quickly ran inside. Gildas unsheathed his sword. A thick plume of smoke blew into them; Ange began to gag from the smell of it.

'What is it, Tata?'

'Quiet!' hissed Gildas.

The smoke suddenly cleared. Bensah threw his hand over Ange's eyes to make sure she did not see anything as his own stomach began to churn from the sights in front of him.

'Start running trader. I will follow you. Head towards the

outcrop of rocks up there. Yours and the girl's hides will fetch a high price here.'

Bensah ran off just as the doors of several huts began to open. Bensah saw the skins stretched on sticks and the charred remains in the ashes. A misshapen child's face stretched in an immortal scream looked at him. Stuck between two sticks and pierced by a third were a torso of ribs and the arms of a babe. He sped through the village. Ange vomited on his shoulder as the smell clawed at her throat.

Gildas cut down a villager running towards him with a fork. Another threw an axe; it bounced of his leather vest. Effortlessly Gildas lopped the man's head off. Then he was surrounded by a dozen villagers. One catapulted a rock which missed his head narrowly. The Graan clansman came to life. Roaring at them he slashed his sword. Blood mixed with burnt flesh. Gildas eyes flashed as he saw each of their faces. Finally, only a man and boy stood before him. Grabbing the man's throat, he thrust him near to his face and spat into it.

'What are you doing?'

The man did not show any fear

'We had nothing to eat. Ranik takes all our crops and still demands payment to feed his armies. We only use the second child from the family. Leave one to live. The skin, it brings a high price with the court. They make gloves and cover their chairs for the women's chambers. It is soft you see. Your friends. They would be valuable.' Gildas saw the man's eye glint with a potential bargain to be struck as he smiled at Gildas with a rotten mouth. 'We could negotiate.'

Gilds ran his sword through him. The boy ran away.

Taking a log from one of the fires he began to light the huts as he ran through the village. The fire soon caught quickly leaping amongst the thatch rooves. Gildas raced up the hill towards the rocks. He saw Bensah in the distance fighting off two men. Nekoda had latched onto another man. The villager ignored the vicious snapped of Nekoda as he groped for Ange who sat high up in a tree. She was screaming. Gildas flew into them and instantly hacked at the villager reached for Ange and then brought another down at the same time as Bensah slashed the third man's throat.

Bensah was heaving 'Thankyou brother. They nearly had me.'

Gildas nodded satisfied. He reached for Ange. She tentatively took his hand. 'Come girl, if I wanted you dead it would have been before now.' He noticed that she had the prism in her hand. She quickly hid it again in the pouch when she saw him looking.

'It was to help Tata.'

'We must make haste; the smoke will alert the nearby villages. Beware of the serpents warning girl about that treasure. I fear it is more of a curse then a blessing.'

'In all my days as a trader of all things, that is has been the worst of what a person would do to one another, especially the babes. You have seen that before?' asked Bensah watching Gildas cleaning his blade on the grass.

'In times of famine the old, weak or young are used as food. That has been a practice of the Matavians for many cycles of their people. The court even considers the flesh a delicacy at feasts. The locals found the skin bitter, so they learnt to make gifts from it. Your indigo hides are rare and would have fed this place for a full cycle of a moon with the coinage they would bring.'

'What will we do to find supplies?'

'We will hunt in the forest trader. Come it is nearly dark. I want to get to the woods for shelter otherwise we will become the hares being hunted in open fields.'

Ange had seen the things the villagers had done, and she had also seen the savagery of Gildas. These images raced in her mind and along with the callousness of Sa, dread consumed her heart, perhaps it would only be her left. It would have been better if she had died in the village with her mother, at least she would be at peace now with their ancestors.

2
The Zhang

'Spider you never change.'

The old woman eyed the assassin carefully. She scanned the scar that ran along the finely sculpted cheekbone to the mouth causing the lips to contort into a mild sneer. The old woman felt the creaking in her bones as she tensed waiting to find out what Ko's protégé wanted with a washer woman.

'Well Sa-Tuc what is it that brings you here and who do you work for now? I thought all the servants and people of Ko would have been devoured by the Matavian devil.'

'Ranik lacks subtlety in his attempt to scour our lands. He is like the magnesium salts of the Dragon festival, a searing lance of heat that extinguishes as quickly as it started. Most of the people fled to other territories but they will return as Ranik's spreads himself thin and he can no longer defend the lands he has annexed.' Sa replied.

Sa-Tuc sat across from the old woman on a tree stump. She watched her craggy lips suck on a clay pipe. She was well into her ninetieth summer now and her name was Mosanna Li. Her hands were gnarled from years of service to the Ko family and reminded Sa of the dead trees that had collapsed onto the forest floor; withered, grey and twisted from their slow demise. One hand was crippled with only a thumb and middle finger that could be used. It had been a punishment from the Empress when her linen petticoat had not been starched enough.

'Ko is dead spider. Subtle or not he is driven by spirits that have been dredged from the shadows. Sorcery is at work and will not be defeated by the levers of political whispers or stealth manoeuvres.'

'The Ko dynasty will rise again, Mosanna. The dragon lies dormant beneath the river of spilled blood. It will feast on the bitterness and rise again.'

'Under whom the fop Kado? He cannot be found. The soldiers have searched for the heir to hang him out to the world and show the death flames of the mighty Ko Kingdom.'

Good thought Sa, they do not know of his whereabouts.

'Another of the Lords will rise against Ranik. There is too much wealth to be had and greed will find a new slave. Mo, I need to exchange these ducks for trader coins. I also seek information.'

The old woman took one of the coins and tested its veracity by biting it. She got up and went inside. Sa thought she could almost hear the bones grind inside the worn body. Returning with a small sack she pulled out a handful of bronze discs with a hole punched in the middle. Sa handed over all her coins and counted only six of the discs.

'That is not enough. You can melt the gold.' Sa spat attempting to intimidate Mosanna.

The old woman placed a few more of the bronze discs in Sa's hand. 'I have one more request Mo. Where do the monks keep the ancient scrolls of the Sindrax Dynasty?'

'That will require a payment Spider.'

'I have no more to give.' Sa began to get edgy. Mosanna's mouth cracked into a sneering grin. One tooth stuck out of the black hole.

Suddenly Sa felt an arm around her neck, and another twisted her hand up behind her. Sa struggled but gave up quickly after appraising that her assailant was stronger. Mosanna came towards her and thrust a knife towards her throat.

'What are you seeking Spider?'

'I seek my old guard. They are scattered, I am without a suzerain to serve, so once I gather enough, I will sell our services to whoever needs us.'

'The assassin of Ko becomes a mercenary eh. So why do you want the ancient scrolls of Sindrax?' The point of the dagger pierced her skin threatening to penetrate more deeply.

'Would Lord Ranik not give a worthy price to know of Ko's treasures, buried far away from his Palace for times such as these? Perhaps we can make a deal. Come now has the spider ever given her prey a chance not to be eaten.'

Sa saw a glint in the old eyes and the dagger retracted just slightly. Mosanna nodded and the unknown assailant eased his grip.

'Tie her.' Sa felt the twine go around her wrists.

'I see that my suspicions were right all along about Ko's hidden wealth and cache in the ancient caves of the Dragon. Their whereabouts only known to Emperor and Heir. How to find them was always the key and it seems you now know Spider.'

'I am not sure if the scrolls will contain the knowledge, but it will do to start with. I once took the life of an old servant of Ko and as the last of his blood drained, he whispered the scrolls of Sindrax. I knew that the servant had been sent to check the caves after reports of Lord Tsang and Hosinax were conspiring against the Emperor. The scrolls location is unknown. But I am sure many secrets would have been revealed on the pillows you lay in your youth Mo.'

Mosanna lit her pipe and chuckled to herself at the ease with which Sa-Tuc spoke of killing. She had never seen a creature so nascent at bringing death; like a spider that must devour to survive even killing her younglings and mates and at the probing question of the information she may or may not have to divulge.

'Mo, what are your terms?'

'Ginda will go with you to where the scrolls lie and return them to me. If they are not returned to me than I shall request my own price from Ranik himself.'

'This Ginda is skilled with a blade why not send him alone now that you know of their value. The old mantis could be wealthy indeed.'

'Because to get to where they are kept, he will need your skills. He cannot read the ancient texts. The monks will not reveal how to read the secret riddles to show the location of the scrolls even under the pain of death. He is strong but not learned.'

'If it is a long journey perhaps you will not live to enjoy the reward.'

Mo laughed sensing Sa's attempt to guess the distance of the scrolls' location.

'It seems we need each other assassin. Ginda tie her to the stump and come with me.'

Sa felt the bonds on her wrists tighten even as she struggled to undo them. Ginda knew his work. She attempted to listen, but the old woman was too cunning to the ways of Sa and they had gone out to the path that led to the village. As they walked back the grandson held the arm of the old woman as she resumed her seat on the old wicker chair.

'Ginda will lead you to where the scrolls are kept and return them to me. If the knowledge is useful then we will split the price sixty forty. The deal favours me assassin. Take it or leave it.'

Sa nodded her agreement. 'We leave today. Loosen these.' She put her hands up to be untied.

The two women eyed each other carefully. Sa's face broke into her contorted smile. Mosanna Li studied her again; the twisted smile reminded the old washer woman of the first time she had seen that face. The grubby urchin being brought to the kitchens after she had been discovered in the orphanage. Dishevelled and sore ridden but under General Doan's tutelage polished to an exquisite gem rising to become the confidante of the Dragon Emperor. So far, she had never been defeated by an enemy in a fight. Sa-Tuc was an ally worth having, for as an enemy you were sure to discover her true talent. The price for the information contained in the ancient scripts would be valuable indeed to whoever was willing to pay for it, Ranik or even one of the remaining Feudal Lords.

Not all of them had been found and executed.

'A partnership between the spider and the mantis? You are honourable Sa-Tuc?'

'Are you Mosanna Li?'

The old woman chuckled.

———

Sa looked at the monk far up the cliff face paying homage to the sunset as it descended over the destroyed lands of the Drax Empire. The sounds of his chanting were refreshing after the long silent trip with Ginda. His tongue had been removed long ago. Sa wondered what he had seen or heard to warrant such a punishment. Normally this castigation was for traitors or servants who had seen too much but were still useful. Perhaps his grandmother's plots had led to the infliction of such a wound as a warning to stop meddling.

It had come as a surprise to the assassin that the scrolls were kept in the main temple of Sa Dom. Sa had been privy to most of the machinations and cogs of Ko's rule but never the location of the cache of wealth accumulated since first generations of Drax or even how to find them. The legends surrounding the vast caverns first carved out by the Prime Emperor Sindrax one hundred deci cycles ago. The horde of treasure immeasurable against anything of renown in the world. It was believed the first Drax still lived there that had mated with a Princess to form the people born of Dragon fire. Sa thought of the jewel which had been entrusted to Ange. How insignificant the Drax treasure was compared to the power which lay around Ange's neck. The vision of those rulers so blind to what now haunted the lands, even the mystique of the Dragon seemed insignificant when placed next to stone wrought by these unknown spirits. Perhaps a new destiny was to be fulfilled at the hands of Ranik. But perhaps that was the purpose of this invasion by the rulers of light and dark. To wake the dragon once more and swallow the tyrant and his ensorcelled mind. To purify the dragon flame so it may rid its' progeny of corruption and greed for petty stones and trinkets. As Sa reached the path that lead to the inner sanctuary of the temple her heart swelled with anticipation that not all was defeated. As the great sea serpent Vipax had said, there were allies who would help.

She and Ginda began to climb but instead of going towards the usual entrance, Ginda pushed back some ferns revealing an unused stairway. He went ahead. The climb was so steep that it was like scaling a ladder. Eventually they reached a table of rock. Sa looked down at the main entrance to the temple, half a league below. The monk had disappeared with the sun letting the moonlight glint on the polished granite of the dragon's head which adorned a doorway. Ginda pointed towards another break in the black granite above them. A platform like the one below had been carved out of the rock, but it looked like a normal crevice in the cliff face. There was no stair way or ladder, they would have to rock climb using only uneven surface of the cliff face. Ginda went first. He gurgled as he gestured for her where to put her feet and hands.

Stepping into a cave, Ginda grabbed Sa and shook his head to indicate not to go forward. He found a brand of twigs and heath on the wall and lit it with some flint. He pulled it across the wall. There were symbols painted evenly along it, stretching from the ground to halfway up to the roof of the cavern. This was why Mosanna needed her: to read the way into the sacred chambers. Sa examined them carefully and soon realised that some of them could be deciphered. The way to the chambers was set with traps for thieves. Taking the torch off Ginda she studied them carefully memorising the symbols. The first row at eye level she thought she may understand. The logo for the Sindrax lay in the middle of flames pointing toward their right.

'This way Ginda.'

Three tunnels came into view like black eyes. Sa veered towards the far-right hand side. A cool breeze met them as they walked further into the mountain. The tunnel began to narrow to the point Ginda had to hunch over. Then it suddenly opened out into a deep chasm with slim bridges crisscrossing over it; each of them identical in width. The bridges led to an unbroken wall of rock with circular doorways carved into them. Sa peered down at the stonework of one of the bridges but did not go any further. She saw the palpating masses of tiny dragons entwined in slumber.

She gestured to Ginda to not make a sound. She pointed to the creatures that formed the footpaths across to the rock wall. Only one of the doors lead to the ancient texts. The tiny dragons were the key to show which one.

Ginda looked at her in surprise. He clasped his hand over his mouth.

Suddenly Sa started to whistle. It was lilting tune which gently echoed in the chamber. There was a sound of fluttering. The tiny dragons began to awaken. The creatures separated, many of them yawned as they stretched their wings and then flew up in a hyperbolic swoop to reform into one bridge wide enough for Sa and Ginda to cross over the other side.

Sa stepped onto the bridge of Zhang dragons gently. It was solid as a rock. She saw their eyes watching her as she walked across.

Walking along the wall she found three concentric circles carved into the wall. She carefully inspected them and finally placed her hand on the left one in the third ring from the edge. The wall glided smoothly into a recess in the rock. Inside was a chamber with shelves of rolled parchment from floor to ceiling. Two tables stood in the middle with a stool underneath each. Ginda went to walk in, but Sa caught his arm.

She took a rock and rolled it across the floor. Suddenly something flashed down and landed on it. Sa thrust the torch on it and a tiny dragon sat hissing at them.

Sa pulled out some salted pork. Another one flew down and they fought over it viciously. The Zhang were no larger than a hand but were ferocious. Their mouths revealed razor sharp fangs and their neck fans had poisoned barbs on each spoke of cartilage which would wrap around their prey.

Entering the chamber, the two dragons retreated to their roosts with the scraps of meat. Sa closed the door so she could speak without disturbing the creatures outside.

'Look for scrolls marked with the symbol of a dragons head and sword behind it. Like this.' Sa showed him the underside of her sash. 'Be quick, the Zhang will be hungry again soon.'

Ginda got busy looking over at one wall of scrolls and Sa went to another. Ginda grunted as he pulled out two large parchments. He took them to the table and unrolled them. Sa came over and looked at them both.

'Keep this one, not that one.' Soon Sa also found what she wanted as well. She unrolled it while Ginda was busy still looking. It was the one she needed. Ginda bought more over for Sa to inspect. Above them came the sound of fluttering and small squeaks.

'That one. Quickly they grow restless.' She placed the two parchments in her pouch. Ginda stopped and grunted, gestured that he should take them.

'We will change when we get outside.' He hesitated but suddenly one of the Zhang swooped down towards him clipping his head. Blood tricked down onto his face. They both ran out towards the bridge. The dragons followed them out after them letting out high pitched screeches. Far away the same screech could be heard in response coming from above. Reaching the bridge Sa carefully walked across with Ginda close behind. The two Zhang started to peck at Ginda's head. He gurgled in panic and began to lose his footing. He grunted loudly as blood dripped down from the cuts and torn flesh. Suddenly the footbridge disintegrated beneath them. Sa leapt to the other side to avoid falling into the bottomless chasm. Ginda fell. The Zhang speared after him, chasing the scent of their prey and next meal.

Suddenly an almighty flutter of wings and screeching came swooping down towards her. She ran towards the tunnel. There were hundreds of them following her. They began to batter her almost forcing her to the ground, but she managed to get inside the tunnel. As the tiny dragons flooded in pursuit clawing at her feet, the sound of a whistle broke through the cacophony.

The melee stopped and the dragons retreated. She waited. Another whistle. Peering out the dragons had taken to their slumber once more in neat ropes across the gaping crack in the stone floor. There were a few still tearing at what remained of Ginda. Some hissed at her as they sat just near the entrance of where she lay but did not attack her. Then a monk appeared before her. He walked through them silently as the compliant pets manoeuvred around his robes and sandalled feet. He looked at her.

'Who are you?'

'I am Ko's assassin, Sa-Tuc.'

'You were stealing the sacred scrolls Sa-Tuc that incurs the penalty of death.'

'The Ko empire is destroyed for now Dragon master. I seek information to restore his kingdom. Does not the heir to the throne lie here, Kado Kodrax?'

The monk nodded. 'What is it that you seek Sa-Tuc? The scroll you hold is very ancient, from the First Dynasty. You will not understand the script.'

'Dragon master, more than just Ranik fills the oceans and rivers with blood. A demon from the spirit world has come and the First who made covenant with the ancients, perhaps were given knowledge of how to destroy this demon. I seek the scrolls of Sindrax to locate the caves of the Dragon but also any knowledge of the first covenant made in the land now known as the Iron Coast which may help in the battle against this demon.'

'We have sensed a disturbance in the heart of the mountain for many moons. Show me what you have taken.'

They walked back over the bridge. The monk looked old but walked nimbly across the bridge even amongst the Zhang hissing and spitting at his feet. A horde of them had settled on a ledge below. He whistled and they suddenly lifted into the air. Sa saw the pure white skull of Ginda lying on a ledge below.

'The scrolls come with the penalty of death assassin if they are ever removed from this chamber. Even Ko's formidable weapon will not be able to leap over that chasm without her hide intact.' Spoke the monk warning Sa that there would be no way to escape with the texts.

'I have learnt the ancient calls which woke your pets Dragon Master.'

'Yes, but the riddle lies in knowing how to put them back to sleep once they have feasted. The taste of blood removes the spell and it must be re-learnt each time. They would have followed you out and to your tomb assassin' retorted the monk.

Unrolling the parchments, the monk inspected them closely.

'Ah yes the armoury of Ko. For your uprising Assassin. The caves of the Dragon are found under the feet of Jun in the great mountains to the north. I am not certain you will find them though. Only the heir to the Dragon may touch this treasure. You must chronicle what you find there if you live to talk of the treasure so that it remains in our memories. It can only be reached beneath the sea with the help of the dragon's breath.'

'But how was the treasure stored there?'

'Why slaves were bribed to swim there and leave the treasures in the arms of the ocean.'

'To die as they delivered it?'

'Their families were well compensated Assassin.'

Sa's mind took in this information. Kado was the key to the treasury but how. There must be another way into the armoury. Sa could not accept the myths of sorcery were its only way in without drowning in the bay of Drax waves.

The monk unrolled the next scroll. He placed the torch nearer and began to read. He ran his finger through the old text.

'It makes a reference to the dark and its lords but nothing about how to destroy them. There is a gift that resides here on the earth that is most precious and the ancestors of the ancient may be called to spill their blood, the blood from the covenant, to keep it from being lost. Prime Emperor was drawn to a power deep within the rock beneath our lands. It was where the bedrock of the citadel was laid. Where the Emerald city stands.'

'I know of what you speak. But what of the demon that has come here?'

'No there is nothing written about a shadow, only that the sun has the power to release the gift and destroy the dark but also the world along with it. This knowledge is old and lost to most now. Indeed Sa-Tuc, how does the assassin of Ko become known to unseen spirits who seek to call the bonds laid down with the first peoples and their ancestors? You are a foundling, not of royal blood.'

'The Ko family are of the ancient blood that is spoken about. Kado needs to be restored. The spirit of our hearts and desires gathered the descendants of the first tribes and has bestowed this gift to an easterner of the lands of Choasa. My purpose is still not fully known. We seek refuge far away from here and hope to rally an army. An alliance of the northerners and Draxus hope to protect the keeper of the gift until the fate of the gods is determined. They lie within the jewel for it was the Lord of Arglethium that rose and destroyed what remained of the Drax City. It had slumbered with one half of the jewel inside its bosom to keep it hidden from the demon deep below in the heart of the world. It was this power which drew the first Emperor to build the citadel of Drax. This god of rock and earth was awoken by the call of its brethren. The one called Ascendant. But these brethren battle now for dominion over its power. We fear that our fate lies in who is the victor in their realm. And while they battle the shadow Voloc grows stronger here, with no spirit strong enough to thwart it.'

'So perhaps the end days have come.'

'No, not until the greatest of these spirits is finally defeated. Is there nothing written about a weapon or sorcery that will weaken the demon?'

The monk perused the texts once again letting his knobbly fingers trace the letters.

'No, only that when the end has come all will be awakened and the first of all the blood will mingle in a river of destruction, even the creatures of earth and sky shall be called to witness. Destinies shall be forged in the fires of destruction and remain unbroken. The gift is both a blessing and a curse. It will awaken the blood of the sun, stone, and water and all will be called to battle.

'Will the Dragon rise?'

'Yes, it speaks of the Dragon Lord who first came; whose flame shall once again render all to smoke and ash. The dragon flame will awaken to meet its destiny but not its victory.'

He rolled the scroll up again and placed it back in the wall.

'You can never take these from here Sa-Tuc. Even the Emperor dared not take them and destroy them. I will take you now to his son. He has matured in his time here.'

3

Hendra Valley

Ange was surrounded by overwhelming waves of colour and thunder. She could hear the lady's voice; it was so sad, pleading for something to stop. A voice answered the calls of longing but it pierced Ange's mind like a blade. A massive shudder rippled around her causing her to fall over. A creature larger than the elephants of home strode past her. It looked like the lizards that would skitter along the desert except it was massive. The tail alone towered over Ange. She tried to scream but no sound came.

'Keeper what are you doing here?'

The voice was familiar, but she could not see anyone. Suddenly Ange was shrouded in darkness. She felt something watching her. She began to whimper with fear as cold fingers seem to work their way into her mind.

'The deceiver shall find you feeble one and bring it to me. It will know the scent of your blood. The clay you stand upon shall be doused in it. I will hold the memories stolen from me and then I shall become what was my destiny.'

She felt the icy whisper gently breathe against her ear.

She turned to run from it.

All a sudden she was wrenched into daylight and Bensah's face was looking over her. Nekoda licked her on the cheek and she hugged the dog tightly.

'What were you doing? Was it a dream, sister?'

Ange felt for the pouch around her neck and noticed that a tip of the prism had come out. Her neck was sore, and a blister was forming where the stone had been resting. She hoisted it back into the pouch and shivered. She would have to be more careful. Feeling drained she pushed Bensah and Nekoda away.

'I am hungry Tata' she said as she stood up.

Gildas returned from scanning the fields from an outcrop of boulders near where they had made camp. Their escape from Farag had been at a quick pace to put as much distance from the village as possible. Some of the townsfolk had followed but Gildas slayed them with ease. The smoke from the burning huts drifted far into the sky in a thick black plume.

'More will come graanar, the smoke will signal the other villages.' Spoke Bensah.

'Ay, trader it will.' replied Gildas.

'We cannot risk fire, so we will have to eat these.' Ange held some roots and suedes she had found amongst the bushes.

She sat and began to rub the vegetables with a rock to remove the skin. Nekoda sat near her but she ignored him. She threw one each to Bensah and Gildas as well as Nekoda. She bit into hers and spat it out instantly. The bitterness burnt her tongue. Nekoda whined with disappointment. 'These are better roasted.'

'Sister, you need to eat.' Bensah grimaced as he chewed the tough flesh.

'I know Tata but' her voice trailed off not wanting to speak openly especially in front of Gildas.

Ange stood. She looked across the plains below them with the aching sadness she had felt when Tessi was taken away by the slavers. The voice from the prism came to her causing the same stab of fear as if it had followed her. She would need to be stronger, but her body was too weak. The god seemed to believe in her but why. The god was more powerful than her.

'Ange come eat. We will need to keep restore our strength with food while we have it.'

She reluctantly came back to the two men. Bensah threw her another type of root. 'This one is less bitter.'

Bensah looked at her, the nightmare had shaken the girl.

'Did the god of the dead flesh and green eyes haunt your dreams Sister?' asked Bensah.

'I am not dreaming, Tata. I cannot feel or smell in my dreams. The world is real.'

She took a bite of the suede.

'Yes, these are better Tata.' She smiled slightly at Bensah.

'How far is it until the pass of Shadaraq, Graanar?' Bensah changed the conversation mostly to avoid asking more about Ange had meant.

'At least twenty days. The main roads are full of Matavian soldiers and men from the land of Unstaadt. I noticed one of their camps south east of here. We will be seen easily as the main guard will have outlying scouts for at least half a league. We will need to head directly through the valley of Hendra. It will be hard going, and we will need to be wary of the creatures who live there but we have no choice. Still it will harden us for the trek to my lands, the ice will try to take you; cut you down. It senses your weakness.'

'Ay the desert is the same' replied Bensah.

They watched Ange wander off with Nekoda throwing a stick and the dog bringing it back.

'How did you know the girl? You are not her father.'

'No, her father and I were traders together. We grew up in the same village. I found her when the plagues came to our lands. Her sister was taken by slavers.'

'You have traded in more than just goods. I saw the mark on your wrist.'

Bensah rubbed the scar on the inside of his left wrist.

'Hmm, many summers ago now. When the great dry came and all crops failed, this was before I had been fledged as a man, the men from my village needed to find other ways to survive. Our tribe was feared by the smaller ones around us, so slaving seemed the easy way to make trades for food. We did not mistreat them though like the northerners. Once the rains began again and we could grow crops and feed our animals we stopped it.'

'Why the scar?'

'It was punishment for those to remember what we did. After that, our village moved further south to the lands of the Chenak plateau.'

'Why the girl? You could have left her there.'

'I don't think the spirits would have let that happen, do you? I remembered the brutality of those days when I was a trader of my people; girls like Ange were tormented and then put to death as amusement for the wealthy nobles. I remember a girl

I had sold, from a neighbouring village, she was like Ange in her body. I remember the merchant who bought her, had her perform at a meal to make fun of her. She was put through this until she died from just being exhausted. No rest until she dropped dead from being taunted. The merchant clapped me on the back and paid me handsomely to make sure I found more of them. When I returned to my village, I saw her mother and family, they asked what had become of their child. My scar is well deserved and hardly payment enough for my deeds. Perhaps by being here now it will appease Ancrid for those times.'

Gildas watched the traders almost black eyes scan the movement of the girl and the dog.

'We put children like the girl to death. They are no use and cannot fend for themselves if the storms come and we are snowed in.'

'Yes, we once did the same, but the elders began to find use for them as midwives and carers for the motherless.'

'The northerners you speak about are they from Unstaadt?' asked Gildas.

'Yes, brutal even to their own kind and all around them.'

'They came from my people, many generations ago. Ranik will find them to be a strong weapon. I noticed their banner amongst the camp of his soldiers at Drax city. We will need to go through the Vale of Hendra. It will be the quickest road to Shadaraq. We will risk being seen if we dwell too long in the trader route. Stealth and pace will be our strongest allies for what dwells there.'

'You will make the girl and me brutal warriors yet Graansman.'

'Good. I fear it will be needed.'

The sun dipped low in the sky with a weak twilight.

'Trader, I will watch until the moon crests overhead and then you can watch until the dawn.'

Bensah nodded. He put his satchel under his head and lay back with his cloak wrapped around him.

'It should be cold by now. It is leaf fall isn't it?'

'Yes. Something keeps these lands hot.'

Gildas looked at the pale red glow behind the ranges to the west. Ever since the battle with the gods at Drax city the sky had been tinged with a dark pallor.

Ange came over and lay down near Bensah. Nekoda sat on his haunches to remain on watch. He yawned at Gildas as if in comradery.

Gildas took a small dagger out and began to sharpen it with some flint. Silence was everywhere, no birds or the sound of a breeze amongst the trees.

Dawn crept towards them reluctant to disturb the night.

Ange noticed that they had been walking downhill since they had begun their trek at dawn. The terrain slowly became rockier with no definite path to follow. She had not slept as her mind had been plagued with the voice and memories if what she saw in the realm of the jewel. She had lain with a sense of doom which was splitting open before her like the vastness of the red deserts of her lands.

'Where are you taking us warrior?' she asked.

Gildas turned and looked at her. She was becoming better at the trader tongue. He kept walking without answering.

'Answer me or I will not go any further.' She stood defiantly on a rock. Bensah stopped and looked at her and then burst into laughter at her insolence to the Graansman. He could cut her down with one swing of his hand.

'We are going through a valley. We cannot take the main roads now. What is it sister? Your father would have whipped you for such defiance.' Bensah replied as he reached up to carry her, thinking she was tired. She stepped back from him.

'Do you know who I am Tata. Do you know what I carry? If I fail, then what will happen to all this? You and Nekoda. All of this. Even this warrior who brings his weapon and skills of war trade will die.'

Bensah looked at her confused. 'We must keep going. We cannot waste time. That demon could awaken at any moment. The warrior is all we have, so we must follow him.'

He reached up and grabbed her she struggled and slapped him on the face.

'Let me go, I will make my own way, I must be strong and be ready. Carrying me makes me weak.'

Bensah let her go and followed her stunned by the slap. Gildas had stopped up ahead and was watching and thinking how the girl needs to be thrashed. She does not know how lucky she was to have the trader bother with her at all.

They began the descent into the valley. The valley stretched for almost a league and had an eerie quiet to it as the rock repelled the sun in defiance to its warmth. Its walls were formed of serrated quartz and marble, pure white and razor sharp. At the bottom stood an impenetrable forest of conifers. It looked from the sky like an eye glaring back at the sun. The crevices between the jagged stones seemed alive to Ange, watching her like they knew all that had happened to bring them here. She shivered as they began to climb down. Bensah offered her a hand, but she refused. She would beat this place and not be swallowed into its emptiness.

They had made it halfway down when the sun began to dip below the lip of the high rocks forming the ridge where the Vale of Hendra began. Black shadows yawned out of the crevices.

'This is too slow trader; we will have to carry her.' Spoke Gildas as he and Bensah waited for Ange to reach them

'She will not let me.'

Gildas grunted in annoyance. 'I will check for a cave.' Nekoda went with him.

Ange placed each foot carefully on the treacherous rocks and slid down. She was exhausted but kept telling herself there was worse to come. Eventually she reached the ledge where Bensah stood. Sitting down she pulled a cloth from her satchel and dabbed her bleeding hands. She took some salt and put it straight on a gash in her weak leg. Tears came to her eyes as the salt worked its way into the wounds.

'Here let me help.'

'No Tata, don't you understand, I must do it.'

Gildas returned and saw the wounds.

'Enough of this brat, it will fester and then you will not be able to walk at all. We will carry you the rest of the way. It is still a long way to the edge of the valley. We need to be in the cover of stone and shadow before the sun falls.' Ange began to protest as Gildas grabbed her. 'Do not worry the ice will harden us all or we will die in its embrace.' Gildas strode into the mouth of a cave. Inside was veiled with wall of darkness beyond the reach of the pale daylight.

The night settled and Ange lay down to sleep despite the pain in her leg. Begrudgingly she knew Gildas was right. She had been looking at his shape at the entrance to the cave; he was so large that he virtually blocked the whole opening.

She woke suddenly but something held her down. It was Bensah's hand. She could feel his head shaking telling her not to make a sound. She looked and saw Gildas was cinched up against the wall. Piercing yellow eyes appeared at the entrance of the cave followed by a second set. A sniffing sound came. Gildas restrained Nekoda with all his might to prevent the dog giving chase. The figures moved on. Gildas let Nekoda down.

'Muzzle it or it will try and chase them' hissed Gildas.

'Who were they?' Bensah placed the mask over the dog's snout.

'Fendaan, they live in the caves. There will be more of them as we reach the heart of the valley.'

'Why didn't they see or catch our scent?'

'I don't know. They may be younglings not yet trained well enough to hunt. We leave at first light.'

'Wont they see us during the day?' asked Ange

'No, the sun blinds them so they live in the very deep caves that reach almost to the other side of the valley. The daylight will hide us.'

'Have you been here before Graansman?'

'Ay, it was when I was making my way south to the merchant's boats, many summers ago now. I met two of the Fendaan and nearly lost my life. They are exiles from Unstaadt but over generations have learnt to live here. They were hunted down by their people's armies and so came to hide in the caves that underlie all this rock. Overtime they could only bear the dark; that is why their eyes are like the mountain lions. By nightfall we should make the forest. There are no entrances to the caves down there. It was where I took refuge.'

Bensah carried Ange on his back until the sun reached its zenith when they rested a bit. Her leg while it looked ugly had healed over. She peered into a long thin crevice which was beneath where they walked and wondered if those people were down there. Gildas hoisted her up and easily began striding along the rocks. They had kept the muzzle on Nekoda and hoped nothing caused him to bark. The echo would penetrate deep into the rocks and would alert the cave dwellers to them. Soon small bushes began to appear amongst the white harshness around them. Just as the sun dipped below the edge of the basin on the second day, they entered the forest. It was cool and moist, soothing compared to the rocks. They kept walking until Gildas stopped and plopped Ange on the ground. That night, no one slept as they heard the calls of the Fendaan. Bensah and Gildas held Nekoda's jaw shut as he struggled to answer almost endangering them all. Yellow eyes appeared at the edge of the forest, but they did not draw into the trees. As soon as first light broke over the valley Gildas grabbed Ange and told Bensah to make haste.

'We need to get to the path that leads out of the valley before nightfall. That was too close. They sensed we were here.'

'Why didn't they enter into the trees?'

'I think they think the forest is cursed but they know we

have to climb through the rocks again to leave the valley so they could be waiting for us at the other end.'

Gildas and Bensah ran. Ange bobbled roughly on Gildas back. Her mind raced as she wondered what she would have done without Gildas. She would be dead by now. Even Bensah would have not known the danger that waited in this place.

Gildas crashed through the ferns. He scanned frantically trying to remember the way out. Suddenly the canopy above cleared and he looked to see where the sun was. He stopped; it was past the midday. He looked around and saw a pond and suddenly his memory came back to him; it was where he stayed when he took refuge. It was not far now.

'Hurry! We are almost safe.'

The sun eased its way again toward the horizon with no thought of the desperate travellers below.

'We do not need to climb again for the path leads to flat lands toward the trader route through a gap where the white rock ends.'

They quickened their pace, but Ange looked up at the black mouths above them and thought she saw yellow eyes watching. She heard Gildas heaving with exhaustion and tightened her grip to let him run more smoothly. He felt her do it and sensed her fear.

'Almost their girl.' He wheezed.

Bensah could see the end of the cliffs. He let Nekoda go to run ahead, he would warn them if anything waited at the other end. He eyed the sun; its rays had gone from yellow to red and would soon leave them. He prayed to the god Ancrid to protect them this bit more.

The sun set as they were a hundred strides from the end of the caves. Gildas was at full speed and heard the whistles and calls above them. Nekoda barked when he heard them. They would know where they were now. Suddenly yellow eyes appeared above them and began to make their way towards them.

Bensah was keeping up but he was not as strong as Gildas and his trader body was wearing out. He could hear Nekoda barking up ahead. Suddenly hands shot out and latched onto his legs. He stumbled full tilt into the ground. He kicked furiously to dislodge the claws off his legs. His foot connected with a head. There was a grunt. Getting up he started to run again but he saw Gildas had already made it to the fields beyond. Ange was on his back and had started to scream. It was too late when Bensah saw the eyes suddenly appear ahead of him, he ran straight into the wraith thinking it would disappear like mist. He put his head down to try and ram its chest, but it was like solid rock. A wild screech came from the mouth and more pallid grey hands caught Bensah and pulled him down. He fell while thrashing his arms and legs trying to escape the creatures as their yellow eyes surrounded him.

Suddenly an arrow flew past and hit one directly in the head, then another. The Fendaan fell on Bensah and he was struck with a rotten smell. The skin was sweaty and grey. The horde turned to see Gildas running at them, bow in hand. Nekoda leapt into the air and tore the leader's throat out. A cry came from the black mouth, sounding like an animal in its death throes. It was answered with more of the same. Bensah got and up and thrust his sword into the back of one of another and Gildas finished the other one off.

'Quickly trader.' They ran as the mouths of the caves above glowed with more piercing yellow lights. The screeches became deafening as they reverberated off the rocks.

They ran into the field and kept running for half a league until Bensah collapsed in exhaustion on the grass.

'Tata!' screamed Ange thinking he had died. Gildas stopped and went back to him. He could taste blood in his mouth.

Bensah rolled over heaving 'I am alright. Is it safe to stop?'

Gildas nodded. Putting Ange down, she ran to Bensah. Nekoda came loping up full of life and drool.

'We are safe. They will not leave the valley. They fear and loathe all outside it. One day I will return and slay them all but only after I have caught one of them and seen it in full light.'

Bensah looked at the scratches on his legs from where the hand had grabbed him. Ange came over to him with her pouch of salts.

'Oh, Tata look how white your bones are.' She chided as she washed the gouges in his leg. 'This will hurt but it works.' Bensah pulled away as the healing mineral worked its way in.

'Where did you get that Sister?'

'I found a lot of old crab shells in the water gods caves. After I touched a few of them I noticed it healed a cut on my hand. So, I ground it up and put it in a pouch.' Ange replied.

'I am glad you did.'

Gildas came back over to them after scouting near the end of the forest to see if the Fendaan had followed.

'They have retreated.'

Ange took some more of the roots out.

'Will it be ok to make a fire?'

'Yes, we are at least a league to the next town. I think we need some meat.' Gildas strode off.

Ange gathered some sticks.

'Tata are you ok?'

'Yes sister. It will pass. If your crab salt heals as well as the crabs tasted, then I will be fine.' He smiled grimacing as he felt the healing pricks of the ointment.

Ange ate as she stared into the plains distracted, not tasting the roasted hare Gildas had caught. The voice from the prism ran through her mind and each time it was like it was just near her again. It was like the screams from the people in the rocks. It would know who to seek when the time came. The fear that had struck her heart when she saw Bensah fall, had been like the darkness in the prism. If she lost Bensah as well, they all could have fallen, the northerner also, her mind raced. The last thing she saw before leaving the world of the spirits appeared before her; the great god from the earth was bound in chains by a monster on a throne and the lady was bound to a tree with a searing wind tearing her to shreds. The gods of this world were losing and every step she and Bensah and Gildas took seemed to bring them closer to death. The images blurred with the yellow eyes of the Fendaan. Her legs twitched with fear wanting to run and escape back to her mother. She could not defeat these spirits or the malice that now surrounded her. How will she fight, with what weapon or strength? Sa Tuc came to mind. The assassin, she was little like her and yet she had heard Bensah and the warrior talking of her with respect and fear. She fell asleep thinking of Sa; perhaps the assassin could teach her to fight.

4

Heir

'Now! You are slow for the progeny of the Dragon!' barked the monk at Kado.

They began sparring together with sweat spraying off both men. Kado wheezed heavily as his lungs scarred by years of smoking in the dens, struggled to gulp the air his body needed. But the monk brought the anger out provoking Kado to shoot three quick blows into the monk's stomach. The primary was too wiry and toned however and he floored Kado in one quick flick of his staff.

'Enough, Kado Kodrax you have done well today.' Kado lay writhing on the mat nodding.

'Thank you Master.' He gasped out. Elder Jhodin looked up and saw the dragon-elder and Sa standing at the entrance to the chamber.

'Sa Tuc, it has been many moons. You have been spared from Matavian blades.'

'Yes, for the moment Elder.'

Kado got up. He stared at the servant of his father not quite believing she was alive. Sa bowed slightly as he looked at her.

'I have no kingdom to inherit now Sa Tuc, so there is no need to bow.'

Kado began towelling down.

'Why are you here assassin?' he asked tersely.

Sa hesitated not wishing to speak in front of the monks. Kado nodded at both teachers politely indicating that they could leave.

'I am here to take you away from this place. I journey north on a quest, but I also seek the heir to the Kingdom Draxus, so the great Dynasty shall rise again to meet the invader of the of the great lizard's land.'

Kado ignored her as he bathed from a bucket of water.

'Ranik will hunt you down if he knows you are alive. Rebellions are beginning to rise already. The Feudal rulers can be bought. They will unite under the Drax banner for the right price.' Sa persisted.

Kado scoffed

'Sa Tuc has finally lost her mind. The Lords will squabble amongst themselves as Ranik slowly usurps their lands and wealth. They were only loyal to the leash my father placed on their greedy necks. That has gone now but is easily replaced by the Matavian. You are chasing a lost cause. Let the dynasty of the dragon whither with some glory still intact.'

'You have recovered well Kado. Your eyes are clear for the first time in a long time.' Sa spoke.

'Perhaps the veil draped upon my gaze by my father has finally been lifted assassin. Gone with the zephyr of defeat along with his ashes.'

'I have come to ask that you follow me north. I am travelling with people to seek refuge amongst the northern clansmen. It will be safer there. A storm is coming that is greater than what has passed.'

'The Clansmen are fierce they will not accept an easterner in their midst. I think you are lost indeed assassin.' Kado replied.

The gong tolled for the midday meal.

'Join me Sa Tuc as an old friend. We can eat here.'

Sa nodded. There was a small table and chairs near a window carved out of the granite cliff. The view from the window revealed a vista of the southern stretches of the Drax Kingdom. In the distance the smouldering ruins of the Emerald Citadel paid homage to its demise.

'I cannot linger long here Kado. I am to meet the others by the next full moon at the base of the northern mountains. We will take the road that leads to the ice lands.'

'Have they paid you for their protection?'

'The spirits made our lives forfeit to this quest.'

The food was bought in, a simple dish of fish and rice. The austerity and the difficulty of getting supplies to the temple since the invasion had meant that the food was even blander than normal.

'I miss the food most of all. The suckling piglets at the Moon's Harvest festival.' Kado heaved a sigh of regret as he put a clean robe on. Sa noticed the bruises and scratches on his back and torso.

'It is part of the illness from the poison as it leaves the body. I had nightmares of being chased. They seemed so real that my body bears the scars of the torment.' He spoke as he noticed Sa looking at him.

Sa looked at him 'What chased you in your dreams Kado?'

'A scorpion at first. But there was something more potent on the edges of my dreams which was willing it. I could never see what it was. And then there was this spirit, like a woman, but not real more a phantom.'

He began to eat, grimacing at the taste. 'Catfish is so bitter.'

'The people I go to meet can tell you of their dreams Kado. They like me have also met this phantom. Kado I want you to come north with me. It will be safer there. You are right, there is something that stands behind the scorpion, but it dwells now here on this world not in the shadows of dreams.'

Kado looked at her. He felt that he did not know this Sa. He saw not fear but insecurity in her eyes. He stopped eating.

'What are you talking about, assassin? Sa Tuc spooked by a nightmare. I do not believe it.' He taunted playfully.

'The spirits that made this world have awoken but in doing so a demon from the great darkness has come also. It is this shadow of malice that haunts your steps. The phantom you see in your dreams is one of them. The woman in your dreams is the spirit of our hearts and desires. She and her equal and this demon seek the blood of the ancient people who first walked the lands. The fate of us all rests now in the battle of the gods in their world and to keep the demon from destroying this one.'

Kado laughed 'Sa, have you been keeping the dens busy in my absence. Hmm I think we may be able to pair up, I grow bored here.'

'Enough Kado. You make light of something that if it finds you, which it will for the blood that flows through you is of the ancients also, it will destroy you. But it is not your death it seeks but the power the demon will draw from you to grow stronger. It also seeks a potent stone of power. It has been entrusted to one, a desert dweller from the lands of Ancrid City. It is this girl who now guards the gateway to these gods. The demon will rule them if it seizes this stone. If the demon controls this weapon its strength will be too great to be conquered. All of those who the spirit visited have blood of the first tribes. I believe there is something in the covenant first made by your ancestors can protect against this shadow. Your ancestors and now you have been blessed or cursed because of this stone. The phantom could have snatched the stone by now, but something thwarts it.'

'Hmph, I will destroy myself in the end Sa.' He finished the last of the meal. 'Still I cannot stay here and become a monk.' He looked at Sa grinning ironically. 'I still get the fevers at night so I am not sure if would be able to travel with you just yet, particularly such an arduous journey. Why don't we go to the eastern province of Lord Yun? He was always a loyalist. He would see the value in providing refuge to the former heir to the mighty Ko dynasty. He has defended bravely against Ranik and I have heard he remains safely locked in his Keep on the eastern shores.'

'I can only stay another night and then I must leave. There is nothing here for you Kado. With time we may convince the Lords to unite under you banner again. It is more important we take Ange to safety in the north. There is only one other called for his ancient blood who can defend her against this malice which haunts all our steps.'

'So, you want to add to the misery with a fop like myself.

Sa Tuc you are a glutton for punishment.'

'I have been told by the spirit to take you with me Kado. I can train you. You are strong now. I see a light in your eyes that had long been dimmed. Come with me and I will show you what I speak about.'

Kado looked at Sa and studied her face. Scarred and weathered, not one pretty feature. Her eyes bore straight into him. Kado could never conquer her. She was solid as the walls of this mountain but ever loyal to him. So many indiscretions that Ko had never known about, Sa had tidied them up. Never a thankyou was uttered from his lips just drunken salacious words. And even now she sought him out to save him. Something had penetrated that wall of rock to make her seek him out. He stood and gestured to take Sa's hand.

'Come old friend I will show you how the monks have trained me to be sharp and swift. Perhaps even better than you Assassin' winking at her.

She stood as Kado cleared the mat. He threw her a stick. He matched her for five blows only and then she bested him. The slightest of grins formed on her face.

'You see, assassin I would have fallen after the first blow not so long ago.' He was laughing but it soon turned into a coughing fit. Sa looked at him and wondered if he would be strong enough.

'I will need to rest often Sa Tuc.'

'We will leave on the dawn Kado Kodrax.'

The pink rays from the dawn crept their way into the chamber from the window. Sa stood looking down in the dense forest below. She wondered about the demon and the others.

With men such as Kado chosen to be the ones who will stand and fight, it seemed that fate had already decided who would be the victor. The elation of hope when she found the scrolls was now replaced by a gnawing doubt at the sight of the prince.

Kado stood before Sa wrapped in a sandstone coloured tunic and pants. The tunic was well cinched at the waist and contained a sword and dagger. His black hair had been shaved by the monks. He and Sa almost passed for twins but for Kado standing a foot taller. His pack was near his feet. Sa was talking to one of the monks. He had only seen him once before at Sa's arrival. He gave Sa some rolled parchment and bowed as he left. Sa placed it inside her apron. It was valuable whatever was written on it for her to place it so close to her body.

'Come Kado, we have far to go yet.'

He hesitated, feeling a little perturbed at stepping out into the world. He had been here for almost six moons now without leaving. The Grandmaster stood at the entrance to the temple.

'Grand master your guidance has been invaluable to me once again. Do not bow to me now, for I am Kado Ko, traveller on the road. I fear this may be my last sojourn Grandmaster. Ranik's gaze will come here soon, what will you do?'

'The temple has withstood the rise and fall of many tyrants from the lands below, this one will be no different. Word has come that Ranik does indeed look this way, so your departure is welcome to us and fortuitous for yourself. Ranik will not defeat this place, its secrets are only known to us. Perhaps your next visit to this temple will be as the new suzerain of the lands. Farewell, Kado Kodrax and Sa Tuc, safe be your journey and may the breath of the dragon be kind to you.'

Kado was bemused at the thought of him returning as a suzerain, his father was despised by all that knew him. To rally the Drax Lords again and territories would be like making Sa Dom Mount move. Bowing he and Sa made their way to the far side of the temple.

'We will have to travel by day to avoid the shadows. As spouses, we will not be noticed.'

Kado bowed facetiously 'As you command wife.'

By nightfall they had already reached the village of Knedron. It was bustling with activity and being a trader town, it had a mixture of the Matavian culture with the Draxus descendants.

Kado looked pale and Sa had noticed him falling further behind.

'We will rest here tonight on the outskirts. We can buy supplies at Shadaraq.'

Kado nodded obediently. They threw their gear behind some shrubs. It was early autumn and the nights were still warm. They ate some dried meats and bread. Kado lay back looking at Sa.

'Why did you come back for me?'

'I have explained that.'

'But there was nothing to behold you to me, even this spirit that told you to seek me there was no real need for you to find me.'

'What am I if I have no lord? Besides Kado you have not witnessed what I have seen since the last turn of the summer moon.'

'I am no master to follow or lead, you know that. My father was right about me. I have not the prowess or strength of mind to lead a kingdom of people. You know me best Sa Tuc. At twenty-five summers, I will not change.'

'Yours and mine fates seem bound together since we were children. I will see this last war until the end and the world's destiny is decided. Would you not prefer me on your side Kado?'

He laughed 'Indeed I would prefer it assassin.'

Sa lay back and dozed a little. She had been calculating how long her journey would be to the Shadaraq pass. Kado had lain back and appeared to have fallen asleep.

A twig breaking woke Sa from her sleep. It was deep in the night and completely still. The sky was clear of clouds and the stars were brilliant in their watch over the lands below.

Sa sat up and noticed a possum foraging in her backpack. She shooed it away but not without it absconding with some food. She looked across expecting to see Kado, but he was not there. Instantly alert she scanned the bushes around to see if had gone to piss. After a few minutes she stood looking towards the lantern lights twinkling from the outskirts of Knedron.

The ale house was full of soldiers, merchants, madams, and the tricksters trying to rip all of them off. The Matavians were the rowdiest. Sa also saw some of the Unstaadt guards, the scythe and vulture insignia on their leather burkas was distinctive. For Ranik to have them in his pocket would add to his domination. Moving around the far wall different threads of the chatter amongst the crowd came to her. At the very rear sat some old men with distinctive square haircuts and indigo eyes. It gave way they were from eastern most parts of Ko's Kingdom known as Gaxonne Province.

Cinching her way behind them she leant over and whispered

into one of the old men's ear. He was puffing on a long pipe and playing dice. He reeked of smoke and years of whiskey like rotting trees in the forest.

'Dhai Ma, old Fox, you still stink like a whiskey vat.' The old man chuckled as he puffed billows of smoke around both of their faces.

'The phantom of Ko, lives.'

'Where are the lily houses in this place? I seek a merchant to give him a message.'

'Assassin you have lost favour with the world, a messenger girl now.'

'Food is food. Knowledge is useful.' Sa replied.

'They are on the far side of the village Tuc. Be careful, they are full of soldiers. These usurpers have discovered the joy a den can bring and fill their bellies and minds and never leave. Ranik may be defeated yet.' He chuckled and rolled the die again. She threw him a coin and made her way to leave.

The streets were bustling as the morning goods were being bought by bullock trains. Sa saw rows of people in chains. Soldiers whipped them and dogs savaged the weaker ones. These were not new images to her mind but now the people at the end of the Matavian lashes were the ancestors of the dragon. She looked back towards the ale house; no one appeared to be following her. Taking a short cut in the back alleys to avoid the melee on the streets, the smell from the lily urns soon met her and she followed her nose the rest of the way.

Dhai was right, the soldiers lay everywhere in a hazy stupor along the gutters and streets around the houses. Children rifled through their pockets to find coins. She went in and could barely move or breath the vapour was so thick. She began to search the cots. The high paying guests would be kept away from the rabble. She moved to the rear where red curtains partitioned off rooms. Sa peeped in stealthily searching for Kado. Leaving she went to the next three dens along the street and still did not find him. With the dawn the streets began to full. It was becoming more difficult to walk around the village freely. Someone would notice her soon and ask questions.

Entering the main road, she walked to the other gateway which marked the edges of the town to see if Kado had gone to buy supplies. Just as she was turning to head back to their camp Sa noticed a house standing apart near the edge of the river. It was two storeys and leaned toward to the right. There was the familiar plume of smoke surrounding the building but strangely there were no soldiers or beggars waiting to be given the leftovers from the paying customers. Sa headed over to it. The door was painted red and a rotten sweet smell permeated from behind the closed door. She opened the door and was greeted with a narrow corridor. There were closed doors along it until it ended abruptly with window covered in some sort of thin leather curtain pulled taught across it. A mark was on it, it reminded Sa of a tattoo the Unstaadt wore on their forearms. The doors were so numerous that it seemed impossible that rooms were large enough to fit anyone in them. She quickly counted ten along each side of the hall. She had started to feel giddy from all the fumes in the other dens and this place was particularly heavy making her stomach and head spin. Every breath she took seemed loud and slow to her. She heard a moan up above her. Taking the stairs to the second floor the layout was the same as below. So many doors, why? Normally there were just curtains. The moan came again; it was further down the corridor. Placing her hand on the dagger, she listened and followed the whispers. She opened the door closest to her and saw a man on the bed with two girls. The cloying smell hit her hard and made her stumble. She remembered what the sweet smell meant; the weed Gorung. The healers used it to mend the soldiers and cut off their arms and legs that would not heal. Smoked like poppy seed it was far stronger and made you lose any feeling and stopped you from moving, but you did not fall asleep like you did with the lily.

'Who is he, general?'

The girl had a scythe in her hand was ready to slice the man's head off. The girl looked around and saw Sa. A man suddenly came from one of the corners behind the door ready with his axe. He had the black eagle insignia of Matavia tattooed on his chest.

Sa flung the dagger at the man's face and hit him directly in the throat. The girl came toward her, but she lazily twisted her neck. The man groggily called out. Sa went over to him and tried to rouse him. She slapped him. He was filthy with bruises and sores all over him.

'Who are you? How did you get here?'

He looked at her, not understanding what was happening. The whites of his eyes were blood red, an effect of the Gorung. Sa left him and retrieved her knife from the general's chest. She wiped it clean. Closing the door, she took the key from the inside and locked it and threw it out the window at the end of the corridor. She heard giggling in the room just adjacent.

Bracing herself for another attack she opened the door quietly. It was dark in here and heavy with smoke. A girl sat on a man, naked. Searching the room there was no one else. Sa grabbed the girl and pulled her off the man, squeezed her neck enough so that she blacked out. On the bed lay Kado. He had a dreamy look on his face. Sa looked up when something caught her eye. An iron frame hung from the ceiling with cogs to lower it down towards the bed. Off it hung hooks with razor sharp barbs. This place was like a slaughterhouse. Sa tied the girl up. She needed to wake Kado up to get him out of here. She slapped him across the face to rouse him. He looked at her and smiled.

'Let me oblige Sa Tuc' Kado spoke with a groggy voice as he tried to grope her waist.

'Wake Kado, we need to leave here quickly. This place is a butchery for the depraved.' She hoisted him to the side of the bed. He sat there lazily and began to lie down again. She opened the curtains to let some light in. There was an urn, seeing that it was full of water, she picked it up and tipped it over Kado. He roused.

'Quickly get dressed.' She threw him his clothes. He slowly started to put on his trousers. Sa heard footsteps on the stairs. She went to the door and locked it and waited behind it with her hand on the dagger.

Kado happened to look up as he put his shirt on and saw the grappling hooks swinging above him. He also saw contorted leather masks in frames hanging around the walls of the room. They looked like faces. He threw up on the floor and then proceeded to finish dressing. He looked across at Sa and wondered what she was doing.

Sa eased the door opened; the corridor was clear. She grabbed Kado and began to guide him down the stairs and towards the entrance. The silence was pierced again by the footsteps and knocking behind locked doors. A thick wail echoed behind them as they descended the stairs. Kado stumbled. Sa hoisted him up and raced towards the door.

When the morning light of the dawn hit Kado's eyes he threw up again.

'Hurry! This is the playhouse of the Matavian and Unstaadt generals.' Suddenly two large men semi naked and drenched in blood came out of the door of the torture house.

'Run rabbits. Flee! Live a little longer and enjoy one more dawn.' They sneered.

Kado finally roused. He looked at the men and saw that they were painting stripes in the blood on their chests. A girl bought out quivers of arrows and cross bows adorned with an eagle's head.

Sa saw the forest that surrounded the village. 'We will go there and make our way back to the camp.'

'What are they doing? There is no battle here.'

'They are getting ready to hunt us and they are my match Kado. You must run hard and fast. Do you understand?' She pulled him along with her and noticed that he had no shoes. He stumbled frequently as they entered the outskirts of the forest. The soldier's war cry pierced the dense silent understory of pines and fir trees. It chased them into the shadow of the forest.

'Quickly Kado!' hissed Sa she squeezed his hand to urge him to hurry.

They were cornered a few hundred paces from their camp. Kado looked at his feet and saw all the blood. The Gorung was numbing the pain but he knew that it would hurt eventually. The two generals stood before them with their crossbows ready. The blood on their torso's and faces had been washed off by sweat. They were massive broad chested warriors; ready to be satisfied with a kill after the chase. Sa crouched in readiness as the first general aimed his cross bow directly at her. Slipping the dagger down into her hand she flung it at his face, it connected as the crossbow shot off a barbed iron bolt. Sa caught the bolt and jumped at the second general. Kado darted to the left as the Matavian hesitated from trying to decide which target to aim for. Sa rammed the bolt into his neck. The crossbow went off and connected with Kado's shoulder. He called out in pain and collapsed. Then suddenly more bolts were flying as the first Matavian got up. He stared at them with one eye socket oozing blood with Sa's dagger wedged where his eye should have been. Sa pulled the bolt out of the one she had just killed and leapt at him. The soldier got her by the throat before she could make the lethal stab. Kado could see what was happening and got up. The pain was dulled by the drug in him, but everything kept going black as the blood began to poor out of his shoulder. Sa was beginning to go limp as the hand constricted tighter around her throat. Suddenly the hand let go and the soldier collapsed. Two bolts lay directly in his chest and neck. Sa looked across and watched Kado fall over with the crossbow underneath him. She ran to him and heard the ragged breathing. She got him up and half dragged him back to their camp. No one had followed but the generals would be missed – soon a bounty would be decreed, and the hunters would seek revenge and glory.

'That was close Kado. You must be stronger than this.' Sa was binding his feet in clothe after tending to his shoulder. Kado noticed she was shaking just slightly. He took her hand to feel it. It was cold. He went to touch her face, but she pulled away from him. He persisted and placed both his hands on her face. He held her so she could not look away.

'Ever the ice queen, why do you bother with me? I cannot be what you ask Sa. Why are you doing this, risking your life for mine when it will mean nothing in the end.'

Kado pulled her close and forced a kiss on her lips. She tried to pull but he was stronger than she thought. The sensation confused her. She hit his injured shoulder and he let go. He had a slight smile on his face.

'I bother with you Kado, for the Ko dynasty hauled a sewer rat from the gutter and made the name Sa Tuc something to be feared and mastered. The spirits of this world and a demon of another have set their gaze upon us and we will never be able to run from them in this world or in their kingdoms so we are forced to choose which of them to serve. The demon will rise again Kado, it only needs to walk amongst these here and it has all it shall need to rule this world. The Unstaadt and Matavian lust for blood and domination will feed its purpose and give it strength.'

'We will all serve that purpose assassin, for I saw the hunter being hunted today, and nearly be bested by her own kind.'

She looked at him and knew he spoke the truth. He was still holding her hand and looking intently at her. She could never guess when Kado Kodrax was being true, but she thought just for a moment gratitude lay behind that gaze.

'We will leave in the morning.'

'What will I do for shoes?'

'I will find some in the village tonight. You must rest. The Gorung will wear off soon and you will know the depth of the wounds inflicted.'

She showed him two iron hooks that she had removed from the flesh of his back while bandaging his shoulder.

'They were almost ready to make you their suckling pig for the sacrifice Kado.'

He shivered at the sight of the grappling hooks above the bed.

'How long does the Gorung last Sa?'

'It would only have spared you for another hour. That's when they have their fun.'

5

Shadaraq Part One

'We cannot go around the caravan. It is too long.'

Gildas came back to where Bensah and Ange were sitting. They were hiding behind rocks in the shadows of the twilight. Before them was a long trail of slavers, traders, and merchants with soldiers from Matavia and Unstaadt escorting the outside. The procession lasted at least half a league in two directions. It was the final four leagues toward Shadaraq in the north east and the trading route to Doanda in the west.

'It is a risk, but I think it will work. Wait here.' spoke Gildas out loud as his thoughts escaped his lips.

Bensah and Ange looked at Gildas as he stood and darted behind the bushes further along the road. Bensah had been scanning the crowds for any sign of traders from Ancrid or Chensai.

'I haven't seen any of our people Tata.' Ange spoke guessing what Bensah was doing.

'No, it doesn't bode well Ange. Perhaps we are the last.'

'I can't believe that it is true Tata, but you are right, there should be Chensai merchants and there are none.'

Nekoda strained on his leash in anticipation that they maybe hunting again.

'Sit Nekoda.' Ange pulled him toward her. She lost sight of Gildas as he blended into the crowd below them. 'It is interesting the westerners choose their own now to be slaves as well as the people from Drax.'

'Hmph, you noticed how many are westerners as well.'

'Yes, why is that?'

'It has existed everywhere, but these poor fools will I expect be food for the proclivities of the nobles in Matavia and Unstaadt.'

'They will run out soon and then what will they do?' replied Ange.

'True enough Sister. What will they do? Their minds are consumed by violence. This demon only had to come and sit and watch like a lizard waiting for the flies to come on hot summer nights. It only had to wait for its feast was already prepared.'

She had been searching some of the faces of the women hoping she would see Tessi again. As the sun sunk low on the horizon the memory of Tessi came back to her in the desert. Ange thought to herself that she needed to accept she would never see her sister again. A sharp prick would catch inside her chest whenever she thought of Tessi. It was like something wanted to speak out. She just could not believe her sister was dead, but would she want her to be alive with the fate that may have awaited her. Tears welled in her eyes at this thought.

'Let her go, let her be in peace with Ancrid.' Ange whispered.

Bensah looked at her.

'It will ease Ange' was all he could say.

'I know but I still don't believe she is dead Tata. I do not know why but I sense she is still here, and I need to find her. I think there is so much more to come Tata, that this will be the least of what pain I may know.'

Bensah looked at Ange and saw how the girl had grown quickly in the time since the plague had struck their homes.

Gildas returned carrying a set of shackles and a leather lash belt.

'Put these on me and expose your branding Trader if we are stopped. She can be your wife and I am the prisoner escaped from Banrock. I have its scars.'

Ange and Bensah baulked at the shackles.

'We can't delay. If we don't begin the trek on the northern ice sheets, then it will be unpassable come the winter.'

'I think we will have to Tata.'

Ange wondered what branding Gildas was talking about on Bensah. She picked up the shackles. They were heavy and the abrasive metal pricked the flesh of her fingers. She placed them around Gildas' ankles. He stooped to let her put them on his wrists. The click of the pin locking the bracelets cut through the stillness of the night.

Ange saw the scars that Gildas had on his ankles and his wrists. She tore some cloth of her shawl and gently placed it under the metal.

'Your wounds will re-open warrior from the heaviness of these chains.'

Tears began to run down her cheeks as she thought of Tessi.

'Oh, sister I know they wouldn't have been as kind to you as I am to him.'

She stepped away from Gildas sobbing. Nekoda barked in disagreement and snarled slightly at Gildas as he handed his weapons over to Bensah to hold including the sword from Tarentess.

'Shoosh Nekoda. It's what we have to do.' Ange patted him on the head to settle the dog down.

Gildas looked at the Ange. For the first time since they had met, neither anger nor impatience welled toward her.

'Ay, you speak the truth of this world, so little is given back when one act of kindness is given. Perhaps it is ready for destruction at the fangs of the shadow demon.' He replied testing the shackles would not fall off.

'Why is it like this?'

'I don't know. I rose to greatness and fell just as quickly and now these gods seek me out again. We say in my lands the Ice Mother blesses and curses.'

Jesse's memory rose in his heart and with it came pain for the first time since he had watched her dying on the floor of his hut.

'Trader they will expect you to whip me. You will be an ally returning a rogue from Banrock. We will join the vanguard before dawn.'

'What are these people below? Where are they going?' asked Ange.

'Ranik must be moving the battle front to the west. The road forks twenty leagues from here. The western territories are vulnerable from the north, especially the Aeserean lands.'

The memories of his own invasion of Aeserean territories came back to him. The Aesereans' weak spots would be easy to find Gildas thought to himself. They were peaceful but vain

people. Their elegance sometimes blinded them to the viscious-
ness of the outside lands. He smiled a little at the memory of
their secret weapon. Perhaps Ranik may still receive a surprise
when he invaded.

On the dawn the trio moved down into the into the traffic
of the caravan. Ange walked between Bensah and Gildas. The
sounds of slaves being whipped as well as the cattle and sheep
protesting at their capture permeated throughout the entourage.
Ange felt the air beside her split as a mercenary lashed an ox
laden with goods go past her. She startled at the sound of it
and again when the man looked at her and snarled something
in a tongue she did not understand.

By midday they had stopped to take a meal. The slaves were
herded into the shade of some fir trees that lined the path. Bensah did the same with Gildas and Ange and gave him some
bread and water.

'Here desert dweller, this'll pick yur up and keep ya chattel
goin. He is a biggun, takin' him back to Madame Banrock?'

A man, Matavian judging by the accent, threw Bensah a
cask. He took a swig and nearly gagged on it. He had not had
any brew for many years and even then, he was not partial to
it. The grog made a man weak.

'Offer it to me. He wants me to get drunk so he can watch
you flog me' whispered Gildas.

'Here northerner, its more your taste' Bensah handed the
cask to Gildas.

Gildas swigged as well and almost spat it out. He nodded
his appreciation at the man as he handed the cask back to
Bensah.

'There's some of ya ice skins from the north, the ice gods musta driv' yer out.'

'What do you mean?' asked Bensah

'There's some of his lot up ahead. Two I counted.'

He held his hand up with only a thumb and pinky finger.

'I'll wager they wouldn't mind bettin' themselves against one of their own in a fight.'

Gildas sat back against a tree trunk and wondered if it would be safe to find them. If they were like him, exiles, sometimes they banded together but if they were still graanar seeking fortunes then it could be dangerous to be found alive by another clansman.

The whips cracked for the caravan to move again. They moved into formation with ease. Ange was wilting fast from the heat. By sunset she had almost collapsed. Where the scorpion had bitten her became red and sore again. She almost fell to the ground but Bensah caught her as they were nearing the end of the long walk.

'They will expect me to whip you if you fall sister.'

She nodded but worried about how much more she could manage. She took some bread and water to Gildas and then sat away from him again with Bensah.

'You should sell her, the cripple, she is not worth the bread and water.' Spoke the same Matavian. 'Her hide will fetch a high price from a noble woman of Ranik's palace. How much for her?'

'Move along trader, she's not for sale. I'll make my own profit when I'm ready and to the right buyer.' Bensah spoke.

'It is heard that Ranik has sired two indigo loaves himself

with a slave. He better keep 'em away from the queen, she might cook em up and wear em.' Another man spoke who had been sitting nearby. The merchant and his friend chuckled.

Gildas kept eating his bread. Suddenly an old woman with a ladle and iron pot appeared beside him. Her lined face and missing teeth were only outdone by her bright head scarf and tiny specs of broken glass and beads entwined in her hair.

'Some possum stew?'

Bensah nodded. As she stooped to give the ladle to Gildas she saw his tattoos and scars on his wrists.

'Been shackled many times clansman.'

'Maybe old woman. What about it?'

'Breed em tough up there in the icelands.' She turned towards Bensah and Ange to offer them some as well. 'That little un of yers, 'ow much? We use the crippled ones as entertainment in the villages. We nice to em, be sure, espeshell if they make a lot for the family.'

'This one is spoken for. Off with you old one' replied Bensah.

Gildas was looking across at the group of Unstaadt traders sitting around a fire. A few of them were maimed or deformed in some way. The girl would probably fit in, he thought to himself.

'Go on she ain't goin' to last the rest of the way without more tending. We have to goes round the great hill of Jank.'

'Why what has happened?' asked Bensah.

'The roads blocked. Its caved in. The great jaws of the drag-on in the bay opened after the mighty quake in the eastern lands which now joins ours with a bridge rubble. So ya cripple she will not make the city, another quart moon's travel – not likely she'll make it. So, how's you thinkin'?' the Matavian leered at Ange. She cringed as she saw his black eyes boring into her.

'Desert dwellers are hardier than you think old one' replied Bensah.

The old woman hesitated a moment staring at Bensah. He looked directly at her wondering what else she wanted. He noticed she was looking at the brace where he kept the sword of Gildas. She waddled off towards a group of soldiers playing dice. Gildas started to think about how to get away from the procession. The detour would delay them even more. The old woman was right the girl would not last that long either. He looked at Bensah to come over. Nekoda followed him and nuzzled his hand as he squatted pretending to check the shackles.

'The road is blocked ahead, and we will have to walk around it. It will delay us too long. There are a group of clansmen ahead. Do you know how to play the die? Go find out how things lie in the north and if there is another way to Shadaraq. A quiet way.'

Bensah got up and ordered Nekoda to stand guard and walked off. Nekoda barked happy to be sitting near Ange again and settled down near her. She scratched his paw with her finger and rested against the tree to sleep. The dog stayed sitting up on watch. The stars came out in their number equal to the noises of the caravan around them. Soft murmurs broken by loud cheers as the winners roared their success in the gambling tents. In amongst the night sounds could be heard the chink of the chains and shackles that held the captive in place.

Bensah walked slowly among the various traders holding the hilt of the sword. He saw a group of men around a cleared bit of earth. The dark small shapes of the dice flew up. Pushing through the crowd surrounding the men, he saw that it was only soldiers playing. He could not discern anyone with the distinctive tattoos of the Graan. Moving on he heard loud roars further ahead. The moon was out again but it still did not cast enough light. Following the noise, he heard a baby start to cry, it was gypsies. The old woman was walking around again with her pot of stew.

'Wiry old witch! Trying to scout out more things to peddle.'

She looked across at him as if she had heard him muttering. Her eyes were piercing and knowing even in the dim light. She nodded and then began to speak to a young boy.

Bensah eventually came to where an even larger crowd stood outside a makeshift tent. The rattle of dice in a timber cup came through the opening as the noise of the crowd suddenly dimmed. He began to push forward towards the open flaps. Inside was well lit with lanterns and in the middle were two circles of players. There were slaves being used as bets as well as gold ducks and any collateral that could be wagered. Bensah's eye caught two men standing to his left. They had shaved heads and around their necks hung the distinctive teeth from the ice bears that lived in the far reaches. Their arms were covered by their hide jackets.

'Holla up!' One of them called the die to play. Bensah heard the distinctive guttural sound of the Graan. The game played out with one of the clansmen winning. The winning Graanar stepped away with a sack full of ducks and knives and a boy of the Drax territories.

'Enough Tyl, I have my fill.' Spoke the other.

He left and made his way to the entrance. The other nodded and threw in another bet. The clansman brushed past Bensah. The die thrower called for another entrant, but no one volunteered. Bensah decided to play, if only to get near the other graanar without being too obvious. The die thrower nodded but then put his hand up to stop him.

'You must remove your weapon, place it at your back.'

Bensah hesitated, the sword from the Keep was irreplaceable. He wrapped it tightly in the leather girdle that carried it and put it against one of the poles that held the tent upright. Taking out some of the beads that he had bought with him he threw a string into the loot as the die thrower handed him some discs with burn marks of different shapes. The four dice were thrown in the air and as they landed two of them came out the same as Bensah's. The die thrower gave him more wooden discs. The game went on until someone won their chosen prize. Soon the circle had dwindled and Bensah had won so many tablets that it was impossible for him not to win. The remaining clansman clapped him on the back and offered him a swig of brew made from the igret root.

'Ay tis good. Desert man you are cunning like the lizards that live in your sands.'

'Another Graanar. I have one I am delivering back to Banrock.'

'I am Tyl of Clan Timmo. What is your prisoner's name?'

'Gildas. He did not speak of a clan.'

Bensah knew the legends of the Gol lord and thought it better to not tell the graan his full name.

'We tired of the ice bears and storms and became merchants of various goods in the south over twenty summers ago. Axl and I are brothers and make our living in trades as well. Fairer days and smoother women in the south eh trader.'

He clapped Bensah on the back and swigged heartily from the jug.

'How goes it now, in the north?' Bensah relaxed a bit not sensing any tension in Tyl. 'I was looking to do some trade in Shadaraq but wasn't sure if the routes were closed that far north.'

Tyl offered him another swig and he took it.

'Ay, we only journey every second summer and leave supplies. The winter storms are too fierce now and many of the younglings were dying. Our chieftain has moved the tribes to the eastern shores, so the bone and fur trade is lessened to Shadaraq city. Shadaraq is still open for trade. There is much still to be won there, especially now with the tyrant beset on ruling all but the Icebear herself.'

'So, the routes north, have the storms blocked them?'

'Nay yer can still make the pass but any further than that yer need to walk closer to the great cliffs of the white claw and then head to the east.'

Bensah nodded. He noticed the tent had cleared and some boys were pulling out the pegs to let the canvass down. He got up as did Tyl.

'It's a bitch graanar that we have to detour now, my goods are looking weak. We will have to spend more to keep em fat for the road to Shadaraq. How about yours? Is there another road to take?'

Bensah stooped to collect the sword and noticed it was not there. Suddenly alarmed he scanned the tent to see if it had been kicked out of the way by the crowd. Nothing.

'What is it?' asked Tyl finishing off the last of the brew and re corking the jug.

'My sword, it's gone.'

'Fuckin Matavian traders, sons of the cursed. It has probably been sold on three times by now. What are its markings? Axl and I can keep an eye for it.'

'I can reward you graanar for your loyalty on this. The sword …' he hesitated still unsure who stood before him the mercenary or the clansman. 'I will take you to my captive. He will explain its value.'

Bensah led Tyl towards Gildas and Ange. It was quiet and he saw that the other slavers had moved away from them. Bensah was glad as he did not wish to be overheard. Gildas looked up from under his cloak as Bensah and Tyl approached.

'Gildas this is Tyl of Timmo. Your sword has been stolen.'

Gildas stood to his full stature, head and shoulders above Tyl. Eyeing the graanar carefully to decide if he could trust him. Tyl stepped back slightly taken off guard by Gildas size and piercing look. He nodded to him.

Gildas held out his hand in the gesture of all the graan to make a bond. Tyl placed his hand in Gildas' and felt the strength of the man before him as they shook on it.

'You are no prisoner Graanar. What charade is being played here?' Tyl looked at them both wary with his hand on his axe.

'You are right. We are seeking passage to Shadaraq clansman and the sword is a potent gift. We came across the caravan and knew we would not escape with our lives, so we hide ourselves as slaver and prisoner. The sword was a gift given by a witch. It is blessed and cursed. I need to get it back.'

'Ay, I can help but what is a graanar doing with two desert dwellers?'

'We seek no trouble but once we are able to escape the Matavians we will continue on our way.'

'What does the sword look like? The gypsy would have sensed the witch's stench on it.'

'Its hilt is pure metal harder than iron and coated in white metal in the shape of an ice bear's head. The blade is bare but for a diamond at its tip.'

'Axl and I have not had battle for many moons. I am willing to help a Graanar even an exiled one.' Tyl stared at Gildas waiting to see if he would react to being called an exile.

'Ay an exile returning home' Gildas icy stare told Tyl that there would be no more explanations.

Bensah took off the shackles and the cloak. 'You will pass as one of their group Gildas. Here is my blade and axe.'

The men walked out into the night. The noise of the dice games had subsided and now only the hill owls could be heard hooting intermittently. Tyl and Gildas walked through the camps casually. Gildas looked at the people around him scrutinizing everything, especially when he saw a group of Matavians with the old woman sitting with them. The moon went behind the cloud making everything too dark to see. His search would have to wait until the day.

'It is too dark and will draw soldiers to us graanar. We will search during daylight.'

'Ay, Axl and I will search as well. If it is found, we will make our way back to you.' They shook hands.

Upon reaching the camp Gildas went towards the tree where Bensah and Ange were sitting. He saw the girl was asleep but Bensah was only slightly dozing.

'How goes it Northerner?' whispered Bensah as Gildas sat down.

'It is too dark. Tyl has gone to his brother.'

On the dawn the caravan had begun to snake its way off the road towards a path not well worn in the fields of Mt Draag. In the distance a dark shadow seemed to block the way they had been on and work its way up the side of the Hill of Jank. It looked like a giant beast had bitten into the mountain.

Bensah walked ahead of the others at a fast pace, so much so that Ange stumbled a few times. After picking her up a second time he pulled her close.

'Get up on my shoulders and look for the old woman.'

Ange climbed up onto Bensah's shoulders. Their search was fruitless that day, on one occasion he had thought he seen the clan of traders but lost them again in the crowd.

That night Gildas covered his face and body with a torn cloak and left Bensah and Ange to seek out Tyl in the gaming tents. He soon found it, surrounded by a large crowd had gathered with roars disturbing the night.

Stepping inside he saw Tyl playing with more slaves as their wages. He nodded to Tyl and inspected the collection of things in the centre of the betting ring. He could not see the sword.

'Throw the die master, I'll bet the shit of the pig I ate today I can haul the lot.' A man boasted drunkenly to his mates behind him. They roared in agreement. Gildas noticed they were Matavian soldiers. The man had been winning based on the number of tablets he had sitting in front of him. To boast a wager of all that the booty was a big risk, for it meant not just winning all that lay in the booty but losing it all even though it was not yours to lose. Deadly fights had been known to occur when the other punters loot had been won by the die master. The dice flew up into the air. The silence of the crowd followed it as the punters waited for the dice to land. On the last throw all four dice hit the ground and rolled in unison, star, moon, hammer and three axes. The Matavian roared in triumph as he displayed all the combinations on his discs. The other punters including Axl groaned in annoyance at the loss of the slave he had won last night. One of the Aesearean traders pulled his sword out to threaten the soldier.

'It was rigged!' he yelled. He made a move at the die thrower who stood back. Gildas saw that he had a small dagger concealed in his sleeve. The soldiers who were already on the ground divvying up the loot looked up. The crowd tensed, anticipating a fight, and moved away from the contenders. The soldiers stood up and took the defensive positions they were so used to. Droplets of sweat began to form on the man's forehead as he realised, he was outnumbered.

'Caleb toss the old bastard a toy to settle him down.'

The soldier that had made the punt rummaged through the pile of goods and found some pendants carved from the jade of Jadah Ranges.

'There ya old timer.' He flung the jewels at him. The man sheathed his sword and gathered them up. The crowd jostled him as he made his way out of the tent. Gildas stood for a moment and was about to leave when something silvery caught his eye. Looking again the one called Caleb pulled the sword from underneath a shield.

'Hey Donax, Gunta, look at this beauty.'

He held the sword aloft. Gildas watched intently and almost jumped when he heard Tyl's voice behind him.

'Is that it Graanar?'

'Ay, it is.'

'Fine it is. I think we will need to take this outside.'

'Axl this is the clansman. The one I spoke about.'

Axl looked at Gildas intently. He was not Gildas height but was twice his width. He was the younger of the two but judging by the scars on his arms and face he was the warrior.

They walked out and waited until the soldiers emerged. Some of their servants had come to help them carry it all. The one with the sword began doing broad sweeps and poses.

'This is a well-crafted tool. I do not know these marks. Gunta do you know whose smithy would have forged this?'

The soldier inspected it closely 'It is too dark Caleb. I will look in the morning.'

Caleb made a joke and the soldiers began to move off. The rest of the crowd dispersed as the die-throwers closed the tent.

Gildas came from behind the tree and stood in front of the three soldiers.

'It is well crafted indeed, by my smithy in the north. But I will have to take it off you as it was stolen from me just last night. Whoever wagered it in the tent had no rights to it.'

'Yeah and me mother's Queen of Matavia. Leave off scum! We don't trade with mercenaries and slavers.'

Gunta came forward.

Gildas stopped him moving any further by placing his hand directly on his chest. He had removed the axe he carried from his vest. Gunta flicked his hand away and instantly unsheathed his own sword. All six men instantly stood ready to kill anyone willing to take the first blow. Caleb decided to use the newly won sword. The moonlight sparkled on its blade and gave it an unnatural shimmer. He went at Gildas straight at his chest. Gildas tried to arc down with the axe but missed. The sword came up and should have severed his arm but instead it bounced off him. It threw the soldier off balance. In his humiliation he roared at the others.

'Kill them.'

The melee began with Axl and Tyl flying into the other two. It was an even match for size, but the soldiers were skilled combatants and could not be underestimated.

Caleb recovered and went for Gildas again. The axe met the blade this time and was cut cleanly in two but when it should have gutted Gildas it simply glided off. Caleb hesitated and then tried the blade on a rock jutting out of the ground. It simply sliced through it like it was bread. Gildas saw what happened and remembered the assassin's words in the Keep. Throwing his axe back in its strap he ran headfirst at the soldier who tried desperately to swing down and cut Gildas head off only to be rammed in the chest. Knocking him over Gildas wrestled the sword out of the soldier's hand. He felt a surge of power move into his arm as the ice bear's mouth moulded around his fist. The blade suddenly shone a brilliant white light, blinding everyone except Gildas. Full of blood lust Gildas killed the three soldiers so quickly that Axl and Tyl were still in mid swing when their foes collapsed under them and their heads rolled down the hill. Gildas stood a moment and then rousing he realised Axl and Tyl were staring at him and the sword. A crowd was coming over to investigate the light. Gildas quickly tried to put the weapon back in its sheath but it resisted like it still wanted to battle. Gildas tried to let go but could not.

'Help me the cursed thing won't let go.'

Tyl came over and tried to remove it but as he touched the hilt a bolt of white light hit Tyl squarely in the chest and threw him hard against the tree.

'Hold it out graanar.' Gildas extended his arm and Axl swung a massive arc with his axe but when he connected the same thing happened only this time it was with the same force, sending the clansman flying even further.

Gildas began to anger as panic rose from the crowd looking at the spectacle and the three headless Matavian lying on the ground.

'Enough, cursed son of a witch, cease this.'

Suddenly the ice bear's jaws released his hand and the blade became dim. Gildas stumbled as he suddenly became free of the hilt's grip. He looked at the crowd and growled at them to leave. Getting up he went to Axl and Tyl.

'Eh graanar, that weapon likes you. I hope I never have to fight you eh' spoke Axl as he got up off the ground.

'We will need to hide the bodies. These three will be missed soon' spoke Tyl as he wiped his axe down.

'Brothers, I need to leave here, do you know of a way to Shadaraq that will keep me concealed.'

'Go back to the hill of Jank, you can walk around its new mouth, you are alone it will not hinder you. The path that lies there is narrow, but it can be walked by a few still.'

'Who are you graanar? You are no trader with that sword, and I have never seen a clansman fight like that since our rites with the ice bears.'

'I am nobody, but I have some goods that need to be delivered safely and this sword was given as part of my payment. The woman was more than a witch, she was a spirit of the nether world.'

Gildas held his hand out and was met by the two clansmen in a gesture of bonded blood.

'Go graanar, I see the torches already of the eagle. We go back to the north this cycle once we pay our debts. Will we see you there Gildas of clan?'

Tyl asked as he let go of Gildas hand.

'I am from clan Clotte. Perhaps, brothers.'

'If you decide to go into Icelands than the chieftain Jarrod of Gol rules and has moved our people to the eastern shores. You will need to follow the Whitefang or Raajn will take you.'

'Jarrod of Gol is chieftain?'

'Yes' Tyl eyed Gildas.

Gildas heart thudded after all these cycles a Gol still ruled the Icebear tribes and it was his brother Jarrod. He sensed Tyl had figured out who he was. 'Graanar, may we meet again.'

Axl and Tyl nodded to him.

As Gildas began to make his way back towards Ange and Bensah he heard Axl ask Tyl if he felt like fighting a bit more. Gildas smiled to himself.

6

Shadaraq Part Two

The fire raged around the bodies of the dead generals. The vulture of Unstaadt and the eagle of Matavia danced together as the winds battered the banners in the night sky. The soldiers revelled in the blood and stench of the burning flesh blessing themselves before the hunt to slay the warriors that had killed their knights.

Jek, Gurna and Kan of Unstaadt had been chosen to give chase. They readied themselves as the scars of death were burned into their back with embers from the funeral pyres. One of the body's skull slipped to the side as the flesh melted and disconnected the head from the body. The skull grinned as the lust of the flames engulfed it and the funeral descended into its frenzied orgy.

'These wrappings will not do Tuc. My feet are bleeding again. The wound in my arm aches deeply also.'

Kado trailed behind Sa feeling sorry for himself. They had made good time despite the wounds Kado had suffered.

'We will need to buy snow paddles for the icelands so you will have to keep using them until we reach Shadaraq.'

'How far is it to the place where we meet your friends?'

'It is at least another quarter of the moon but only because we will have to avoid the main roads and villages.'

'But I cannot walk with these things.'

'We cannot stop Kado, the bodies of the generals would have been found. The smoke from their funeral pyre smeared the dawn grey this morning. The soldiers will seek revenge for their deaths.'

They had steadily been climbing a hill that was part of the ranges that surrounded Knedron. Kado was puffing heavily and wishing he were still at the death house with the girl. She was particularly good. He had been thinking of her during the night. Suddenly they reached the summit and a vast plateau stretched out before them. In the distance the northern peaks could be seen like a grey shadow that divided the sky and earth. The two huge mountain peaks which towered over Shadaraq lay to the northwest. Sa pointed towards them.

'We are headed towards them Kado. They are considered the tallest any person can climb. I once heard of a legend long ago. A great warrior from the south called Manon the Tall scaled them bare footed. He reached the top bloodied from the dagger sharp edges of the granite slate that they are made from. His hands and feet were shredded, and his skin flayed to the bone on his arms and legs. The eagles that nest there picked the ragged flesh off him until he died leaving the stone stained with red. The peaks are named after him: Redblade and Blackspike. Nothing grows on them. Their northern faces are barraged with raging storms which bury their feet in razor beds of black granite and shards of ice. Manon cursed the mountain on his death and ever since thieves and brigands have hidden, dwelling in the black chill of the rock. Waiting to slay any travellers.'

'Well we shall be suited to the dwellers there, an assassin and whoring lily user. Do you think they will welcome us?' Kado caustically added in his agitation and pain. The Gorung had worn off fully now and the pain from his wounds was gnawing at every thought.

'Come we will track around the eastern ridge of the table-lands below. We will have more shelter and there is a stream that courses from the Knedron Hills where we can replenish our water.'

They began to climb along the slope that led down again. Kado stumbled behind Sa. After a short while Kado stopped and fell to the ground.

'I cannot go any further Tuc! I am flayed to the bone like your hero Manon.'

Sa stopped and looked at her charge. The sun was at its zenith and a long time until dark when they could find proper shelter and make camp safely. If Kado kept stopping, then they would be too exposed to any pursuers.

'Wait here.'

She ran off into the brushes that lay at the top of the hill. Kado looked at her searching the ground amongst the rocks. She really was so loyal to him most would have left him behind by now he thought.

'Take those off! I will wrap them again and put some of this on the cuts. It is like the Gorung plant but not as strong. Can you move your arm?'

Fortunately, where the arrow of the general had lodge was only shallow and was healing well. She helped bathe his feet. They had not festered yet due to her care, but the cuts were deep. She crushed the weeds and placed the paste on the cloth then covered his feet. The burning sensation eased to a mild sting then numbness. She rewrapped the bandages and then strapped on the sandals she had taken from a villager's hut onto his feet. She held her hand out to hold him up. He got up and curled his arm around her waist and pulled her close to himself. He traced a finger along the scar on her face. He kissed her once again but held her for longer. She pulled back from his face without a reaction.

'I cannot be one of your women Kado. I do not know how, and it will diminish our resolve to face what awaits us. Show restraint, be stronger.'

He held her looking at her intently wanting more. She gave a minute nod curious as this had never happened before. This time his lips pressed with more passion. Inside she felt surprised at not feeling more repulsed by it, her whole life had been a violent existence honed into a weapon of inflicting death with stealth precision. Tenderness had been replaced with control and discipline. He let her go.

'You did not fight me.'

'I would have killed you Kado if I didn't want you to.'

He grinned slightly realising that it could have ended much worse for himself. He watched her again as it occurred to him that even if the world stood at the edge of its death and he along with it, Sa would still be standing next to him.

They reached a cosseted section of wood on the eastern

ridge by the time the sun set. Sa had not seen anyone following them. A stream gurgled to the surface for a hundred paces or so then it dipped beneath rocky culverts into a deep reservoir below the ground. The large fang ferns draped themselves over it creating a cathedral of cool relief in the summer and moist reprieve from the biting winds of winter. Sa had busied herself with catching some fish. Even her stomach was rebelling at the thought of more rice cakes.

'Do you think we are being followed?' Kado was fondling the tip of a frond that had sat on his shoulder. He pricked his finger on the tip and noted the thorn that jutted out. It looked like the fangs that the fighting dogs in the palace used to bear. He realised how the ferns had gotten their names and the valley.

'I am not sure. I hope to make it as far as the outlying towns from Shadaraq. It is a city walled in completely by thick granite walls, but there are makeshift villages that have sprung up around it. We can hide there while I scout for the others. The security will be strict and no doubt Ranik's arm has reached that far. You will need to keep guard with me tonight Kado.'

They sat opposite one another. Kado watched the north and Sa looked to the south.

'Most likely the soldiers would follow the same route as themselves. The ones chosen to avenge their death would be expected to die or bring our heads to be placed in the notorious prison of Banrock to place in the walls as trophies.'

Kado sat listening to Sa whisper in the darkness. He thought to himself how the temple had felt serene, but in the world all things became a decision about who was friend or enemy.

'Do you think this world wants to die but just doesn't know how to Sa?'

'I am not sure Kado. It seems death is everywhere, and I am one of its loyal servants.'

'Not all of you is Sa.'

Sa got up to refill her water satchel.

'Sit next to me Tuc. Keep me awake.'

She sat and took some more water. It was too silent around them. There should be animals coming to drink. This was the only water source around here for many leagues. She pulled some fronds off one of the larger palms and whittled it down so that it was a straight length with only the thorn at the end. She threw some more to Kado.

'We can use them as darts to hunt for animals and as weapons.'

'They are not large enough to harm anything.'

'I have found some banaroc root when I was tending your wounds. A tip of one of these ferns dipped in its pulp will kill a man.'

The moonlight shone on Sa as she sat upon a rock high enough to be above the canopy to watch. Kado had dozed off. He had lasted longer than Sa thought possible for him. On his chest sat a quiver of fern stems with the thorns still intact. She had crushed some of the root and placed it in a leather pouch for him. A reed of water bamboo had been hollowed out for him to blow the darts through. They would practice tomorrow. The weak rays of the dawn broke through the ferns canopy. Sa stood and looked across the flat disc of land they were circling. They would be well covered from the tableland below, hopefully their journey would go unhindered she thought to herself. The silence of the valley worried her again. The animals had been becoming scarcer since she had left the water spirit's Keep. Sa had to go further to find meat and the fish were less plentiful in the streams. Perhaps the world was dying or had the demon awoken and begun to spread its poison. As the sun rose Kado woke startled realising he had fallen asleep.

'Come Kado.'

He got up and gingerly began to check his feet. They were healing. He slung the pouch and quiver over his back.

'I am sorry for falling asleep.'

'It will get easier with time.'

Kado saw them first, three figures on the horizon. The soldiers were behind them, not far from where they had made camp. Kado had climbed onto a large boulder to try one of his darts on a mongoose he had seen at the base of a tree.

'Hurry, keep below the ferns.' When the sun finally set, they had climbed to the tip of a large conifer to wait in preparation for their hunters. After what seemed most of the night, the three warriors passed underneath their prey as silently as the moon began to shine. All Kado and Sa saw was the pale reflection of the metal of their blades. Sa watched until she lost them to the understorey of the forest and waited until the dawn.

'Where are they Tuc?'

She did not answer Kado as she had lost sight of them.

The huge oak they hid in towered one hundred men above the ground. The tree had been their best defence. It gave them a clear view all around and no one could climb from below without being seen or heard. Something cracked below. Kado was alert instantly. His mind had fully cleared after the fog of the den of Knedron and his body was learning to do without sleep. He readied his bamboo and waited. Sa had seen the assailant but waited. It was a good test for Kado.

Kado could see the man's eyes watching him. He blew and saw the fang bite into the brawny neck of Gurna. He made a rush at Kado but just as he reached out for his foot his hand went limp and he began to gag. Kado watched the man dying. Suddenly a lasso wrapped around the dying man's neck.

'Help me Kado, don't let him fall to the ground.' Kado started at Sa's voice behind him. He had become mesmerised watching the poison work its way through the man's skin. It followed the trace of the blood lines in his neck and into his eyes, turning the whites black. They hoisted the limp body up and tied it to a thick branch.

'The others must be close' hissed Kado. His chest thudded from the shock of coming so close to death and defeating the soldier.

'Not necessarily, the Unstaadt assassins have been known to work alone to purchase glory only for themselves at the end. He must have sensed we were following. I think the others would be here by now of they knew of our whereabouts.'

'What will we do?'

'Wait another day then leave. If the others know of us, then it is best to stay here. They are impatient for a kill. They will not wait long.'

'Why don't we hunt them and be rid of them Tuc. They will follow us regardless so why don't we finish the job.'

'We were lucky Kado with this one. We may not be so

with the other two. Learn patience Kado.'

'We may as well die hunting them rather than living in further fear. This demon of yours Sa, it awaits us also.' He grinned excited now that he seen how effective his darts were.

Sa studied Kado's face for a moment, seeing the glint in his eye and realised it was the first time she had ever seen Kado with any passion for fighting or defending himself. Perhaps you will be your father's son, yet she thought. His first kill had awoken the Ko Dragon. She nodded in agreement at his proposal.

'We will rest here tonight Kado and begin tomorrow.' He kissed her cheekily again and smiled as he looked across the plateau beneath him. Kado felt alive and for the first time he could see clearly without a veil of shame cloying to him. Far away in the distance the twin peaks of the path north silhouetted themselves.

The night in the tree had not revealed their prey which meant that they had been able to have a moments rest. The body of the soldier had bloated and stared at Kado with bulging eyes still dismayed at his fate. Kado stooped over the body and cut the left little finger off the body. He looked at the ring, an eagle's head with a ruby for an eye. Inside was a mark from the smith that forged it. The silver of the ring was unblemished suggesting it was newly cast. He wondered if this was forged from the wealth of the Ko mines. They resumed the route they had intended to follow but looked more closely for any signs of the other two. He plucked out the ruby and stowed the ring and finger in his pocket.

'Are there any other paths to take to Shadaraq?'

'Only along the plateau, it is a straight road for the traders. They would not have gone that way. It is too easy to be spotted. The death marks would stand out amongst the other soldiers and word would easily reach all tongues of their presence. That would inspire hatred in some and spur on others to seek glory in vengeance. They tread the same rock and stone as we do Kado.'

They met their assailants four days later just on the outskirts of the shacks that surrounded the merchant city. The last of the Fang Fern valley had retreated giving way to the black granite beds that were the feet of the northern ranges, worn down over millennia by the same stream that now flowed beneath it. Each pursuer saw their prey and waited in the ailing light of the leaf fall sun. Kado looked at them and threw Gurna's ring at the one called Jek. He caught it and spat on the rocks.

Lifting his massive arms, he roared readying himself for battle. Kado got onto his haunches. He would need to be quick. Kan came running from their left and threw an axe directly at Sa. She dodged it easily but the Unstaadt then bought down a massive metal head with spikes splintering the rocks. Sa's foot slipped as the granite shards gave way. She leapt towards him hoping to land a cut into his face or throat, but his massive shield made from the black metal of the iron coast swept her directly into the face of a boulder. She gasped as the wind was knocked out of her and again when she hit the ground.

Jek saw Kado lying on the rock and warily made his way towards him. He snarled at him as he heaved the mighty blade directly for his skull hoping to splinter it into a thousand pieces. Kado rolled away quickly and kept doing so frustrating the frenzied attacker even more. A few darts got off but each time Jek deflected them away with his shield. Foaming at the mouth his sword came crashing down in a barrage of strikes and sparks, each time Kado barely missed them until he began to tire. Suddenly Kado dove through the soldier's massive legs and squashed into a gap between the rocks. He worked his way down until he wedged between the two massive boulders. He could hear the water below trickling. Jek stood over him. As he raised his sword above his head and roared, Kado noticed the size of the man's scrotum hanging beneath the loin cloth. Gently manoeuvring the bamboo tube, he blew three fangs straight into the sac and braced himself for the sword blow.

Sa hit the rock a second time as Kan had collected her with his mace and whipped her threw the air. She was too dazed to see what had happened to Kado. So far nothing had broken. Landing again on the flat bed of stone she drove her dagger into Kan's foot just as his axe swung past her head. He picked her up again and lifted her high above him with both hands. As he turned to show Jek his killer blow he watched his comrade fall into the crevice with mouth foaming and blood pouring, from his nose. Kan roared and shook Sa so hard she thought her back would surely break. She began to black out from the pain as his hands dug into her neck. Kado managed to move Jek enough to see what was happening. Crawling out, he took the axe from the dead soldier and threw it directly at Kan. It lodged in his chest momentarily and then fell to the ground. He walked towards Kado. Pulling the bamboo shoot from under him he saw that it had broken. Kado grabbed a handful of the deadly thorns. Kan swung Sa around like a rag doll to use her as a weapon. Taking a wide arc, he swung her body towards Kado. His head collided with her body stunning Kado and snapping Sa's ribs. As Kado fell he grazed the poisoned fangs along Kan's leg and blacked out.

The night sky seemed to ripple as Kado opened his eyes. His head throbbed and he could not breathe properly. He tried to turn over but realised something heavy lay on him, then he saw Kan's blackened eyes staring at him. He heaved the monster off himself and looked for Sa. She was lying on the edge of the crack. Her legs and arms were splayed. Rolling her over he could see that she was breathing and tried to rouse her with gentle taps on her face. She did not move but she was breathing. He felt over her body to find any wounds then he tenderly picked her up and took her back towards the path covered over by the forest. He made a bed for her to rest upon and dribbled water from their bladders into her mouth. Her breathing was the same. He sat back and waited.

Sa's eyes opened to the rising sun. It stung them immensely so that she instinctively put her hand over to shield them. As she moved, pain shot through her.

'Kado' she croaked.

'Well Tuc still not dead.' His humour could not disguise the relief in his voice.

Her face broke into a crooked smile 'Water. I cannot move.'

'Rest, they are both dead.'

'How many days has it been?'

'Only a night Tuc, it is safe, rest. We are safe now.'

'We must bury them, for others may find them and it will start again.' She had turned her head to look at their slain hunters, but needles of pain shot through her. 'Am I broken?'

'I don't think so.' Kado pinched her toes and hands. She moved them reflexively.

'Rest Tuc, I will get rid of the bodies.'

Giving her more water he made sure she was comfortable then walked towards Jek and Kan. Taking the massive mace of Kan he pushed them towards the open crack between the slabs of rock. He prodded the bodies down until they fell into the reservoir below. He heard the satisfying splash as each body was swept away to the depths of the river which ran beneath Blackspike and Redblade.

'Where were you to meet the others?'

'At the northern most gate on the full moon.'

'How many of them?'

'Three. A girl and a man from the eastern deserts and one graan warrior from the north. Oh, and a mongrel, bred from the wild dogs of the dirt of the desert.' Sa smiled slightly at the memory of Nekoda.

'Rest Tuc, I will find us some meat, and cook it eh. No more of being hunted, we shall feast like a princeling and his vassal should.'

She dozed off with that thought and slept for three nights as her body healed. Kado stood and looked towards the faint shimmer of the dusty industriousness of Shadaraq.

'Here Tuc, eat more. Can you sit up today?'

Sa eased herself up. The crunch of her ribs had lessened. The threatening bloom of pain swelled and then settled quickly.

'I feel equal to you today Tuc. We have our battle scars and the commiseration of our wounds to dwell upon.'

'Indeed Kado. I am indebted again to the Draxus. I would have died if not for you. Twice now.'

Kado smiled and lightly kissed her on the cheek. He offered her his hand to assist her to stand as she finished eating the pieces of meat. She stood hesitantly.

'As dragonflies hover
Over a deep pool
I ascend into stillness
Lighter than air
Weaving as a spider
Webs silent and strong
Without fear
Fear is the doorway to defeat
Defeat is the path to weakness
Weakness is the step to destruction
Destruction is the door to death
Fear is death
Be still
Be strong
Be true
Ascend above fear
Rule death
Be a dragonfly
Be a spider
Rule the air
Rule your fear.'

Kado listened to the mantra of discipline. As she uttered the final words of the dragon fly prayer she leapt into the air. Her movements were fluid and her aim accurate as she snapped a small frond off a fern and held it aloft in her toes. Such graceful precision, his father had been wise, to see the jewel under the muck of her beginnings. She was dressed in her under tunic revealing her thighs and arms. They were covered in scars, new and old. She was almost unworldly in her resilience thought Kado. Only four dawns had passed, and she was already back to her usual self. As Sa sat down next to him slightly panting, he offered her some water. She took it. Some of it dribbled down her chin. He wiped it off with his thumb.

'I will be ready tomorrow, Kado. I can see Shadaraq from here.'

'Yes, I will scout today for your friends and make sure the route is safe. I have not seen any soldiers.'

'Take the path which runs along the southern edge of the road. It is hidden and soldiers will not use as it is too narrow.'

Kado slipped his arm around her waist again. This time Sa met his gaze.

'Do not distract yourself Kado. We are still hunted by the demon and we cannot let ourselves be off guard.'

'I know Tuc. But do you not desire tenderness rather than this brutality that has become the hide which covers our flesh. Are you not hungry for nourishment and fulfilment from all the beauty the world can bring if we would just stop and seek it? Let this be a pause to slow the death of the world.'

She did not answer him but relaxed against his arm. He pulled her to him, and she let him lay her on the ground. Lying near her gently he loosened her tunic. She let him do it, but her body was rigid, ready to fight. He saw the alertness in her eyes. He pulled away but she took his hand and placed it on her.

She would let him be there for this moment. He undid his loin clothes and felt for hers. He gently stroked her and felt her respond to his fingers. He kissed her again.

'Why do you want me Kado Ko? I have no memory of tenderness. I cannot feel the same things as you. I fear in the end I will hurt you.'

'Our lives have always existed on the edge of an abyss gouged out by the hatred of others. One wrong step could mean our end. I am tired of the hatred this world seems to grow. Let us know this tenderness together in case that dark place rises again to destroy us once and for all.'

Sa closed her eyes as Kado penetrated her untouched body knowing how close that abyss had been her whole life.

<h1 style="text-align:center">7</h1>

Blackspike and Redblade

Paval sat on the ice ledge above the darkened passage and watched the lonely traveller. Fools, this was an easy pickin', he thought. The snow had not come yet so the great wash of the Draan River gushed from the northern base of the mountains spitting forth from its underground entrance. As it did so it carved a ribcage of large icicles along the path that led to northern lands. The ignorant traveller did not know that you could walk above the massive spikes of rock and ice without being seen. Paval the thief giggled as his excitement built watching his next victim beneath him. He edged slowly towards him. He waited until the prey had walked under a bridge of ice formed from rocky outcrop then as he re-emerged Paval jumped screaming loudly. He thrust his axe into the man's head causing them to both instantly fall to the ground. Paval kept jumping on him in happiness.

'Oi that's enuff o that, yer mad bastad.'

Two others came down from the same entrance and began rustling through the dead man's clothes. He had only one large pack on his back and it was full of sheep skins. Yaun took a machete out to make room for the sack inside his coat. Sten stood up and kicked the body fair in the head.

'Dam ya useless load of shit. Onnag will be pissed again.'

He was rubbing the side of his head where a large lump had formed from the last time, they had come back with nothing.

'Come on we better get back, the sun's already on the shy side of the mount.'

The three thieves collected the body and hoisted it into the raging Draan as it coursed its way to the eastern ocean almost two thousand leagues away. The body smashed against rocks and then slid underneath the water lost forever to whoever may have known its face and life. An eerie silence came back to the passage as the sun rays closed behind Blackspike enveloping the passage in darkness.

— — —

Gildas worked his way through the markets towards the black obelisk. He could not see the assassin. It was where they were supposed to meet. He had been cursing under his breath at all the soldiers.

'They are like fucking flies on a carcass, trader.'

Bensah turned to look at him.

'I know, Ranik's arm grows long. We will need to find lodgings somewhere.'

'I remember a place. Not far from here. They will offer shelter for us. I will begin to gather the furs we will need for the passage.'

'How long will we wait for Sa?' asked Ange

'Only a few days, girl, the more we delay the closer the winter draws near.'

Gildas rubbed a cut on his arm. He noticed Ange looking at him.

'I wonder how the soldier is Gildas?' she had a smile on her face. The soldiers had soon caught up to them on the Hill of Jank but fortunately only a few had been sent to find them. Gildas had not used the sword and become pinned by one of them. The girl and dog had come from behind and knocked the soldier out and then maimed his leg so he could not chase after them. He remembered the girl copying him as he watched her clean the little dagger on the grass.

'Ay, girl, I still owe you some lessons.'

Making their way out of the busy market districts the people thinned as did the huts and stalls revealing the massive stone wall that surrounded the city. It dominated their view in all directions. It soon became oppressive to Ange, she felt more caged here then she had with the desert or even Hendra valley. A beggar caught her leg as she walked past. Looking down at his eaten face from the beggar's disease, she looked into his eyes. All around she could see the oppressive stone wall as it seemed to magnify in her vision trapping her and the filth of the city it contained. She yanked her leg away and grabbed the pouch around her neck. His face reminded her of the lands she had passed through to reach Shadaraq. She gave him a piece of biscuit. Nekoda growled at the beggar but Ange pulled him away before he drew attention.

Soon they stopped in front of a barn like house on the out-skirts of the bustling central square.

'Stay here while I speak to the landlady' spoke Gildas.

Not long after he came out and led them behind the house to an empty barn. It had no walls only a thatched hay roof, but the ground beneath had been swept clear of dung and straw.

'Luck's wife is with us desert dwellers the owner has just sold her swine and has room. She and her son will be leaving to buy more but we should be gone by the time they return.'

The trio began to make camp under the roof. Bensah tied Nekoda to one of the beams that supported the roof and fetched some water for the dog. Nekoda whined as he stretched out onto the dirt. The nights were still warm enough but a bite in the air could be felt when the northern zephyrs came down from the towering peaks.

'A bairn Gildas, I'd have thought even you had ya limitations. An' which demon of the underworld spawned that mutt.' The proprietor had bought them some food and hessian sacks to sleep on.

'Ay, mother she is to be a maid for a noble. The other we will see. The dog keeps em under control.'

'Well then an empty swine pen won't do for a noble's hand-maid. Come girl I have a room for you.'

Ange looked at Bensah and Gildas fearful suddenly.

Gildas stopped chewing the bit of gristle he had in his mouth thinking if it would be ok.

'Ay, mother. It will be good if you can clean her up before I deliver her.'

Ange took the woman's hand. They felt calloused; she had known hard work in her life.

'Come Zack will place a bowl and ladle ready for ya to sup

on while I draw ya a bath. How'd ya get caught with one such as Gildas?' Ange did not answer but looked back at her two companions. They both nodded for her to go.

Bensah sat back against one of the beams and continued to eat the stew.

'How do you know the woman?'

'She takes lodgers and asks no questions which is why she is still alive. The grog houses are usually the best place for mercenaries to pick up friends. Gerty was still suckling her boy as a service maid in one of the alehouses when I lastl stayed here.'

'Where have you been?' asked Bensah

'I was in Banrock prison, captured for brawling and killing an Aeserean noble's servant.'

'How long?'

'Fifteen winters.'

They did not speak again that night. Gildas lay back on his roll thinking of the years that had passed. Bensah wondered how the clansman had managed to escape a place like Banrock. The spirits had been watching him even back then.

Ange sat in the copper tub enjoying the warmth of the water. Her legs stung slightly as the soap worked its way into the wounds but the herbs in the bathe were soothing.

'There are some fresh linens for yer and the suppers ready' Gerty spoke as she placed crisp white undershirt and towel on a table.

She sat down at the table. Gerty and her son Zach were there already eating. The smell of the soup made her mouth water.

'So little un, yer didn't tell me how you caught up with the northerner.'

'My family were killed by the plague and Gildas found me in the desert along with Tata Bensah.'

'As long as he is good to yer, these invaders from the south, are mean bastids child, if yer get sold to em, you come runnin here. Do yer hear. Come to Gerty.'

Ange nodded.

'Quick eat, mama's soup is the best in Shadaraq' spoke Zack.

Ange smiled at the toothy grin of Zack and then greedily ate the soup and delicious bread.

Ange woke to find no trace of Gerty and Zack. She found a plate with a bowl of milk and some bread and honey left on the floor near her bed. Ange gobbled it down and went out to Gildas and Bensah.

'The northerner has gone looking for goods and he will check for the assassin.'

'I hope she comes Tata. We will need her. She will need to teach me to fight Tata and you as well. The demon will look for all of us.'

'I know. My bones are telling me how many moons have passed and I am not as blessed as the northerner. The northern road will test us Ange. I have heard the legends of the storms and winds that scream death at everything that stands before them. If we survive them, I think we will see another spring in Chensai.'

Ange was not so sure. She fingered some of the beads Bensah had given to her and Tessi, so long ago now.

'I should have given these to Gildas to trade.'

'You smell like one of those pale puffy royal women. Turn you into a high lady yet, sister.' Bensah was grinning at Ange in fun.

'Maybe I'll become a queen one day and rule the land and kill the demon and stand with the gods.'

She stood up and pulling out her dagger she began to stab the air with the same moves that she had seen Gildas doing.

'I can make better moves with my short leg, Tata, see if I dip and fall this way an enemy can't guess which way to strike at me.' She beamed at Bensah as she performed her contorted defensive fighting moves. Bensah got up grinning and started to spa with her. Nekoda stood wagging his tail and barking hoping to be able to join in.

Gildas found them on the ground drinking milk and sweating from their play fighting. He threw three large coats down and several pickaxes. He looked at them both and shook his head.

'Well clansman, any news?' asked Bensah. Ange got up and got a bowl of milk for him.

Taking it, he drank it down, finding it refreshing.

'The assassin was not there but a companion stood waiting. He did not give his name, but he had her belt of the royal staff of Ko. She lies wounded. They were hunted by soldiers in revenge for killing their generals. I said we would wait until the next full moon waxes but if she is not recovered by then we would need to leave with or without her.'

Ange stood hearing the news of Sa and suddenly felt the fear again rise in her heart.

'Can we not go to her and help her heal. I know of herbs that will help and Tata, he remembers the ways of our tribes.'

'The messenger said she is healing quickly. It will give us time to gather more supplies.'

Ange grabbed Gildas arm and making him look down at her.

'Do you understand northerner, she must be with us. We will wait for her.' Gildas looked at the intensity of Ange's eyes. He could not tell if he saw fear or she knew something he did not about the need for the assassin. He suddenly felt her nails digging into his arms

'Ay girl, I understand but I heard talk that disturbed me. The gossip in the grog houses told of Ranik being under an ancient sorcerer which had awoken. He had unleashed more of his militia to conquer the western lands. They will be passing this way to make a stealth attack. We cannot linger for too long girl or the demon may catch us. Your skill with the dagger might become the talk of the grog houses as well.'

He half smiled at her but the look of concern in her eyes only relented slightly.

'Here come try this on.' He pulled a hide coat made from the pelts of the marmoset rodents. Its sleaves were too long but it was the right length.

'I will make boots and gloves for your hands and this will do as your head covering. Trader try yours on as well.'

Soon they all stood in their fur coats and masks looking like ice hunters from the north. Ange made gestures of spearing fish and began to giggle, but she soon became too hot in the afternoon sun and took it off. The pelts were turned inside out so the warmth of the fur lay against the skin and the hide protected from the wetness of the ice. They were soothing on the skin and felt in-penetrable against an enemy's spear or the frigid air of the north.

'What about our feet?' She asked.

'I will need to find some timbers to make gliding on the ice easier. I will go tomorrow there were too many soldiers in the markets today.'

'Food?' asked Bensah

'I will buy dried meats but there will places we can fish as we need. I will teach the ways of the graan, trader.'

Bensah nodded as he took his coat off.

Gildas stood at the obelisk on the seventh morning waiting. The evening before had ended in an argument with the girl. He was adamant about leaving on the next dawn with or without the assassin, but the girl had started crying again and then threatened that she would not go if we did not wait for Sa Tuc. In the end he wanted to rip the cursed stone off her neck and throw it away after she had threatened him about leaving it here for Ranik to find. The trader had restrained them both. The girl grew more headstrong everyday perhaps it was the charm of the prism he thought to himself. Standing in the hot sun he became more agitated as the heat and the congestion of the markets grew. A lot of soldiers were coming in. They would be noticed soon. Scanning the crowds, he soon saw two figures shrouded in black. The small one limped slightly, while the other one seemed to be scanning the crowds looking for something.

'You made it.'

'Yes, Graansman and you waited. Why? That was not our agreement.'

'The girl refused to leave until you came. Are you able to travel? The ice will be unforgiving. And you? Who are you?'

'We can travel. It is better not to talk here. When do we leave?'

'At the dawn. I want to be through the pass of Shadaraq before nightfall. Come I have collected everything we need.'

Kado stood back, still amazed at the size of Gildas and a little intimidated.

When they reached the home of Gerty, Ange flew towards Sa Tuc and hugged her. Taken aback at the display of affection she pulled Ange away and looked at her.

'What is it Ange? The warrior said you would not leave without me. I am not important here. You must be hidden from the demon as should the gift. If this happens again and it is only the graanar here, then you must obey him' Ange felt Sa's fingers dig into her arms.

'You are to teach me to fight Sa Tuc. What would I do if everyone is gone and I am left to protect the lady's gift? I cannot fight like Gildas and Tata, but I can be like you, quick and little like the sand lizards of home.'

She said it so simply that Sa did not know whether to laugh or not. She nodded.

'When I am well, I will teach you to fight.' Sa sat down feeling the pain ebb slightly in her chest and back.

'First Sa Tuc, who is your companion?' asked Gildas.

Sa nodded at Kado to answer.

'I am Kado Ko Drax, former heir to the throne of the Ko Dynasty, now fellow traveller and companion to the Assassin of Ko.'

Kado bowed slightly in deprecating humour at his demise

from such an auspicious position.

'So Tuc you have bought the heir of Ko amongst us to give Ranik even more reason to hunt us down.'

'The spirit asked me to find him Gildas. Kado is thought to be dead. If any hunt us it is not for him but the dead that lay behind us.' She smiled sardonically remembering the defeat of the warriors.

'You are thin boy' Gildas spat on the ground annoyed again. It was a complication he had not expected.

Kado thought how much like his father Gildas was but with more battle scars. Ko had been the strategist and general not the warrior in the mud and blood.

'We shall rest tonight and feast well. I found a suckling pig in the pantry. Will our landlady mind Graansman?' Bensah announced trying to break the tension as he sat piercing the piglet with a skewer ready to roast.

'Nay Gerty will not mind' replied Gildas.

The group sat down waiting for the pig to roast. Ange sat near Sa feeling more hopeful with the assassin nearby.

'What happened that you have been hurt Sa?' she asked.

Sa looked at Kado.

'Three Unstaadt warriors chased us because we killed two of their generals.'

'I have healing salts Sa. I made them from the crabs in Lido's dwelling.'

Sa grimaced as she moved against the pole she rested against.

'I will try some Ange.'

Ange took some of the minerals and put them in a mug to dissolve in water. She placed it over the fire to warm.

'I am not sure how it will taste but it is very strong.'

'Thank you.'

'Sa you are to teach me. I have learned some good strokes from Gildas, but I think you will be better.' Ange continued in a matter of fact manner, not seeing the smile which broke on the other's faces at her innocent slight about Gildas.

'I will Ange. I will teach you the dragon fly mantra and all I know but I think the ice will teach all of us first though.'

Bensah handed each of them some stripped roasted flesh off the pig. They ate in silence enjoying the richness of the meat.

'This reminds of the harvest moon festival. So long ago now. Never again' sighed Kado.

'I still don't understand why we have all been called to this quest?' Gildas asked as he lit a pipe.

'Neither do I' replied Kado. 'I was haunted by dreams of a scorpion driven by something deeper and more menacing. Perhaps it is this demon which has brought destruction that invades my dreams, as if I were living them.'

'Ange do you see or know more since you have been given the stone?' asked Bensah.

'No Tata. It is potent. I walk in the realm of the spirits and only hear the sounds of war' Ange choked a little 'I saw the mighty god of this world bound in chains.'

'What else have you seen Ange?' asked Gildas. His jaw tensed thinking of the god he had seen at the Drax Citadel chained. It was a bad omen indeed.

'I sought the ancient scrolls of Sindrax. There is no mention of this covenant and likely it was made before even the flame of the dragon was awoken in the Drax people' spoke Sa.

'When I touch the prism, I feel it call to every part of my body. I feel like it goes into my heart and my flesh and bring it to life. It is as if it is part of me and I am part of it. I also see shadows as I see the light and the spirits as well. Our blood, the blood of our ancestors was spilt when this jewel came here with Norbu. It made us. The same thing that made it made us. And I think the shadow. The reason the shadow wants it is to destroy the thing that makes us. That makes the sun, the sky and the dirt and this pig and this desert dweller now entrusted with it. It also holds the world of the gods. It has its last moments. I am not sure but ...' Ange trailed off thinking of all she had said.

'How do you know this Ange?' asked Bensah.

'I am not certain Tata, but it explains that with all of us together the stone remains stronger in its power and helps stop the shadow and the god of green eyes from destroying the other spirts. It keeps it in the same state as it was when Norbu first forged it. We are the remnants of its memory except back when it was brought here Norbu and Lido and the gods of fire and wind lived among us. So, it lay like the stones beneath our feet, asleep and only moved by wind or water. Now the spirits have gone, our blood has awoken it. This is what draws the demon and makes the shadow so destructive. Part of its creation became bound to our ancestors.'

'I feel this same bonding when I use the sword of Tarentess. It is as if I am no longer flesh and blood but become the mountain itself.'

'This is why you must teach to me to fight and I must find a way to Norbu to free him and the lady. I am not strong enough yet to defeat the shadow.'

No one replied to Ange.

'Was it deliberate for the gods to make this happen or is it by chance?' asked Bensah.

'Perhaps that is what I will learn Tata. Mata once told me that when I was born, I made her see only what the gods and stars could see. Perhaps that is my use, my purpose to see beyond those stars and find out why this fate has come to our lands and just maybe stop it.'

Bensah looked at Ange and felt pride swell inside him at the strength in one of his people especially, one such as Ange. A deep wisdom had seen Ange and protected her, kept her alive for this time now.

'We understand so little in this world Ange' spoke Kado.

The fire died down.

'We should get some rest.' Gildas had heard all the girl said. Within his bones he felt the breaking of all his life knowledge being swept away. They stood on the edge of chasm of doom or something beyond what their eyes or minds could understand. Either way this world and their lives were finished, and something new was about to be birthed into existence or annihilated.

Ange stared at the massive iron gate that was the northern entry point for the city. In it were carved scenes from a great battle on the mountains that stood above Shadaraq. The final scene showed a man the size of a giant slumped over the peaks of the mountains. There was script written along the top of the archway, but Ange did not understand it.

'Gildas what does that say?' she asked.

'Beyond these gates lies the tomb of Manon the Great,

conqueror of Redblade and Blackspike, cursed by his tongue and blood. Gateway to the great ocean of ice. May you prevail traveller.'

Kado looked at the intricate detail of Manon's conquest and thought they will be having their own soon enough. As the reality of passing into the northern wastes drew the thought of what was to come had begun to weigh heavily on his mind.

They stood waiting to pass through the ominous exit but a large contingent of Matavians and Unstaadt soldiers were arriving, blocking any access to the gates.

The group looked heavily burdened as they had packed the furs and shoes inside rolls. Ange nearly tipped over from hers but managed to balance the pack.

'This is taking too long' Gildas muttered to himself. Soon the bullock trains and wounded began to dribble in signalling he dregs of the procession. Gildas headed towards the entrance. As he and Ange walked past looking straight ahead, they did not notice a soldier on a litter. A putrid smell came from one of his legs. He looked up when he felt something brush on it, pain shot from his foot to his groin. As he looked up, he stared straight into the Ange's face but could not remember where he had seen her before. Ange looked away quickly realising who the soldier was and pulled her shawl over a bit more to conceal herself.

'Quickly Gildas!' She pushed his leg slightly. He turned in irritation and as he did so saw the soldier looking back at the pair of them. He picked Ange up and began to walk faster. The others followed. Bensah saw Gildas recognise the soldier from the Hill of Jank. He hurried Sa and Kado along. His face was entirely covered and managed to slip by without being noticed. They reached the gates and slid past the massive iron columns that held them upright.

'How far to the pass?' asked Bensah, 'I think we were seen.'

'I know we were. We can hope the man will die before he remembers who we are. We head for the trees up there toward the north. Quickly the sooner we are away the better. The crowd follows the west road.' replied Gildas.

They were soon draped in darkness as they walked under the canopy of the massive conifer forest which stood at the base of mountains. No light came to them again until thin slivers of sunlight broke between the icy roof of the pass as they walked under the great stone feet of the mountains. As they left the cave and entered the pass, they were met with blasting ice winds and reflections glinting back and forth off the snow covered red and black granite.

Sa tensed as they stopped to put on their furs and paddles. Something was watching them, and the silence agitated her after the bustle of Shadaraq. Nekoda trembled from anticipation sensing what lay ahead. Bensah had placed his muzzle on as the barking would have echoed for leagues through the crevices in the cliffs.

'We are watched warrior' Sa whispered.

'Nay not here, further along. The scum that live here dwell in the caves above a bridge of ice that forms over an outcrop of rock. We will need to be ready with our weapons as we approach. Ready for another fight girl?' He looked down at Ange.

Ange nodded with bright eyes, filled with as much courage

as there was fear. They began to walk along the narrow road formed naturally between the two peaks. On the eastern side stood Blackspike and on the western stood Redblade. Their boots were fashioned into a frame of twigs entwined so that they could glide on the ice rather then walk. Ange was surprised how smooth it felt under her feet. In single file they followed each other through streams of sunlight broken by the solid rock plunging them into shadows as deep as a moonless night.

Paval saw the little one from above and licked his lips. So long since a youngling had passed this way. He used to play with some of the ones they had trapped before. Only they would tire on him quickly and he would become angry and smash their heads with rocks in frustration. He followed as they neared the bridge. He saw Sten and Yaun waiting above him as well as Dog and Tridek. The big one would be hard to bring down. Sten nodded at Paval and suddenly like a snake pouncing he flew down the side of the cliff and pegged a rock directly at Gildas as he came out from under the bridge. It misfired though and glanced off to the side only scratching Gildas face. Paval saw the warrior glare at him with rage and swallowed hard. Suddenly a blade stuck in his neck as he saw the others fly down their ropes to their victims. Blood spouted all over Paval's face and into his mouth as he fell past Gildas. Sa swooped on Paval's body as it hit the ground and removed her dagger.

'Quickly run!' bellowed Gildas. He reefed Bensah's arm and pulled him close to him 'Run ahead and bury the girl in the ice. The coat will protect her. It will be soft near the river's edge.' Nekoda snarled straining wanting to attack.

Bensah grabbed Ange and bolted along the passage. He let go of Nekoda and the dog bolted directly for their pursuers.

Dog threw a pickaxe at Kado, but he glanced it off easily. He stepped behind Gildas quickly as the warrior sparred with Tridek. Kado took his darts and began to shoot them at their assailants. They kept missing, the only exposed place he could aim for was their faces. Then he felt a blow at his back. He turned and saw a third thief standing behind him ready to strike again. Kado spat a dart off quickly and got him in the eye. The hammer came down a moment before the poison began to suffuse into Yaun's body. Kado fell reeling from the blow. Gildas hauled him up and pushed Kado along to run. The passage was narrow with bends obscuring their view to only a few paces ahead. Kado flew as fast as could along the passage as he heard Gildas grunting behind him.

'Up above!' came the roar behind him. Kado looked up and there hung another. Kado shot off the dart, one connected momentarily but he pulled his sword out ready. Placing his foot on a small outcrop of rock Kado launched himself up towards the thief and plunged the dagger into the man's chest. It barely penetrated the thick leather burka he wore but the poison on the blade managed to finish him off. Kado propelled himself at a full leap to get even further ahead. Looking back, he saw Gildas sparring with the first two. One of them lost their arm then his head as the mighty graanar axe came down. They ran forward trying to avoid arrows and rocks as Sten attempted to bring them down from above. Two more thieves scaled the granite and dropped down behind him with crossbows spewing metal barbs everywhere. Suddenly the passage opened out into a massive expanse of white land, broken by the ribbon of black water of the River Draan. Sa and Bensah stood facing the entrance of the passage waiting for them.

Sa saw Kado's eyes widen as he ran towards her.

'Bensah, Sa, ready yourselves!' Three Matavian soldiers poked through a gap in the mountains feet where the river gushed out.

'Ahh chunt bastids' groaned Gildas.

The four stood back to back as the soldiers and thieves surrounded them.

'Thems our spoils militia! Leave 'em to us!' shouted Sten.

'Nay we seek their heads for payment for some of our own' one of the soldiers barked back.

Sten looked at the quarry before him and thought Onaag would be happy with some of those leather rags them soldiers wore as well.

'Well let's see who walks with the spoils' he snarled quietly.

The clash began with Sten launching himself at Sa. She crouched and easily deflected the clumsy attempt on her life. Gildas held the other two thieves back as Bensah and Kado took on the soldiers.

In her cocoon beneath the snow Ange could hear the scuffle and grunts and then blood plume through the ice covering her. She pulled out her dagger ready just in case.

Sa saw Kado being pulled to the ground by one of the soldiers about to inflict the lethal blow. Sa's dagger sliced through his hand as Kado's slammed into his chest. Gildas had managed to dispatch one of the brigands but then, two of the soldiers rounded on him.

Bensah meanwhile stood his ground over Ange's temporary grave waiting for the remaining Matavian as he raced towards him. The Matavian came at Bensah swiftly thrusting his massive sword with ragged teeth for a blade directly at his head and as he did so his foot sunk into the ice just to the side of Ange's head. Bensah looked down fearful that he may have crushed the girl. Suddenly the soldier yelped in surprise and pain as a dagger poked through his foot. It disappeared and shot up again. Losing balance, he fell over. Bensah quickly plunged his axe into the man's head. Nekoda came pounced on one of the thieves. Its thickened hide deflecting the clumsy blade strokes from the overwhelmed soldier.

'Keep down again sister. We're not finished yet.' He scuffed the snow over her again and went towards the others. Four on four but the soldiers and thieves were more battle ready than himself and Kado. One of the thieves threw Nekoda off and attempted to slice the dog's head off but Sa kicked him directly in the knee and Kado bought his dagger down into his neck.

Gildas soon took out the soldier behind him and whipped the remaining thief's head off in one move. Sten began to make a run towards the entrance near the waterfall. Kado and Sa gave chase. Behind the gushing waterfall of the Draan, Gildas and Bensah watched Sa and Kado play with the thief briefly in their Draxus style of fighting and then one of the figures collapsed with a spray of red penetrating the white wash of the water.

'It's easier just to run em through with a blade trader' Gildas grunted as he cleaned his axe on the edge of the river.

Bensah was pulling Ange up out of the snow.

'Or a dagger in the foot' replied Bensah grinning at Ange's quick thinking during the melee.

'We will make camp further along the river; we should be able to make it to Blackspike's toe by dark.' He looked at the sun in the sky and saw it lay just past its zenith. 'Hurry.'

Gildas began to walk ahead while the others gathered themselves together. He and Bensah pushed the dead into the river.

Sa stumbled briefly as the pain of her own wounds broke through the blood lust from the fighting. Kado caught her.

'I am ok Kado. I can walk.' She stood breathing heavily.

Ange watched the bodies of the dead be gently pushed along as its black surface of the river. The darkness of the water reminded her of the crushing void that had enveloped her when she had delved into the prism making her shiver at what now was to come. Roused by Nekoda's wet nose nudging her hand she began to follow Gildas' trail in the snow – nothing broke the blankness until the horizon met the grey sky.

8

Shadows of Oblyquixiton

The Aracnine stood on the red dirt of the cavern swaying in silent unison. They felt the force of the Caemexa within the rock as they watched the bones of Voloc melt back into it. The black fur of the wolf it had inhabited flew away into the shadow of the ancient cavern. The guardians would wait now until the winds were ripe for re-awakening. They felt how diminished the world had become since the loss of the demon and the custodians from the world of heavy light. To the Aracnine's eyes this world was chaotic and purposeless. The silence of the demon's prison was something to be desired and the need for the creature to break its chains made no sense to them. It had been ordained many millennia ago at the time of the schism between Oblyquixiton and Caemeris that the Aracnine were created to watch. They were the keepers of memory. The ones to see when dark and light, emptiness and movement had bled together, and creation began. They had seen the fell creatures that were spawned from the void and the chains which controlled them. They became the urns where the chaos and order were remembered. They became the weavers of time. But they

118

had grown bored with their purpose and asked for a time when they could worship and bow down in obedience to something instead of existing on the edge of creation. The voice came to them in the silence 'Their patience would be rewarded in time' with a vision showing the First of the Aracnine of when that time would come.

Finally, all trace of the wolf had decayed except for its skull. Its empty sockets stared at the cavern around it. Belmaris was still strong and had done its work to rid the world of the beast. First scraped a talon along the snout leaving a slight singe. It stirred the air into a circling wind around the guardians causing an image to form of the time Magmeris had died at the hands of this demon. They the weavers had been searching for the breech for eons but were too late. Across the scored darkness lay the obliterated remains of the mighty sister to Belmaris. In it lay the shadow eating all the light and letting none out. The guardians had wrestled with the shadow for its insolence to breech its void. The beast grew strong chewing on the dead star around its feet. 'The void existed before the Caemeris and it shall return to me.' The voice snarled at the Aracnine. Finally as it ate the last shining spec, a chain began to form in the emptiness, link after link entwining the guardians and shadow until the links formed in the bones of their chests and pierced the shadow straight through its black heart. Suddenly the bonds of hardened light wrenched tightly, chaining the gaolers and their captor together. The shadow screeched and the guardians pulled. Despair tore through the ancient creatures as the vision of the emptiness of eternity stretched ahead, forever chained to the shadow with no reprieve or release burned into their memory.

First raised its talons and a cry tore its face in two bursting through the weave of created matter up towards the first reaches of Caemeris and into the emptiness where it once lay.

'What of our reward at times end?'

But no answer came in the darkness as shadow and gaoler lay shackled and the screech of rebellion was swallowed in the emptiness of Magmeris' tomb.

The image melted away as the guardians stepped away from the skull on the dirt and took their place along the cavern's walls. First could feel the chain inside its empty chest and called again

'What of our reward at times end?'

The cavern returned to its silence like the grave of an animal that had wandered too far from the sun and died within its walls. The emptiness pulsed beneath the Iron Desert with the only signs of life the footprints of little rodents scampering trying to hide from the great lizards that sunned themselves on the rocks. Belmaris baked the red dirt and the iron it contained, but try as it might, it could not melt the metal to form a mirror to reflect its rays.

— — — —

Voloc had been its first name when the void spewed it forth into the realm of light. Its memory was laden with the death of the First Star Caemaris, mother of Magmeris and Belmaris, far away from where they now lie. Voloc seethed at the beauty it contained. Eons it existed, still and lifeless, with only the memory of the mother's death to fill its mind. For the cruelty of the void to the offspring it bore was the vision of its own emptiness but Voloc had been corrupted for the great star had left its mark in its being, and always that light burned driving the shadow to lust for its destruction so that eventually at the end of time all trace of the searing pain of the great star's memory would be gone, and only the darkness remain.

Voloc lay limp and almost transparent so that not even its gaolers could see where it had fallen. The black specs knitted together to form the shadow, darker, and darker against the blackness until its claw came to its chest and felt the chain that lay there. The blackness coalesced around the chain that bound it and soon its eyes took shape; lifeless, no blood yet from the newer creatures, which thrived on the Belmaris' glow. Soon the shadow stood and saw the light again that had been extinguished just after its birth and roared in vengeance at its eternal enemy.

Silence clothed the malformed creature as it waited. In time the gaolers would find it. A memory formed; a face, a prisoner had found its way to the shadow's voice and stayed. It shone brightly in the dark, even brighter than the first star and it sent agony into Voloc's mind. It was a god made by the makers of the light, but the prisoner had spurned its creators. The dark had seen the eyes of the god seeking its own glory and lost to the vision that had been its purpose. Voloc stepped forth when the light had weakened from the loss of one so bright and took the prisoner devouring its memory and destiny for its own. The pain seared through the shadow and its chains of bondage formed another link inside the imprisoned god plummeting it to Voloc's cage, to lie in captivity as the shadow grew in strength again. Then a new cry in the darkness could be heard in the eons of time that passed. Something searched for the prisoner, a woeful voice full of grief and pain. It came close but never found Voloc's lair. The chains rippled with the sorrow of the call and the ceaseless quest for the lost god but so dark had the god's mind become it no longer felt the sorrow; only reeled from the pain the light caused when the voice had neared the throne of bondage the god sat upon.

Then with time Voloc saw another world that had been born of Belmaris' heat. The world basked in brightness and it grew before the empty eyes of the shadow causing the ancient memories to flare again. So began the wars of creation as Voloc the destroyer sought to halt the dawning of new creatures into the void. But the caemexa of this new world thrust the shadow back again and again. Then as the last battle was waged Voloc on the brink of being hurled back to its cage by the mighty custodian of Arglethium, was freed by the Aracnine. Behind the guardians, chained and rotted by its prison, they dragged the god imprisoned by Voloc.

As the shadow and its quarry were hauled back to its lair, Voloc heard the mighty Norbu, custodian of the new world cry, 'My brethren'. Then Voloc saw the custodian reach out to another. This other's haunting lament which had torn the dark heart of Voloc to shreds, was awash with tears. The god had stirred and in that instant all knowledge of its creation and destruction had been imparted between the gods. It was captured by Norbu and crushed into a bright stone of light. Then the chain wrenched and Voloc and the Descendant of Caemeris were swept back to their cage.

Eons passed and the sorrowful voice came close once more,

the shadow sought it out and found the remains of the god's memory now contained within the sorrowful lament. Voloc also saw the light burned with the same brightness as the memory of the First star. Voloc knew that all the power and the life of Caemeris lay in the jewel wrought by Norbu from the tears of this sorrow. The shadow neared the god and pulling away some of the blackness that filled the god's mind to let it remember what it had once been. Voloc spoke of betrayal and vengeance and maligned the light that the god remembered and then it let it hear the sorrowful cry that called in the emptiness. The god sat staring into the red eyes of the shadow and thought of death and hatred with the same malice as its gaoler. Descendant wept when it saw its destiny shatter before it. Descendant roared its grief into the silent emptiness when it heard Ascendant's lament echo far out of reach. Descendant saw the jewel which now contained its power and destiny wrenched from it by Ascendant and Norbu. Anger seethed in the god's mind.

Voloc finished spewing its venom into the god's mind and waited for the stars of light to become weary.

The blackness knitted together until the faceless shape began to form as it remembered now what had sent it back to its bondage and it remembered the last thing that happened on the world below. The red eyes flared into life peering across the void and the cry of Voloc's rebirth screamed the death of the First Star and its offspring. It bellowed through the emptiness in great tidal waves of malice destroying everything it touched. Even the fell creatures born of Voloc's reign felt the wrath of their creator and were obliterated into the darkness, macerated, and forgotten.

The Aracnine woke again when they heard the call and moved off the cavern walls where the skull still lay. The First reached down and picked up the bone and lifted it to the roof of the cave. Its talons burned into the bone and chanted the ancient litanies to call its prisoner back to its gaolers. As it held the skull, time stilled, slowly the Aracnine watched the beast form in front of them. The last thing restored were the red eyes in the vault of the head. It howled as it walked to the entrance of the cave across the iron desert and night sky. The shadow placed its snout to the dirt and sniffed it. It could smell the raw dense light hidden within the dirt, all the power which could be used to bring the destruction which had created Voloc.

Looking towards the horizon Voloc saw the coast and where the people lived. They would work and forge all the metal that was needed. It sniffed the air searching for the jewel, but it could not see it; not yet. The Keeper had hidden it well. It took to the desert and the Aracnine followed again as Voloc began its reign on Arglethium.

The black shape moved quickly down the red cliffs that surrounded the village Ferren. It was like many of the other villages that dotted the iron coast, situated upon undulations of red sandstone cliffs with deep bays for the trading ships to moor, interspersed with long stretches of beaches of pink sand. The sand was mined and melted into diamonds.

'Round them all up and set them to dig the dirt' the shadow rasped to the Aracnine.

Voloc looked at the ocean and watched the currents ebb at its feet. The water spirit had gone, and nothing stood in its way now. The prism remained hidden but with time it would find it when all the hidden places were laid open for Voloc to see. Shrieks of terror echoed across the still air. Voloc peered towards the noise. The guardians were herding the villagers together and binding them with chains they formed in their talons. Already one of them was leading a group back across the desert towards the caves. It would begin there, the destroyer thought. A stinging pain niggled in its paws as the first rays of dawn touched the hide. It waited for as long as it could but soon the burning became too strong. Again, Voloc the destroyer was ransomed to the night until Belmaris could be extinguished.

The shadow followed the guardian and their prisoners to the ancient tomb it had awoken. It stood in the darkness waiting. Voloc had smelt the ancient blood that ran here amongst the iron sand people. As it spilt over the sand and rock with their digging the shadow could feel it ebb to life within the bones and fur it now lived in – erupting in waves of power through its being. As the first pile of rocks was laid at its feet, the beast looked within the banded stripes of the rubble. Soon the rock began to change shape into a shield and metal vest, then an axe.

'The next' it commanded.

Another villager rolled a boulder beneath the towering wolf like god. Voloc's red eyes flared and again the same happened. Soon a pile of armour and weapons lay at its paws.

'First, have them take these back to the shores ready for the ships when they come' Voloc then lurched at First and seized its throat. Dragging it to its knees it held the Aracnine like a vice. First felt the emptiness tear into its form. Then suddenly the beast stepped back, letting the creature go. First stood to its full height, a faint glow ebbed around its form.

'Continue here' commanded Voloc.

First swept its great talon swept across another pile of rubble and more weapons melted into shape upon the dirt.

Voloc stood at the shores and howled into the night. Its cry spread across the waters rippling the surface and back across the land. Voloc's dirge of birth and domination was heard by all that stood on the red sands of the iron coast. Soon a canoe came paddling towards it.

'To Ranik' it growled at the rower.

It transformed into a shadow shape of a man as it stepped into the canoe. In it sat two soldiers, they steered the canoe towards a tall ship with the eagles flying in the wind. It set sail for the Bay of Tears. Voloc went beneath into the darkness of the hull as the sun greeted the sails over the horizon.

As the great ship moored in the still moonlit waters Voloc sniffed the air as it headed toward the White Palace. It gulped the perversion and malice that pervaded the hearts of those dwelling within in the stoney walls. It found the old man. He looked pale and wizened as if the work he had been set to do gnawed away from the inside. A candle flickered as Voloc entered.

Ranik stood up from looking at a map of the Aeserean Kingdom. He had forgotten the intensity of the red eyes.

'My Lord you are restored.'

'Yes servant. I see you make war on the lands of the setting star Belmaris. How long before they are taken?'

'They are hardy fighters and the territory is full of valleys and forests making it difficult to openly battle against them.

My army gathers to the north at the base of the ranges and will seek to attack from the lesser known paths. The City of Esteron lies in the centre of the valley of Aeserea. If my soldiers invade from the western passage th …'

Suddenly a snarl came from across the room and a dark claw locked around Ranik's throat.

'Send your ships south to the land you call the iron coast. It is there weapons and armour lie for the soldiers to use in battle.'

Ranik gasped as the claw let go from around his throat.

'Yes Lord.'

'Have you any news of the Keeper of the jewel I seek.'

'Nay my lord. I will summon Faad, he has just returned from inspecting the armies gathered for the invasion.' Ranik rang a bell.

'Send for Lord Faad.'

The servant that came in noticed how cold the room was.

'My lord let me light a fire for you.'

'Nay I am fine. Quickly fetch Faad.' The servant left but hesitated near the corner of the chamber that lay in shadow as if sensing something was there.

'Hurry boy before I lash you' roared Ranik as the tyrant felt the claw form around his neck again.

When Faad entered he felt the iciness of the air and a feeling of dread formed with in his bones. The night he rode to Ko's palace and had watched the demon run beside him as a wolf returned to him. Faad knew the demon had awoken as soon as the air hit his lungs. Faad had barely stepped into his chambers when he had been summoned by the shaken servant boy.

Dishevelled and pale he bowed to Ranik as he felt eyes boring into his mind.

'My lord has something happened to summon me so quickly.' Ranik looked beyond him. Faad smelled the foul breath as it neared his ear. A dark shadow in the shape of a claw moved onto his face.

'Let me see.'

Faad felt the fear and bile rise in his throat as Voloc saw all that captain knew. Images raced until one word seemed to stop it all and freeze the piercing pain that had been shooting through Faad's skull. The words a great warrior and a desert child drifted through the sea of images.

'What was said of these clayborn, soldier?' Voloc turned Faad towards him.

Faad's legs began to turn to jelly when he saw the red eyes and wondered why Ranik had struck a bargain with such a creature; their destruction was at hand.

'It was the gossip of the soldiers; a fight broke out after a die match went badly and three Matavians were killed. As the thieves were being pursued one of the soldiers was wounded and spoke of these two. The girl stabbed him with a dagger. It was later that he saw them at the northern gates of Shadaraq. There was also gossip of the graanar using a weapon full of the light of the sun.'

'Why that place, where does it lead?'

'A passage lies there that leads to the great northern lands beyond the mountains. But it is treacherous, they would not have survived the trek through as the brigands and murderers make their home and feed off the unwary.'

Voloc let go.

'Servant what is this land made of, these icelands.'

'It is the northern wastes lord. It is bound by ice and raging wind storms all year. It is the top of our world. I have heard rumours that only a few times a year does night fall. The sun dances along the edge of the world but never sinks below it.'

Voloc chuckled deeply, 'Oh little Keeper of the tears, perhaps you will thwart the mighty shadow.'

Ranik looked at Faad who had become deathly white not understanding.

'Can it be invaded?' choked Ranik.

'The land is cruel and unforgiving and the graanar are formidable in their strength, more so in their lands. It would require a massive army to survive the trek north and then to battle. But Lord there is nothing there of import, it is all imprisoned in ice' replied Faad.

Instantly the claw squeezed around his neck, almost making Faad black out with the force.

'The jewel goes there to the protection of your star. The warrior will guide its Keeper safely through his lands' Voloc spat.

'Faad send soldiers to follow this girl. At least we can know where they are until a way of regaining what our master seeks.'

Faad nodded and then made to leave. Voloc looked his way and Faad felt the probe again but it let him go. A weight lifted off his shoulders as he left Ranik's chambers. The world would be turned upside down by this demon to find this thing it desired. The northern icelands could not be conquered. The Graan lived within the laws set down by the wind and the ice. Faad remembered the moment at Ko's palace when the bright light had blinded everyone and the power that had forced all of them to the ground. The demon was intent on destruction only and the jewel would allow it to do it. It had no desire to rule or conquer this world but to see it die.

'Get rest servant for you march to war' Voloc hissed at Ranik. The tyrant collapsed on the floor clutching his mind.

Voloc strode the empty passageways of the White Palace its mind probing every person contained within the walls. It came to a chamber and felt drawn to two very warm hearts, fragile but brimming with ancient blood. The hearts beat in rhythm with one another peacefully and strong. Moving into the chamber it saw the babes asleep in the womb. Voloc went to the babes and went inside their minds. Their mother and fathers blood coursed strongly but the mothers would win in the end. Leaving the babies who remained peacefully oblivious to the malice that had come near to them, the shadow went to the mother and drank fear again. It saw Ranik ravaging her in the memories. The perversity of the man on top of the girl amused Voloc. Entering both the minds it found they were the parents of the younglings. Voloc persisted with the girl. Tessi felt the icy claws in her mind and froze.

Voloc saw the desert and the little girls playing together and the sorrow that filled Tessi's heart; the death that had come at the hands of Voloc and the decay that lingered in the girl's memory. The shadow saw the fear that emanated from her at the sight of Ranik and the queen. It pricked the heart to taste the ancient blood and felt energised. It saw the confusion which lay in the heart for the children inside; a desire to protect and care for the younglings and loathing as well at their father and creation. A desire to be rid of them and end the curse of their creation. The confusion washed over Voloc. The shadow touched the tiny hearts and scored them with a mark of its memories. 'Younglings you will be birthed in the time of Voloc's reign. Long shall it live. You will be formidable, born of caemexa and oblyquixita.' Then Voloc drank in the sorrow for another, the Keeper that kept the gift it sought, born of the same blood, sisters.

'You will be useful clayborn youngling.'

A deep chuckle left the dark shape that had settled over Tessi as it went to find the queen.

Tessi kept her eyes closed and curled into a ball, paralysed, and sobbing at what had just been near her. She had felt it linger over the image of Ange and the babies.

It had been easy for Voloc to find the queen. Her heart was as cold as the shadow and did not resist its presence. She lay on the bed asleep. Her mind was filled with the void as her dreams had died long ago with her children. What remained were empty shapes drifting in a sea of lost happiness. The bitterness in her heart was like the chain that sat in Voloc's own chest; forever bonded never to be dislodged. The anger and loathing the queen held toward the babes in the servant's womb was sweet to Voloc and it drank it in, so much so that its form thickened and did not feel the first rays of the dawn touch the shadow it cast.

Retreating down to the vaults of the palace the shadow waited again for the day to pass. It thought of the queen and the babes and the keeper of the prism most keenly. Voloc let its mind go back to its birth and remembered the power coursing through it as it devoured the placental remains of Magmeris.

'Your blood and precious token are mine Caemeris' came the murmur from the cellar below. While above Tessi's mind reeled with nightmares of her babies and the queen's bloodied hands holding a dagger dipped in their blood over their dead bodies.

The Queen looked into the dawn rays and her eyes were as red as the sun itself, she felt power coursing through her body and the barbed talons of Voloc plunged into her heart.

9

Concubine

The girl came first followed quickly by the twin brother. The bloody mess that lay over them was deftly cleaned off as Sala, the hand servant of the queen, washed them in the copper tub. Their violent conception and the chaos of birth slowly cleansed away in the water to reveal the fragile beauty of new life.

'She is bleeding. Rags!'

Tessi was in a stupor of exhaustion. Her eyes roused when she heard the cries. 'Show me.' At barely sixteen summers Tessi did not know what to feel for the babies as Sala carried them over to her.

'Boy and Girl' Sala indicated with each arm tucked around the babes. Tessi reached forward to touch them but suddenly pain shot through her pelvis as the mid wife Hanni pressed down on her abdomen to staunch the blood. She heard the tyrant's voice booming in another chamber. Too exhausted to care, the usual knot of fear she felt whenever she heard him did not form as she blissfully sank back into unconsciousness.

When she woke, she felt the dull ache in her legs and

buttocks. She tried to sit up, but a fresh rose of blood broke through onto the sheet.

'Lie still it is too soon. I will bring them to feed.' The two little babes were bought over to her. Hanni helped rearrange her dress and attached one of the babe's mouths to her breast. Instantly the child began sucking. Tessi squirmed at the sensation. Soon both babes were happy suckling. Mixed feelings of loathing and warmth came over her as she knew these children would always be a reminder of the curse which had buried her family and ravaged her life. They finished feeding. Hanni took them and placed them in the cribs. She did not want to let go of them now. She kissed the boy on the head 'Your name will be Noab' and to the girl 'and your name will be Angette.'

'Oh no Lord Ranik will name them as he does with all he has sired. Although you are favoured amongst his concubines, they will hold rank above any of the other babes.'

'To me they will be known as Noab and Angette.'

Ranik came into the room with the queen. His face was more drawn these days. He had launched war against the Western Territories and now minor rebellions had begun to break out in the feudal provinces of the Drax Kingdom. Tessi tried to sit up but was still too weak.

'Look my dear, are they not strong. They look like the milk and chocolate sweeties that are made for the summer festivals.'

The queen stood, stony faced. Her porcelain white skin and black hair only made her demeanour more severe. She had endured years of barbs and personal anguish at not producing more children, but she had learnt to hide her pain from Ranik, if only to diminish his cruelty towards her. He would not toss her aside nor would she give him the satisfaction of standing down from her throne. They both knew the people's loyalty and the guards were bound more to her ancient lineage than to the House of Ranik. It was their mutual loathing for each other and her wealth and connections which sustained their marriage and throne.

'They will be my legacy for the empire I build. Once again I will restore the great Matavian houses to their rightful suzerainty.' He tickled Noab on the nose and giggled as the baby squirmed at his touch. Noab opened his eyes and Ranik saw that one was green and the other brown.

'Look at that, a perfect brew of the East and the West. Is she not strong my dear to have survived my ravages and still bear me children? After all, not many do, do they? No, she is special this one. As the banner of the Matavian Ruler spreads across the middling lands so will his progeny.'

A lascivious grin spread across his face as he said this. Tessi cringed in fear at the words as she felt the cage of his perversions close around her. She tried to look at the children to forget for just a little while.

'The people will never accept the offspring of a desert dweller as their ruler. You are a fool Tias.'

Tessi stared at the couple as they stood over the babies, wanting to take them and run as far away as she could from these monsters that had enslaved her in a simple barter at Ancrid City. Something so many had endured with no thought given other than to the few coins that signalled the lock on the chains that they would then endure. Tessi's heart ached as it threw her memory back to the last time, she saw Ange. The lonely figure lying under the Boab, in the great desert near their village was clear in her mind. She closed her eyes trying to shut out the grating voice of the beast that held her captive now. She tried hard not to respond when one of the babies let out a squeal, but her instincts overrode it as her body wanted to take the child and hide it. Hanni pushed her back as she got up to go to Noab. She shook her head at Tessi warning her not to move while the tyrant was still here.

'Stay my dear and enjoy them. See the new empire before you. All things must change. After all the delicate nature of the wombs of your family, seem to lack the fortitude required for a ruling monarch' Ranik taunted at the Queen.

His eyes flashed at his wife with a delighted malice as he left the chamber. Her face grimaced slightly at the barb about her barrenness since their babes had died. By his hand she thought. She formed a fist and dug her nails into the flesh of her palm from the spiteful hate rising in her throat.

She turned as she heard the concubine stir. Tessi had sat up wanting to protect her babies but could only watch the little bundles as Hanni took them and placed them into the cradle near the window. The queen went towards them but stopped and looked out over the ocean.

'Are you well recovered my dear?'

Tessi startled slightly at the sound of her voice. It was thickly accented as she spoke in the trader tongue. Hanni had been giving her lessons with Matavian but she still missed words when anyone spoke quickly.

'Yes ma'am.'

'Good. I remember the first days after the birth of my children, my body was worn thin, but it will pass. The desert people of the east, that is where you were bought from was not it, are strong. Of course, those first years as a mother were my fondest memories until the babies were taken from me. You are only a child yourself, like me. Be careful! Always watch that your children are safe. We wouldn't want any harm to come to them.'

Tessi watched the queen with widening eyes as she had walked over to the crib and began stroking the babies on the crown of their heads. Her fingers looked like white claws to Tessi; long and slender with nails painted red, as though they had been dipped in blood. She got herself up and swung over the side of the bed. The bleeding began again but she ignored it as the panic began to rise. The queen had started to hum a tune, and the stroke became fiercer, Noab stirred and began to cry.

'My lady!' Tessi cried out as she half collapsed getting out of the bed, the queen ignored her and continued to hum. Just then Hanni came in when she heard Noab's cries.

'Mistress Tessi, get back in bed. My lady.' she curtsied, 'I will tend them.'

The queen stopped and nodded at the midwife.

'You were the midwife who tended to me as well?'

'Ay my lady. Oh, dear mistress we will have to re-wrap you.'

Hanni curtsied quickly and then shot into the bath chamber to fetch some rags when she saw the blood seeping onto the floor from between Tessi's legs. The queen left without speaking only humming the tune.

'Poor dear' Hanni whispered, 'She ain't been right since her own were taken.'

'I am frightened Hanni. Will she hurt my babies? What if Lord Ranik wants to take them away.'

Tessie began to sob as the old midwife changed her rags. She softly tried to settle the young girl but deep down she was right. She had seen the queen become more bitter as time passed. And the babes were a threat to the queen's lineage spanning many generations in the Matavian Kingdom.

'Shoosh, rest now, you will need your strength.' Hanni finished cleaning up and checking that the babies were settled went to her rocking chair in the room where her bed lay. She was old now, almost sixty summers and while the thrill she felt each time a new babe came into her life still made her heart sing, she was weary of the world they would grow up in. A storm was brewing for these two little ones. It was the way of the Matavians; a brutal bunch with Ranik now becoming the most brutal of them all.

Tessi sat feeding Noab near the window that overlooked the ocean. She watched the moonlight twinkle on the surface. Being a desert dweller, the ocean was a frightening mystery to her. Noab gurgled a bit with a full belly. Tessi snuggled into him before handing him to Hanni and then she began to feed Angette. The tiny little hands now chubby and perfect in every detail gripped the swaddling cloth and the bright eyes stared at Tessi's face, watching her.

'They are thriving child. The feast will be very great indeed for their naming day. The Lord is feeling generous normally the babes of his mistresses are not given such a dedication.'

Hanni busily changed Noab and placed him in the cradle as he fell asleep.

'What names has he chosen Hanni?' Tessi was gently stroking Angette's head.

'That will remain unknown until the time of the ceremony.'

Tessi felt the fear rise in her again as a strange premonition came over her as though her children would be swallowed by the white palace and the foam of the waves that beat at its foundations. As if by giving them new names they would become unknown to her.

'Hanni, I have nothing to wear to the ceremony.'

Hanni hesitated slightly as Tessi handed her Angette.

'The concubines are never present at the naming day. You will not even be recorded as the mother. It is considered improper, and an insult to the queen.'

Hanni saw the tears begin to form in Tessi's eyes 'I will be there to tend to them. The ceremony will only be the turn of the glass and then I will bring them back to you.'

Tessi grabbed the midwife's arm 'Oh Hanni, you must keep them safe. I am so afraid that he will take them.' Tessi half sobbed. The old midwife took Angette to the cradle and placed her beside Noab. When the baby was settled, she took Tessi to the bed.

'You need to rest again. You must understand, these are the Lord Ranik's children, all the slaves that bear his babes and even the queen are treated the same. But the babes will know you are their mother.'

Tessi did not believe her but lay down on the bed. The waves were soothing tonight but sometimes when the winds from the west would race across the world and the ocean would heave its way up the side of the white walls of the palace Tessi would lay shivering hoping they did not wash up and sweep her away. Hanni bought her some tea which made her drowsy. She listened to the pulse of the waves beneath as she fell asleep thinking of her children and wondering would become of them.

The queen stood at the right-hand side of the throne to Ranik. Her hand was placed lightly on the back rest.

'Let it begin.'

Hanni and another of the wet nurses took the children to an altar that had been placed in the centre of the banquet hall. She un-wrapped their cloths, instantly Noab began to cry setting off Angette as well.

'Leave them.' snapped Ranik.

The priest came down from the platform with a knife. He took the knife and circumcised Noab. Instantly the child screamed in complete distress. He wrapped the bleeding member and began to chant. The hollow cries of the children reverberated throughout the great hall magnifying off the white marble. Ranik gripped the arm of his throne as the squeals of distress jarred his ears.

The priest held the boy towards the throne.

'Do you Lord Ranik ruler of the lands of Matavia, claim, this boy as your progeny, sired from your loins to be bearer of your name and heir to your throne.'

'I do.'

'And do you Lord Ranik, claim, this girl as your progeny, sired from your loins and to be bearer of your name and heir to the throne.'

'I do.'

'This boy is so named Tias the Second and this girl is so named Mordraag the third.' He smeared oil on their foreheads and ushered the midwives over. Hanni quickly wrapped Noab up tightly to staunch the bleeding. There was applause from the assembled court as the screaming children were carried away.

The Queen stood frozen as she watched the babies being carried back to their chamber. The words of the priest piercing her heart like needles. 'Heirs to the throne and the numbering, they were not the second or third of the same title.'

'Let the feast begin.'

Ranik stood smiling as he went towards the great banquet laid out in honour of the children. He motioned for the queen to come as well.

'Come my dear, it is a joyous occasion is it not?' He sniggered like a child, making her lip curl in disgust at his churlishness. Soon enough he was drunk with a young girl sitting on his knee. She looked barely past fifteen summers. She struggled but he was too strong for her.

The queen saw that Captain Faad had returned and was seated across from them both. He looked haunted and aged since the last time she had seen him. He had barely touched his food.

Ranik was trying to kiss the girl and they both spilled onto the queen.

'Lord Faad, will you accompany me to my chamber.' She rose disgusted.

'Yes, my lady.'

They adjourned hearing Ranik's voice in the background. 'Take the brat to my chambers, I'll teach her how to behave. Wine!'

'You have rested Battle Master. The battle in the west. Are the preparations in place?'

Faad hesitated 'Yes my lady. The contingent is large and strong. As for the weaponry I have not held stronger blades before.'

'So, victory will be swift?'

'Perhaps m'lady.' A strange look came into his eyes, like a memory came back to him. He shivered slightly.

'What did you see Faad?' She whispered in his ears. They had been lovers on and off and she could sense when he kept something from her.

'I do not know, but it walks the earth and seeks death wherever it goes.' They reached the door.

'Stay I will soothe your fears.' He went in with her as she guided him to her bed. Her alabaster skin almost glowed in the moonlight as she removed her gown. Her body had never changed in all the time he had been privy to her seductions, not even after the birth of her children. He wondered again what sorcery the queen dabbled in. He felt inside her as she straddled him. It soothed the heaviness which now lay on his shoulders since the demon had touched him but never satisfied his heart. He stroked her skin as their thrusting quickened, faintly her eyes seemed red in the dim light of the room. His mind went blank as she bent down to kiss him.

She gracefully rose of his heaving body and walked over to her dresser and opened a small draw hidden at the back of the mirror. Removing a small red velvet pouch, she took out two gold cylinders. On them were engraved the initials T and M. She took a lock of hair from the pouch as well and placed it against her cheek.

'Tais and Mordraag. How dare he.' She growled under her breath 'They will never replace my darlings. None shall be heirs unless they are mine.' Her voice cracked just slightly. Faad came over and wrapped his arms around her.

'What are these?' Noticing the cylinders in her hand.

'They are the bones of my children encased in gold to preserve them. Their little fingers and toes forever with me.' Faad grimaced a bit. 'How dare he steal their names and memories. Spawn of a slave child to be heirs to the great kingdom of Matavia. I will not let it be.' Her hand clenched on the bones and Faad felt her body stiffen.

'He is a fool! You know the great houses will not accept those children. He has written his own demise.' The queen hissed.

Faad took the queen's hand as she clenched the souvenirs of her babies' remains.

'Why do you dwell on this sorrow Giandra? He knows the pain it causes you and yet you let him keep pulling it like a hook. Let it go.'

She rounded on him and slapped him across the face. Faad grabbed her hand as she went to hit him again. He stared at the woman he was watching descend slowly into malicious insanity. But then perhaps he would follow as his mind churned with haunting shadows after the meeting with Ranik and the demon.

'You can go now.' She turned her back to him. He felt her skin almost become frigid under his hand with the venomous command dismissing him.

The queen went back to the dresser and stowed the bones back in their pouch along with the hair. She stared for a long time in the mirror fingering the necklace she had worn to the ceremony. It was made of white tapered shells with almost a pearl like sheen. Her earrings were the same. She was thinking of her babies and how beautiful their little smiles were as they lay in their cots and their tiny mouths contorted with the rigours of death. The necklace needed a pendant to complete it she thought. In another few months, by the next summer solstice, those younglings will be just ripe.

Tessi woke the next morning and saw the babies asleep in their cradle. Her head ached from sleeping for so long and her breasts were heavy with milk.

'Ah feel better now deary.' Hanni came over with Noab. He grizzled still from the circumcision.

'What is wrong with him?'

'It is tradition for the Matavian people to remove the skin of the men's members. It is done when they are newborn, so it heals quickly.'

'My people do that also Hanni.' Hesitating 'What did he call them?'

'Tias, the Second, after himself, and Mordraag, the third. She was the first queen of this land many generations ago when Lord Ranik's ancestors invaded from the west.'

'Mine are better. Do you know that Noab is the name of the serpent that lives in the desert and Angette is the name of the precious stones along the riverbed of the mighty Choasa? They shine with all the colours of the world when the midday sun strikes them and are as strong as a mountain's heart. The stone and serpent Hanni – hidden strength and endurance. That's what it means to be a desert dweller.' Tessi snuggled Angette into her.

Hanni nodded happy that the girl was less fearful on the dawn. The old nurse kept her dismay at the names Ranik had chosen for the babies and the boldness to name them heir. If by chance the queen was to be with child again then these babes would not be able to take the throne. The old Lord was playing games.

10

Ice Mother

Gildas ran through the lands of his birth with the speed and agility of the ice bear. He knew the feel of the snow under foot, when it was like a rock, when it had been freshly laid down and when it was thin and likely give way to a massive opening to the ocean that lay beneath the frozen surface. The knowledge of the ice and its unforgiving ways kept the Graan strong and formidable even in times of peace. For the first time in twenty summers, he felt the bond of the clansman to the ice. In his time as Chieftain, he only wanted to wage war on his enemies and had forced the Graan to become like the ice bears, unconquered and elusive. He had forgotten the great mother shared power with no other and her retribution had struck him down along with Jesse and his heir.

The others followed the huge warrior, not speaking of their exhaustion. Even Sa had begun to feel the deep ache in her bones as the winds cut through the fur coverings. But they endured never succumbing to the ice or the pace Gildas set.

'Another league away lies the ridge of the Whitecliffs. We will find shelter there from the wind.'

Ange had been keeping up. She had stubbornly refused Bensah's offer to carry her for a bit.

'Tata,' she said indignantly 'We have many more leagues to go. The snow is easier to walk on then I thought. It holds more firmly than the sands of our land.'

'Ay sister, but the cursed cold makes up for its one kindness.' They continued with Bensah keeping ahead slightly to slow the pace down. Bensah could see the changes in Ange and knew if they survived this trek then nothing would stand in her way. He realised how much kinder the desert had been to his people. Even in the baking heat, the ancient Boabs had stood fast and provided some water as relief, but here, the relentless ice and wind allowed nothing. He had tried eating some of the snow, but it burnt his lips and tongue as if in protest to his need to live.

Bensah also missed the vistas the desert gave and sense of time. Here the sun never set, and the perpetual daylight and brightness gnawed at his mind, making him crave for the night. A blast of wind caught him from the side throwing him off balance slightly. Kado caught him before he completely toppled over in the makeshift boots.

'Thank you Kado, I cannot figure out where I am, it is daylight but no sun. I cannot even remember how long we have been travelling for.'

'I know, the dreams I had in the temple came back to me when we last rested. I nearly wept for the darkness in them. Come or we will lose the others.'

A massive cliff of ice rose suddenly before them. It was formed from two glaciers splitting apart and the north eastern shelf pushed higher above its western counterpart. Everyone peered above them. Ange could not see the top. Nekoda whined at stopping, enjoying the pace they had been running at. It felt like he was one of a pack again. He had run alongside Gildas wearing a fur muzzle making his already massive jaws look twice the size. He nudged Ange who had pulled up next to him. She collapsed onto the ground, gasping for air. Her legs and chest throbbed. She saw Kado looking at her.

'I never ran like that in my homelands' she beamed at him pleased at keeping up with everyone.

Kado smiled back at her, not knowing what to say. He was amazed at her being so little and so strong. She reminded him of Sa.

'We will dig some shelter here beneath one of the ridges. A storm is coming from the west.' Gildas pointed to a smudge of grey in the distance. 'The western winds are deadly. We will not survive their fury out in the open.'

The large Graansman began to hack away at a buttress of ice jutting out from the cliff. At its steepest it stood more than three times the height of Gildas and twice that width again.

'Dig at the base the snow is soft here but will pack hard once we delve down into it.' Everyone began to dig and soon an entrance began to take shape. Gildas went ahead as they went deeper until suddenly the snow gave way altogether and opened out into an empty cavern. Its roof was shaped into an arch over a space that was large enough to snugly fit all of them. Icicles hung from the roof, Gildas snapped one off and sucked on it as he went into the newly dug shelter.

'What is this?' asked Ange

'They are frozen flows of water when the cliffs were first

formed. For a few days in the warmer season the snow melts revealing the Claws of Whitefang. But for now, it will be our shelter until the storm passes.'

Gildas went to the entrance of their hollow and began to rebuild the snow to cover the opening. Soon most of the light had gone except for a gap at the very top to allow air. Bensah relaxed a little as he felt the warmth of the group begin to ease the ache in his back.

'We will need to ration our food. Supplies are still many days away. Once we are past the Whitefang then the steppes open out to fields covered in snow rather than frozen sea that we now travel across.'

'How do you know the time of day in these lands, Graansman?' asked Bensah

'You can't for the sun remains too high and is hidden by the clouds. The light is a reflects what lies behind them. It is the fever of the ice that often kills the uninitiated in the snow not the cold. They wander lost and eventually their head fills with the empty vastness around them. If the Graanar goes on a trek, the time he is away is called the Gronaag; lost time in the trader tongue.'

Bensah nodded understanding how the ice fever could happen.

'At least the sun rises and falls in the desert' he spoke quietly relishing the memory of heat.

As the storm careered into the cliffs Ange jumped at the ferocity of the wind's howling. It seemed alive with fury. Their cave held fast but eventually the shaft of light from the entrance was snuffed out leaving the group in pitch darkness. Nekoda nuzzled deeply into her thigh. She could feel him shivering.

'This place will hold. Sleep while we have warmth and shelter' Gildas voice resonated in the ice cavern.

'How long will it last for?' asked Sa.

'Days at most. It was not the wind of Raajn. Those storms will rage for a whole cycle of grey light, like your leaf fall.'

Gildas sat back and let his mind drift. He felt like he was back in the cell in Banrock. A picture of the witch came to his mind. He wondered in which realm she now sat. Did she know where they were? He noticed the others were silent as he began to doze off. The last thought he had was of Jarrod and himself standing in the forests of Enan. The sorrow in Jarrod's eyes belied the pale fury of his face. Gildas wondered what his younger brother looked like now and what he would do when they met again after so long.

Sa was running through the mantras in her mind as Kado settled near her. His arm was draped across her waist. She did not remove it but wondered what would come of their bond. Sa was still not sure what she and Kado would do once they had reached the territory of the Graan. She felt that hers and Kado's destiny lay elsewhere. If the beast rose again and they defeated it then Kado would then face the battle of reclaiming his throne. She felt Kado pull her closer as he murmured something in his sleep. She was grateful for extra warmth and relaxed more.

Ange felt the prism hanging around her neck. She had had no more dreams of the realm of the gods since being in the icelands. A surge of warmth passed through the pouch and onto her flesh, lessening the cold from the frigid ice beneath. Pulling out the pouch she looked inside wondering what had happened. It was like something called to it. She touched it with her finger. The miasma of colours within its facets were tinged with a shadow. The demon was awake once more. She shuddered as she quickly placed it inside. Time was running out for her and everything else.

Sa you will need to teach me quickly to fight. Assumpta, Norbu, Lido, where are you? Your ancient enemy lies here with us with only me between it and its victory, Ange bit her lip as she thought of the gods and the shadow. The emptiness inside her gouged by the fear of what was to come grew even more. Would it grow so large the demon could leap directly into it and snatch the jewel? She gulped with panic and hugged Nekoda tightly. He licked her on the cheek to comfort her. But it was no use. Ange knew she was alone and it with every passing moment Voloc would draw closer to her.

'It is safe to go out now' Gildas voice pierced the silent cavern as the wind subsided.

'Our rations are running out graanar' spoke Bensah aching from lying down for so long. 'How long have we been here?'

'Not long, I think only a day and one night by the southern territories, trader. We are fortunate.'

Ange heard Nekoda chewing on the icicles that had formed at the base of the cave. Gildas began to dig at the entrance. As light broke into the cave Bensah and Ange both audibly breathed a sigh of relief.

'Is it safe clansman?' he called out.

'Yes, gather everything, it is clear.'

Gildas stood now at the tip of the arch of ice they had taken refuge under. Everything looked the same except for more snow underfoot. He took a breath at the freshness of the air around him and felt glad to be back in his land. He wondered if the Graanar would be as welcoming as the snow and ice. The others began to poke their heads through, and he helped them up onto the new ground.

'We will reach the edge of a vast frozen lake one hundred leagues from here. It has fresh water trapped by deep walls of ice keeping the salt of the eastern oceans away. There will be food there. Fill your casks with the fresh snow that has been laid before it hardens. It is the sweetest water to drink as it comes straight from the tits of the clouds.'

Halfway to the lake Ange fell over suddenly as her legs cramped. Sa picked her up and asked Kado to carry her. Looking the assassin directly in the eyes 'I do not need help. I will be ok. Let me be.'

'Conquer what you can Ange but accept help when it finds you. You have too far to go yet and you have already proven your courage and stamina tenfold. Death is a worthy opponent to be defeated by, but only if it is justified in its victory.'

Ange nodded feeling another cramp begin. Kado picked her up and they continued.

The lake was only discernible from the rest of the tundra, by a small hump of snow that continued in a long vague line arching away towards the north. When they reached the lip of the lake Gildas tapped on the surface of the ice plate. A cracking sound echoed around them as the axe handle hit the hard surface. He slammed his axe in again. Shards of ice flew up into the air. He continued until he had gouged a tunnel leading down to black water.

'The fish will be hungry.'

Taking the axe, he nicked his thumb slightly and let some blood drop onto the leather strap. Dunking it in and out of the hole, he then placed his thumb directly over it to let more drip into the water. Suddenly a set of black jaws shot up through the gap snapping at the strap. Like lightening Gildas whacked the fish with the blade in his other hand and flung it out onto the snow. He cracked its skull and instantly the manic jaws closed shut. He then threw the carcass back into the water. The others watched as the frenzy of feeding began to spill up over the well onto the frozen sheet. Gildas quickly made a neat pile of black jaw fish for them to feast on.

'That will do. Remove the heads and pile them over there. The belly is the sweetest flesh.'

Ange and Bensah found eating the raw fish turned their stomachs but they swallowed it as their empty stomachs roared with hunger.

'The black jaw fish is a delicacy for us. Are they in abundance here Gildas?' asked Kado as he scooped another fillet into his mouth with relish.

'Only for a short season.'

He looked suspiciously at Kado not wanting to tell him too much. To the Graan they were easy food to stay alive on when they trekked the massive wastes. But a lucrative trade had developed around the carp, mostly by the cunning of the clansman not to let the southern traders know of their abundance keeping them at a high price in the markets. The Graan knew the traders would risk the vastness and dangers of the journey if there was coinage to be made.

'Come here, each of you are to fill a small pouch with the poison in the fish. It may be useful later' commanded Gildas. 'Now just beneath this fin, massage it like a tit and you will see the poison come out. Careful with it, it can kill a bear.'

Gently massaging it the venom oozed out at a slow pace making it easy to pour into the leather purse. Ange looked for something to use. She nearly pulled out the prism in her excitement at being included. Bensah threw her one of his coin purses that was empty now.

'Hang the rest of the carcasses on your waist belts, the flesh will not rot in the coldness.' Gildas had six of them hooked on to his coat.

'Gildas I do not have any arrows to dip the poison in' asked Ange.

'We will make some when we reach my tribal lands.'

There was a slight glint of respect in Gildas eye as he looked at Ange. She was tough like the clan wives.

'How much further is it to your lands?' she asked.

'At least five hundred leagues. It depends if the storms follow us. The only safe passage is to stay near the Claws. That will take us east rather than a straight line but there is no other way. Come let us go with fat bellies.' Gildas almost looked cheerful as he slapped himself on the stomach full of the carp.

Sa wondered how Gildas picked the direction of their journey as she still could not get her bearings in this tundra. She raced along ahead between Ange and Gildas trying to see any mark in the sky that showed whether they faced east north or west. But all she could see was a slightly duller white of the snow clouds that fed the tundra. She sped up to catch Gildas.

The cliffs had passed into a blur on the horizon, sometimes she caught glimpses of it ahead of them then they would be to their left.

'Warrior, how do you know where we are going?'

'I have walked the length of the cliffs many times, I know the path it sets without seeing it. My land lies above on the eastern ridges where the snow eases letting life live on its fringes. Even an unseasoned traveller if they survived would soon find a way there. Look in the distance where the clouds meet the earth. What do you see?'

'Nothing it is as blank to my eyes as an artist's canvass.'

'The curve of the world. You can run in circles and never lose yourself assassin, eventually you will return from where you began. Remember that if a time calls for it.'

Sa looked again but could still not see what Gildas spoke of. Truly the Graan were born of the ice.

Ange kept up with the others as she felt her body adjust to the shoes and snow again. She was pleased with herself and her heart had swelled at Gildas' approval. She let her breathing flow in rhythm with the gliding movement of her legs. Little puffs of warm air broke through her balaclava of fur. The snow had been drifting down slowly tickling the exposed part of her face. It was wondrous to her eyes that it existed at all. Her mind drifted off barely feeling the cramp beginning to grow in her weak leg. She was gliding along the snow and Nekoda raced alongside her. Her crippled body did not matter here as the snow helped her manoeuvre more easily. She thought this must be how the other children felt when they ran with ease and swiftness like the cheetahs. Her mind filled with snow and white and the cutting iciness of the wind. She let it drift back and forth between the others and Nekoda's paws padding on the ice around her. Her heart soared as she increased her pace. She wished Tessi and Mata could see her now. Nekoda's grunting became heavier as she went even faster. Suddenly a massive gust of wind propelled her forward and she went spilling head over heels into the snow. Winded and dazed she took a moment to clear the ice from her face. She vaguely heard yelling, but it seemed to be far away.

'Nekoda why did you do that for?' thinking that it was the dog playing. Getting up she was thrust over again causing her to black out as her head connected with a hard slab. Suddenly a massive roar and yellowed teeth followed by foul breath met her. Screaming she realised it was not Nekoda at all. A hand yanked her by the collar and dragged her away from the approaching bear.

'Be quiet' Gildas hissed into her ear as he slowly began to back away. Ange looked up and saw a massive ice bear rearing up onto its legs. There were two cubs behind her, larger than her but dwarfed by their mother. The bear towered over Gildas at least by his height again. Another roar emanated from its mouth and Ange could feel it vibrate in her chest. Little darts came flying but simply bounced off the thick fur. Sa and Kado were getting ready to try it again.

'Enough it will only enrage her more. Step away' Gildas called to them.

Gildas looked behind him desperate to get away from the bear. It was rare for them to be hunting so far south. The cubs were growing braver as well, heading towards Sa and Kado.

Bensah stood ready with his axe. She came down with such force from her pose of aggression that the ground shook beneath Gildas. The Graan were generally swift to kill any threat but for many generations they had left the bears alone mostly out of superstition that they became the spirits on the howling winds when they died.

'Kill it Gildas with the poison.' called Bensah.

'It will not penetrate the hide.'

A massive claw swiped at his head barely missing it. He darted away towards the lip of snow that showed the edge of the lake. The bear followed.

'Run to the edge of the lake.' He shouted. He kept running until the bear was almost upon him and Ange. He took out the sword and instantly it welded to his hand. The bear reared up again.

'Get behind me girl and run straight ahead. The rest of you run. Ice Mother I do not wish to kill you.'

He bought the sword down and slashed at her paw. She roared in pain and the blackness of her eyes shone in anger at the Graanar's insolence. Sa and Bensah came near to help Gildas. The bear looked at them for a second. Gildas took a glance at her midriff. She ran at him he bolted away trying to outrun her.

'Get the girl and run from here!'

The bear thumped down just behind him to show her strength. Tiny cracks began to form under her feet. The two cubs came from behind, swinging their heads to show their anger. They mimicked every move of their mother as they began to thump up and down to show their aggression.

Bensah looked back and saw Gildas slip over as the bear got him with one of her paws. He was trying to thrust the sword inside her, but she was overpowering him burying him completely in her massive belly of fur. Bensah threw Ange to Kado and ran back to Gildas. He began to shout to distract the bear. It used to work with the lions and jackals back home, but the bear ignored him as she thrust herself up for the lethal blow to Gildas. The clansman skittered quickly from under her along the ice. He slashed the sword across her throat sending blood spraying onto the snow, but it was not enough to fatally wound her.

Bensah leaped with his axe thinking Gildas blow would slow her but the blade caught in her massive shoulder muscle and he was thrown back onto the ice.

'Bensah run!' screamed Gildas. His feet slipped on the slurry of blood and ice as he tried to get up to reach Bensah.

Bensah felt the claws and teeth clamp onto his arms and shoulders and then he was falling. The mother turned to look at her cub's first kill. Gildas skittered on his back to flee from the behemoth. He watched the blood stain the white ice and the cubs rip the trader to pieces. He heard the screams further away. The mother slowly backed away swinging side to side warning Gildas that even though she had fed her young she would still attack.

'Run now!' Gildas looked momentarily as the great mother sat contentedly watching her cubs learning to feed. He saw the trader slowly disappear into the mouths of the gods of the graanar. She had been teaching them how to hunt. He ran towards the others. Sa was holding Nekoda and Kado held

Ange as she screamed wanting to get to Bensah.

'Hurry, he will not be enough for them.'

He ignored Ange and kept running. Kado picked her up but she struggled too much. She got away and started to run back towards where Bensah lay. Gildas caught her and slapped her across the face. Stunned she went still. He threw her over his shoulder and sprinted away from the carnage. Sa struggled to stop Nekoda from getting away but managed to hold him. He growled viciously at Gildas and Sa, snapping at them both. Ange hung limply over the warrior's shoulder.

'Fast now, go for the middle of the lake, the ice is thinnest there and they will not follow.'

They ran for more almost two leagues until Kado collapsed with exhaustion. Gildas stopped and placed Ange gently onto the ice.

'We should be safe here. Assassin do you have any brews to calm the girl when she wakes.'

'Nay clansman. Why did you not kill the bear? You could have slain it.'

Gildas hesitated. Looking intently at Sa and Kado and then down at Ange but did not answer.

Ange awoke in the darkness of another cave that instantly felt cold and empty surrounded by howling winds deafening her thoughts. She rubbed her cheek and wondered why it was sore and her eye swollen. Then the image of Bensah came back to her and she started to cry. The bears were on him. She had seen them coming towards him, but he did not hear her cries of warning. Nekoda snuffled against her hearing her stir in the darkness.

'Here Ange, have some water and fish.'

Sa's voice came to her, but she felt hatred rise in her heart. They were all here but not Bensah. She batted the cask away. Sa left the fish near her but Nekoda gobbled it up.

'Let her sleep. We still have many leagues to cross before we reach my lands and even then, I will need to find out if we are welcome.'

'You should have killed the bear Graanar' Ange hissed in the dark at Gildas.

'The ways of the Graan have been for as long as we have dwelt within the ice. Our ways and the ways of these lands are the same. To change them for a glimmer of unknown spirits to our world that have chosen to forsake us so that we must now run like hunted rodents and battle for a victory against a demon they bought with them. A victory that lives on a fine thread of hope and shrouded promises. Nay I will not slay the mother of the ice that has suckled my tribe for a thousand generations on such a dim vision.'

Resentment welled over the numbing grief Ange felt toward Gildas.

'Tata ran back to save you.' She whimpered as the tears clotted in her throat.

Gildas heard what Ange said. What was done is done he thought but it was true the trader had gone to help him.

'There is a reason why the trader has gone.' He finally answered without knowing exactly why it was necessary to kill off the protector of the girl. 'Sorrow and solitude can be a source of strength, desert dweller. If my exile taught me any-thing it was this.'

Ange deep down knew as well that at some time Bensah was not going to be with her. The shadow of Voloc rose again and this time if felt like it feasted on the carcass of Tata. Closer and closer it was coming. Stroking Nekoda she quietly sobbed with the image of Bensah lying in the snow struggling against the cubs. Then Tessi in the arms of the slavers and her mother's bloated infested body.

'What news have you of your people, clansman?' asked Sa almost agreeing with Gildas. The gods had never fully revealed their purpose, nor their destinies and their motives were questionable like all who wielded power over others.

'I am hopeful. My brother Jarrod still lives and sits at the seat of the Elder chief. At the least I may be able to bargain for the protection of the girl alone and the rest of us seek out our own fates.'

Kado sat eating the fish without hunger as the lingering image of Bensah stubbornly remained in his mind. He like Sa wondered why the clansman had not killed the bear. To hear him speak with such reverence of the beasts of their lands surprised him. Gildas was no ordinary exile. What had happened to cause Gildas to leave his lands? He had seen some of the tattooing the Graan used to mark the warriors under the scars and wounds of his massive arms. Gildas had been someone great at one time. He remembered the scholars showing him the markings of the clan elders and their chieftain warriors. Gildas had the same markings. He had now seen the bond the clansman had with their homeland. Even banished clansman, it was said, that when death neared, always trekked back to their lands to die in the ice and become one with it. Kado also remembered the strong trading links the Ko dynasty had formed with the Graan and thought perhaps a bargain could be struck if Gildas life was still in forfeit.

'I think we should rest before the last part of our journey' spoke Kado.

Bensah's eyes and that of the ice bears blended together in Gildas' mind as he sat thinking of the day. He knew the others would be asking themselves why he had not killed the bear. But in the end, it had been his Mother and protector since his birth. It had been that bond he had chosen over the newly formed company. Now they would know the deep bond of the graan to their lands, not even the threat of a demon could break it and never the life of a foreigner. Was it this bond the gods wanted to exploit? They knew Gildas of the Graan would rise to defend the life of the ice over all else. If this Voloc dared, a mighty foe would face it, buying the gods time to defeat their enemy. Gildas wondered what the purpose was of the gods and why they had been thrust into their wars. Perhaps there was no destiny only chance and this was their fate to accept or conquer.

Ange fingered the prism wanting to crush it She touched the prism around her neck and squeezed it wishing she could crush it in her hands and let the raging winds blow the dust away. Anger toward Gildas roared inside her mixed with the cutting grief of losing Bensah. Resentment and a deep desire to see it all finished began to form in her heart.

'I am alone Mata and Tessi. But I will fight before I die, if only to see the mighty boabs and Choasa once more.'

Gildas heard the whisper and the deep sob of sadness from

Ange. You grow stronger everyday Keeper of the gods. Perhaps we will make it after all, he thought as closed his eyes to sleep.

163

11

Elder Chief

The hoar frost had been softer this year allowing the few conifers and elderberry bushes poke through their white veil sooner
than previous cycles.

'Oi Han and Jano! Come now and gather the baskets' she
called.

Two young boys got up from lying in the snow trying to
trap a marmoset. They had found the entrance to its den and
thought it was a good opportunity to practice for the initiation
rites. They left the trap set up and decided to come back later
after they had helped their mother.

The trio walked back to the village each laden with full
baskets with seeds and nuts.

'How long before the trap is sprung Jan?'

'I have seen that rodent often in the woods it is old and will
not be easily caught. The older they get the more cunning seeps
into their bones' replied Han.

'Ay it is old. I have seen the white on its whiskers; it will
wait.' Caelwyn smiled slightly. The old rat had lived there for
at least four summers now. She had seen it often scampering

into the village raiding some of the vegetable stores. She had even fed it on one occasion. She had called it Laanan, the night thief. The boys would wait a long time to catch him, especially with its feasting in the vegetable stores. The traps were designed for the frightened and hungry rodents of the wastelands who half-starved reacted to the smell of food before looking for danger.

The boys and their mother stashed the baskets in their family hut to begin the sorting. Other groups had come in from the woods as well.

'Do you need us to help mother?' Jano asked eagerly waiting to be let out of the chore.

'Nay not this time, there is too little' Caelwyn replied.

'We had twice that many last cycle' spoke Jano.

'I know. Trading will be tough this time with so little to barter with.'

Han and Jano ran back towards to see if they had caught the wiry old marmoset. Caelwyn pulled the lids off the baskets and tried one of the berries. They were bitter and would need to be used for medicines. She would ask the other wives what theirs were like and perhaps she could barter some furs, so they at least had some for the feast when Jarrod returned.

Later that evening as she sat stirring some broth for the evening meal the boys returned with two fat pups rather than Laanan's hide. She smiled at the small victory for the rodent. The boys had not skinned them yet as they wanted Caelwyn to check the furs.

'Sit and eat.'

She got up and inspected the pelts. They were young and

not fully formed so the prized thick down that the rodents were used for had not matured. But still it showed promise that the boys may do well at the rites.

'Keep practicing, the down is not fully grown, see here. A pup needs to grow as long as my arm and have the white of its whiskers poke through. See they are still brown around the nose.'

'Another winter and it will be ready for culling. But you did well to capture the cubs, they are the quickest.' The boys slurped their broth feeling happy from their mother's praise.

'Jak said that the Graan should farm the rodents' spoke Jano with a mouth full.

'Jak's full of northern winds' replied Han.

'Yes, his father should know most of all about the problems of the rodents being kept captive. It was Janis that first tried to breed them here in the village, but their fur loses its quality and becomes brittle. They are like the Graan, born of the ice and bonded to it for their survival.' Caelwyn gave the dead animals back to the boys and her skinning blades for them to practice removing the hides.

'Your father is expected soon. Give them to him as a gift.'

The cacophony of the dogs barking and cheering tore through the wide-open tundra as Jarrod's entourage arrived back in the middling light of day. The clan wives greeted their husbands with loud calls of celebration as the men threw their spoils from the hunt. Jarrod went to Caelwyn and the boys with open arms. Caelwyn bowed slightly in respect to Jarrod's position as the Elder chief of the Graan. He rubbed Han and Jano on their heads roughly. Each of them held up their catch.

The hide neatly peeled off and the fur washed and dried.

Jarrod took them and felt the quality.

'Hmm, younglings, you were fast to catch them.' He gave them back impressed and hopeful.

A giant clothed in a massive cloak of ocean dog furs came up behind them all.

'Chieftain, it is decided that the council will be called tonight. The chiefs are here already. Mother fortune has smiled on us' spoke Unta son of the chieftain of Clan Clotte.

'No Unta, rest yourselves, tomorrow will be soon enough for the clan meet. Let the men see their wives and younglings.' Caelwyn spoke up, not intimidated by Unta's position or size. He looked at Jarrod.

'Nay Caelwyn, there is much to discuss, and it is best to do so while it is fresh in our heads.' Unta nodded and walked off.

When they arrived at the hut the strong smell of roasting meat met them. Jarrod felt his mouth water. The trek had gone along the south eastern ridge and mostly their diet consisted of the carp. The two rodents sat staked on iron bars, smoking over the coals. Jarrod removed his massive fur coat and boots and sat down on the rugs located away from the door. He lay back and let his mind and body rest. Suddenly Han and Jano jumped on their father in playful wrestling. He took their blows good naturedly. He felt his body resist as he pretended to be wounded from their punches. His and Jano's hands became entangled but the boy's hand was half the size of his father's and he soon became exhausted trying to conquer his father. Jarrod relaxed a little realising how much this journey had taken its toll on him.

'Come go and fetch some water to drink. I have used the last for your father to wash with.' Caelwyn called happy to have Jarrod back. A small knot always formed in her belly every time the men went hunting or to trade. The ice was treacherous and the winds of Raajn could sweep up behind a man without him knowing and scour his flesh to the bones.

In the corner near Jarrod sat a bowl of slightly warmed water. Fine tendrils of steam rose above it as the herbs in it gave a slight scent of the great conifers that surrounded the village. Jarrod removed his undershirts. Caelwyn took a cloth and washed his back as he splashed water onto his face. His beard was almost grey now, but his hair remained dark. Scars ran from his right cheek down to his shoulder and there were contorted patches of pulled skin all over his torso and back. Caelwyn was towelling him off when he turned suddenly grabbing her waist and smelt her.

'You have been in the forest today.'

She nodded enjoying the strength in his arms and the roughness of his beard on her neck and face.

'I think the smell of your husband goes better.' He kissed her fiercely. Caelwyn was small in stature but sturdy like most of the Graan women. They were not known or required for their beauty but their hardiness to endure their lives spent on the icy wastes. They kissed deeply enjoying each other's taste and warmth. Caelwyn pulled away and gazed at her husband's grey eyes.

'I am glad you are safe. But you need to eat as well. You have become scrawny from your travel.' She cajoled plucking the flesh on his back. Jarrod smiled and kissed her once more.

Caelwyn went to the cooked carcass and pulled it off the

iron stake. She placed it on a wooden slab and handed it to Jarrod.

Jarrod helped himself to a succulent leg of the marmoset and slurped some distilled root milk.

'What news from the south?'

'I will speak of these things at the clan meet. The wives should be present as well. But let us rest for now.'

Han and Jano came bounding in with a pale of water each. Sitting near their father they helped themselves to some of the food.

'How far did you go father?' Jano was the more curious of the two and Jarrod knew he was about to be bombarded with questions.

'As far as the ranges meet the great ocean and inland from there for hunting.'

'What does it look like?'

'Jano let your father rest.'

'When the great spikes of the mountains first greet you and the blackness of the frigid ocean washes at their feet your heart soars at the majesty and lordship they have over the world. They are the gate keepers of our lands and protect the rest of the world from the wrath of the winds of Raajn. One day when you are fully initiated your heart and soul will be struck with fear by their strength and beauty.'

'Did you see any of the great ice bears?' asked Han.

'Nay they live in the lands where the ice meets the sun.'

Caelwyn interrupted noticing Jarrod yawn slightly. 'Come boys to bed now. All the children old enough are being sent into the woods to find more berries and nuts tomorrow.

You will need to be gone before the end of night shade.'

They got up and went behind a screen of hessian at one end of the hut. It only contained some furs thrown over some roughly woven mattresses stuffed with down and fur. Caelwyn came back out once they had settled. She heard the clack of a game of knuckles being played as she pinned the hessian back into place. It was still a long twilight and a pale glow suffused the hut through the open gap where a curtain hung marking the entrance. Jarrod had laid back and closed his eyes. His back ached slightly where he had slipped trying to capture a large sea dog out of the raging ocean. He had managed to hook it, but it pulled him almost into the tidal wash.

'I will gather the Elder wives for the meeting.' She kissed him gently on the forehead as she left. He grabbed her hand not wanting to let her go.

'Later husband. You didn't find another to your liking on your quests to be so hungry for one as worn and stout as me.' She smiled slightly at her teasing.

'And you woman, another did not tempt you with darker beard and stronger back!' He watched her leave.

The day finally ended leaving the village in a duller grey then the day. Jarrod walked towards a large circular hut located in the village centre. He was draped in the Elder coat, a massive white rug made from the pelt of a male ice bear. He carried a spear intricately chiselled from its bones and the point made from the jawbone honed to razor sharpness. It could be used in combat not just as a ceremonial staff. The cloak was made when a dead bear was found. Only then would the Graan dare to violate the sacred hides of their god.

He entered the hut and was greeted with a smoky haze and the smell of burning pine and coal. Altogether the full council consisted of eight chiefs from each of the clans of the Graan and their wives or daughter. The chieftain wives were held in higher position to the rest of the Graan women. All the Graan even the Elder chief, were required to care for their own needs and provide for themselves. Jarrod sat and shouted the call of the chieftains to gather.

'It is the fortune of the ice bear that we are all here tonight. Clan Clotte, Gol, Hadraan and Nimmo have returned from a trek south to hunt but also to seek tales about the wars of the southern peoples. We have seen how the harvest has failed for this cycle of cold but also the traders we barter with for goods and weapons have become worthy of the axe for their weighty prices. I have seen graanar against graanar over the cost of lint and grain.'

There was emphatic grunting at Jarrod's last comment.

'It seems it will not get better. The tyrant called Ranik, who I remember my father often cursed, has risen again. He has conquered Emperor Ko. A clan that had laid its rule on the middling territories for a thousand cycles is now dead with no heir to its throne. The wealth of the Ko mines is plundered by Ranik and a few feudal Lords who remain alive due to their sworn oaths of loyalty to him. All this wealth is now made into the weapons for the armies of Matavia and Unstaadt. It seems now Ranik has turned to the west and seeks dominion over those lands as well.

'But this fever to attack the western provinces will require all his might. I have only seen it once, but its land is full of deep valleys filled with forests. To move an army so large quickly and in stealth would be impossible' Hadrin of clan Hadraan spoke up.

'What does it mean for us, Jarrod?' Unta of Clotte spoke 'Will the Graan need to fight?'

'I do not know. If the westerners fail and are devoured by the tyrant then he may turn the eagle towards us. We have nothing here that Ranik can want but we have grown fat on the goods the southerners bring to trade with us. It is not just this war Ranik brings upon the southern lands, but plagues have swept like the winds of Raajn across the desert plains, killing most of the peoples of those lands. These people were the slaves to the overfed nobles of the Ranik's palaces.'

'They will seek others' interjected Caelwyn.

'Ay, wife it is my fear, for the Graan are hardy and strong but not wealthy so the only riches we have are ourselves.'

'Brrraaaack!' cursed Hadrin 'The Graan are bonded to the ice and it alone, no man may own us.' The clansman spat on the dirt of the hut. His massive arms went taut at the thought of a Graanar in chains. The chiefs Knut of Kaan and Brago of Bregt got up and roared the battle cry at the same thought, all collectively cursing Ranik's name.

'Ay, clansman, we will die and feed our younglings to the ice bears before we wear the bonds of other masters.'

The circle of chiefs clashed their axe heads together to signal unity. Jarrod breathed in at relief that the clans would unite so readily. His rise to Elder chief had caused divisions which had spilled over at times into petty battles. Jarrod had overcome many threats to his seat as elder chief. Threats which could with time erode the other strength of fealty to each other. Jarrod had proven time and again his loyalty to the Ice Mother and his strength in battle.

'My brothers and sisters, I need a blood oath from each of you that if the time comes and we must fight for our lands and lives, that the Graan will rally together as one. We will show the cursed usurper what might and terror the Graan hold within their hearts.'

Jarrod stood and raised the staff and shouted 'Graanar!' The chiefs and wives stood and shouted back to their Elder and the sound of their roar echoed through the forests and into the turbulent clouds above them. Han and Jano stirred at the sound of their father's voice.

Jarrod took the staff and cut his wrist on the inside. The dark blood welled quickly. Each of the chiefs and their wives stood before him. Each of them touched wrists sealing their bonds with mingled of the Ice Bear clans.

'Gol with Clotte

Gol with Hadraan

Gol with Kaan

Gol with Bregt

Gol with Nimmo

Gol with Vallyx

Gol with Timmo'

Blood mixed with distilled root milk on the sleeves of the great bear cloak as the brew was passed around the circle of chiefs and clan wives. The sacred bowl had been made from petrified wood shaped like a bear's claw. Caelwyn sat beside Jarrod slightly dizzy from the broth. She was proud of her husband for she remembered the bitter fights for the Elder chieftain's seat and the bad feelings towards the Gol clan after his brother had fled. Gildas had nearly led the Graan over a cliff in pursuit of domination like this tyrant that rose in the south. But Jarrod had weathered that anger and had risen to be the new ruler. The wives left as the men began to sing the battle songs of old and the younger chiefs of Bregt, Kaan and Vallyx sparred drunkenly together.

Seven dawns later the wound on Jarrod's wrist had begun to heal. This scar lay above another, the one when had taken the blood bond when he rose to become Elder chief. He had taken the staff over eighteen summers ago now and it would remain his until the ice took him. Three of the clan chieftains were ready to leave. The reins of their sleds strained as the dogs were eager to race along the tundras to their villages. They were the outlying clans only seen at specials gatherings and battles. The clans of Nimmo, Vallyx and Timmo made their lives on the shores of the great ocean. Their prowess on the water and ice was renowned among the Graan. Their fishing skills were taught to all the Graan younglings so with each journey south they took back the children old enough to learn their ways. Caelwyn and three other mothers hovered over the younglings from their village. Five children had been chosen to go and live with the northern clans and learn. There was no sadness on the part of the children but excitement at being chosen but also to ride with dogs was a great honour. Soon the call came to leave.

'Polax, safe fishing and fat purse for the Timmo' Jarrod embraced Polax the eldest after Clot and Unta and the one with closest kinship to himself.

'Ay, the tit of the wet mother never dries for the Timmo, Nimmo and Vallyx' Polax laughed.

'Nino, and Van, again may the ocean be generous in her bosom to you and your kin.'

'Ay Jarrod, we are ever blessed' replied Nino.

'Vallyx clan is loyal to the Gol whatever happens. It was in our great grandfather's time and so it is now' spoke Van.

Jarrod embraced Nino and Van. He watched the sleds leave sure in his heart that the Graan were united if war came to them.

Hadrin came over to Jarrod and slapped him on the back.

'It is good Graanar that we are united, but I think it is time to begin the initiation rites and for us old men to lose our belly fat eh with some practice. If war comes, we need to be ready.'

'Ay Hadrin, prepare the contenders for the rites and send word for the axe games to begin.'

'The plains of the white cliffs shape the most fearsome.'

Jarrod grinned at the comment and nodded.

'Begin with the young Graanar first, they have the most to learn and will need time to season.'

Jarrod returned to his hut where Caelwyn lay on her litter sewing a torn sackcloth. She looked a pale.

'Are you with child again wife?'

'Ay husband, but it seems it is not happy to be here. It kicks and rebels at my every turn. I fear it sees the dark clouds of Raajn's wrath on the horizon.'

'Hmm, so it could be. We saw much blood shed at the hands of the southern tyrant. It is also rumoured that he is in league with a demon which drives his hunger to war with all it sees.'

Caelwyn sat sewing not reacting to Jarrod's words. Her mind drifted back to when she was a little girl hearing her mother and father speak. It was in the days of Gildas when he had conquered the Unstaadt invaders and enslaved them. She remembered her father talking of the brutality of the Gol lord and that he would destroy their people.

'He is like your brother.'

'Ay, I sense the same but more. Even Gildas only wanted to battle for the sake of it and searched for the one enemy that could defeat him. If the loose tongues of the taverns of Shadaraq are true, then more evil lies beneath this destruction.'

'We will fight as always husband until we die in the ice.'

'When will the youngling be born?'

'It will be a winterspawn child.'

'No wonder it kicks to get out. To be spat out in the dead heart of our winter I would cry for release sooner as well. It has taken many summers for you to bear again after Han and Jano. Two again this time wife; they almost cleaved you in two. Are you sure you wish this bairn to be born?'

'Only the one. And yes, I miss the softness of a fledgling skin. The boys are almost gone from me. This body and spirit have been blessed again with the Ice mother's claw to birth again. Nay I am not broken yet husband.'

Caelwyn went about her chores that day with a heavy mind about the impending birth of the child within her and the memories of how she nearly did not survive the last time she was with child. Jarrod was right to be concerned. It had taken the twelve summers for her to fall again thinking she had finished as her body approach its forty fifth winter. She felt the sudden kick and sat again to rest. She had been preparing the wreaths for the initiation rites. The mothers of the boys being sent out would throw them into the forests to ward off the ice ghouls of the tundras. Jano was ready but Han may need to go again. Jano had been second to come out but was the stronger of the two and larger. Han looked like her people whereas Jano was fair and had the ice blue eyes of the Gol clan.

Han and Jano stood before their father on the next dawn laden with their traps and furs. Jarrod stood almost twice their height and towered over their young heads.

'Be wise and brave, the rodent is quick but dull in its wits.'

'Yes father. We think it will be a contest between ourselves, the others are smaller and have not shown much in our games in the forest' spoke Jano.

'Arrogance can blind you not only in the ice but also to opportunity' replied Jarrod.

But Jarrod knew the boy was right. The others including Han were runts compared to Jano. He looked at his son's eyes and saw the Gol clan reborn again and the hunger for victory. His grandfather had it as had Gildas. It was as if the ice was their birth mother.

The twelve boys waded their way through the forests of Enan to the edge of the great tundra. Jano felt this heart surge with the thrill of what he was about to do. He knew he would be the victor. He had been ready for this day for the last two winters. He looked at his brother Han and nodded.

'Ready brother? You and I will show the pride of the Gol clan.' Han nodded as they clasped each other's right hand to leave. The others had begun to make their way in their chosen direction. Jano was going towards the plate of the Whitefang, Han towards the eastern shores.

The snow had begun to thicken as Jano neared where he was going to make his camp. The plateau that he walked upon was completely flat except for a small undulation that stretched for half a league. Under its summit lay a collection of small tunnels where a tiny waterspout had been frozen in place by the winds of Raajn one winter. Jano had remembered it from many years back when he and Han had been out hunting with their father. Jano remembered the pups of the marmosets poking their noses through the ice curious about the outside world. He also remembered the ones with the little black patches. The rare ones most valued for their pelt. Walking over the rise he stopped about halfway down the slope and began to dig his shelter. It was harder than he expected jarring of his hands and arms each time the axe gouged into the ice. Soon however a small cave began to take shape, just large enough for him to fit into it. It was completely silent as he stopped to rest and eat some nuts. He thought of his father's words that the land ruled the Graan and the clans do not forget this. It is the only reason they have remained alive for generations. But as he scanned the horizon with eyes matching the iciness around him, he knew he would one day rule the white lands and the ice bear.

12

Invasion

Derek ran through the tall forest towards the city. Blood poured out of his nostrils and mouth. His right arm hung loosely at the side as the dislocated shoulder grated bone on bone with every jolting step. He thought briefly about Jack and Connar but refocussed quickly to get to the river before they discovered he had escaped. The intermingled screams and laughter had hidden the noise of his fall to the ground when his bonds had been cut by a jagged branch. He had hesitated momentarily wondering if he should try and free Jack. But his comrade had shook his head and mouthed for him to run. Turning away Derek had heard Connar scream as his wrists and arms broke from being strung to the tree. The soldiers had been swinging Connar back and forth, betting on how long it would take for his bones to break. 'Don't let them hear you scream as well Jack' he thought as he ran into the dense forest. Suddenly the forest cleared and the river Nordra flowed before him. It was calm as most of the melt water from the mountains had already flowed through towards the Southern Ocean. His home was not far now. Wading into the water he felt instantly soothed by it.

He stopped to wash his face and tested his shoulder. He gingerly felt where the bone jutted out towards the skin and then taking his forearm he wrenched down and in, popping the bone back into its position. His eyes watered with pain and suddenly he threw up into the water. He stood letting the bone ache ebb away and the yellow bile disappear in the current. The sound of the Matavian dogs echoed behind. He instantly began to wade to the other side of the river. He thought of Jack and Connar as he ran into the open fields that surrounded the city for a league in all directions. It is too exposed he thought for the enemy to risk being seen. Relying on this he sprinted across the furrowed paddocks longing to see the walls of Esteron City.

— — —

Joab had concluded that his favourite past time was enjoying a cup of herb tea, cinnamon biscuits and transcribing the holy texts into a new language. The nuancing of the mantras changed with each translation and made him wonder how this would present itself in the new society that would adopt their ethos. Today was particularly enjoyable as the sun had come out and was dancing on the cobble stones in the central courtyard of the palace. The light pierced the gaps made by the leaves of the maples red leaves. The summer cycle in Esteron had been especially hard and long this year with many babes and the old dying of the grippe which had come from the Doanda Ranges. Everyone was relieved when leaf fall arrived. A curse to weaken the lands of Aeserea had been how the gardener of the palace had dogmatically put it. Joab was not so sure, but the coming from plagues affecting the far eastern deserts and the tyrant's ascent and war mongering had been undeniably quick. He conceded that perhaps sorcery was at work. His mind drifted again to the destruction of the temple and loss of his brethren as he sipped the tea and watched light play on the ground. Only a handful of his order remained. They had met once and decided to go into hiding until the power brokers had run their course and the victor established. Joab had already been installed in the Palace of Esteron and the others had gone to the more outlying reaches of the Aeserean Kingdom. At least the demise of the order by Ranik had reinforced Queen Nene's belief that the preaching's of Ira must be holy for the despot to seek the destruction of its followers and its sacred place. Getting up the corpulent monk sighed heavily and stretched his back and legs

'You are not a young monk anymore Joab' He said to himself outloud.

As he was about to sit down again the bell rang for the court to assemble. The Queen had summoned her advisors and a few trusted friends that morning meaning himself. These meetings had been more frequent of late and had begun to bore Joab. He had no advice to give on politics or warfare and resented the loss of time he could dedicate to the translations. As he entered the hallway leading to the throne room, he saw a young soldier walking with Lord Cotus Medret, First Knight of the court and armies.

'Brother Joab, good to see you in fine health.' Lord Medret often made jibes about Joab's physique; Joab being overweight as much as Medret was muscles and sinews. The Knight was a huge imposing man of over twenty hands, indeed the horse he rode needed to be especially bred to carry him. The soldier that accompanied him was tall but skinny, a youth in his first year of service. He looked pale and dried blood streaked on his face and neck.

'Thank you, my Lord, her Highness does look after me well.' Joab nodded to acknowledge the young soldier but neither Medret nor the man responded with any introductions.

The interior throne room was set to the side of the main court and was used for smaller gatherings, mostly war councils and private family meals. The chamber was austere in its decor of timber panelling and red curtains to adorn the walls with a large oak table placed in the far end on a dais. The only indication that the room was reserved for royal gatherings and the elite nobility was the throne placed at the centre of the table. The throne was hewn from an ancient walnut tree after a battle many generations ago. Its arms and legs were ornately carved with two large timber poles extending from the back rest chiselled at the ends into lion's heads. Queen Nene was already seated upon the chair. Her brothers the princes Draved and Dronagh were seated to the left and right of her. The Knights of the Calvary Lords Yonan and Warick were also present and seated. Of course, the diplomats Tern and Laude were hovering over maps at the left-hand end of the table. They gave Joab a cursory glance and acknowledged Medret. Joab thought to himself as he bowed before the Queen this was a council for war and his presence was unnecessary. He made his way towards the far-right end and sat. Noticing the queen's pet lioness lying on the floor he bent to rub its belly before sitting.

She purred and rolled on her back happy for the attention. Sitting down the monk began to meditate. Medret and the soldier remained standing.

'My Lords, thank you for making the time to be present here again, too soon unfortunately but disturbing news has come to me and I require your counsel. Lord Medret please.' Queen Nene gestured for the knight to speak.

'Thank you m'lady. This is Derek, soldier of the first rank who was stationed on the edges of the great forests of Vran. He is here by his own valour and strength of body. His two companions did not survive the brutality of the Matavian soldiers who captured them. He brings grave news for our lands and people. Speak Derek.'

Lord Medret was ever the dramatist thought Joab. He noticed the awkward angle the boys right hand seemed to rest. The brutality of Ranik's men was unsurpassed and the monk shuddered to think of what had happened to the other soldiers.

'Ira give them peace and protect those of us here.' Joab prayed.

'Your Highness, Matavian and Unstaadt ranks were seen on the borders of the forest of Vran and southern fields of Hendra. We saw two legions camped there before we were captured.'

Derek swallowed hard thinking of Jack and Connar. 'I escaped but, we all know of the Matavians barbarism, my comrades did not.' Derek's voice trailed off.

'How many?' asked Lord Warwick

'I counted at least three thousand warriors. The camp seemed to stretch as far as we could see. There were as many eagle banners as that of the black vulture of Unstaadt.'

'How is it that such a large contingent was not sighted before now?' asked Laude.

Derek looked at Medret for an answer intimidated by the diplomats piercing gaze.

'Our lines of information were severed in the melee that Ranik has created since the Ko Dynasty collapsed. Your Highness we were preparing to send another but since then the news has come Ranik has managed to manoeuvre what appears to be a large part of his army towards Aeserea' replied Medret.

'How can Ranik have such legions to spare when reports come of his malice advancing on the Ko territory, the invasion of Irasia and he sends bulwarks south for restocking of the minerals needed to make weaponry. Unstaadt warriors while tenacious are few. He knows our strength here. It would take all his might to consider invading our lands and to succeed in annexing it.' Lord Yonan spoke.

He took a swig of ale that had been set down after speaking to calm his nerves. His drinking prowess was well known, and his ruddy bloodshot nose and cheeks testified to the years of practice spent in the ale houses.

'Yes, the despot has declared an open act of war towards me and the Aeserean people. Is it madness that drives Ranik to such arrogance, for the army needed to defeat our own would take all his? And ever, the natural defences of our lands the great forests of Vran to the east and south protect us while the cliffs of the Jadah Ranges hinder any movement of great numbers of soldiers and weaponry. While he has been a shadow in our midst, he has never been foolhardy enough to attempt a direct attack' Queen Nene spoke.

Joab noticed the Queen's hand gripping her sceptre tightly. The strain in her voice matched the concern in her face.

'Cotus have there been sightings of the Eagle's head along the north Aeserean Coast?' Prince Dronagh stood. His large sword banged against the table making Joab and Derek jump.

'I have sent a kite this dawn when this soldier bought word. We should know by the next morn, my lord.'

Medret gestured for Derek to stand near the side entrance. Medret went to sit near Joab.

'Soldier if there is nothing more for you to report, you may leave' Queen Nene ordered.

Derek bowed deeply, he still had blood crusted on his face and clothes and was beginning to feel faint from hunger. 'Thank you, my lady. I will only say they appeared swiftly as if the night hid them and then we were captured. They were as silent as the jaguars that live in the Vran, so we did not see if more soldiers marched towards the first camp.'

Nene nodded and clapped her hands. Instantly a man servant appeared from behind a curtain that partitioned off a private room for use by the royal family.

'Eric take this boy to the apothecary and nurses to tend his wounds. Prepare a letter with a purse for the families of the two soldiers who did not return.'

The servant bowed and took Derek by the arm. Derek stopped briefly and turned to the table of nobles.

'Your Highness and Lords, I heard the soldiers jeering my brother Connar before I had managed to get away. When he asked how they hoped to gain victory, the forests alone would defeat their army, they replied, we fight to destroy not to win.'

Queen Nene got up. The words chilled her. It must be sorcery that drove Ranik's thirst for dominion over the lands of the earth. Nothing made sense, the Ko dynasty, the destruction of the Irasian temple, his ships sailed in large numbers with armoury from the Iron Coast. The people of the eastern deserts were being devoured by plagues and those who survived were enslaved. Lastly for Unstaadt to form an alliance with Ranik was unheard of in her memory. Her father had approached the ruler of the Unstaadt many years ago to form an alliance against Matavia, but they spat at the offer and threatened to slaughter the younglings of every village. Nene remembered the messenger vividly, he had vultures sitting on his shoulders as he threw their diplomats heads on the floor of the court.

'The alliance with the Unstaadt rulers, it must be coerced. They are fierce in their independence and can match the Matavians in brutality and determination. They would fight to the death rather than be ruled by an overlord from another territory.'

'Sister whatever drives the madman's purpose his gaze comes to us. We must be ready for war.' Prince Dronagh spoke up.

Joab had seen the young prince mature greatly over the last cycle and realised how the Queen had become more reliant on his counsel. She would need him thought the monk.

'The armies are well prepared your Highness; a stealth attack amid the forests could well see us take the advantage from Ranik. I feel it has come to the Aeserean's to destroy this tyrant once and for all and break this insatiable hunger to rule all that his eyes can see.' Medret looked around the table to read the faces of the others.

'We are beyond diplomacy your Highness. To send an army of such size signals only one thing, invasion of your sovereign lands and a lethal intent to your person as its ruler.' Diplomat Tern looked directly at the Queen. She stared back, not breaking his gaze until he diverted his eyes.

Sighing heavily, she walked back towards her throne.

'And if the worst is true, Ranik's ships lie in the docks of our beloved shores of the coastlands …'

'Then we are at war your Highness, and it will be a fight to the death. I am hopeful even if the news is not favourable that victory will be easy against an army stretched so wide.'

'Sister remember we are the warriors of the forests and mountains, the Matavians only know warfare on the open field and they are clumsy brutes to say the least. Our numbers are enough to send Ranik's army back. If the coast is under threat as well, then we will have the blades and arrows to defend our lands also.'

Dronagh had stood moving to look at the maps the diplomats had bought with them. He was dressed in his riding regalia, a tall imposing man Dronagh was honorary First Knight of the cavalry but due to his young age was commanded by the more experienced soldier Lord Yonan.

'Lord Medret, I will prepare the royal writ, giving control of the lands and city to the rule of the army for the length of the battle.'

Medret stood and bowed towards the throne.

'Go now ready the city. Diplomat Tern please begin preparing the writ and rules of battle.'

'Yes, your Highness.' Tern and Laude both left as did the

others of the council. Draved hesitated to see if his sister required his presence. She waved him to go.

The stone walls reflected the silence of the room and seemed to pulse with tension of thunder clouds about to burst. Joab made to leave but suddenly the Queen spoke.

'Brother why did Ranik destroy the temple?'

'I do not know your Highness. The mineral he sought was in far more abundance elsewhere and more easily dug from the earth.'

'The tyrant seeks something.'

'But what my lady? He is driven by madness and will ultimately find his own death. How can he defeat all the world?'

'If he takes this kingdom then what is left but only the gypsies and the empty icelands above us.'

'My lady I am deficient in giving you advice on this matter, our order only teaches us to seek harmony and peace to make this life bearable for the injustices that afflict so many. I believe Lord Medret has seen many battles with Ranik over the time of his service and knows his enemy well. Insanity drives the tyrant and it is this that will be his undoing. His armies are too stretched and the insatiable desire for wealth that he digs deep from within the earth only destroys its fecundity for providing food to the soldiers. I will make offerings to Ira that the victory will be quick and loss of life few.'

'Brethren I wish it were so but my dreams have been filled with the blood of many innocent lives and always I see blackened and burned earth with nothing alive not even the madmen who began it. You know on occasions I don the dress of my attendant and a scarf and go into the markets and taverns to hear the idle gossip of my people. It helps me understand them.'

Joab nodded for he had on occasion seen the Queen exit by a secret door from the interior gardens that only the nobility was allowed to use.

'Many of the sailors and merchants that travel to the Iron Coast have bought back stories of the creatures that enslave the people of those lands. One story talks of a black beast with eyes redder than the great fires that ravage the woods and forests. It shuns the light of the sun, so it runs at night and devours anything that it finds. Its great claws burn the sand and make it brittle like glass. I asked where it came from and the answer came 'The great tombs of the ancients gave birth to it. They lie beneath the heart of the desert.'

Joab looked at Queen Nene and saw that her gaze was far away and slightly fevered like the image of the demon's birth haunted her vision.

'I asked again of this place in the desert of the southern lands and a sailor showed me where on a map. 'Maiden,' stated the gnarled old sailor 'nothing but the sand lizards and this demon can live in the heat of those lands. The fiery heart of the sun laid its claim many generations ago.' Come here monk and I will show you where the mouth of the demon's mother lies.'

They went across to where the diplomats had left their maps. Unrolling them she placed her long index finger directly into the heart of the Iron Coast.

'Does this not look familiar brethren?'

'Yes, your highness, it is where Ira's great pilgrimage began.'

'I think it is no coincidence that this demon and your holy

messiah both began from the same hole in the ground and then since this demon has risen, the Irasian temple has been destroyed.'

'The elders of the Iron Coast believe that the caves below are gates to another world, where the spirits that first made the world left when it was completed. Perhaps their beliefs are true, my lady, only it's not just the benevolent spirits can enter through them.'

The Queen began to walk towards a small window located directly behind her throne. She looked out beyond the wholesome ploughed fields to the majestic forests that made up the eastern borders of her lands. She stood for what seemed to Joab a long time. He was about to rise and excuse himself thinking the Queen no longer wished to speak with him when she suddenly spoke again.

'The demon has come for something and he uses Ranik to find it until it is strong enough to hunt for it itself. I know the brethren do not believe in the gift of sight like the witches of old but my dreams, as malicious and terrible as they are, always contain a dot of light, like a small jewel shines in the darkness. Did you know my great-great grandfather wed a witch? Queen Jana. It was not well known; indeed, it is thought she placed a spell over King Freidyn to take the throne by his side. Ever since, the women of our family have had sight some stronger than others; mine lies in my dreams. When news came of Ranik's annexation of your holy temple for no other reason than to dig for a mineral that lies in greater abundance in his own lands I grew suspicious. In my dreams a shadow lay at the heart of all the destruction and it scratched at the bedrock to release something buried within it. I decided to send some of my most trusted soldiers to search the ruins of your temple when they were deserted. Deep below the smashed rock they found a crystal pillar surrounded by stone walls. One wall had collapsed allowing the sea to wash in but the rest of it was still standing. Those remaining stone walls were intricately carved in a text unknown to us in this land. The soldier removed a piece and bought it back to me.'

Nene handed Joab a brick of the stone. It was covered in the intricate details of an old text.

'Do you know what it says?'

'It is one of the Mantra's of Ira but not all of it is able to be deciphered.'

'When I learned of the stories of the Iron Coast and the connection to your founder I began to delve into the stories and gather ancient texts of the great pilgrimage.'

'My lady it is sacrilege to the brethren for any person not of the Order to read or possess those texts. But continue.'

Acknowledging the admonishment, she continued.

'Very little is written about his time there particularly with the elders of those lands, almost too little. And yet there is much detail of his courageous journey, crippled and maimed upon his return the lands of the temple. He came back a different man both in his body and spirit. I believe he saw the face of the gods and it was this vision that crippled him. I also believe the demon seeks, a gift for people entrusted to your holy founder kept safely for a thousand generations of brethren in your temple. A covenant perhaps for the gods to protect us.'

Joab looked at the queen and wondered if she had become

over wrought with fear of ruling a land neighbouring one such as Ranik and now she grasped at the slightest thread of hope which may relieve her of her fears.

'My lady, I know of no such covenant or gift, our order endeavours to remove the fear and tumult superstition invokes in the daily lives of the ordinary people. Reason and introspection of the self is our way. Our prayers and mantras are formed so that they are attuned to the daily rhythms of life.'

'Joab, the tongues of the ale houses also whisper of a mighty god who was released from the earth after the Ko palace fell. It stood thirty hands spans tall and was bedecked with precious stones and gems. The earth quaked under its feet and the wind and fire raged, driven by a dark shadow all around until the earth was laid bare and only blackened dirt remained but the god did not fall. No, I believe the battle that rages towards us is more than a madman's desire for power. I believe the spirits have come here to decide our fate.'

'Yes, your Highness, if the tongues can be believed then perhaps a gate to the world of the spirit does exist and has been opened. But I have no knowledge of it or of this covenant with our beloved founder and those of the spirit world, and any record would be lost to the rock and water that is our temple now. I remember my last meeting with the great Abbot Paulus, his eyes were haunted by something. At the time it was thought to be a fever but perhaps he knew of what was to come. Certainly, in the time of Abbott Vronius, the peace of Ira, seemed distant and ever a shadow seemed to follow his step. Brethren would disappear and many sightings of a demon in the woods with red eyes staring back were spoken of by even the most stoic monks.'

'There is no way we can win a war against gods and demons if they choose here as their battlefield.'

'If the idle talk and your dreams are true my lady, then you will not win. But until these spirits show themselves to the world then your soldiers will go to battle believing they fight a madman they can defeat.'

Queen Nene nodded.

'My head is full of death and blood that runs across the lands like the ocean. We will need allies, once all the battles have been fought, whoever remains standing will need to unite.'

'My lady, this is counsel you need to seek from your knights. I am a cosseted scholar who sits behind ancient texts and muses on the meaning of the words. If this world's fate is to be decided in our time then perhaps the wisdom of Ira may be of comfort 'If courage is set in the heart before fear, then the thorns under foot on the path ahead will be a mere scratch and not a bloody wound.' Our world had a beginning my lady, so it seems that it must have an end. You and I have our places set before us and will do what we must. We are of this world, but it was not made by us nor will it be our place to save or end it. We exist because it does.'

'Your words are humbling rather than comforting. You are dismissed brethren.'

Joab left. It was true the end felt near to him, ever since the temple had been destroyed. The utter ruins of it when he beheld the toppled columns of the prayer chambers had left a stain on his heart. It had been this vision that had made him hasten the translations to the common tongues so that some wisdom could be preserved in the world even if it became steeped in darkness.

Queen Nene woke the next morning after only managing a few hours of rest. Her dreams were more terrible then they had ever been. She had felt watched. A knock came at her chamber. Jocelyn, Nene's attendant went to the door.

'My lady will not receive visitors now. Can it not wait?'

'It is urgent message from Lord Medret and Warick they wish a meeting with her highness before the morning meal.'

The queen came to the chamber door, dishevelled. The messenger boy noticed the dark circles under her eyes.

'I will receive them in the blue chamber. Send word for the Princes to come as well. Oh, and have Eric bring tea.'

The boy nodded slightly shocked at seeing the queen in her nightdress and long red locks draped around her shoulders.

After the messenger had left Jocelyn quickly went to draw a bath for the queen.

'Leave it dear, I will not bathe this morning, come braid my hair.'

Queen Nene sat down as everyone was assembled. 'Speak Cotus.' She waved the servants away and began to pour the tea for herself and the men before her. The ritual gave her a feeling of calmness

'Matavian ships have been sighted off the Aeserean coast. The assault will be from the north and the south.'

Without saying anything she handed the cups of tea to each of them.

'How long before we are ready?'

'Sister, reinforcements for the coast are ready to be sent. Lord Medret awaits your permission. Already forests are filling with our soldiers. The Matavians will have no choice but to push through it. We will be waiting for them.' Spoke Draved

'Empty the cities and villages of the old men and women and children under eleven summers. All others are to be trained in warfare or to provide supplies to the soldiers. This land now fights for its existence.'

As she spoke, she pulled two scrolls from within her apron.

'Lord Medret the writ of War has been completed. This land is now under your control.'

Medret bowed deeply 'My lady.'

Taking the scroll, he placed it in his leather undervest.

'I have prepared another writ for the cessation of battle. It is in the event I am dead, or we are defeated. I have given each of you a task to fulfil and have as would be expected handed the sceptre of rule to Dronagh, being the next in succession.'

'You must retreat to the groves of the lioness until this is war is ended.'

'Yes, Draved I will begin preparations to leave and lead the old and young to the safety of the groves. Stand!' The soldiers could hear the tremble in their Queen's voice.

Eric the attendant handed the Queen her sceptre. Medret stood to his full height and placed his right hand on his chest 'By my life and blood.' Nene nodded and accepted the oath of Medret by placing her sceptre on each shoulder. Dronagh, Draved, Yonan and Warick all stood and swore their oaths alike and each were blessed by the Queen.

'I smell smoke.' Draved went into the royal council room and towards the windows.

Looking out he saw black plumes of smoke rising on the far side of the river. Suddenly a bright burst of flame appeared towards the southern end and dark shapes seemed to be jumping along the treetops with the fire spreading quickly behind them.

'Curse this sorcery! The forests are burning. How does the spark catch? The leaves drip with the rains of the clouds they make above them' spoke Dronagh.

Tears formed in Nene's eyes, the beloved forest, their protector was being eaten alive. It was as if she could hear the trees screaming in her head. She saw a dark shape jumping along the trees and then the sparks take hold. Suddenly something came crashing through the trees stopping at a gap in the dense forest on the edge of the river. Then it started again bleeding into the crystal blue water. They were soldiers carrying a large battering ram; followed by hundreds more. Nene's heart thudded in her chest.

The bell in the watch tower sent its peal across the valley and fields. Nene watched the peasants stop their harvesting and run towards the city walls.

'Prepare for the Queens departure.' Nene looked at her brothers and then at Medret. He stared at his queen.

'Even if you fight fiercely my knights and with no other thought than to show the cursed tormentor the ways of the just and brave, I fear we will not win this battle. The pits of deaths dungeons have been opened and their gaolers are in the purse of Ranik.'

'Ay my lady but it is of no use to run for they will follow. You and the Princes must depart to the groves and we will stall their advances. Take your people to safety.'

'My captain I will stay and fight with you. Dronagh you will defend our sister for the throne will be yours. Sister it is my time to become the Knight of the mighty houses of Aeserea.' Draved could see the objection in Nene's eyes but she relented.

'Of course, my brother, bring me a tally of the soldiers you behead; a necklace of their ears.'

13

Clan

'We are heading for the forest on top of the cliffs.' Gildas shouted back to the others following. The cliffs soared almost a league above them. Ange saw the skeletal conifers clinging desperately to the stone beneath the ice.

'The forest protects the villages from the winds of Raajn. My grandfather used to call the wind the old washer woman, here to cleanse the land.' Gildas puffed heavily as he stopped to rest. His last memory of this place was standing on the precipice with Jarrod and falling from the top and landing on freshly fallen snow.

They had been following the bulwark of cliff face for at least three leagues hoping to find a place safe enough to climb. Near the forests the plateau edge gradually dipped so the climb up at its lowest point was only half a league high.

'Is this it?' Sa asked

Sa and Kado came behind him with Nekoda and Ange following. Ange sat down and leant on Nekoda panting in unison sending quick bursts of steam into the air. Ange had not spoken in the whole time since the fight with the ice bear and she had barely eaten as well. Her face was gaunt. She tasted blood again in mouth. She touched a thick scab which had formed on her from the frigid gusts of wind. She stayed near Nekoda as the others walked towards the cliffs edge.

'It is the edge of the Enan, and the lowest point of Whitefang. Once the daylight is brighter and the wind dies down, I will climb up and secure a rope at the top.'

'It is still half a league Gildas. Is there no other way to your village?' Kado swallowed hard looking at the slippery ice that covered the rock face.

'Nay, the ridge runs all the way in a circle, see, look how it curves and in one point they are so high a man cannot even see their end. We will camp here for now.'

His massive arms swung his axe into the ice once again to make a shelter. Kado and Sa helped. Sa stopped and turned. She saw Ange lying with her eyes closed on Nekoda's belly. Her melancholy had worsened.

Sa strode over to her and squatted down.

'Get up and help Ange. You will freeze on this ice.' Ange grunted at being disturbed and curled up into a ball. Sa tried to pull her up by her arm.

'Stand girl, you can grieve all you wish when this life affords you the luxury but until then we need to keep going. Your grief cannot be the demon's deathblow to us and this world. Let go of the trader he shall not return. He has been set free.'

Ange curled up even tighter and ignored the assassin. Sa tried to grab her again to stand up, but Ange suddenly turned towards her and slapped her. Stunned at her aggression towards Sa she broke into a million tears of sorrow.

Sa looked at her unsure what to do. Nekoda quickly started licking the tears off Ange's face. Kado came over. He bent down and hugged her.

'My father used to tell me not to cry when the servants I played with were punished by their masters for even the most trivial things. He said they were not worth the tears I shed when I saw them die from his cruelty. But I still wept for them. Your sadness will pass Ange but for now we need to be safe from the wind. If not for us, help dig for Nekoda. He needs you to help him like you do him. Put the sadness into the ice, it was the one who took Bensah from you.'

Sa looked at Kado and knew in her own way she cared for Ange as well, but it was like a brick wall sat before her. A wall built by every put down and scalding slap until in the end Sa Tuc watched the world from outside never feeling she belonged to it. Never to understand the motives that drove a person's hope or desire. Perhaps it as this that made her so skilled as an assassin. At no point could she relate to the lives she took so easily. She went back towards Gildas who had grown impatient with the girl. His loyalty to the ice bears stood equal to the girl's bond to the trader. Sa dug thinking of Kado; the indolent salacious prince understood the girl's sadness more than she did.

Ange walked over with Kado and began to dig, piling snow into mounds beside her. Nekoda sat behind her keeping her warm. Tears trickled down her face, but she persisted like the others until their shelter was made. Inside they ate fish. Ange lay back down to sleep. A dark cloud had fallen over her, like she was walking inside the prism but this time there was an emptiness, no sound or movement. It was the space where Tata should have been and Tessi and Mata. A deep empty burn lay within her. Ange began to feel anger, real anger at all that had been taken from her. She even began to hate the lady who had come to her. All of them were to blame, the shadow demon and the gods. None of them cared. She closed her eyes ignoring Nekoda's nudging to play with him.

Kado watched her curl into a ball. He had done that many times in his life. He thought he saw a tiny smile curl on her face as Nekoda persisted in pushing her with his snout.

'Have you climbed the wall before Gildas?' asked Kado.

'Ay.' Gildas had begun to eat another cod knowing that there would be ample food on the plateau once they reached it.

Kado rolled his eyes at the recalcitrant answer and persisted.

'So how long will it take, the surface looks slick with ice.' He probed.

Gildas stopped eating, irritated at the questioning and looked directly at Kado 'There is no other way, prince. I will go first and then I will throw a rope down to hoist the girl up. You and the assassin will follow. How long that takes is up to you.'

Kado sat back annoyed at Gildas obstinate logic and the cliff. Both as implacable and intimidating as each other he thought.

The sinews in Gildas arms and neck strained with each precarious step. He had climbed perhaps one hundred spans. He would wedge the pickaxe into the rock then he would hoist himself on an outcrop. He had scaled the walls of Banrock prison with oozing wounds and broken bones but the fall there was not as great. Perhaps the sacrifice of the trader would be enough for the favour of the ice mother to help his feet grip the cliff. He had not mentioned to Kado the number of times a graanar had died trying to scale the plateau. Nor would he tell them of the pass that lay a thousand leagues to the north where a tiny gap allowing passage to the steppe above. But it was too far and the winds of Raajn collided with the great ocean making the passage often awash with waves that stood as high the cliffs themselves. They would not survive 'the flesh grinder' as his grandfather used to call it. His leg slipped suddenly but he caught his toe on a small ledge. He exhaled heavily as his leg trembled beneath him. Then with one swift move he jammed one axe then the other and heaved again. Each time the axe tore into the surface the chink of the ice breaking echoed across the empty land. All Gildas could hear was his breathing and the tip of the axe grinding under his weight. Soon enough he saw a root of a tree hanging over the edge. He dared to look up and the stalactites of ice were hanging like a beard of an old man from the top of the ridge. With one last monumental heave he dug the pickaxe into the frozen bark and managed to swing himself up onto the plateau above. He lay for a moment panting into the air. He tried to stand but his arms and legs trembled beneath him.

Drinking some water, he stood and looked down to the others. They were black specs from where he stood. All around him was the silent stillness of the forest standing as black sentinels on the precipice, warning the barrenness that it could advance no more.

Gildas went to the trees and chose the one with the broadest trunk and tied the rope securely around it.

As he tossed the rope, he called to them 'Send the dog first to test its strength.'

Suddenly a high-pitched squeak met him. He saw a tiny figure hug the dog. He watched as Kado and Sa tried to put the rope around Nekoda, but Ange blocked them. Nekoda began to bark to protect her. Then one of them, he could not see which one, grabbed the rope and began to climb. Ange and the dog stood away. Kado waved his arms in the air in a sign of frustration clearly worried at Sa's courage to test the trees strength. Gildas began to heave helping her climb. Sa scaled the wall effortlessly with the help of Gildas. She nodded her appreciation when she reached the top. Moving behind Gildas she stood and regarded the trees.

'It looks like old bones in a grave.'

'Ay the trees on its northern face never bear leaf, the winds of Raajn, scour their branches clean. Oi next Ange' he shouted.

Kado tried to grab her but she refused

'Brat child, the village can't be soon enough.'

Spitting on the ground he roared 'Now girl!' sending ripples across the expanse. They watched as Kado managed to secure the rope around her waist and tugged hard before she could undo it. Gildas gave a mighty heave surprising Ange and making her flail helplessly against the face of the cliff. She screamed and kept trying to catch the icy wall but could not gain any purchase. Kado was yelling something to her but the only thing Gildas and Sa could hear was Nekoda barking. Sa watched Gildas massive arms and legs straining as he quickly hauled Ange up towards them. They would be dead now if not for him she thought. He swore suddenly as the rope hitched.

'Go see what it is!' he commanded Sa. She peered over and saw Ange wedged beneath a small outcrop of rock. Her struggling had caused her to swing too far to one side.

'Ange push yourself away from the rock. Gildas cannot pull you up.'

Sa saw Ange's arms try to reach the ledge above her, but she could not reach it. She simply hung limply underneath it. Gildas began to walk to the left to pull her along the face of the cliff away from the ledge, the rope dragged along the jagged surface, pulling Ange away from it. Suddenly the knot unravelled around her waist. Screaming she managed to grab the end of the ropes. Sa saw what happened.

'Gildas stop, the rope has come undone.'

Gildas heaved but saw Ange's grip loosen on the rope from the sudden jolt of his pull.

She screamed terrified looking straight down towards the sound of Nekoda's barking. Gildas steadied his grip.

'Hold girl. I will haul you now.'

He pulled slower and looked at the rope glide smoothly over the rim of cliffs edge. Sa lay down on the ground as Ange approached and as soon as she could she grabbed her collar and hauled her over to safety. She could feel the girl's body was wracked with shivers of terror. Sa took off her coat and threw it over her to help get her warm again.

Gildas began to twine the rope again ready for the next.

'Send the dog!'

By the time Kado had stood on the top Ange was still lying on the ground with her eyes closed. She had not even moved when Nekoda nudged her. He whined again pressing his nose into her face. Ange rolled over and rubbed his cheek and reluctantly sat up. She hugged him fiercely.

'It's just you and me Nekoda' she whispered to the mongrel. He licked her to tell her he agreed.

'Come there is still another day's journey to my clan.'

Gildas stooped and picked Ange up. He threw her over his shoulder as he led them into the forests.

Soon the trees became so dense that dirt beneath them could be seen in patches where the snow could not penetrate. Branches clawed at their thick hide coats almost as if the trees wanted to hold them prisoner. Gildas stopped put Ange down.

'We will rest a little. We have travelled well into the heart of the forest.'

Gildas began to pull some inner branches and twigs off the trunks and place them into a pile of kindling.

'Desert dweller do you still have your flint?' Ange looked at him with vacant eyes momentarily before reaching inside her jacket to pull out a little pouch. Inside were the two flint stones.

Soon the fire was raging and the last of the fish was frying happily. Everyone warmed their hands and feet near the bright licks of flame. It was the first real heat they had felt since Shadaraq.

'It is strange that these trees live at all here clansman', spoke Sa.

'Ay it is many generations of graanar in age this forest. It was told that it stretched all the way to the mountains that cut the north from the south but slowly the ice has eaten the trees and eventually even this part will succumb to its hunger.'

'How much further?' continued Sa.

'One more day and we will see the end of the Forest and the dens of my people.'

'Will we be welcome clansman?' Kado eyed Gildas speculatively.

Gildas hesitated before answering. 'I do not know. I was banished from my clan many summers ago but the news that my brother is Elder chief may mean fortune's hand stays with us a little more. It is on his blood bond to me that I will ask for welcome.'

Suddenly they heard a branch crack and some voices. Gildas doused the flames and everyone huddled down behind the trees. The voices neared. They were speaking the native tongue of the Graan. The figures were short in stature. Gildas guessed they were the boys sent out for their rites and were returning. Each of them was comparing the pelts. Suddenly Nekoda let out a bark and everyone froze.

Gildas saw the two boys drop to the ground and withdraw their garrotting blades.

'It came from over there.' They inched on their bellies towards the group. Gildas stood and took Nekoda with him as there was no use in hiding. When the boys saw the massive form of Gildas their eyes bulged. They stood instantly in defensive stance readying their blades.

'I am graanar' spoke Gildas.

One of the boys stepped forward and removed his large fur hood. Instantly they both saw the same ice blue of their eyes and each knew they had a blood bond with the other.

'Your name graanar?'

'Gildas Gol.'

Jano had heard the name but could not remember seeing him in the village before. The clans were made of many blood relatives and not blood, but the younglings always took the Chief's name. Bonded pairs were allowed with cousins removed by one clan parent but not immediate clansmen.

'I have not seen you at our clan gatherings, and where is that beast from?' pointing directly at Nekoda.

'Nay I left to trade in the southern lands many summers ago and this is my pet. My companions are a desert girl and merchants seeking new trinkets. Come out.' Gildas waved to the others to come from behind the trees.

The boys became alarmed again when they saw the others emerge.

'Your names?' asked Gildas, seizing the advantage.

'Jano and this is Han of the Gol clan.'

'You are in the first rites.' Gildas looked at the sacks on the ground. Han stood protectively over them.

Jano nodded suspiciously.

'We seek shelter in the village and nothing more. Your haul is safe.'

Han and Jano looked at Ange first and her crooked stature, she looked directly at them without flinching. Then at Kado and Sa.

'You know the ways of our tribes, graanar. Permission to enter is given by the Chieftain.' Jano stood defensively, still suspicious of the strange group before him.

'Ay, we will follow until the edge of the forest and I will wait until the Chief decides. You must go and claim your place in the rites and warn them of my coming' replied Gildas.

Jano nodded and said as he walked backwards away from Gildas 'Gol or not, if you come with battle in your hearts, then your heads followed by your bodies will be tossed to the great ice mother.'

Gildas grinned slightly at the boy's posture of aggression and nodded 'Ay it is understood.'

The boys walked away facing them and then once they were out of sight began to run to the village.

'Come we will be greeted soon enough, once my name is spoken.' Gildas gestured for them to follow the boys.

Nekoda barked after Han and Jano but the only reply was his echo. As they began to trek through the forest the dog followed the trail closely leading a direct path towards the clan's village. Soon the forest began to thin again and eventually the white expanse opened out as it did on the glaciers beneath Whitefang. But this time it was broken in the distance by tendrils of smoke and round thatched huts. In front of the huts a group of men with swords and axes stood in a line waiting. Nekoda sensing a threat bristled but Gildas held him tightly. Sa made sure the muzzle was secure.

Four men approached. Gildas placed his axe on the snow as a gesture of peace. He nodded to the others to do the same.

'I seek shelter for me and my goods. I am of clan Gol and request treaty with the Chief.'

'Come.' replied one of the men. He eyed Gildas carefully. Gildas looked at the man but did not recognise him.

They walked through the village. Gildas saw his family home where he was born. He saw the Elder hut, the same as he remembered, located in the inner circle of the village, protected by the rest of the clan's dwellings. He saw Jarrod standing before its entrance with the Chieftain warriors surrounding him.

Sa slipped her small dagger down from her sleeve to rest in her palm. She could sense from the unyielding stance and expression on the clansman's face Gildas was not welcome. Sa and Kado looked at one another beginning to get nervous.

'Elder Chief' Gildas met his gaze and knelt before his brother and leader.

Jarrod knew it was him from a distance. Gildas the great warrior stood above all others in the thousand generations of the Graan. As he watched him approach, he thought to himself how the ice bear ever favoured the strong and brave, even one as brutal and tarnished as Gildas.

'Your life is forfeit Gildas Gol. Why have you come back? Does the former Elder Chieftain thought long dead, return for the clan retribution as deserved by all traitors to the Graanar?' Gildas stood but the warriors around Jarrod motioned offensively not to come any closer.

'I am he, and my life is forfeited to the clan Gol and Graan. But I seek shelter for the ones that stand with me and call upon the blood bond to bargain with the Elder Chief as it was with the ways of our fathers.'

Jarrod nodded. 'Bring them in when their weapons are removed.' Jarrod had noticed Sa's manoeuvre with her dagger and wondered who she was. The southern merchants brought their own guards for protection and rarely carried weapons themselves and never brought their women.

Jarrod sat on the bear throne which elevated him above the

rest inside the hut. Kado and Sa sat behind Gildas and Ange. Nekoda had been tied up outside and was barking furiously. Around the edge of the hut stood the Graan warriors, as rancorous and unforgiving as the Whitefang they had just scaled.

'Speak' ordered Jarrod.

'I ask that only the first of the Elder warriors stay to hear my treaty.'

Jarrod nodded after a long pause. 'Jank, Tommo and Ikdad stay.'

The three hefty men stood closer to Jarrod in case of any attack. Gildas still stood two head lengths above them. His scarred face and height were menacing even when he attempted to lower himself before the bear throne.

Jarrod gestured with his hand for Gildas to begin.

'I will speak in the common tongue so the others will know what I say. This is Kado Kodrax, son and heir to Emperor Ko, now slain at the hands of the tyrant Ranik, Sa Tuc first assassin of the Ko Palace Guard and Ange Tsaed of the eastern deserts.'

'Brother your exile has put you in wide company.'

'How this has come to be is a long tale and I will only say that the reason for it lies with the same reason that Ranik brings destruction to all rulers of the lands in the south. The tyrant of Matavia seeks a stone of magical potency or at least the demon that has taken hold of him does. The stone has been given to the girl by the spirits that seek to thwart the demon's power. I have brought her here to be hidden until they return, for the demon shuns the light of the sun which never leaves our land. I seek no shelter for myself only the boon to leave and return to my exile. It is only for the girl and the royal status of the other two that I ask they be allowed to remain until the world's fate is decided.'

'Gildas, you were brutal and almost led the Graan to the precipice of annihilation .When I hear word of this tyrant, I think of you also for I wonder if it had not been the death of your wife and child by your own hand that stopped you destroying all who stood in your way. It took no demon to set you on that path only the lust for death and glory that drove your sword into many men. Why should I believe you? And how is it the mighty Gildas Gol now runs with princes, demons, and gods? Are you dead and one of the ice spirits plays games with the Elder chief?'

'Nay brother it is me, your sword will draw blood if it pricks my skin. I have seen this demon wolf and have been tossed to near death by it, as have all these. The gods that follow it also seek the stone and even now fight to bring back the one who can destroy the demon. If it possesses the power within the gem, this black spirit would be unstoppable even by those who created it. Ange show them the stone.'

She looked at Gildas with hatred, you killed your son and wife and Bensah her eyes accused the clansman. Gildas knew the others would be shocked at this news of who he was but soon it would end, and he could leave.

'Show them the stone girl or we are all dead.'

Reluctantly Ange removed the pouch and took out the prism. It glistened slightly in her hand as the flames from the small fire in the hut were caught in its facets. The prism began to warm slightly as if drawing the heat of the flame into itself.

Suddenly it burst forth with great shimmering lights filling the whole hut with its iridescent beams. Ange felt herself falling into the brightness again. She pulled back but could feel herself weakening. Gildas and Kado and Sa saw figures fighting and massive waves of lightning and thunder but coloured like the rainbows that came after a storm. A deep booming voice broke the silence of the tent followed by an almighty roar. Ange collapsed and the light disappeared as the prism rolled from her fingers. Gildas checked her. Heat radiated from her skin. He picked up the prism, but it burnt him. Quickly he placed it back in the leather pouch. Kado and Sa went to her to see if she still breathed.

The chieftain guards poured into the hut ready to attack. Tommo and Ikdad had hurriedly got up to protect Jarrod, thrusting their swords at the company sitting before them.

'Sit back assassin, prince. Leave her' spoke Gildas. A sword hovered near Sa's face

'Leave brothers, it was but a talismans trick performed by the desert dweller' spoke Jarrod.

Jarrod got up and walked towards Ange. Nekoda was barking so ferociously he started to lose his voice. Kado suddenly understood why Sa had persisted with the girl. She carried around her neck the key to the world's destruction and a gateway to a realm unknown to any who lived.

'I was many things brother, but I was never a liar. The world fights more than the men made of it. The graan are blessed and cursed by the ice and sun, both of which thwart this demon. Again, I treat with you as clansman and blood kin for protection and shelter for these three.'

'Those are true words Gildas, you were never a thief or a liar.'

Jarrod looked at Ange, she was panting. He noticed the small burn mark on her hand. He kicked back her coat and noticed her withered leg, bound with sticks to keep it from giving way on the ice.

'The desert dwellers are kinder to their misborn then the graanar, eh brother.' Jarrod looked at Gildas as he got up.

'Ay, she is strong for she trekked from the blade and the spike of the great peaks. If you let her stay, she will keep her own needs with work. She has a strong back.'

'So, these gods hand the world's fate to a cursed desert dweller, broken graan chieftain, assassin and a throneless prince. These spirits, are their names known to us?'

Sa spoke 'Our monks of the high temples have ancient scrolls of these spirits coming in the first days. But their names are unknown, and they remain hidden as custodians of the earth, wind, fire, and waters. Two higher ones have come also but we do not know their name or purpose. Many things have been revealed to us that lie in the earth but now our lives are forfeit to their whim. The gem contains their full power placed there by the god of earth and stone.'

Jarrod looked at Sa. Gildas had called her the assassin of Ko.

'Why did they not fight their battle here with the demon? It seems they war amongst themselves and have abandoned their believers.'

'We do not know. The girl may know more. It was she who was chosen and seems to be the only one able to touch the rock.' Gildas stopped before saying too much.

'Fetch the wives to take the girl. The other two, take them to one of the empty dens on the edge of the village. Place a guard outside.'

Kado and Sa were escorted out roughly. They both looked at Gildas not sure what was happening. He nodded to show there was nothing to be concerned about. Soon two women came into the hut, the older one ordered one of the clansmen to carry Ange. They bowed before Jarrod and eyed Gildas suspiciously. The older woman's eyes suddenly went wide when she recognised who he was.

'Be gone woman, tend to the youngling.' Jarrod commanded her gruffly. Sitting down he waved all but Tommo, Jank and Ikdad out of the hut. 'Sit all of you.'

'So Gildas you have brought destruction again to the graanar.'

'It was not my intent to return here brother. I was compelled to it. The god came to me while I was in Banrock prison. The demon chases our ancient blood lines; the girl, me, and the prince. Most of all though it lusts after the power of the spirits contained within the stone.'

'It was thought the great mother of the ice had taken you saving us the effort but the gaolers of Banrock eventually chained you.'

'My life now or before is of no import. My presence here will open the old wounds and clan war will come of it. Let me go Jarrod. The assassin will protect the girl.'

'I cannot let you go Gildas, my position as Elder chief commands me to seek clan retribution. If Clan Clotte hear of you being alive and slipped from my grasp again, they will seek revenge on all Gol. They are too powerful, second only to us. I have fought hard and long to bring honour to the Gol clan. You will be placed on trial. Half the Chieftains are only a day's ride with the initiation rites. I will send for the fisher tribes to call judgement upon you.'

Gildas stood and clenched his hand near where his sword would normally be and looked at Jarrod. Tommo, Ikdad and Jank got up and withdrew their axes ready for an attack.

'I will escape brother, not even Banrock prison could hold me.'

'I will have the others killed and this stone will fetch a price in the markets. Think upon it carefully.'

Gildas growled but stopped himself moving closer. The brothers looked at one another for a moment and then a tiny smirk crossed Gildas face knowing he had been beaten.

'You have the spirit of the bear in you Jarrod, you do our fathers proud. What of the girl?'

'Does this demon know where she is?'

'I don't think so, we were followed only as far as Shadaraq and killed the thieves that live in the passage to the icelands so their tongues would remain silent.'

Jarrod picked the pouch up and could feel the warmth through the leather.

'And this demon cannot bear the sun?'

'Ay until it is at full strength then the sun is its enemy and the icelands are protected by deep spirits that live in the water beneath it. These spirits seek time to restore their order.'

'If Ranik is so driven to find this thing he will look this way. The graanar always defeat their enemies on their lands but sorcery is another thing. Why back here Gildas?' There is room on the expanses; you could survive until these gods of yours fight their battles.'

'Me yes, but not the girl and she is the only one to bear this stone. Even now it burns you. Also, Ranik may well seek dominion here also. It is better to know what you fight brother than die foolishly.'

Jarrod nodded beginning to feel the stinging in his skin. He tore some fur from a mat on his chair and wrapped the pouch in it. The burning stopped.

'War will be certain to follow you if this magic stone remains here. It need not be this way.'

'Believe me brother this demon is real. I have stared in its eyes, felt its claws and teeth shred the flesh on my back. I saw the mighty god of the earth rise from the deep heart of the world and wrestle with this wraith, but it commanded the spirits of wind and fire. Their fury melted rock to crystals as shiny as the icicles of the deep caverns of the claws of the cliffs. Men will be devoured by this whether they wish to battle or not. I do not lie brother.'

'I believe you. For the great Gildas Gol to seek shelter and protection for a maimed desert child at the risk of his own life and cross the icelands to his certain death then sorcery and magic must be at work here. I will need to meet with the village council but for the moment she can stay.'

'And my freedom?'

'I think we have agreed to the terms of our treaty brother. Take him to the pen. Bring food.' Gildas let Tommo and Jank grab each arm and bind them tightly behind his back with leather straps.

'Gildas, it was good to see you kneel before your Chief. I remember a time when you would not have done so. You do our fathers proud also' spoke Jarrod.

Gildas nodded at his brother as he let the clansmen lead him away.

Nekoda had gone with the others to their hut on the outer circle of dens. Sa and Kado looked across at Gildas bound and being escorted to a pen that stood on its own away from the other dwellings. The gaol was a square construction made from mud and leather walls that only reached three quarter of a man's height leaving a gap between the walls and the thatched roof. In the middle was a large tree truck worn in places from a chain that was wrapped around it. He let them sit him down and straighten his legs out for the shackles to go on. His hands were bound to two iron stakes on either side hammered into the massive trunk. There was enough slack in the chain so he could bring his hands to his face. A bucket of milk and some bread scraps were left to him and a hide for warmth. Jank and Ikdad then stood outside. As Gildas sipped the milk he noticed Kado had come over. Ikdad stopped him and warned not to come any closer.

'Well Gildas, will your blood bond buy us some time? Would the graanar be willing to fight if needed.'

'My brother will speak to the village council, but I think you will have shelter for the moment.'

'And yourself?' looking down at the shackles.

'That hasn't been decided yet.'

'I remember who you are now. My father and his generals had said they wished they had gone to war with the great

Gol lord, a fitting enemy to sharpen their blades upon.'

'There are fiercer enemies in the world to fight prince. I am nothing now. Go back to the hut. My brother will send word when he has made his decision.'

Gildas sat back and finished his bread and milk. The taste was the same and instantly bought his mother's face to mind. He had lost the memory of it so long ago but now her smile and eyes came back to him more clearly than the sky above him. He sat against the tree and rested.

14

Temple of the Lioness

'Hold your lines' shouted Medret.

Medret was riding before the two thousand strong cavalry which stood behind the soldiers fighting off the first legion of invaders. Pulling his mare into line with the staff captain he looked towards the lifeless city. The people had emptied towards the deep valleys of the forest on the eastern side of the river. The seasoned war hero knew not all of them would find refuge with the Lioness. Once their lines broke then the Matavian scum would soon catch the slower ones. Medret could smell death in the air. His horse shook and snorted in anticipation for the battle to begin; her black armour contrasted against her white coat making her more menacing in its stark contrast.

'Wait' He whispered under his breath.

He looked briefly over to the south western edge of the forest or at least what was left of it. Marching toward them were at least two legions of Matavians and Unstaadt soldiers. In amongst them were the three black creatures that had destroyed most of the sacred forests of Vran. The venerated trees that had stood since the dawn of the earth were now scorched to black stumps.

'Wait' he breathed again.

'Pull back' came the roar from Draved. One of the creatures scooped up two men and tore them in two. Its claws barely missed the prince.

'Cursed demons, go back to your master.' He stabbed its foot.

It looked directly at him and suddenly a massive arm swooped towards him. He ducked and weaved his way around it to plunge his sword in again. It turned but then seemed to lose sight of him and continued forward tearing more soldiers to pieces.

'Pull back' Draved shouted as he waved the men back towards the waiting cavalry.

The Knight General had seen the prince's brave but futile assault of the creature. There was no defeating them. The horses strained and snorted against their riders stamping their hooves wanting to run.

'Just a few more paces.' Medret glanced quickly to the left and saw a brief flicker of red. 'Good they were ready'

Then everything stilled around him as he watched the lines of fighting and spouts of blood draw closer.

Medret raised his sword. As he brought it down, he shouted 'Horse masters!'

The foot soldiers on the fields suddenly scattered. In the distance the rows of invaders turned into a disturbed anthill as lions appeared from beneath their feet ripping them to shreds. Those who outran them ended up falling into the dens of the great cats beneath the crushed wheat fields. The carnage made Medret fiercer forcing the anger and hatred for their long-time enemies to rise in his chest.

'Die!' he screamed as he beheaded three-foot soldiers with one swing of his blade. In the melee he noticed the rear flanks of invaders turn to the south but then they seemed to fall back on themselves. Looking across he saw more of his riders coming from both sides being led by Warick and Yonan. Their advancing surge forced the Matavians back towards the open pits. So crushed were the invaders from their huge numbers they had no room to manoeuvre. Their bodies disappeared in gushing spouts of blood as the lions fed and the cavalry stomped and slashed. Medret saw two of the lions climbing one of the demons but it merely plucked them off and flung them to the ground. The creature continued towards Warick as he led the second wave of riders. Medret saw his old companion gracefully out step the creature on his magnificent black steed.

Medret blazed into action again and soon the two cavalries met up forming a bulwark of horses, lions, and foot soldiers. They kept pushing forward toward the great river Nordra at its deepest point. The torrents of water swallowed the soldiers as they fell into its clutches, smashing them into its bed of jagged rocks.

The screams of the Aeserean's calling for death to the Matavians was matched by the roars of the lions. Soon the low rumble of the river's flow pervaded the battles cries. Medret, Draved, Yonan and Warick each saw the white foam of the rapids and raising their shields and banging their swords in unison began to drum their army forward pushing towards their beloved river. The Matavians pushed back but each time they reformed new pits would open releasing more lions breaking their ranks.

Yonan looked to his left and the most satisfying sight met his eyes, dead bodies covered in the red eagle racing down the river.

'Keep pushing, men!' He yelled but it was cut short as a massive arm swung down and broke his body into a thousand pieces. His men attacked the creature with vicious blows of revenge, but none survived its talons.

Draved saw the gap opening ahead toward the north and fought his way to Medret

'The cursed scum begins to thin toward the north. I will lead my men to the pass.'

'May the strength of the great lion be with you' shouted Medret.

The young prince saw the veteran knight bring three Matavians down in two graceful strokes. His great mare reared above his head and stomped on the soldiers to finish the kill. The prince nodded at his captain and forged on through a group of Unstaadt warriors.

Medret watched the prince slash a dozen men alone without so much as a graze on his body. He will be a mighty leader thought the knight.

Soon the cavalry had swung around to the north trapping the Matavians between themselves and the river. The water ran red with the blood of the dead but while the invaders were thinning so were Medret's soldiers. He decided that it was now that they should follow the prince.

Nene heard the cries of the war and prayed to the spirit of

Vran and the Lioness that victory would be theirs. She thought of her brother and hoped to see his face again. The passage under the city was damp with the musty underbelly of the kingdom. It snaked its way underground for over a league towards the base of a gorge where the Nordra and Hunjasat met on the edge of the Vran. The passage was full of children and the old that could manage the journey. She could hear sobbing again from those who had left behind members of their family either to fight or to die. The torch lights flickering made it even more sombre. Occasionally the passage would have an opening leading to another passage. Pale shafts of light filtered down towards the pilgrims accompanied by a musty odour. The overhead gushing of the river in the deepest caverns was deafening making the children whimper with fear. The passages lead to the cages where the lions were kept. Nene felt sad for her precious lions, great warriors themselves, being sent to do battle and die for their masters. The Aeserean's had always bred them for such a purpose. Her pet Ushan had gone off to fight also. A small tear came to the queen's eye when she watched the beautiful cat stroll off with Yonan. I hope you feasted well Ushan she thought to herself. The monk Joab had not come either. He said he needed to finish his translations as a legacy. Nene had commanded him to leave with her, but he had been firm.

'My lady, I thank you for your hospitality, but I have sensed the end of things for a long time now. It is better I leave something for the people who will live so the wisdom of Ira remains in this world. I will be a burden my lady. I am a scholar not a soldier to fight and I won't live caged under the bonds of a tyrant.'

She had accepted his answer and left him; her fondness for the chubby monk causing her heart to ache when she thought of what awaited him. The passage suddenly rippled with the noise of massive thud.

'Hurry people, we must reach the forests as quickly as possible.' A hundred soldiers had been spared to be their guard for the journey.

'Sister I will take a dozen men to go ahead and scout that the passage has not been breached.' Dronagh gripped Nene's arm fiercely. She could sense the tension in him and the urge to battle.

'Dronagh go. We will meet at the grove. Bring our brother Draved safely home.'

A small grin spread on his face. He squeezed her arm in gratitude at being released to fight.

'Yes, at the grove sister, may the Lioness protect us.' He turned to the remaining soldiers.

'Split into two's and go back amongst the villagers and hurry them along. Once the Matavians breach the city they will discover the passages.'

'Yes sire.'

Nene went on ahead quickening her pace. Soon however the screams began to echo behind signalling they had been discovered. The Queen saw a soft pallor ahead and her heart leapt with joy.

'Hasten people we are close. Run for the protection of the great ferns and trees. They will hide you until you reach the entrance to the grove.'

Stepping out into the fresh air and daylight, Nene sprinted

for the heavy undergrowth. This part of the forest had been untouched by the demon's fires and soon the villagers were lost to each other amongst the dense greenery. Nene led a group of twenty as they headed deeper towards the black wall of rock which formed a ring of stone for half a league. Nene's legs pumped beneath her as her chest burned with exhaustion. At forty summers she wearied more quickly, and her legs had forgotten the pace of their youth. The Queen prayed for the strength of the lioness and stamina of Ira to get her to safety. A large boom sounded startling a young woman and her baby beside her, causing the woman to scream and the child to cry.

'Soldier take the child, or they will hear us. Run with him girl, get to the temple.' Nene commanded.

The woman nodded in half a stupor as the soldier grabbed her baby. He smothered him into his shoulder as the piercing cry was just about to come. The mother followed quickly behind him. Heaving with exhaustion Nene saw the black rock jutting from underneath a cluster of massive ferns. Moving along the wall she saw the soldier she had sent ahead suddenly appear out of a gap.

'My lady, this way.'

Nene called a group of mothers and their children to follow her.

'Quickly now!'

She squeezed through into a narrow passage crushing her breasts and back as she edged her way along. The sigh of relief she felt when the passage gave way to the caverns of Vran echoed throughout the vast labyrinth. Small torches were scattered along the walls to break the black stillness. Across the far side a gap in the wall pointed to one of the entrances to the heart of the mountain where the sanctuary of the Lioness lay.

'Be careful my people. The pool below hides a floor of jagged rocks, sharper than the fangs of the Lioness. We are almost home.'

When Nene stepped onto the ledge that overlooked the oasis of forest where their refuge lay, she praised the Lioness and Ira. The sun shone brightly stinging her eyes as it pierced through the hole in the mountain side and onto the pilgrims as they made their way to the protection of the walled in grove. Waterfalls glistened as they spilled through the leagues of solid black rock that surrounded them now. Nene quietly hoped it would be enough to weather the Matavian curse. She looked at the massive carved head of the Lioness overlooking the sanctuary.

'Protect us great mother' prayed Nene.

The murmurs of the villagers settling into their camps and the constant arrival of more escapees broke the tranquillity of the sanctuary. Nene had come here often to dwell on things in her own heart and the day to day politics of ruling her kingdom. The bloody battle and scourge which forced her here now at least seemed dimmed. The sun sunk quickly, leaving grove illuminated by the waning moonlight washing serene water and ferns in a veil of eerie foreboding. Nene sat on a boulder and scooped some water from a stream to drink; it was fresh and sweet tasting. The rain began to fall lightly on her brow, but Nene knew it would be torrential soon.

'Come take water and go to the caves above us, the lioness calls to the clouds to water her garden and to shed her tears at the destruction of her mighty forests.'

She looked around as more of her people arrived exhausted and frightened. Some stood looking in awe at the magnificent place. Nene guessed that less than a thousand had made it here. She thought of the battle and wondered how Draved and Dronagh were faring. So young still, they had been born when she had reached womanhood. They had barely known their father the king, so relied on her to tell them stories of his prowess in battle and kindnesses to those who toiled for his kingdom.

Nene lay down on the woollen blanket she had carried with her and listened to the rain and waterfalls streaming over the rock and stone. A dozen soldiers and few older boys had been placed as guards in the passages that lead to the grove in case the Matavians managed to find their way here.

The pass that wound from the plains of Vran to the feet of the mountains was steep and windy. Draved and his contingent sat waiting. They could hear the chink of weapons and armour of Dronagh's sortie clashing with the war cries of Unstaadt. Draved's heart thudded in his chest as the anticipation of killing their mortal enemies grew.

He saw the yellow lion on the shields flashing between the green foliage as his brothers marched. Suddenly flickers of red and black appeared. Draved whistled. His men leapt onto the path from the undergrowth slashing viciously at the Unstaadt warriors. Arrows rained down from the trees. Dronagh's men had stopped further ahead blocking the Unstaadt from spreading out so they were trapped from the front and rear and to the side.

Draved grabbed the head of one of the soldiers he had slain

and threw it at a companion advancing on him. He took off the ears of both men and placed them in his pocket thinking of Nene. The poisoned shafts of the arrows began raining down on the outnumbered Unstaadts leaving piles of bodies causing Draved to trip over them. The brothers met awash with the blood of their enemy and exchanged their collection of ears.

'Nene will be pleased.' Dronagh smiled at his brother.

'What now?' Draved heaved as he remained alert for any stealth attacks.

'Continue on towards the mountains, Medret and Warick will make their way as best they can. We are outnumbered and will need to search for victory another day. The demons that walk with them cannot be killed by our blades but at least the river is thick with the blood of the Matavians beasts.'

Dronagh offered his brother a swig of whiskey which was taken with gratitude.

Turning to his men he rallied them. 'Stake the heads along the path to remind them who they fight then we make our way north.'

'We will take the path of the kings to the refuge. Safe passage brother.'

They interlocked arms at the elbow in the traditional manner.

'May the claws of the great cat protect ye.' Draved tipped his helm as Dronagh marched off with his men disappearing quickly into the forest.

Turning to gather his men he saw the demon first and the heads of the eagle and vulture coming along the path. He gripped his sword and readied himself again.

'Archers into the trees' he hissed 'Steady men, flee the demon we cannot defeat it.'

He eyed the general of the Matavians, his helm forged in the fashion of an eagle's head.

'You first' the young prince whispered. They clashed swords but the strength of the man unbalanced Draved. He stepped back to avoid a thrust at his chest. Taking the advantage Draved plunged his sword into his head and tried to finish him off but the massive warrior's strength was too great and deflected the blade with his shield. He spat at the prince. Arrows began to fly in the melee. The general caught one in the neck instantly sending blood spouting. The general finally collapsed in front of Draved. Suddenly one of the demons swooped his claws down near but Draved only felt the whoosh of the air as it barely missed his face. He could feel the squelch of the dead bodies as he ducked between the creature's legs. Four of his men were thrown clear along the path as it kept pushing forward. Draved wondered why it just kept moving instead of staying where the fighting was. Medret's war cry suddenly came to his ears causing a massive grin to spread across the prince's face.

A cry came from the Aeserean soldiers 'The great Knight of Esteron.'

The leaves of the oaks and ferns became stained red as the soldiers hacked at each other in vicious hatred. Medret and Warick greeted Draved, all of them barely recognisable they were so covered in the blood and entrails of their enemies.

'One of the demons pursues Dronagh.'

'Ay we cannot dally here, more of this cursed Matavian rash

are coming. They have stormed the city' spoke Warick.

A massive clap of thunder came across the skies from the direction of the city. 'Ah they found our gift. That should give the queen more time' spoke Medret.

Draved nodded and called his men to follow into the thick underbrush of the forest. Medret and Warwick moved forward until they saw the boulder that marked where their path lay. They waded in silently so that by the time the Matavians reached the same spot they marched by with no sight of their enemy.

Medret's horse whinnied as he took off the bridle and saddle. He patted her nose and shooed her into the forest to eat. 'It is too steep here wife and living in a mountain is no place for one such as you. We will ride into battle again.' The moonlight filtered on the back of the magnificent white mare.

The passage that led into the mountain was well hidden and difficult to navigate once inside the rock. He ushered his contingent through, only a few hundred he counted. They would not have survived another clash. As the last soldiers were about to enter, they began to roll boulders across the entrance.

'Sweep the dirt to hide our steps.' The boulder closed over the entrance with no trace of them. The silence of the forest resumed oblivious to the hundreds of men making their way through the rock.

Draved finally saw the base of the mountain with relief. They had begun to smell smoke not long after they had left Medret. The demons were burning the forest again to flush them out of hiding. Soon it had begun to choke them and obscure their sight. Frantically he searched for a mark that signalled the way inside but all he felt was sheer flat granite. Suddenly he felt the carved sign, but it was too late, a group of Matavians emerged from the forest. Pulling his sword out his men rallied near to him.

Draved saw his men fall like leaves around him as the three demons emerged in front of them collecting a dozen at a time and ramming them into the earth. Draved managed to escape their glance.

'To the death!' yelled Draved to rally his remaining army.

'To the death!' came the roar back.

The prince could feel his blade and shield heating up from the encroaching flames. The frenzied attack of his soldiers against the demons, seem to confuse the creatures making them reign fire down even on the Matavians. Soon the screams came from their enemy more than themselves. Draved foamed at the mouth as he slashed and cut at everything coming toward him. They could not give way the secret passages for fear of condemning his people to slaughter. The captain of the Matavians came screaming toward him, back aflame and helm so hot the skin on his forehead blistered. A broken shaft of an arrow protruded from his neck. He grabbed Draved by the throat and rammed him against the rock.

'You are one of the princelings? Where is your queen so I can taste the flesh of her heart?'

The fire rippled across his back, but he seemed impervious to the pain. His face oozed blood and clear fluid as the skin began to peel away exposing bone.

Draved tried to thrust him away to stick him with his blade but the massive warrior was too strong. His vision started to go dim as the general slowly choked the life out him. Flailing in desperation as the last bit of air in his chest he grabbed his dagger and plunged it into his eye. The captain laughed as he stepped away with the blade sticking out.

'Die infernal beast' screamed Dravad.

The general slapped the prince to the ground and turned to one of the creatures.

'Take him and find where the other of his kind have gone. They hide somewhere in the mountains.'

The great talons wrapped around the prince who lay dazed on the ground. Four of his men attacked the creature but to no effect. It simply swept them away into the flames. The captain grabbed some dirt and doused the flames. He gingerly felt where his skull was exposed and Draved's blade. His mind registered the pain, but he ignored it as he pulled the dagger out. The flesh on his face was eaten away. Death had found its table to feast on. He continued to fight knowing it would be his last battle.

Draved could feel himself bobbing in the air as he began to wake. His hands scraped along rocks. His head pounded from the slap the general had given him and he could barely breathe. He brought his hand up to loosen something that was clamped about his body. He felt the dry skin, like gravel, a fine red dust came off. Looking up he realised he had been captured by one of the demons and it was scaling the cliff face. Struggling he felt the grip tighten making him almost blackout. He could see the smoke and fire and the soldiers fighting one another below him, becoming smaller as the creature seemed to fly up the mountainside. Run he tried to scream to the men below him, but nothing came out. Soon the smoke cleared, and he began to feel lightheaded as the creature climbed higher and higher. He noticed the other two were following. They would find the precious sanctuary he thought and the only hope of their people surviving began to slip away. He reached for his sword and tried to jab the creature, but the blade simply sliced through the leather skin with red dirt falling out of the wound.

By the time the creature reached the opening to the grove he had nearly passed out from the height. He felt sharp pains in his chest where his ribs were broken. Looking up he saw the edge of the rock and began to scream to warn them below.

'How many Cotus?'

'We are depleted badly my lady, but the loss was one of ours to a dozen of theirs.'

'Any news of Draved?'

Dronagh had just returned from the far eastern passage. Between himself and another soldier they carried a young man with blood gushing from his leg.

'No news sister. Nurses here' Dronagh called.

He lay the wounded man down and began to wipe the blood off his tunic. As he stood a fine spray of dust fell around him, making him sneeze. He looked up and his heart filled with dread. Above him in the gloom of the night he saw the red eyes of the demons staring down at them. Suddenly a white face appeared between them.

'Run!' came Draved's croaky cry echoing down toward them.

'By the lioness is there no relent from the fucking curse of Ranik' pleaded Dronagh.

'Run!' Draved screamed even louder.

A thousand faces looked up and screamed. Panic set in as people tried to flee into the caves to hide.

Nene saw the monsters and then saw her brother. A great sob of fear and grief left her lips. Suddenly they began to crawl over the edge and climb down towards them. He screamed with the pain as the claws wrapped around his body.

'Cotus we will not defeat them.'

'Nay my lady for they do not bleed from cuts of a blade. They are not of this world.'

Suddenly the creature that held Draved let go. He screamed as he fell to his people below. His body landed with a dull thump on the ground not far from where Nene and Medret stood. Nene gasped with horror and ran to him. His face was so pulverized nothing was recognisable except for his brown hair. Dronagh pulled his sword in anger and grief at the sight of his brother's body lying on the ground.

'Pull your swords brothers and sisters. Stand and fight.'

Nene stroked Draved's hair and sobbed quietly over him. She cursed Ranik and the gods who created these monsters.

The three Aracnine landed on the ground simultaneously and stood over the Queen and Draved. Dronagh came at them with his sword but was batted away with a casual blow. Medret, Warick and three soldiers advanced on the one near Nene to stop them attacking her.

She stood and looked directly at the flaming red eyes. 'Where are you from and what master do you serve?'

It lifted its talon and placed it on the Queen's head. Medret hacked at its arm but it ignored him.

'Kill me creature, your cowardice is matched by the darkness of your heartless bodies. Tell me what victory is it for a god to squash an ant?' pleaded Nene.

Nene braced herself for the lethal blow as darkness met her mind briefly but suddenly the talon released. All three of the creatures seemed to look up as if hearing something call. Looking back at Nene and the people around them they screeched causing everyone's eardrums to split. Blood poured from the villagers' ears making them collapse in pain. Leaping to the cavern walls the creatures climbed to the opening at a lightning pace and disappeared into the night.

Nene fainted on top of Draved. Medret dropped his sword and went to the queen. Her face was burnt from the where the claw had touched her skin. He pulled her off the dead body of Draved. A small groan came from her as she began to wake.

'Quickly tend to the Queen.'

Nene's attendant raced to her. She bent down crying and began to dab the wounds on her mistress's face.

Stepping over to Dronagh the prince stared blankly at Medret; his neck broken. Medret closed the lids of prince's dead eyes and sat on a rock nearby.

'By the lioness Ranik I will take your black heart and head and have them studded to serve as a footstool for the lion once our protectors have feasted on your carcass. May all your kin be cursed and meet their death at the blade of an Aesearean for all ages. Are the passages safe?'

'I have sent men to check the entrances. Smoke comes through the eastern entrance, but no fighting can be heard. What will we do Lord General, we are trapped like wild hares in their dens for those beasts to come back?'

'Ay, I do not know. Send a skeet to find how the coastal people have fared. Scouts will need to be sent out to see where the Matavians lie.'

'The princes?' asked Warick tentatively

Medret shook his head 'The Queen lives but is branded with a mark of the demons.'

He watched them gently place Nene on a litter and carry her towards the grotto she had taken as her bed. He had served her father and watched her grow to become the fair Queen Nene of Aeserea more favoured then her father and subtle of mind.

'You will live fair one, the lioness dwells in your soul. You have survived the touch of a fiend of the dark. Nothing can defeat you now' whispered Medret.

Revenge bloomed inside him more than any rose or desire before. He realised the depth of his love for his Queen and his lands.

Nene woke thirsty. She felt where the bandages had been placed to cover her wounds. Ellen one of her attendants gave her some water.

'Rest my lady, nothing more has happened.'

'My brother Dronagh?'

'The princes are ready for burial your highness.' Medret walked towards her and offered his hand.

Nene took it and stood up. Her face burned as the tears began to stream down into the wounds. She took the knight general's arm and joined the burial procession. Draved and Dronagh had been wrapped in makeshift death rags.

The passage to the crypt was oppressive as the suffocated torch light barely flickered on the stone walls that led to the tombs of the Aesearean rulers. Draved and Dronagh sons of Cedric the Great were placed inside a coffin carved out of the wall above their father. Nene waited in vigil until the rocks had been cemented in place. Each stone slowly entombing her brothers.

'Come my lady, you need to rest.' Medret took her arm once more.

The light of their sanctuary revived her briefly. Two skeets flew down startling some of the villagers now on constant watch in fear that the creatures would return.

'What news Cotus?' she asked.

'The battle still rages along the sea, but the scum is being met with the fierceness of our lioness. They have not advanced much beyond the City of Strad in the south. Esteron is destroyed but they do not linger. They will make their way north and attack from the rear.'

'The people can be warned. It is a seven days march south.' Nene was sitting near a stream. She let her fingers dangle in the soothing gurgle of the water as she looked at all the people. They numbered fewer than two thousand and most of them were old and young. 'There are too few of us to help them.'

'Ay m' lady. I will send word to them in the south. Lord Warick has taken some men to rally the westerners. If the sorcery that makes the demons walk with them has left, then there is hope of a victory yet.'

'We will wait then until the fate of the Aeserean people is decided Cotus.'

'Ay my lady. I will take your leave now I wish to fortify the passages.'

'Ellen are the wounded being tended to sufficiently.'

'Yes, my lady, they are well settled.'

Nene walked to her litter in the grove. Lying down she closed her eyes. Draved and Dronagh faces came to mind and tears welled again making the burns on her face sting more. The memory of the beast touching her and everything going black came back to her. She remembered seeing the heart of the creature; inside it lay a chasm of profound emptiness with chains embedded and leading to a figure watching. They had been caged by spirit that now wished to destroy all things here. The creature sought something just as Nene had foreseen. It wanted the blood of ancients whose ancestors still walked and the power which had been given to them. As Nene began to dream, her grief for Draved and Dronagh was consumed by a terror of what was yet to come.

15

Judgement

Ange woke to the usual pallor that the icelands called dawn. She went outside the hut they had been placed in and looked around her. Some women and girls were already out milking snow cows. Their thick fur hides obscured the fact that they were cows. Nekoda nudged her hand. She smiled when she saw the mutt. He still had his leather shoes on and his ocean dog vest. She saw the place they had put Gildas. He was standing stretching as much as the chains would let him. Her heart filled with anger again. The image of Bensah dying came to her mind and tears formed. She felt a hand on her shoulder, startling her. It was Sa.

'Have you eaten Ange?'

She shook her head.

'I do not think it is wise to wander too far.'

They went back into the warm hut and sat together. Kado was asleep on a rug.

Sa noticed the tears in Ange's eyes.

'What frightens you the most?' Sa handed Ange a bowl of milk with some ground nuts floating in it. It was bitter and salty, not sweet like the milk her mother used to make.

Ange did not answer. She did not want to start crying again. She put her hand to her neck to feel for the prism.

'Where is it Sa?' suddenly alarmed.

'You fainted after you showed it to Gildas brother. He must have kept it.'

Ange jumped. 'No, I must get it back. It was given to me.'

'We can go later and ask for it. Ange how much have you seen?'

'Not now Sa.'

Ange raced out of the hut back towards the centre of the village. Sa followed her but the girl was quicker than she expected. Nekoda was bounding behind, barking which set off the sled dogs. On hearing Nekoda a group of clansmen began to walk from an open field where they had been practising defence manoeuvres. Sa noticed three of them were the ones guarding Gildas' brother. Jarrod was also among them.

Ange entered the large den looking for the man they had been brought before but it was empty. Stepping outside again she scanned the village hoping to see the Chief. Nekoda snuffled around her thinking it was a game.

'What are you doing girl?' Tommo grabbed her before she sped off. Ange barely understood him, his accent was so thick and guttural in the common tongue. 'You are not free to walk the village.'

He picked her up and began to take her back to the hut.

'I will take her clansman, she got away from me.' Sa was holding Nekoda back as he growled at the great native of the ice. She knew he would kill Nekoda in an instant if the dog attacked.

'Look after your brat better.' He almost threw Ange at Sa but as she landed instead of walking with Sa she began to walk away from their hut towards the outskirts of the village. Sa went with her holding Nekoda as he barked their presence all through the humpies. Children came running out to watch.

Ange saw Gildas watching from his prison. She went up to him.

'Where is it? You know I must keep it. That is what she asked me to do.'

Looking down at the girl he saw the fear in her eyes as they both knew what now lay in the world and what it meant to lose the gem.

'My brother the Chief took it. He will not let you have it until it is decided whether we can stay.'

'I will explain to him. He saw what it was.' Ange hissed back.

He noticed the warriors were walking towards his pen. Jarrod was leading them. Sensing that Ange may do something rash he grabbed her.

'Go back to your hut girl. We are not welcome here. If they send us away, then they will give the stone back. They will consider it a curse. But if you cause trouble, they will kill us all.' Gildas saw the anger rise in her eyes towards him as she pulled away from him. He understood the hatred a person could feel towards another.

Nekoda yapped at Gildas to remove his hands. He batted the dog away as it nipped his arm.

'Take the dog and go back.'

'What is this Gildas?' Jarrod stood at the gate looking flushed from fighting.

'It is nothing Chief, she thought she had lost her gem.

She will go back now and wait until our fate here is decided.'

Ange flew at Jarrod 'Where is it? It is not yours. It was given to me by the lady to keep safe. The great god of the world Norbu made it before you and I were even the grains of dirt which shaped us.'

Jarrod tapped her away knocking her over. She had fight in her if nothing else he thought.

'It is safe. I have seen its power and that is why you shall not keep it until your fates are decided.'

Jarrod looked at Gildas in chains. He said nothing but averted his eyes quickly. He wondered what had happened to Gildas to break him.

'Take her back and keep guard until I call the clan meet' Jarrod spoke to Tommo as he walked off to his hut.

Ange withdrew a dagger she had hidden in her under shirt.

'I will fight for it Chief. You don't know what you carry.' Ange ran to get in front of him. Nekoda growled and leapt at Jarrod. Gildas seeing it strained to stop the dog attacking but Sa managed to grab him in time.

Jarrod stopped as Ange menaced the blade at the massive man. He feinted to the left, she met him and then to right and she met him again, but this time managed to cut his hand.

'Give it to me. We will leave here and find another place.'

Jarrod darted forward but she swiftly outstepped him and tried to dig the dagger into his thigh. She missed and Jarrod caught her arm and twisted the dagger out onto the snow.

'You are quick with your blade. You would make a good Graan wife. You and the merchants may leave but Gildas owes blood to the clan. He must stay.'

'We will leave but give me the stone.'

Sa interrupted 'Ange enough. Come with me now.'

'No! Don't you understand, the demon can't find it while I have it for it must be given freely. It cannot see it. That is why she gave it to me. I must have it back or it will come. Our ancient blood dims its power and stops its call to the demon. It is why we were called, Gildas, Kado and me. For some reason me especially. Don't you see Sa it can't lie with anyone else. It was Norbu who made it from Assumpta and now Assumpta has given it to me.'

'But the ice and eternal sun thwart the demon Ange, that is why we came. Chieftain please we will not disturb you more.'

'Get back to the hut girl.' Gildas growled at her.

'No!' Ange screamed as Kado picked her up. She struggled too much though and Kado dropped her.

'Hold. Is this true Gildas?' asked Jarrod.

'I do not know brother; the girl has been entrusted with it. We are only here to protect her. The beast cannot run in daylight but neither has it been tracking us in the night or haunting our dreams. How do you know this girl?'

'I can see its eyes searching in the dark when I look into the stone. It searches all the time, but it does not see me walking beside it as I look for the lady.'

Sa exhaled. So that had been the reason Ange was given this potent gift she would remain hidden from the demon.

'Do the gods know you are with them when you look in the stone Ange?'

'They have seen me there, but they fight.' Ange started to shiver from being out without her coat on.

Jarrod looked at her and then around him. Most of the clan had come out to see what was happening. Han and Jano stood with their mother.

'Bring her to my hut. Tommo and Ikdad bring Gildas as well. Tie the dog. The rest of you get back to your chores.'

'Who is the cripple father? She almost bested you with her dagger.' Jano jibed at his father as he and Han and Caelwyn walked with Jarrod back to their hut.

Looking at his hand where Ange had slashed him 'The desert teaches their younglings well. Perhaps she could teach you two' looking at Jano with a glint of humour in his eye.

'Why are they here Jarrod?' asked Caelwyn

'We will speak inside.'

Caelwyn laid out the bowls with milk and almonds. There was some smoked fish as well.

'Has your brother brought a curse back on the Graan?'

'Not of his own will. He would not have returned here without cause.'

Ikdad brought Gildas and placed him towards the door of the hut. He saw Jano and Han sitting with a woman. Jano eyed him closely and Gildas thought he will keep the Elder chief staff in clan Gol.

Kado, Sa and Ange arrived. Tommo waited outside with Ikdad.

'Sit. Have you taken food?'

They nodded. Caelwyn stood and motioned the boys to stand as well.

'Nay stay Caelwyn, Jano and Han. I am not Elder Chief at this meet.' He looked back at Ange and the others. He pulled the stone from his vest. It was still wrapped in the fur of the bear hide. 'Tell me everything desert dweller.'

'I do not understand it all either. But I know that for some reason the demon has not been able to snatch this jewel from me. I can see in the god's realm and they war with each other. Perhaps Norbu and Assumpta the lady who called all of us, battled to free Lido, and the spirits of wind and fire. I know though the longer it is not in my care, the easier it will be for Voloc to find it.'

'And you Gildas, how is it that you became part of this?'

'It is our ancient blood that binds us. The demon and the witch draw's its strength from it but most of all the stone. Once the demon has the stone's potency then its enemies can be destroyed, along with us.'

'So, do you intend to run until these gods or spirits choose to return. It makes no sense to let this demon loose on our lands with no way of fighting it. If the world is destroyed before your gods return, then their quest is in vain. It will find you eventually. Once it has razed all the southern lands it will look here.'

'Ay Jarrod, nothing here can destroy it. Only these spirits that have risen seem to match its strength. Something lies inside that will ensure they can defeat it and we are here to keep the stone hidden to give them time. But also Brother if the time comes it may well be all those who remain may need to join in battle to destroy the shadow or thwart it until the gods return or the world's fate is decided. This battle is about destruction not conquest' spoke Gildas.

'For now, you may stay until Gildas fate is decided. I have

called the clan meet and will expect them to be here on the next dawn. If this stone brings war, then the graanar will meet our enemies as we always have. Our lives are guided by the ice and its mother and she has offered succour and protection in return. This demon may yet learn the wrath of the ice bear.' Jarrod tossed the stone to Ange. She quickly un-wrapped it and placed it inside the pouch around her neck.

'Thankyou.' She looked directly at the large Chieftain in front of her. 'It was none of our choosing to bring this demon upon your clan. My mata and pata are both dead and then my sister was taken by the slavers. Bensah was my father's friend and he found me, but your great ice bear took him as well. Gildas was chosen to protect me but now death is near to him also. I see where I will walk alone with this gift until the gods or the demons take it. We will stay until Gildas' fate is decided and then we will move to where refuge can be found. I thank you for your shelter and food.' Ange looked to the ground as her heart thudded in her chest. She had realised after Bensah died that one by one the others would meet their end until it was only her and the black shadow standing in a pool of blood with the prism between them.

'Ay girl. One such as you would not live here amongst us. We give our misborn as a sacrifice to the mother of ice. You are twice cursed, first your shape and now to be made the bearer of a weapon of these spirits that fight for its power. You will need your strength and courage girl for it seems you are alone in this.' Ange nodded as she felt the fear and hatred engulf her again for what had happened.

Jarrod stood looking at her with a glint in his eye for he

could see the fear that lay behind hers 'You have been taught to fight girl. My hand still bleeds from the prick of your weapon. Who is your tutor?'

Ange smiled just slightly 'Sa and Gildas.'

'Perhaps you should practice more while you are here. Han and Jano can join you with the assassin.'

'I will not fight with a crippled desert dweller father' Jano objected.

'Did you not see what this cripple did Jano, she fought the bear to protect her jewel. I think you will find she will teach you. Go, there is much preparation for the clan meet.' He looked at Gildas and knew in his heart Clotte would not send him to exile.

Gildas sat listening to the clashing swords and shouts as the warriors resumed their weapons practice. In amongst it, he could hear the thatched brooms sweeping out huts and the women counting their hauls of nuts and fish to feed the clan chieftains when they arrived. The high-pitched squeal of a girl and boys voices also broke through the bustle. It was Ange and Jarrod's sons sparring. He stood up to watch through the gap in the wall. Ange high kicked at Han, he feinted a blow to her stomach, but she whipped around it and managed to push his legs from under him. Gildas could predict all their moves but the girl was getting faster and more determined. Ange was right, one by one they would die until it would only be her standing between the demon's victory or defeat. Why had they chosen her? The destruction or survival of their lands now rested on a maimed desert youngling.

'Up now Ange, draw your lead arm down so the weapon

remains hidden and use the other to distract the enemy. Good again.' Sa stood watching the three children with her arms behind her back, patiently correcting their mistakes.

'Oi!' came the squeal of Han as Ange forced him to the ground and dislodged his axe. Jano annoyed at being there at all went for Ange as she steadied herself over Han. Quickly she ducked beneath his broad stroke of his blade and barged directly into his stomach. Keeping with the forward momentum she pushed him over onto the snow and landed with her dagger poised for the lethal blow. Jano lay underneath her winded. Recovering he hoisted her off and got up.

'Enough! Han get up.' He spoke in his native tongue but Ange and Sa both understood from the anger in his tone that the sparring had ended.

'Well done Ange you are getting stronger and more subtle.' They walked in the opposite direction to the two boys. Their path took them past Gildas' enclosure. Seeing him watching they went over to him.

'The graanar aren't used to being beaten by a woman Assassin.'

'The clansmen are rigid in their ways. It will be their doom' replied Sa.

'Nay, what choice does the ice give us. If the women do not tend to food, then we die. The younglings would not survive the ice lands without the shelters we build. The men are for fighting and the fishing and the women tend to the hearth. That is our way.'

'Your crimes must have been great Gildas for retribution to last so long?' Sa asked.

'Ay they were. I would be no less merciful if I were the Elder Chief.' He looked at Ange 'You know more than you have told us girl?'

'No Gildas. I have only searched for the lady in the hope she will return soon. I do not want anyone else to die.'

'The mother of the ice never takes without giving back. The trader's death will not be in vain.' Ange did not answer Gildas.

'Come we will rest a while. A storm seems to be coming.' Sa pointed to black clouds forming in the distance.

'Ay get shelter.'

As Ange and Sa walked away Sa wondered at Gildas, a calmness seemed to exist where once she only saw the warrior seeking his next war. Perhaps being back in the land of his birth had stilled his agitation. She knew they would be leaving in a few day's and he would not be with them. She wondered how they would hope to survive without him.

Kado had risen and was sharpening a small knife he had found at the base of his sack.

'Well warriors, how goes it?'

Ange lay down on a rug 'I bested them.' She looked shyly at Kado.

'That is cause for celebration Ange, but we only have ice and smoked fish.' They both giggled.

A flap on the door blew open as the wind picked up outside. Sa got up 'I will get Nekoda.'

The three of them sat around the fire with Nekoda whining and being restless as the fury of the storm overtook the village. Ange found the flames mesmerising as she watched them flicker almost in time with the howling winds outside. She soon fell asleep inside her furs and began to dream. She and Tessi were playing near the stream. Tata and Mata came up behind them and sat on the long straw that had not been harvested yet. Her heart ached with the loss of it all. On the horizon stood the black dog howling but only she could see it. She kept pointing to it, but they were ignoring her. The red eyes looked directly at her as if it were real, but its gaze seemed to extend beyond her. She turned to follow where it looked. She saw a figure on a throne waiting as well. It saw her as well. It stood ready for battle also. Before its feet lay figures chained straining to be free and beyond it was the memory of light long passed and forgotten. Why us? Why me? She asked the figure on the throne.

'Because in you lies the strength of Caemeris stolen from us the first created by its vision' spoke the figure.

Sa and Kado stood watching as the sleds of dogs arrived in the village in a cacophony of barks and shrill whines. The howling set Nekoda off also. The echoes raced across the tundra and forests. As each of the Chieftains alighted from their sleds Kado was amazed at the size of the men. Giants of the ice was the name he called them as they gathered around Jarrod. The last sled arrived and on it sat an old man with a younger one standing behind him steering. Upon the back rest was a skull of a bear. Its size and menacing fangs were threatening even dead. The other Graan cleared a path for the old man as he walked towards Jarrod. Not quite kneeling but what seemed to Kado an act of homage the Elder Chief stooped and grasped the old man in a hug. Suddenly Kado noticed Ange standing beside him. She looked feverish and was panting slightly.

'What is happening, how long have I been asleep?'

'You slept most of the day and this lands idea of a night. Bad dreams again Ange?' Kado patted her on the head.

She nodded without elaborating on it. The snow had fallen heavily during the storm and most of the huts were now buried almost to the roof. Ange saw a woman digging her way out. Where the sleds had entered deep tracks had been carved out of the fresh snow. The walls of the tracks were taller than herself.

'Come we will eat. Sa thinks we should have our things packed, as Gildas judgement will come soon and we may need to leave.'

'Will they kill him?' Ange asked.

'The Graan are slow to change their ways and minds on most things. If Gildas had a death pledge on his head when he left here, then I think it would still remain' replied Kado.

'If we are made to leave, we will need him Kado. We will not live long even with the skill of Sa. I also think his destiny lies elsewhere now and his fate is not to end at the hands of his kin.'

Kado grinned slightly at the innocent oversight of any mention of his own knack for survival in a vast icy tundra.

'Sa and I both know this. We will do our best to try and spare him being executed. Go and practice some more. Sa and I have been asked to be present at the clan meet.' Ange whistled for Nekoda to join her as she walked off. She saw the two guards of Jarrod escorting Gildas towards the large main hut where his judges had gathered.

'I hate you, but we need you' she whispered.

Gildas was placed at the base of Jarrod's chair over to the left.

He sat crossed legged. He noticed his leather vest and the sword from the Keep were placed in the middle before the throne. He would either walk with it as an exile or it would be used to quarter and behead him. Gildas remembered the fight at the Hill of Jank. The Matavian had been unable to cut him with the blade. Perhaps there was a way to convince the clans that they needed to let him live. Sa and Kado had been permitted to attend the clan meet. He nodded at them as they entered and sat to the side.

Jarrod followed by five of the eight clan chiefs entered the large hut. The old man with the bear skull adornment on his sled walked in supported by a younger man. He stopped when he saw Gildas. His son tried to move him, but he would not budge.

Gildas stood and bowed slightly to acknowledge the old chief.

'Cursed and forsworn, you are exile. Murderer of kinfolk and graanar' spat Clot of Clan Clotte.

'Clansmen, today I have called you to a death judgement upon an exiled graanar. Many cycles ago my brother Gildas Gol former Elder chieftain of the eight tribes committed an insult to the clansmen and most of all to Clan Clotte when in act of rage he murdered his woman who was heavy with child. It was not only the act of murdering the woman Jesse of Clotte and the buried child, heir to the throne of the ice bear but also for murder of younglings in Clan Nimmo and Bregt for choosing to challenge the rule of the Elder Chieftain. Gildas Gol brought the curse of conquest to the lands of the Ice Mother instead of prosperity. In his time half of our younglings were slaughtered, the peoples who had traded with us for generations had been enslaved. It was the clan wives who challenged this insult to the Ice Mother and were punished by the blades of Gildas Gol with the death of their younglings. It is this breach of the sacred oaths which the Graanar have held deep inside their flesh and bones for as long as we have lived on the ice. It is these acts which I ask for judgement from all of you here. I ask now even though the bones have lain so long in the ground, if the graanar wish to continue the death judgement or let exile be the punishment for Gildas of clan Gol?'

The old man tapped his stick on the floor to signal he wished to speak.

'Chieftain Clotte and father of the murdered, speak.'

'Gildas Gol not only insulted and destroyed the most beloved of clan Clotte and all the graanar, the fair Jesse. He usurped his own father's chieftain chair before the elders had chosen their next clan ruler. It was a sign of the wrath and lust for his own battle glory which follows every step of this accursed. His battle lust almost brought destruction to children of the great bear. My daughter spoke of the death which would follow him. She knew that one day she would die by his hand. Foolishly she believed she could stay his hand. But the spirits deceived her. I have lost my daughter and grandson to the great mother of our lands and she has not been paid in full for the blood spilt. The great mother has always asked blood for blood and it is she that demands that Gildas juice stain the lands. To let him go will bring retribution from the mother. If there is no retribution, may she call the winds of Raajn to scour all of us from her sight.' The old man trembled as he spoke.

Gildas remembered when Jesse spoke of the visions she had

had when they were asking permission to join as mates. He knew now that what Jesse's vision sealed her fate, but the witch knew something else would come of their union. She had gouged out the dormant feelings for her and it was this that had protected him against the shadow wolf.

'Are there any clansman that do not call for the death of Gildas Gol?'

Kado stood as the others remained silent.

'I wish to speak Graan Chief.'

Jarrod nodded.

'I am Kado Kodrax heir and son to the former Ko Dynasty Emperor Ko, now destroyed at the hands of Lord Ranik. The world beneath the graan has changed and lies for the most part in ruin due to this tyrant's lust for destruction. This has been his way in all my memory but now a black spirit has entered this world and its claws lay embedded in the tyrant's heart and mind. As we have explained to the Elder chief this demon now seeks the girl and her gem. The brethren spirits that have followed the demon here have chosen us to protect the girl until they return. We need Gildas to live to see this quest to the end for I fear without his strength and courage we will die and the world will fall into the claws of this demon and to its death. Not even the great mother of the ice would defeat it. We also have been chosen for a fate not yet determined by these gods, not least of which was Gildas. We fear his death at the hands of his kin may bring greater destruction rather than appease those wounded long ago.'

'Elder chief this boy would not know of who Gildas was. He speaks of the tyrant Ranik and his war of death and black spirits. But the Gol lord that sits before us now had the same vision of darkness before his eyes and drove the graanar almost to annihilation. To let such a blackheart loose in the world when it seems already threatened by another would only ensure our defeat. War will come Elder chief if your brother is set free.' The frailty of the old man belied the black threat that came from his lips.

Jarrod looked at Clot and knew the clan retribution would not be dropped. He also remembered the wounds of the infighting after Gildas fled. The clans would chase his brother down and kill any who stood with him. Jarrod's ruling would not change their lust for vengeance.

'You are heard Clan Clotte, but I have seen some of the potency of this thing the demon seeks and Gildas at risk of his life brought them here for refuge. I see a broken man now not the warmonger that once ruled us.'

Kado interrupted sensing that Jarrod would be overruled. He stood again. The old man spat, offended that an outsider was allowed at a clan meet. Kado saw the threatening gesture but continued.

'I make an offer to the graan in return for the boon of leaving Gildas to exile. When my kingdom is rebuilt then in payment, I offer all the jewels and metals the Graan need for either trade or survival. I also will grant that any trade in the precious fish of your icelands, is yours solely forbidding any merchants to seek it.'

'There will be nothing left of your kingdom after Ranik has scoured it of its wealth. The graanar have all they need from the ice' Clot growled.

'I believe this war will come to the clansmen. The only thing that stands between the spirits and our world is this girl. The one Gildas has forfeited his own life to protect. My word is true. My father was a great general and soldier but lacked the subtlety of a merchant. A new era will begin under my rule and the Graan will be the first to prosper from my reign. Ranik does not know where all the riches of the Drax Dynasty lie Chieftain.'

'If it is the worlds end so it shall be, but the ice bear asks blood be repaid in blood and her favour has always stood with the clans because we follow this rule. To forsake it now will bring our ruin sooner than need be. I call for the head and carcass of Gildas Gol to be left for Raajn to scour until his bones are as white as the snow, they will lie in.' Clot and the other chieftains thumped their staffs heavily.

Kado looked at Gildas knowing he had lost the argument. Gildas looked back at the prince and nodded at him.

'What is the Chieftain's ruling?' asked Jarrod.

'Knut of Kaan, blood with blood, as the Ice Mother blesses and curses.'

'Hadrin of Hadraan, blood with blood.'

'Brago of Bregt, blood with blood.'

'What is the Elder chief's ruling?' Clot peered with deep black eyes at Jarrod.

'Kado Kodrax your offer and loyalty to my brother is honourable but I fear a hollow gesture. The Graan have no great need for baubles and precious things as the ice does not require them. And if it is true that this demon ravages the world below us and seeks an end to all who dwell here, then the graan will meet it in battle on the ice and our blood will be the offering to our great mother for the succour she has given to us over many generations. As Elder chief I cannot forsake the rule of the ice and the graan. Blood must be met with blood. On the dawn of the second day Gildas will be staked and then quartered by his own blade. He will be left for the Winds of Raajn to gather his bones and remove him from the memory of the graan forever.'

There was a collective thump of staffs as the gathered chieftains agreed to the ruling.

Kado slumped as he sat down next to Sa. Her mind began to race as she thought of where they may go next with Ange. Her only thought was the temple of Sa Dom and the protection high amongst the Zhang. She had known Gildas would not leave here alive and the calmness in the way he accepted his fate seemed to her that it was perhaps what he wanted; an end to the violence that had ruled his mind and heart all his days.

Tommo and Ikdad pulled Gildas up and walked him out again to his prison. Kado and Sa were gestured to leave.

Ange was sitting in the snow with Nekoda cleaning her dagger and sword. She had finished playing with Han and two other boys. They did not tell her their names. Jano had refused to play again after humiliation at her hands. When she saw Sa and Kado she waved to them. The look on their faces told her that the news was bad for Gildas. Looking across in the distance she saw Gildas being led back.

'Do we have to leave?'

'I think so. On the second dawn he will be put to death.' Sa answered.

'Where will we go?'

'I will ask for passage back to the south. I think there is one place where we can hide until ...'

Sa did not finish because she did not know what to say. Kado began to walk back to the hut as he was feeling the cold again. Ange and Nekoda followed but did not say anything. Ange knew this would happen. The great chasm that she stood upon in her dreams was drawing closer.

16

Exiles and Traitors

Faad watched the desert youngling play fighting with the boys. She is different to the sister he thought, hardier from her life as an outcast. His lips and face were crusted with scabs from the searing chill of the ice. He trudged back to a small humpy concealed with branches from the vast forest of conifer trees. He sat trying to warm his hands inside. One hand still had an open wound from the fur trader who had guided them here, inflicted as Faad's blade pierced his gut.

'What will we do capt'n?' One of the guards, Ulrig had made some porridge. Some of it slopped down the man's chin. Faad grimaced in disgust at his clumsiness.

'I am thinking. We will not be able to steal her. We will be captured.'

Faad thought. The clansmen were not kind to outsiders normally. She would not be easy to take. She would struggle and they would not be able to outrun the clansman on the snow. The distance back to the southern passage was days away with nowhere to be concealed from any pursuers. He could bribe them for the girl feeling the purse of gold he had brought with him.

'We are low on oatmeal capt'n. The huntin' in these parts is likely to let a man die of hunger more than anything else.'

'Yes Ulrig. I think it is time to play our hand. There is nothing to lose now.' Ulrig offered Faad a bowl of the bland porridge.

Faad sat eating and thinking of the Queen and their last night together before he left. She was slipping into madness, a dangerous madness. But then her white skin and supple body came to mind and he felt his body warm at the thought of it under his. Faad was weary of Ranik and his insatiable desire for war, perhaps it would be better for the demon to kill them all.

Kado, Ange and Sa and Nekoda sat inside and listened again as another storm raged around them. Their packs lay ready with their furs. Kado had paid for some of the women to make new coats and boots for them. The three of them had agreed they did not wish to see Gildas dead. They would leave on the day of his death.

'Have you spoken to Jarrod yet?' asked Sa.

'Yes, he will let us use a sled and a clansman will guide us to the common merchant route to the east. There is a passage that leads south where the mountains meet the ocean. And then it is up to you assassin as to where next.'

Sa was about to ask another question but Kado answered anticipating what it was going to be.

'The clan consider Gildas and anything that would walk with him cursed. Jarrod said war would come of it or our throats slit in the night if he let us have refuge here.'

Sa nodded.

Ange looked at them both and lay down.

'Come soon Lady, I don't wish Sa and Kado to die' she whispered.

First felt blinded by the snow. Belmaris' light did not burn the same here as it did in the red dirt. Its gaze was broken, and the shards were like the crystals in the white that crunched beneath them. But the face etched into First's memories were clear. The prisoner had put it there when its screech had called the Aracnine from the creatures inside the mountain. The gift had revealed itself and now that they neared the power of Caemeris the strength and image of its keeper grew with every stride. A roar came from behind, First looked and saw the beast that chased them. It never left their trail. Its potency was ancient like the ones their prisoner fought. But the Aracnine were not of this world and their destruction lay with their creator. First had turned to the beast but its mind was closed to its command and so it continued to chase in the vain hope of ridding the intruders from its lands.

Ange sat in the sled looking up at the white ceiling of the sky. Just briefly she thought she saw some blue poke through. A group had gathered around Gildas' enclosure. His brother chieftain was talking in their own tongue. Gildas stood bound before them.

The group of graanar began to walk towards the open plains that lay to the south. In the distance stood the black stump of a large pine. Ange watched them tie Gildas to it. He was larger than all of them but did not fight them. Hurry Kado, Ange thought as she knew they would kill him quickly. He had gone to gather more supplies. Flashes of Bensah came to her and she began to cry. Hurry she whispered to herself. Sa heard her and followed Ange's gaze.

'He wants to die in his homeland I think Ange. Gildas could fell any of them without a weapon but he does not struggle against his judgement.'

'I know. We are all prisoners in our own way Sa' replied Ange.

'Yes, we are. But some of us choose it freely. I wonder if the regret and shame is deeper than those of us who did not.'

'It depends. Mata said I made her see the faces of the gods when I was born but I brought a cage around her neck and Pata. We were shunned and I was doomed to a life of slavery or begging on the edge of my village. Now I am here with assassins of emperors and former war chiefs and still I am caged. Shame, guilt, or revenge for freedom, are not what matters the most. They are important. But you need to see the cage first then you can decide what to feel and if you wish to be free of its bonds.'

'They are old words from young lips Ange.'

'When you are made to be left alone you have all the time under the sun to think about a lot of things.'

Gildas watched across the tundra to remember his birthlands. He felt the ropes chaffing against the thickened scars from his imprisonment. The snow started to fall heavily. He watched the dense drifts of snow shifting in the distance, but then the snow cleared momentarily, and the spikey crown and red skin became clear. They had found them.

Suddenly struggling against his bonds, he yelled at the gathered Graan.

'Let me loose, the demon comes. A battle comes Graanar bear your axes and blades.'

He looked down and saw his blade from the Keep. It had been rammed into the frozen earth ready to be pulled out by Clan Clotte to slay him.

'Let me loose and give me my blade.'

Everyone turned to see what he was talking about when suddenly screams came as one of the creatures barged their way into the gathered crowd.

'Graanar! Ready your weapons' shouted Jarrod.

'Let me loose Jarrod' Gildas yelled.

'Nay brother. What curse has followed you? Gather and strike brothers. Clan maidens take the younglings to the forests. Wives ready your axes.'

Three of the guardians swept past ignoring the attacks of the clansman. First could see where she was and kept walking. It stomped on the old man Clotte. Gildas saw it heading towards Jarrod as he and a dozen others stabbed at another creature's legs.

'Jarrod!' He tried to heave the stump out of the ground, but it would not budge.

Sa yelled for Kado to come. Nekoda strained in its leash. Sa cut the rope that tied Nekoda. The sled dogs strained so hard the stumps keeping the sled from moving gave way. Sa grabbed Ange out of the sled just as the dozen pack dogs ran directly towards the creatures. The First Aracnine front stood on the pack leader as it picked up two others and flung them towards the trees.

'To the forest' Sa urged Ange.

Putting Ange down they began to sprint. Kado had come out of the hut with arm full of furs. He saw the creature swoop down its mighty talons to collect Ange, but she managed to miss it. Darting to her right she began to run in a blind panic to where Gildas stood.

'No Ange to the trees!' Kado screamed and began to race after her. Suddenly all the creatures seemed to turn to where Ange ran. Sa got herself in between the one leading them. It stooped and picked her up. The strength of the grip forced the breath out of her lungs. It looked at her. Sa could see its red eyes searching. Then it placed a claw on her forehead touching the scar that lay there. A shrill scream came from its jagged maw. The piercing noise did not cease. Sa felt like her head was going to explode. The others came to it and gathered. Then all of them screeched in unison. Sa felt the vibrations and began to feel dizzy. Blood came from her ears as they perforated from the noise. Everything went black.

Ange looked back and screamed for Sa but the noise from the creatures was so great that it drowned her out. Then the screams stopped, and they turned their gaze back to her. She ran blindly until she saw Gildas trying to climb up over the stump to get free. Pulling her dagger out she ran to him. Gildas saw her and slid down so she could reach him.

Ange quickly slid the dagger between his arms and leather bonds. She was sobbing as the blade sliced through. Gildas snapped free and gathered her under his arm 'Is the stone safe girl?'

'Yes, it is' she replied.

The leader strode towards Gildas. It had placed Sa on the

ground as it began to reach for Ange. Gildas pulled his sword out of the ground. Instantly he felt the power surge up his arm. Ange felt the prism fill with heat around her neck. Ange pulled it out and touched Gildas with it. They both felt the strength of a thousand suns bond with their ancient blood. The sword glowed as he wielded it in a great arc at the extended claw. It dug into the red hide of the creature and sliced through its arm cleanly. The creature screamed looking at the wound. The graan had gathered behind Gildas and watched as he fought the demon beast. Each blow piercing the hide. But as soon as the wound was inflicted it healed leaving only trails of red dust on the snow. Ange clung to Gildas as he tried to make his way toward the forest but the other Aracnine formed a circle. Trapped he put Ange down. The guardians began to sway in a chant. The leader picked up its severed claw and reattached it. There was no mark of the blow inflicted by Gildas.

Gildas roared and went into a frenzy of blows and strikes. Ange cowered beneath his mighty legs. The guardians stepped back unsure of the power the creature of clay wielded.

Gildas heaved with exhaustion as they waited. Jarrod ordered an attack but the graanar were flung with no effort into the ice. Nekoda barked and nipped at their ankles but they ignored the dog. Suddenly Gildas felt a hand on his sword arm. He looked down and saw Ange with tears in her eyes. He hefted his blade again, glowing a brilliant silvery white he slashed again. Missing he went to his knees.

'You will not defeat them Gildas.'

He did not want to hear it.

'I will go with them.'

'Nay, child, it will kill you.'

'They will kill you all if I do not. I will find a way.'

'It will force it from you.'

'There is no victory here. I hate you so much and your kind, but I see we are both trapped by this thing and it must be understood and then destroyed. I will leave Bensah and Mata and Tessi and seek a way. It is as the spirit of our hearts Ascendant told me. We are doomed unless we find a way Gildas.' Ange sobbed with fear.

Gildas grabbed her face and let her tears trickle onto his finger. He could not speak, but his heart wanted to explode with anger and grief. He wanted to tell Ange no greater warrior stood before Gildas Gol of the Graan, but his lips remained as immovable as the ice they stood upon.

Suddenly the leader clasped its talons around Ange's waist. Gildas swiped at it but missed. A talon latched onto his head. He collapsed on the snow as he was plunged into darkness. The leader screeched and one of them picked Sa up off the ground. The Aracnine fled with their quarry into the southern tundra.

Gildas roused to follow them but suddenly a massive bear appeared and began crashing its way through the gathered clansmen. It knocked Jarrod over as it went to chase after the creatures. The bear reared up over him to crush him into the snow but Gildas raised his sword and roared at her.

'Nay mother, seek the demons that threaten your lands not the ones who you feed and give succour.'

The blade glinted in the black eyes of the behemoth as fine sparks flew off it, melting the ice.

It roared at Gildas and went to strike him, but he brandished the blade again. 'The god of the stone and mountains forged this weapon, do not dare to defy it mother.'

Roaring the bear stood down and backed away towards the tundra from where it had come.

Gildas turned to give chase to the creatures but they had disappeared into the horizon obliterated by the snow. In the distance Nekoda's barks could be heard as the dog bolted after them.

'Why Sa?' Kado collapsed pale with fear. He had seen now what threatened them all.

Gildas drove his sword into the ground and roared in anger. The power of the sword cracked the frozen earth below sending waves across the village and into the forest. Jarrod and the graan gathered behind him. Gildas turned to them. Some of them stood back in fear that Gildas would attack.

'We are doomed brother' Gildas spoke heaving from the battle and power which had surged into his flesh.

17

Bonds of Light and Memory

The snow fell in a blizzard and began to encrust the red eyes of the Aracnine. Ange shivered uncontrollably as she dangled in the large talons of the creature. She tried to jab the hand with her dagger to make it put her down. But the freezing air made her fingers stiffen and the handle of the blade stick to her skin. The hood on her coat flapped on and off with each swing. She started to scream again in the hope that Gildas and Kado had managed to keep up with the creatures. The wind roared taking her voice with it. Suddenly the jerking stopped, and she was flung over the shoulder of the one who carried her. Lifting the hood up she looked down and realised the creatures were climbing. They had already made it to the mountains she had crossed with Gildas. Higher they went making her feel dizzy. She pulled her hood over and closed her eyes. As they climbed Ange tried to suck in more air but it was like the snow and ice had stolen it, mercifully she blacked out as the air thinned in the high altitude of the Northern Ranges.

Sa stirred from the jolting. She began to struggle trying to free herself from the creature's hold. The talon clamped around her tightened causing her to see stars from the pain.

'Get me to shelter. I will die in this blizzard.' Sa yelled but her she could not hear herself. The screams of the Aracnine had sent her deaf. She saw the creature's head turn towards her but ignored her pleas and continued to climb.

A screech came from below followed by rocks falling. First stopped and looked but could not see as its eyes became iced over. An image formed in its mind. It was Last. It could no longer see and was slipping down the cliff face.

First took its mighty talon and punched it into the side of the mountain until it made an opening. The Aracnine crawled into the space it made. Gently they lay Sa and Ange down on the freezing granite. Sa went to Ange who was unconscious. She knelt and felt the weak warm breath coming from Ange's mouth. Sa wrapped her furs around Ange and then cradled the girl to give her extra warmth. First placed its hand on the floor of their roughly hewn cave. Instantly Sa could feel warmth suffuse into her from the stone. The Aracnine's eyes began to glow red again as the ice melted away from their faces. All of them swayed gently as if chanting in silence together.

'What do you want with me?' Sa felt frustrated by the ringing in her ears.

When they did not respond she shouted again 'What do you want with me?'

Ange stirred at the sound of Sa's voice echoing. Looking at the assassin her heart leapt with relief.

'The demon will kill us Sa.'

'I know Ange. I am not sure why they took me but at least we can try to get away before it comes. Is the prism safe?'

Ange could feel the jewel's warmth and was glad for it. Her hands had defrosted so that now she could make a fist. Sa stood and went to the one that seemed to lead the others. Its height at a crouch still made it taller than Sa by a full body length. Its skin appeared to be made from fine red dust. Its eyes were small but shone brightly in the dark. Could the demon see her and Ange, Sa wondered? Were they telling it what was happening? Suddenly First placed its hand on Sa's head clamping down on it. Sa went to pull away taken by surprise but was held fast by the massive claws. Ange got up and pulled the prism out to touch the creature hoping the power would somehow make it let she and Sa go.

First saw the light of the jewel and stared into it. The wars of light and dark still raged within. Even when the stars had their victory the lust of the dark to consume all things remained. The tumult caused by the breech of their prisoner never waned.

First plucked the shiny thing from the little creature's hands and stared into it. Looking deeply, it saw the chained god and its brethren and felt the potency their prisoner desired so much. The power of all creation lay here and even the light of Belmaris would not withstand the depth of the emptiness that would come if Voloc gained its freedom. First let the image flow into Sa. Sa's mind reeled with the energy that flooded into it. Only for the large talon holding her up she would have crumpled onto the ground. Ange saw Sa's eyes close as she blacked out. She grabbed Sa's shoulder and reefed her away from the creature.

'Give it back to me!' she demanded.

First dropped the prism into Ange's hand. Sa roused again.

'I understand Ange, it is an old feud that has existed at the very beginning of time. The jewel holds within it the very essence of time's beginning. It holds the first spark before all else was wrought. It's the memory of first light.'

Sa looked back at First. 'Your master cannot have this, you and I and her will be destroyed. Let us go and end this thing now. We will hide.'

The red eyes stared back without responding.

'Can't you understand, your master will kill us and you.'

'It is no use Sa; they do not hear you. The prism doesn't even seem to affect them.'

'No Ange. I wonder why not.'

'I am thirsty' spoke Ange as she sat down.

Sa got up and went to the entrance. The creatures made no effort to stop her walking towards it. She went and held her leather cask to capture some snow in it. It melted quickly. Ange gulped it down as did Sa.

'I have some nuts here Ange. But that is all.'

'It may be all we will need anyway Sa. The black wolf will come soon. I think they are calling for him.'

Sa looked at the leader again. Its eyes had dimmed slightly as if it rested. Standing in front of it she took its talons again and held it. It did not resist her touch. Instead it gently closed its claws around her tiny hand and held it. Then it reached out to the one on its left and clasped its arm. The rest of them followed until all the creatures were linked by their hands.

'Speak' came the command in her head.

'Who are you?' she asked

'The Aracnine.'

'Where do you come from?'

'We do not know from where. We are bound to the being called Voloc that seeks the tears of the ascendant. Our memories are beyond the time of Caemeris, but its brightness has blinded us to our progenitor.'

'Is that the name of the stone Ange carries.'

'Yes.'

'Who is ascendant?'

'The custodian made for the hearts of the clay born. Her tears were formed when she was sundered from her spouse. They are made from the first star Caemeris. The ascendant's purpose is to make the clay born seek out what they cannot see.'

'Who is the one the ascendant seeks?'

'The god who lies chained to our prisoner.'

'Who is your prisoner?'

'The one called Voloc, shadow.'

'How is the demon your prisoner? And why do you not command it?'

'See now.'

Sa's mind filled with the image of the Aracnine and Voloc. Sa saw the massive chain spanning the ages that bound them. Sa realised the Aracnine were as imprisoned as the demon.

'Who is the god that is held prisoner?'

'Descendant, the shadow to balance the light of Ascendant. Together they form the sceptre, the gate to Caemeris. The way to Caemeris; the first star.'

'How is it that this god came under the power of the Demon?'

'See now.'

Sa understood what the war was over. It was not just about the demon gaining the power but also to bring the god back to its rightful place but to also show the way back to Caemeris, to find its origin.

'Why do you want me?'

'You are our queen.'

Sa jolted away from the creature after she had seen the image it made. Breathing heavily, she tentatively held its hand again.

'What is this? Who are you?'

'I am First of the Aracnine and you are our queen.'

'I am no queen; I am the assassin of Ko. I am of this world not the world of the spirits.'

'Aracnine were created to serve. Until we have another for our bonds to be given then the shadow is where our destiny lies. Aracnine were promised by Caemeris a queen who will set us free. A ruler made from the remnants of Uchala, the ancient who hid here when the Aracnine were first made. Hidden from the shadow so all was not lost to us and the bonds could be broken.'

A feeling of intense longing washed over Sa. It penetrated her mind and heart with such clarity that for the first time she wanted to weep for the despair it caused. Eons of time had passed for these creatures drawn into the destruction and chaos of the shadow with no chance of release until now. Sa stood away from First and sat down heaving. Slowly the ache of what she had felt dissipated.

'This is not me. You are mistaken.'

The hand went up again to place it on her head, but she

moved away. Sa thought she saw a small tear in the eye of First.

'I am not your queen.'

Ange saw how pale Sa looked and went over to her.

'What is it? What have you seen?'

'They are bound to the demon until they can be freed. They believe me to be their liberator.'

'But how Sa?'

'I do not understand either. We are trapped Ange by all the spirits. Perhaps Gildas is right, they have snared us in their own games and have not come to save the world at all.'

Sa and Ange became aware of the silence pervading their makeshift cave. The guardians had stilled as well. Ange got up and went to the entrance of the cave and saw that the storm had moved away. Light snow drifted down and disappeared in the vast depths below. Ange bent down and scooped some to drink. She took some back to Sa.

'It has cleared outside.'

'We are too high to get away from them here. We would plunge to our deaths.'

Suddenly First stood and screeched. Sa felt it pierce her head again causing her to fall to the ground in pain. First went to her and placed its hand on her again. Sa flinched but it held her firmly.

'Let us go. The demon will kill all of us including you once it has the stone. You know this, you have seen the power it contains.'

'Our destruction lies with our creator. The shadow calls, we will go now.'

'Nay you take us to our deaths.'

'Find Caemeris and the tears will be destroyed. Clayborn and Oblyquixita will be freed from their chains.'

First screeched once more. Ange covered her ears.

'The shadow calls.'

The huge hand lifted Sa onto its shoulder and another Aracnine grabbed Ange as they made their way out onto the mountainside. Ange began to shiver as she felt the cold thin air envelope her. She felt the dizziness return and her breathing become laboured. She looked at Sa.

'I can't breathe properly.'

'It's because we are so high. Soon we will cross the top of the peaks and we will see the sun again Ange.'

When Ange felt the first bite of the warm rays on her face, she roused slightly wondering what it was that burnt her. The brightness hurt her eyes as she looked at the great yellow disc bearing down on them. The Aracnine now walked along the top of a peak which for at least a league was a flat broad table of granite and quartz. It twinkled in places where the sun struck the dormant crystals in the rock. Along their left stood the sheer wall of mountains that trapped the clouds over the ice lands. Ange struggled to be put down. Her belly ached from being held in the one position for so long.

'Stop Aracnine!' ordered Sa and they did.

'It is so warm here Sa.'

Ange lifted her face toward the sun and drank it in.

Sa filled her leather pouch again from a pool of water that sat beneath a thin layer of ice.

'Drink Ange. The water is sweet.'

'Can we escape from here Sa?'

Sa peered across the lands below and saw the small familiar peaks of pure green granite and quartz.

'Further along the mountainside it is less sheer. It leads to the great foot of Jun. I know there are caves we can hide in beneath.'

First went to grab Sa to begin walking again but taking its hand she told it they would walk. Continuing Ange and Sa remained between First and Second as the group formed a line along the plateau. However, such was the pace Ange soon began to slow from exhaustion. Sa saw her stumble. They were close to the place where they could slide down the mountain as the massive abutment of green stone jutted out into the forests below.

Sa stopped the Aracnine as she looked down at Ange.

'The girl is tired First. We must rest or she will not make the journey. We need food, nourishment. We are not Aracnine.'

First looked at the lesser creatures.

'The shadow calls.'

'We will go to the shadow, but we must rest first and eat. We can go to the caves of Jun that lie below. They are not far.'

First stood swaying without responding. Releasing the talon from her head it picked Sa up and began to walk. Sa struggled but it ignored her. Ange fought against the one who went to grab her managing to escape. She began to run but it was futile as the creature took two large steps and caught her easily. The last two of the Aracnine headed toward the edge of the cliff descending the mountainside quickly.

'Yes First, let us go down there. Food and water. If I am your queen, I order you.'

'The shadow calls. The bonds are not yet broken.'

Sa's hope of any escape soon left as they strode passed the foot of Jun to be replaced by sheer vertical cliffs once more. Up in the distance stood the lanky shadows of the two more guardians. As they neared them, First placed Sa down. She saw a pile of rabbit carcasses on the rocks. First pointed to them. Sa picked one of them up realising they had bought food for she and Ange.

'We need fire to cook.' She shook her head as a gesture. With no response she took the talon again and explained.

First placed its hand on the rocky surface. Sa and Ange watched as it began to glow red with heat. The rabbit sitting on it began to smoke. Sa quickly pulled out her small paring knife and stripped the fur off it. The smell of the roasting flesh made her mouth water.

'Quickly Ange get the others.' Soon they both sat bursting with roast rabbit in their bellies.

First screeched to call for them to leave again.

'Are we too far to try and get back to the caves Sa?'

'Yes Ange. We will not escape now. Are you afraid?'

'I am but I knew that it was always going to be this way.'

'Try and rest. We will need our strength to face the beast again.'

First could feel the urgency of the call as they neared the shadow. It screamed in its head for them to hurry. It had waited long enough and now wanted release. The pull on the chains in the Aracnine chest tightened even more. The malignancy of the prisoner seemed to grow stronger as well. First knew once the shadow held the tears then the darkness would bleed out into the land seeping into all that Belmaris kept alive.

Descending into the lands of Matavia the Aracnine sped with their quarry towards the palace of Ranik. The moon was at its fullest and shone brightly over the bay of Tears. Ange's heart thudded as the chilling white walls of the palace seemed to match the fear that coursed through her body. She began to sob.

'Sa I am frightened.'

'I know Ange. Stay close to me.'

'Aracnine stop.'

First halted at Sa's command.

'I will not let the shadow take the stone nor let it kill us.'

'The shadow calls.'

'I will not let your bonds be broken First if the girl is taken by the shadow.'

A screech came from the mouth of First.

'The shadow calls. It cannot take the tears. It must be given. You have been promised to us.'

'You must choose Aracnine, the shadow or your queen. Either way I will not let the girl be taken.'

'Aracnine cannot choose we are servants. The shadow still holds the bonds of our fate. You must choose to accept the blood of Uchala that flows in you and be the queen that rules the Aracnine.'

First pulled away from Sa. They began to head towards the palace. Three guards on night watch stood up suddenly as the group entered the courtyard. Ange saw a woman standing in one of the arches of the balcony above them. Her face was the same iridescent white of the moon. As they entered a passageway beneath the palace, the darkness that surrounded them was thick with malice and fear. Ange began to tremble. She took Sa's hand as they walked with the Aracnine to face the demon.

Voloc stirred when it felt the gift enter the palace, drinking in the power even as it lay around the youngling's neck. A deep gorge of lust coursed through the shadow as it sensed the nearness of the gods that lay within it.

Silence greeted Ange and Sa in the dark cellar. The Aracnine had stood back and began their swaying.

'Why is she here?'

'The promise has been fulfilled Shadow. Our bonds can be broken if it is willed by the ancient power of Uchala.'

Ange could feel the chill in the demon's voice as it spoke to the guardian. Sa could feel the pain begin where Ange clenched her hand so hard her fingers were almost breaking. Slowly the red eyes began to glow as Voloc took shape before them. Sa's heart missed a beat as icy fingers run across it. Ange folded herself into Sa trying not to look at the red eyes. She knew that she would fall into the despair that lay within them.

Voloc moved towards Ange. Its long finger lingered around her neck. The eyes flared as it neared the prism. Ange pulled away trying to stop it coming nearer. Sa gathered herself and pushed Ange behind her and bared a dagger out of habit but knew it would be useless against this wraith.

Voloc hissed at them both and looked directly at Sa. The pain seared through her as the shadow searched her bones and then her mind.

'Ahh ancient indeed Aracnine. The deep blood of Arglethium

has been given to her at her beginning. Her father crawled into her mother and there lay the seed of the ancients. You are ignorant to your strength clay born. As the god drank of Uchala so I will drink of her progeny.'

Sa felt her heart stop and mind go blank but then First grabbed her before Voloc finished.

'Back prisoner, she is not for you. She is for the Aracnine, promised by the ancestor of Caemeris your undefeated enemy.'

First thrust Voloc back away from Sa and Ange.

Voloc hissed and suddenly First was wrenched to the floor on its knees. Screeching it pulled itself up, but its chest bulged as a massive chain link seemed to appear tearing the red hide. The other guardians screeched as well as the pain raced through them all.

'Sa do something it's going to kill them.'

'I don't think it can Ange.' Sa looked quickly behind her and saw the passage was open.

She nudged Ange towards the passage. They ran as fast as they could. The moonlight appeared again as they entered another courtyard. It was not the same one they had come from. Sa saw on the far side a dimly lit passage and raced towards it. Inside was a steep set of winding stairs. The screeching came again.

'Up here Ange quickly.'

'But Sa it will know where I am.'

'I know but we can at least try. It is distracted by the Aracnine.'

The stairs ended abruptly into a long hallway which led to a sitting room. In the distance Sa could hear babies crying.

She led Ange towards it. As they neared the entrance a large window came into view. Hopefully, it would be empty, and they could scale down the wall. A salty breeze drifted along the hallway. They were heading towards the Bay. Sa remembered the Demon shunned the water. Perhaps they could stow away on a ship or the great serpent would come to their aid. Her mind raced as they slowed near the doorway. Sa looked around the corner to see if anyone was in the room. No one.

She motioned Ange forward. A chilling screech roared up from below them. Sa and Ange raced to the window. Sa pulled the tie cords from the curtains and knotted them together. The drop was not too far, and fine pebbles would break the fall. She scanned quickly and saw the docks where the boats lay were only a few hundred paces.

'Ange if the rope doesn't reach all the way let yourself go limp when you fall. We will run to the water. The prism may draw the great serpent from the sea.'

Sa lowered Ange down as far as the rope reached and then climbed after her. Just as she reached the sand the screech echoed through the palace with an almighty crash as one of the walls exploded out onto the water.

Running towards the wharf Sa saw the small skiff tied to the large wooden pylon.

'Hurry in here Ange.'

Sa hoisted Ange in and frantically untied the boat. Sa took the oars and rowed. Sa saw the Aracnine making their way down the white walls as she pushed out into the calm moonlit ocean. Ange screamed suddenly making Sa look behind her. Her heart filled with dread as she saw the blackness within the night and the red eyes glowing on the wharf. She rowed faster trying to escape. First got to the water and began to wade in after them. The water slowed its stride, but it was still gaining on them.

'Ange put the prism in the water. See if it will call the great serpent.'

Ange took it out and as she removed it, the moonlight struck it causing a beautiful rainbow of indigoes and violets to wash over the bay and palace. Ange could feel the shadow calling for it, but the brightness of the moonlight enhanced by the jewel began to burn Voloc. First kept coming towards them. Plunging the stone into the water Ange willed for the golden serpent to rise. The gem burned brightly under the surface.

'Please come and save us.'

The talon of First latched onto the boat almost tipping it over. The water had risen to its chest seeping into the gaping wound. Sa touched the hand and spoke to First.

'Please let us be free. If the shadow takes the gift the gods will not return. They can free the Aracnine and rid the world of this malice.'

'It is not ordained for the custodians to free the Aracnine.' It began to pull the boat towards the shore.

Ange squealed 'Please come serpent.'

Voloc stood on the shore and waited. Sa began to feel her heart being squeezed as the darkness seeped in.

'First stop. I will be your queen. I will renew your bonds with those of this Uchala. I will be the ruler of the Aracnine but on one condition.'

First stopped and turned to her.

'The Aracnine must protect us from the shadow.'

Suddenly the icy finger within her mind and body squeezed hard Voloc heard the words she spoke. She passed out as the searing pain tore through her. Ange wondering what had happened leapt to her sobbing. The prism slipped from her fingers into the boat. First picked it up. Ange stopped suddenly wondering what the creature would do. The red light flared behind her as she saw the demon tasted the power through the guardian.

'Please, I don't understand any of this, but I know it was given to me to keep. I know if it had meant for any other it would not have found its way to me' Ange's voice was barely discernible as she trembled with fear.

First stood in the water and let out a screech that rippled across the night, waking the palace and city. The other seven gathered on the land also screamed their joy at Sa's oath. It looked back at Ange and gave her the prism back. Voloc roared but First turned to its prisoner and screamed its freedom call across the water. Reaching into its chest it pulled the chains out and tore the links apart. Voloc came towards the guardian in the water, its shadowy claws reaching along the surface towards its gaoler. The other eight gathered around the demon. First took Sa and Ange and began to wade back to the beach. Ange's heart sank as she thought it was taking them back to the demon but as it reached the pebbled beach the other creatures closed around the shadow. A guttural snarl emanated from it making Ange cringe with fear of the retribution the voice threatened.

First called across the Bay and then towards the hills that surrounded Matavia City. The surface of the water rippled with the force of its joyous scream. The eight cried their liberation to the skies making the Matavians that had gathered cover their ears from the deafening roar.

Ange looked towards the palace and saw two women and a dishevelled man with guards at their sides. They were looking down from the window where she and Sa had escaped from. One was white and the other was dark. She peered towards the dark woman, tall and slender she cradled a baby in her arms.

Ange became aware of the silence as the Aracnine walked away from the shadow and the Bay of Tears. The icy chill of Voloc crept onto her skin making it sting as the demon tried in vain to take her but as her flesh crawled with repulsion at the touch, the first ray of dawn struck her where the shadow had placed its claws. The dark hand released her letting First flee with the other Aracnine following. Ange called for Sa, but she lay limp in the arms of the creature.

The Queen looked at Tessi. She noticed she was breathing hard and perspiring. The baby wriggled in her arms as she tried to settle it.

'You look upset dear?' The Queen moved and placed her fingers on the baby's head and began to stroke the tiny scalp. Tessi tried not to look at her as the sight of her long red finger-nails stroking Noab's head sent shards of fear into her heart.

'No, my lady, it is my childish fears at the shadows that move within the walls and now hunts at night as well. We do not have such magic in my lands. I must put Tias to bed. The King wishes to take the children to watch the parade later today. Tias has not slept most of the night and will make his Lord angry if he is grumpy.'

'I noticed one of those prisoners looked like she had come from your lands' Queen Giandra probed.

Tessi placed Noab over her shoulder to hide her face from the queen.

'I didn't notice my lady. Please excuse me. I must get him to sleep.' Tessi got up and quickly made her way to the nursery chamber. After she had put Noab in the cradle she sagged down against the wall. She could not believe it had been Ange. Her heart thudded with fear and relief at the sight of her sister being so near. She had survived but what brought her here to be hunted by Ranik and his demon. Why would they want her? She got up and walked to her bed and lay down. Tears welled when she remembered the last time, she and Ange saw one another at the Boabs.

'Oh Ange, what has happened that this curse follows both of us. Mata, Pata, Ancrid of the desert sands please protect us.'

She rolled over trying not cry again. 'Stop it.' she said to herself. Tessi had resolved in her heart not to be weak. She needed to be strong for the babies to protect them from the king and queen. Tessi closed her eyes and began to think of a way to escape. The creatures had protected Ange from the demon. Perhaps she could escape as well and find them. Hanni would help her. Ange's face, full of terror and fear came back to her making her heart ache again for everything that had happened. When will we find peace again, she asked into the empty pale night?

'Follow them' ordered the Queen as she stood watching the creatures and their hostages flee.

'Yes, my lady' The guard responded.

18

Oaths of Blood and
Shadow

Queen Giandra walked into the dark cellar, the light of her torch barely penetrated the thick smoke which had filled the chamber. A puff of air blew out the torch leaving her in complete darkness.

'The sun is still your enemy dark one' she spoke peering into the shadows.

A snarl came from behind her followed by the red eyes. Then she felt the claws around her neck. She could barely breath.

'The girl you chase is related to the king's concubine.'

'I know clayborn. Voloc sees all. Why are you here?'

'Is it the jewel you seek? I saw its light in the water. Such a beautiful ...' Giandra felt her throat constrict.

'You know nothing of what I seek, lesser one. Go back until I have use for you.'

Giandra collapsed gagging.

'Shadow, how will you follow the thing you seek? The creatures that have stolen your jewel race across the steppes toward the ranges. It is more than a night's journey with no cover. Your enemy shall rise to greet you before you will find your prey.'

A deep snarl met the Queen, but she continued with the knowledge that at any time this spirit could squeeze the life from her.

'Send the concubine as bait. It will draw the owner of the jewel out. I will convince my midwife to help her. She will not choose the stone over her sister. I only ask you let me have my wish when your victory is complete.'

'I see the prize you seek lesser one. The deep malice of the void festers within your blood. Beware of such a gift if it is bestowed.'

'None the less will you grant my desire if the gem is returned to you.'

Silence met the Queen for what seemed an eternity.

'Bring it to me!' came the command. The words fell like lead spears on her heart making her gasp.

Tessi sat on the dais watching the parade of soldiers marching by but all she could think of was Ange down on the beach clutched in the hand of the creatures. Ranik sat with Noab on his knee but the boy screamed wanting to be with Tessi. Oblivious to the boy's distress the King cheered loudly and laughed manically as the prisoners from the Aeserean siege were paraded before the royal dais. The crowd flung manure and rocks at them.

Tessi saw Ranik stand and make a speech but she did not listen to the words. The cries of Noab distracted her briefly. She got up and gestured to take him but Ranik shunned her.

'My dear you look so tired. The last few days have been distressing for everyone' spoke the Queen.

Tessi looked at her with the same revulsion she always felt.

'My lady I will take the babe, she is restless today.' Tessi wanted to take Angette from the Queen's arms.

'Nonsense, she is no trouble at all.'

'Hanni, take the girl back to the palace. She looks very drawn. Tias and I will bring the children back.'

'My lady, I am fine I will wait until the parade is over.'

'No, my dear I insist. Hanni.'

'Come my dear.' Hanni took Tessi by the arm.

Tessi did not speak until they were almost to the garden wall that lay beneath her chamber.

'Hanni can I tell you a secret.'

'Yes, my dear. That would be lovely.'

'That night the creatures invaded the castle, one of the prisoners with them, I think it was my sister Ange.'

'No, surely not. I thought you said that all your family died in the plague.'

'I thought so as well until now. Hanni?'

'Yes dear.'

'I want to find her. I want to take the babies and find her.'

'No, my dear. How? Lord Ranik will not allow you to do that. Why he would kill you.'

'I know Hanni, but if I can get to Ange, those creatures, they protected her from the shadow that dwells here now. I just need to find her. Hanni will you help me?'

'No, my dear, it is impossible, how would you take the babies. His lordship is well, you know, an impatient master. I think you need to rest as the queen says.'

'Please Hanni. He will kill me anyway once the babies are old enough. Please I have no one else. The queen ..., she is always in my dreams standing over Noab and Angette.'

Hanni looked at the girl. 'You need to rest then we will talk. You are overwrought at all shenanigans.'

'No Hanni, I will leave without you. I will find a way.'

'The King and Queen will be leaving for the western lands to celebrate the victory there. Perhaps you could search then without them knowing. But you do not know where your sister has gone. No, it is out of the question you will be put to death for trying to escape. It is not such a bad life here.'

'I heard the guards talking about it. Ranik won't send more soldiers to follow them because the creatures are too powerful.'

'Please Hanni. I will go whether you will come or not. I know where to find them. I heard a guard telling the Queen. She sent one of her soldiers to follow them.'

The midwife did not respond she only looked at Tessi.

The dawn rose on the fifth day after Tessi had seen Ange and she stood in the sunshine with a feeling of light hearted-ness. It would be a full day's journey to the steppes that surrounded the valley the city dwelt in. She had arranged with Hanni to meet on the path that led to the garden where she would often take the twins to play. Tessi had stashed a sack with food under a grotto of rocks. Nothing would be missed in all the fanfare of the victory. The feasts alone had left ample scraps for Tessi to store.

Ranik walked towards the horse and carriage dressed in full battle gear with his hair blowing in the breeze, now completely white and brittle, hanging in long spindly strands down his back. The Queen was not with him.

Ranik entered the carriage. He looked at Tessi and a crook-ed smile crept across his face.

'My dear, I shall celebrate with you upon my return.'

Tessi shivered inwardly at the thought of him again. He had barely touched her since the twins were born but they were almost weaned now. As soon as the carriage left, she made her way towards the garden. Once inside the walls she could see Hanni's scarf amongst the hedges. The sun was shining bright-ly and looking at the sky it was completely free of clouds. Her heart leapt with hope for the first time since before the plague had struck her village.

'Hurry Hanni, the Queen was not with the king when he left. She must still be present in the palace.'

'Ay my dear she has taken ill. Oh, Tessi I fear we walk to our doom. Can I not convince you to stay?'

'If we are caught then I will say I made you come Hanni. He will not harm the babes or yourself, only me.'

They headed out onto the path where a small secret gate led out to a walking trail to the foothills. Noab and Angette bobbed in harnesses made of muslin cloth on the backs of Tessi and Hanni. They cooed softly until the natural rhythm of the strides rocked them to sleep.

The rise onto the steppes was gentle and Hanni and Tessi arrived on the cusp of a magnificent sunset stretching across the barren plains.

'Where to Tessi?'

'I asked one of the guards about the nearest shelter and he said straight ahead is the quickest route. Any other way will take longer with no water.'

'We should rest a while dear.'

'Only to feed the babies but then we must keep going to get as far away as possible.'

Tessi noticed the trail by the middle of the next day. The ground changed from course gravel to a sandy surface with tufts of grass crushed by the steps of the creatures. In amongst them were the tiny footprints of two people.

'Look Hanni, you see. These must be Ange's feet.' The nurse could barely keep up with the young woman and secretly hoped it would be over soon. She looked behind her as Tessi sped ahead with renewed hope. In the shimmering distance Hanni saw the small entourage following.

Night crept over them again. Noab and Angette grizzled in their makeshift cots tired and uncomfortable. In the twilight Tessi had seen the grey cliffs in the distance that signalled the end of the steppes and the beginning of the fertile lands where most of the grains were harvested. It was here that lay a network of caves underneath carved out from molten lava eons ago.

Hanni slowed down. 'I cannot keep going my dear, my legs are old.'

'No Hanni we are almost there I am sure ...'

Suddenly a massive arm swung down scooping up Tessi and the babies. Then another grabbed Hanni. The creatures had been on watch and found them. Within no time at all Tessi and Hanni were being put down in a torch lit cave in front of the other Aracnine. Sa and Ange were standing in between the massive legs and arms.

Ange and Tessi looked at one another across the shadowy space.

Ange ran to her older sister and hugged her. She turned Tessi around when she felt the wriggly bundle on her back.

'Ange meet Noab and Angette, my children.' Ange stared in wonder at the babies.

Taking Noab out of the sling she offered him to Ange to hold. The babies saw the guardians swaying nearby and reached out to touch one of them. First lifted a talon and gently touched each of the babies. Tessi held her breath wondering if it would hurt them, but the babies did not flinch. Each of them stared at the other. First saw the mark of Voloc inside their hearts and a vast journey stretching before the younglings. The knowledge passed silently between the babes and the ancient creatures and a foretelling of a destiny not yet made clear. First moved away.

'I do not think they intend harm to you' reassured Sa as she saw the panic rising in Tessi's eyes.

'Oh, Tessi I never thought I would see you again. I thought you were dead' spoke Ange.

'I have wanted to be many times Ange. My heart was so broken and full of sadness at everything that has happened.'

'I thought you were dead as well Tessi but in my heart it never felt like you were.'

Sa came to stand near Ange as she cradled Noab. Ange looked at Sa through a flood of tears.

'Tessi this is Sa Tuc, my protector and friend. Sa this is my sister.'

Sa nodded at Tessi and the babies. She saw the mixed heritage and wondered what torment this girl had been through. The spirits truly watched these two desert dwellers for both to have survived the malice that had consumed their lives she thought.

'This is Hanni the babies nurse and midwife.' Tessi gestured for Hanni to come closer.

Sa looked at the old woman. She noticed how nervous she was not so much around the guardians for she was certain the people of Ranik's court would have felt and seen stranger things than these creatures. Something else lay behind the fear. She kept looking over her shoulder.

Hanni nodded without saying anything.

Tessi and Ange sat on the ground with the children playing between them.

Sa went to their sacks and pulled out a hare to prepare to eat. She noticed the nurse looking toward the entrance.

'Are you being followed midwife?'

Hanni startled 'Ah no miss but it is strange days and I jump even at the slightest thing now. It is welcome flame. I will make some tea. It will help us rest after such a long journey. My legs are old compared to the concubine.'

Sa Tuc strode outside into the night after placing the rabbit on a fire to roast. She was greeted by silence. Two of the Aracnine stood on a ledge of rock high above to keep watch. The steppe was clear as far as she could see. When she walked back in, she noticed Ange and Tessi curled up together asleep. There were two cups beside them half filled with tea.

Hanni had one of the babies on her knee trying to settle it. The other lay in a bundle of swaddling peacefully asleep as well.

'I have made some tea, please try some Sa Tuc. I will take

Noab outside, the fresh air will help.' Hanni slid out past Sa without looking at her.

Sa went to First and spoke to it.

'Can the servant be trusted? Would not all the servants of Ranik be bound to the shadow as well.'

'The Aracnine no longer hear the shadow' First's voice drifted into Sa's mind.

Sa stepped away frustrated. She sensed the midwife had something to hide. Sa lifted the pot of tea off the flames and sniffed it. It was the same aroma as some of the geranium teas made in the kitchens of the Emerald Palace. Sa poured some into a small wooden bowl and drank. It was soothing. Lying back against the rock, Sa began to feel sleepy. She vaguely saw Hanni standing rocking the baby looking directly at her.

She woke, daylight streamed in through the entrance. Ange was shaking her. Her head ached and the brightness stung her eyes.

'Sa wake up! Quickly come.' Standing up she steadied herself against Ange. She could hear the babies crying and Tessi's voice pleading. Sa called the Aracnine. They followed behind her.

As she went outside, she saw the midwife standing with one of the babies, a dozen soldiers and a tall slender woman dressed in black with a sheer veil over her face. In her arms she held the other baby. Her hand, as white as alabaster, stroked the child's head slowly and with deliberate menace. On her index finger sat a silver thimble with a tapered hook at the end. She kept it hovering above the scalp as she stroked.

'Hanni, how could you?'

'Now my dear all will be fine, just do as the Queen asks.'

Sa pulled her dagger out 'Aracnine come!' she called but was cut off as Ange grabbed her arm.

'No Sa, she will kill Noab if I refuse to come with them. The demon has sent her to bring the prism back.'

'You will not defeat the guardians; your master and king could not hold them' warned Ange.

'Of course not, why do you think only my personal body-guard were spared to escort their queen. Now child, what will you choose, the trinket around your neck or your kin's child?'

Ange stood looking at the innocent child in the woman's arms and then at Tessi. She saw her sister's eyes fixated on the silver thimble on the queen's finger.

'Ange what is this thing the demon hunts you for? Why is it so precious to them they would kill for it?' pleaded Tessi.

'It is a gift from gods of the dawn of creation Tessi. It has been given to me.'

Ange looked at Sa then Tessi then the Queen.

'My sister and her children are to be kept safe if I return with you.'

'Why dear simply give it to me and we will leave you all in peace.'

'The shadow will unleash his venom on the world if it gains the stone. Why do you serve its malice when it will destroy you as well?' Sa spoke to the Queen.

'That is not your concern easterner.'

Sa turned to First and touched its arm.

'What counsel can you give ancient gaoler. Your former pris-oner holds the upper stroke and moves close to its purpose.'

'The shadow whispers to the clayborn but the Aracnine no longer hear its words. Voloc only moves within the darkness that already existed in the heart of the Clayborn's malcontent. The gift must be given. It cannot be taken not even after death.'

Sa heard the voice in her head and moved closer to Ange.

The Queen raised her finger ready to plunge the poisoned needle into the delicate skin to let the venom do its work.

'No please. Noab!' Tessi ran to grab the child but one of the guards stopped her.

'I will go with you, but my sister must be kept safe and her children. No harm can come to them. Promise me that Tessi will be safe.'

'Of course, dear. But wouldn't it be better to just give it to me.'

'No, I will carry it. And speak with the shadow itself' Ange looked at the veiled face and thought she saw a snarl move across it.

Ange looked towards Sa.

'I knew this would happen. After Bensah died, I knew it would only be me.'

Sa pulled Ange closer and leant down to her ear and whispered 'The Aracnine say the gem can only be given. It cannot be taken, not even after death.'

'Get them on a horse, we ride directly back to the palace.' The Queen strode off handing Noab to one of the guards so she could mount her black stallion. Tessi ran after her to grab the baby but the guard threw her off and handed him back to the queen. She placed him in a harness safely. His screams were smothered as she covered his face.

'No! He his mine.' Tessi pleaded.

'Ride!' commanded the Queen

'We will come for you. Be strong. I will find Gildas and Kado and we will come for you and your sister.'

Ange cupped Sa's face with her hands 'All is not lost Sa Tuc. I have found my sister again. Do you know what joy that brings me even in this time of deepest shadow and sorrow? I felt it deep within that Tessi had not died and I wondered if the god who gave me the stone had placed a curse on me to make me forget. Make me lose hope. It would be terrible to think she deceived me like that when the gods also ask us to save them. What power lies within me now, to stand between shadow and light and be asked to decide who lives and who dies. Who can wield this power and who must serve it? I go now but you must save Tessi and the babies.'

Sa saw the resignation in Ange's eyes and wondered how deep the fear lay in her heart. The gaze that met Sa was no longer that of a young girl but a soul weary from sorrow and the struggle to stay alive.

'We will come Ange'

Ange nodded as the soldier tore her away and placed her on the horse in front of Tessi.

Sa stood in front of the Aracnine as she watched Ange ride into the steppes knowing that they both stood on the precipice of doom which they had tried so vainly to flee.

'Aracnine, we go north' spoke Sa in the silent pallor of the dawn.

19

Ice Lords

Tyl saw the men moving beneath a ridge of snow on the edges of the forest.

'See over there.'

'Will we kill them for their hides or let the clan have their piece first?' replied Axl.

'Let the Elder Chief find out their purpose' replied Tyl.

Tyl and Axl silently crept toward the camp of Faad. Such was the stealth of the Graanar that not even the snow crunched underfoot. The blunt end of Tyl's blade came down on the Matavian Captain as he lay scanning the village. The soldier Ulrig turned to fight on his back but Axl lodged his axe in his chest in one swift arc. Tyl hoisted Faad up onto his shoulder to continue onto the village. Axl searched Ulrig finding a dagger and a whiskey flask and some coins. Putting them in his pockets he strung Ulrig up on a branch. He slit his throat to let the blood scent attract the wolverines. Pleased with seeing the mangled eagle crest made from the wound his axe inflicted, Axl wiped his blade and jogged to catch up to Tyl.

'The winds of Raajn must have come this way. Look at the

huts.' Tyl pointed to the northern side of the village. The huts were destroyed. Suddenly six clansmen appeared from behind the enclosure that had held Gildas.

Tommo came towards them 'Who goes there?'

'We are Tyl and Axl of the Clan Timmo. We found this Matavian and another lies dead in the forest as we made our way here. We are passing to our lands in the east.'

'Come.' They followed Tommo and the others towards the Elder hut. The whole village seemed to be gathered around it.

'Stand here.' Tommo went inside.

Faad began to stir so Tyl threw him on the ground with a heavy thump. Faad looked up and saw the graanar surrounding him. He went to stand but Tyl put his foot on his chest.

'Don't move scum.'

'Inside. Bring him with you.' Tommo gestured for Tyl and Axl.

As soon as Tyl stepped inside he saw Gildas sitting on a chair with Kado next to him. Jarrod was seated upon the throne of the bear.

'Kneel before the Elder Chief.' Tyl ordered Faad as he thrust him down onto his knees.

'Elder, I am Tyl of Clan Timmo and this is my cousin Axl. We are traders in the south, but we return every second summer to see our people. We only pass through and re supply for the journey to our homeland, but we found two of these dogs on our journey through.'

'Ay Tyl, Axl. I remember you from earlier visits to Gol village. You have missed your father Polax. He left just days ago.'

Jarrod looked at Faad and wondered what else awaited the graan.

'Are there more of these?'

'Only one other who is wolf meat now.'

'By which route did you come?'

'The passage from the blade and spike.'

'Have you seen others along this way?'

'Nay only this one.'

'Tommo and Ikdad take a scouting party out to search the forest in case more lie in wait.' Jarrod ordered.

Tyl looked at Gildas but said nothing not sure of what to make of the situation.

'You have seen my brother before graanar?' asked Jarrod.

Tyl and Axl both answered at once. 'Ay, Chieftain.'

'Brother these two assisted me and the others on our journey north. I am indebted to them. Graanar, I was not straight with you at our last meeting. I am Gildas of Clan Gol; brother and exile to Jarrod Elder Chieftain.'

Tyl and Axl looked at Gildas. 'Your strength with a blade had not diminished Gol Lord. Our father often spoke of your strength and terror. We saw it with our own eyes near Shada-raq amongst the Matavian thieves.'

Jarrod got up and went to Faad. Pulling his head up he looked at the captain of Ranik.

'What is your name?'

'Captain Piotr Faad.'

'Your purpose here?'

Faad looked at Jarrod and then at Gildas. He had seen the creatures from the palace and what they had done. His purpose no longer mattered as the girl had been taken. The Graan would kill him anyway.

'I was sent to find the girl taken by the creatures of the shadow.'

'Are there more coming?'

'It was only the two of us and all that I know of the demon's servants have already passed.'

'Should we kill the scum now?' asked Axl

Jarrod chuckled at Axl's keenness to see more Matavian blood.

'Well you are a dead man either way Captain Faad. Your master would not be kind to a soldier with no use now he as the token he desired and the Graanar have no need of a Matavian wretch. Take him to the pen. Once the scouts are sure no more wait in ambush, he will be given to the ice mother.'

Gildas stood 'Wait clansmen. Captain, you know of the shadow that now rules Ranik?'

'Yes, I have seen and felt its presence in the night' replied Faad.

'Where does it dwell?'

'Deep beneath the palace in the Bay of Tears. The creatures will take the girl there.'

Faad answered the next question for Gildas guessing this is what he wanted to know.

'The King's mind is more bound to the vision of the demon as it grows stronger. As I left to find the girl, Ranik was planning his invasion of the Aeserean lands. The southern lands and eastern deserts are enslaved or dead and the wild men of the far western reaches are easily captured. Ranik's strength comes from the shadow and its lust for the jewel this girl carries will be sated once it has it. It will be unstoppable. The shadow's claws will sink into the hearts of the Graan as well.'

'Why do you tell us so much of your King's plans? Matavians would cut out their own tongues out rather than betray their masters' asked Gildas.

'The destruction Ranik seeks will see the end of our mighty rule as well. The shadow consumes all his will. He sees nothing else.'

Gildas looked at the man on the floor and began to think there may be a way to get the girl back.

'Have you finished Gildas?' asked Jarrod

'Ay.'

'Take him to the pen.'

Jarrod sat on the throne again. Unta stepped towards him.

'Elder, a ruling is needed on the exile. I now speak for the Clan Clotte after our honourable father's death. This demon's blackness stains our lands; a blackness brought here by this cursed exile.'

'What is Clan Clotte's demands?'

'Blood has not been repaid in blood Elder. The debt is still owed to our clan.'

'Ay but we have seen the mother of ice bend her mighty will to the power that my brother possesses. To fulfil the clan retribution now may be displeasing to her. Prepare your mighty father for his death march and the feast to celebrate him. In time you will have my ruling.'

Unta bowed but looked at Gildas with cold eyes. Gildas stared back at him.

'Greater shadows and sorrow lay ahead than Clan Clotte's grief for their chieftain and daughter. You have seen for yourselves what now walks this world and will, as the Matavian said, soon come to the land of the ice mother. I have paid my debt for the death of my son and wife. I will pay no more' warned Gildas.

Unta moved his hand to his axe insulted at Gildas words. Gildas moved his hand towards his blade.

'Enough! Gildas you insult the great Chieftain and his death. I call an end to the meet.' Jarrod thumped his staff on the ground to signal everyone to leave.

The hut emptied except for Gildas, Kado and Jarrod.

'You will need to be gentler with your words brother. The Graan are not won yet to let me free you and if war comes our way, we will need to be united to defeat the enemy.'

'You will not have victory here. The girl and stone must be taken back brother. If the demon gains enough strength to meet the Graan here in your lands, then you are already defeated. Fight with me, meet Ranik in his lands. His army is stretched east and west. He lies naked in his bed. Let Kado and I and the Matavian and those who wish to follow me go seek the girl. I will not let her perish without trying. This power lies with me for a purpose. I will not let it be wasted over a blood debt too many moons old to be remembered.'

'Why the Matavian?'

'He will lead us to the girl.'

'I will call the Chieftains soon for them to choose. I will not set Graan against Graan again.'

Gildas spat in frustration. 'You are weak brother as always.'

'Gildas hold your tongue. We have few enough allies as it is.' Kado grabbed Gildas arm to stop him saying more.

Jarrod turned and stared directly into Gildas eyes 'I am no weakling brother. Have you not learnt that it is your blindness to only consider what serves you above all else that has always defeated you? I have united the Graan under honour and loyalty not with fear and retribution as was your way. Do not think that my loyalty to you lies on more than a fine layer of snow first laid down many winters ago. Your warnings are not unheeded and yes, I have seen the power of which you speak but the clans must choose. The ice bear prevails here, and we live by her rule and no other. Leave me now.'

Kado took Gildas arm to get him to leave. Kado felt the tension in Gildas shoulder as he nudged the massive man out of the hut.

'Gildas we are not in control here. Our hope lies with Sa to help Ange escape. Even if the Graan decide to wage war on Ranik, the demon with those creatures are our bane. What use is it to make an enemy of your people now when it is likely we will all stand back to back as the shadow grows.'

'My sword cut that creature's hide, prince.'

'Where are you going?'

'To speak to the Matavian.'

Gildas went to the enclosure and saw Faad sitting on the ground. The guard put his axe in front to stop.

'Out of my way Graanar.' Gildas brushed it away ignoring it.

'What do you want?' asked Faad.

'A way into Ranik's palace?'

'Hmph, impossible. The demon senses anything that comes near it and if it is the girl you wish to rescue, well she is probably already dead.'

'If she lies dead then Ranik's stinking carcass at the end of my blade will be even sweeter victory. Lead us to the palace so I can at least plunge my sword into your King. You said it yourself Faad, darkness lies in every route, so why not spill the blood of the darkest. If your lands lie burnt and your King dead, then there will be nothing left for those who remain. Get me to the palace so a place can be made for a new leader. They are the lands of your birth.'

Faad looked at Gildas. If any man could fight the beast that now lay claim on the Matavian King this graanar would be him. Faad had seen the power and tenacity of Gildas and knew Ranik would meet a formidable enemy. The shadow would kill him in the end though; the clansman underestimated what the shadow could do to a man's soul with one look.

'What makes you think you can trust me clansman?'

'Nothing other than you are no longer useful to Ranik and failed his command leaving a price on your head. The Graan have no use for you. You are a dead man either way captain. While I can be merciful at times, eh Prince.'

Gildas looked at Kado with a glint in his eye. 'Let me know your decision. I leave here, with or without an army, to dip my sword in the blood of Ranik.'

Gildas left with Kado.

'He can't be trusted Gildas. Besides, it may well be that your brother will order clan retribution.'

'I think he can useful Prince. He wants Ranik dead as much as the rest of us. And besides if the girl lives then the only chance, we have of finding her is to have someone who knows where she has been gaoled. I leave here with or without my brother's blessing.'

Kado noticed Gildas had placed his hand on the sword of Tarentess.

'Will the Graan follow you?'

'Some will. We have nothing now to bargain with Prince. We fight to the death.'

He slapped Kado on the back almost sending him through the air. As Kado caught his breath Nekoda's howls came across the wind towards them from the far edge of the village.

'I will go get him.'

Nekoda stared across the tundra looking for Ange. The dog looked at Kado as he came up to him. He growled slightly but on sniffing his hand the dog relaxed.

'Come Nekoda, we shall leave soon to seek Ange and Sa.'

Patting him Kado stared across the white land before him as well. He tried to feel Sa using the meditations the monks had taught him in the Temple, but nothing came. He thought of their time together. Sa always kept her heart closed and unknowing even to herself, but she had never spurned him.

'Are you still alive assassin?' he asked into the emptiness of the white tundra.

Kado longed to see the mountains and forests of his homeland. His body had begun to crave the poppy again as he knew their journey south would be futile. If he walked to his death it would be better to be in his homeland not in a land of sadists and warmongers or ice laden dunes.

'It would be nice to see you one more time Sa-Tuc. Come Nekoda.'

Nekoda whined at being made to leave but relented when Kado put a harness around his neck.

The pale sun eased across the tundra illuminating the ice just slightly more than the night which had passed. The village and elders had gathered in the hut of Jarrod.

'Jarrod the time comes for your decision. What is your judgement?' asked Gildas standing in front of his brother.

'Clan Clotte seek their blood debt to be paid' spoke Unta.

'Clans Nimmo, Kaan and Bregt and Hadraan, Vallyx and Timmo how do you lean?' asked Jarrod

'For Clan Kaan, we follow the Ice mother' spoke Knut.

'Clan Hadraan, are with Clot and Kaan as we are brothers in the inland cradle of the Ice. We make our bed and our food from the very fangs of the mother. Ever she has suckled us. It would be sacrilege now to forsake her' spoke Hadrin.

'Ay so says clan Bregt' spoke Brago.

Tyl stood

'I speak for Clans Timmo, Vallyx and Nimmo, graanar weaned on the tits not only of the Ice Mother but the Sea Bears who give us food and coin to grow fat upon. I will walk with Gildas into battle. I have seen the blade he wields and the power behind this graanar. The ice bears rule is diminished as the spirits that now bring their battle to our lands grow in stature and strength. Graan fight for victory like the mother of ice defeats the hardness of the land beneath her. If it is to be the last battle, then it will be stained with the blood of Timmo and Matavian. May the Ice Mother and Ocean bless us all and curse these usurpers who seek only destruction and live as scoundrels fed upon rotting flesh of the dead and not the sweetness of victory won between equals of strength and courage. We ask for the blood bond upon Gildas head be ended, so that these new enemies may be struck down or we die in glory with our brother.'

'And brother what of Clan Gol. Where does your axe and blade lie?' Gildas looked at Jarrod once more.

'Brothers, I counsel you to be clear in your minds and hearts. The ice mother is still the bearer of the fortune of the graan. Clan Gol will not follow Gildas the exiled into battle.'

'Jarrod war comes your way whether you follow me now or not' Gildas interrupted Jarrod.

'Silence brother. I have not finished. Clan Gol respect the ways of the ice and the strength of Clot and Clan Clotte. Nor has this Chieftain forgotten the younglings slaughtered by his brother's wretched hands. But we have seen the power of the ice mother subjugated to this cursed Graanar. Darker shadows lie before us and we need to be ready for war, even if it is our end. I sense that for now our loyalty lies with this cursed exile. We will let him be free to fight this shadow with this power given to him. The ice mother cursed him, and she will bless us and Clotte when a time is doomed for her swift retribution on his hide. Let the exile free to live or die for his new gods.

For those Gol who wish to follow the exile may do so, but I will not. The clan's loyalty to the bear and ice shall prevail here even after our bones lay picked. The ways of the Graan will live or die with the bear. So, it was laid down at our beginning and will continue until our end. But I have seen the mother of our lands kneel to her equal and his blade, begotten by the spirit of the earth. For this reason, I will not hold any Gol to the throne of the bear but by their own minds and hearts.'

Unta stood 'Gildas Gol, cursed is your name evermore with

Clan Clotte. The blood debt will never be forgiven. Be warned Elder Chief, your kin divided and almost destroyed the Graanar during his rule and now his return has done the same. All Clans should show their blood bond to the bear. To let any Graanar forsake her is heresy to our ways. Clan Clotte call for any Graan that follow your brother shall be banished from their kin and lands.'

Hadrin looked at Gildas, Jarrod and Unta

'Hadraan call for the elder chief to change his rule or we will ask for banishment as well. Elder you have risked your life to bring the Graan together after their bloodied ways of your brother. Let the curse of your kin end with his death and the Graanar will face the honour of a glorious battle here in their lands with our mother and succour watching.'

'Hadrin, Unta, Knut and Brago your loyalty feeds the ice bear's cubs brothers. But I will not change my rule. I give leave for any Graanar to seek their glory and fortune whether it be in fealty to the mother of our lands or to show their skill in defeating these spirits. If war comes to us, then they may only return to fight otherwise their clans may exile them. That is my rule as Elder and it is final. Gildas and any who wish to leave with him are to be gone by the mornshade.'

Everyone stood as Jarrod made his way to leave the hut. Gildas grabbed his arm

'I ask one boon I want to take the Matavian. He will be a guide to find the girl and the assassin.'

'If you trust the word of any of those scum, then you may take him.'

'Brother, war is coming; if I am alive at the end of this next battle then my sword is at the ready for the graanar.'

Jarrod clasped Gildas' arm and nodded 'Go brother, finish this quest the gods have asked of you. Twist your axe as it cleaves the tyrant's head in two. May the ice bear run with you.'

Unta waited as the rest of the chieftains left. Going up to Gildas he suppressed the urge to thrust a dagger into his chest.

'Our father saw your blood spilled on the ice mixed with our kin Jesse in his dreams exile.'

Tyl placed his hand on Unta's shoulder to warn him not to do anything rash.

'A darker shadow dogs my steps now. Clot shall have his revenge for Jesse, but it will not be done by a graanar's blade. Honour the Ice Mother Unta as I have not. She and I were sundered at my birth as I see now that another god lay claim to me. It is this that pits the great mother and me at battle against each other to be rulers.'

He looked at Axl and Tyl standing behind Unta 'We leave today. Gather any that wish to come.'

'It will be a seven-dawn journey to our lands' replied Tyl.

Unta tore himself away eyeing Gildas as he left the hut.

Gildas whistled Nekoda over to him and patted the dog as he sat down to begin packing his sack. Kado looked at him quizzically

'We head for the eastern seas. Clans Vallyx and Timmo and any others who want to taste Matavian blood on their swords will join us.'

'And the Captain?'

'Bring him to the sled.'

Gildas felt alive again as sped along with Tyl and Axl and

one hundred sleds across the tundra. At least a thousand Graanar stood with him when he counted clans Timmo, Nimmo and Vallyx. It may not be enough to defeat the whole army of Ranik, but it could still wound the invaders.

The land began to rise steeply for a league as they climbed the hill of Hyrdal the Hammer. It brought back memories of Jesse teaching the younglings of the legends of the Graan. Her face smiling and deep blue eyes came back to him vividly.

'Ay Jesse, my blood will be spilt as was yours. I have paid for my lust for battle and now lie caged again by these gods. Why does your spirit wait for me? Go to the mother and be at peace. I will never know the relief of death as my doom now lies to watch rock and stone until the world dies around me.'

They passed over Hyrdal's grave and began the descent towards the ocean. Kado hung on tightly as the sled dipped over a steep ledge before flattening out onto a gentle slope. Nekoda howled in his ear every time the wind picked up setting off the sled dogs. The cacophony gave Kado a headache. He had never wanted the lily stem so much.

When they did arrive at Tyl's village Kado got out of the sled with numb legs and arse. He saw Faad get out of Axl's sled stiffly, his hands were still bound. Nekoda shook himself and began sniffing the other dogs and the new ground they walked on. A breeze blew in Kado's face and brought with it a smell he had almost forgotten, the salty sweetness of the ocean. Over the rise, stood the village of the Timmo clan. It was like the village of the Gol clan in layout and size except for a massive sheet of the black eastern ocean lying in wait to smother the huts compared to snow. It was calm on the morning of their arrival but Kado felt a menacing presence within the deep waters.

'The oceans calmness belies its true power Gildas.'

'Ay it does. If the winds of Raajn blow this way the waves can reach the height of thirty graan stacked head to toe.'

'How do the people survive?'

'If we live to see more peaceful times, I may tell you the secret of the Graanar's ways.'

'Gildas, Prince. Come' called Tyl from outside a main hut. The village had gathered at the arrival of all the sleds. Nekoda trotted over to the dogs and joined them in rubbing their bodies and snouts in the ice to cool down.

'Father.'

Tyl and the older man hugged and thumped each other's chest in the usual manner. Then Axl stepped forward and did the same.

'Son and kinsman three summers have passed and still the flesh of the babe sits upon your faces. This time you bring the Timmo's gifts of fellow graanar and merchants and the cursed eaglets of Ranik. You have learnt to keep strange company son. I see that Elder Jarrod has spared your life exile.'

'Ay Father. There is much to tell most of which has occurred since our arrival in Gol village. This captive is a soldier of Ranik. His purpose will also be explained. Take him over to the pens. Keep him alive' ordered Tyl.

Polax looked at Gildas. He remembered the strength of the man that stood before him. A bad omen came over the chieftain about what lay ahead for the Graan.

'We need rest and the yak's milk father. Our stay is brief' spoke Tyl.

'Come, the fire rages and my wife has brewed her special fish stew this day.'

'Prince, you need not hear this again. Axl take the royal heir to get food and warmth' spoke Tyl.

Kado stared at the ocean and saw far out into the rolling waves interspersed with boats where the Timmo fished. Silently behind the boats a large majestic iceberg floated by. A few of the fishers stuck their poles into it to push it away from their vessel. The pristineness of the white block of ice made the ocean look blacker and more ominous. Kado wondered if this is what would become of the world if the stone were to be taken; a deep blank morass where no life abounded and only silence reigned. He thought of Sa again and his heart ached for her. Even the skilled assassin of Ko could not defeat the creatures which had taken her hostage.

'Axl we cannot linger here. If your Chieftain refuses to help Gildas then we will leave regardless.'

'Ay Prince. No fear, the Timmo clan's blood boils for battles whether it be with the great fish of the black ocean or a feud with men. We are not like the Gol and Clotte who fight over pettiness of rules. Chieftain Polax will not deny the Timmoan warriors a chance to feed their bloodlust. The women tend to the villages when the men go to war.' He slapped Kado on the back heartily as he half thrust him inside the hut. Kado slipped on some ice. Axl caught him easily, surprised at how light the prince was to pick up.

'Emperor Ko was a mighty soldier of your people, but you are not like him' Axl commented as a matter of fact.

'No, he often said that to me himself.' Kado went to warm

himself by the fire. Axl found a jug and two bowls and poured each of them some distilled yak's milk.

Kado held the bowl up in both hands as a gesture to toast.

'Here's to finding my assassin Sa, Ange and to sating the Timmoan bloodlust.'

'Ay to battle!' Axl responded and skulled the drink.

'Tyl and I went through your lands before coming here.' Kado looked at him paying attention.

'Did you go to the city and the Drax Palace?'

'Ay but the place was overrun with Vulture and Eagle. The pits of the dead had been opened on the plains and mountains as Ranik digs to the bottom of the world. Nothing of the palace stands. I think Prince the Ko dynasty still has allies. We made our way to the mountains where your holy men live as we journeyed north. Once there we were offered money to join and fight as mercenaries to attack the soldiers as they dug to stop the pillage of the city.'

'Was it the monks?'

'Nay a group of your people who had escaped the Unstaadt whips and torture.'

'Who led them?'

'Jan or Jang. Your tongue twists the graanar tongue into a lump.' Axl laughed and took another swig and poured more into Kado's bowl.

'Jiang.'

'Ay.'

Kado remembered the Harvest moon festival; memories of himself disgraced along with Princess Yun in front of his father. Lord Jiang red with rage as was the Emperor.

Kado realised that was the last time he had seen Ko.

'How many did they have?'

'Only a few hundred but more were joining. They were moving to the hills or feet of Jun. That is why they wanted Tyl and me; to go in front and warn them of any of Ranik's hoards. Kill as many as we could. The Timmoan name and skill with a blade stretches far.'

Axl laughed to himself.

'This is good news Axl.' Kado smiled and skulled another bowl of the milk. Two young women walked in with leather napkins filled with dried fish and bread. Kado salivated at the bread not having had any since Shadaraq. One of the young women stared at Kado and cheekily winked at him. Kado stared back at her. The Graan women were not refined like the ones Kado had known in his own lands. The girl was handsome and firm he thought to himself but then Sa's face came to mind again.

'Our women are not pretty like the ones in your brothels Prince, but they are better to grind. Stronger.' Axl winked at Kado.

'Yes Axl, I think they are hardier than the middling lands women.'

'You and the assassin ...' Axl asked prying.

'Sa Tuc belongs to no man.'

'Hmph, in that case, try her, she is willing.' Axl grabbed the other girl, she let out a short squeal as he fell on top of her.

Kado stood and bowed to the one left standing 'There was a time when I would have but not now.'

Axl looked up briefly shrugged his shoulders and gestured

the girl over to him as well. She lay down giggling beside him.

Kado smiled and went outside. He made his way towards the shore. An icy blast drove away the cravings for the opium that had been playing on his mind for last few days. The waves grew in strength as the wind pushed them towards the shore. He made his way to a group hauling their nets bloated with fish. Kado heard them laughing despite the bitterness of the wind and turbulent waters crashing around them.

'Can I help clansmen?'

One of them nodded looking at the stranger and pointed to Kado where to grab the net. Everyone hauled at once heaving the massive load further up the icy shore. Women gathered on the higher ground ready with baskets to carry them back to the village to salt and smoke the fish. The Graan began to chant in low melodic rhythm as they slowly made their way up. It soothed Kado's nerves as he worked in time with them. Lord Jiang came to mind. The caves of Jun were a good choice. It was also where his father had kept an arsenal. He also remembered the insult he had caused to Jiang over his daughter. Perhaps there was a chance of defeating Ranik, but he would need to overcome the insult he had caused Jiang and to many of the Drax people in his time as the indolent heir.

20

Wounds of the
Ice Bear

The sleds were filled with supplies squashing Kado and Nekoda even closer together. Nekoda licked Kado's face but the smell of his breath made Kado gag.

'Where do we go from here Gildas?' Kado looked around him amazed at the number that had come. At least a thousand massive warriors stood ready to go to battle.

'South to the eastern pass through the lands of Doanda and then we follow the feet of the mountains until we reach the lands of Ranik. It will be the only way to hide such a large contingent. The Timmoans say most of the Ranik's men march west and down toward the coast. The Vallyxan will meet us at the foot of the great mountains under cover of the forest that grows between the trader route and Unstaadt. There another few hundred will wait. It will be enough to distract Ranik while we search for the assassin and girl.'

Tyl blew a great horn to signal their leaving. Nekoda howled into the air and Kado's ear. He pulled out a leather mask and wrapped it over the dog's snout to quieten him.

'It will be a swift journey if the winds of Raajn do not make their way to the sea. The land is mostly flat.'

Soon the sleds separated with a group racing ahead. Nekoda's warmth and the gentle sway of the sled lulled Kado in a deep sleep. He dreamed of Sa and Princess Yun and the smoky brothels in Drax City.

'Prince wake!' Kado woke startled at Gildas loud voice. He looked around him and saw Gildas standing in front of a group of clansmen. They had their axes at the ready. None of them looked familiar to Kado until he saw Unta.

'You must die. You are a curse and pox on the clans.'

'Stand down Unta. I will not slay thee here. Enough Clotte blood has been spilled because of me. Let us pass and do battle with the shadow that grows in the south.'

Kado slowly got out of the sled. He took his sword with him. Looking around him, he saw at least a hundred men standing behind the Clotte chieftain. He searched for Tyl and Axl but could not find them.

Gildas took the sword from his back.

'Die you cursed black heart and heresy to the mother of our lands.' Unta and three others came towards Gildas with axes swooshing through the air. Gildas cut through them with his sword and decapitated one man and sliced another is arm off. Unta struck him in the back as he twisted around. He grunted with the force of the blow.

'Stand down Graanar or I will kill you' Gildas threatened.

Kado readied himself as three men made their way towards him also.

Gildas went into a frenzy of swings and blows but only maimed Unta. He looked at Kado collapsing onto the ground as the three massive clansmen soon overpowered him. Gildas thrust Unta away and quickly got the three off the prince. Just as he turned Unta's axe barely missed his head but as Unta made the upswing with the blunt head of his axe it hit Gildas in the chin spraying his blood all over the ice. Suddenly the fury with in Gildas unleashed itself. Kado heard the roar of the man and knew it would not end well for Unta. The sword glistened in his hand and for the first time Kado saw how the filigreed handle entwined itself to Gildas' skin.

Unta died instantly as the blade effortlessly sliced through his neck. Enraging a dozen clansmen, they rushed at Gildas, but they were soon thrown back. Suddenly Tyl and Axl came into the melee as a massive clash of Graan against Graan spread out into the hundreds of men. Kado realised that if they did not stop fighting there would be no one left to go south.

'Stop Graanar!' yelled Kado. Nothing happened. He looked around desperately and remembered the horn Tyl had used. He ran and searched the sleds. He saw the massive seadog tooth hanging on the frame. Faad was sitting, hands and feet bound half grinning at the bloody scene in front of him. Kado grabbed the horn and blew nothing happened. He tried again and suddenly the low timbre call broke across the ice and the roars of the fighting clansman.

Gildas stood heaving and covered in blood. He saw Kado coming towards him with the horn.

'Stop or none will be left' yelled Kado.

Gildas looked around him and saw the dead bodies of his clansmen sprawled across the ice. The prince was right he thought.

'Stand down graanar!' His voice echoed across the valley. 'Clan Clotte, leave now or I will slay all that are left. If you wish to come with us, then come as a brother to battle the enemy not to slink in shadows to stab like thieves and brigands. Who is with me?' Gildas held his sword aloft. The hilt was still welded to his hand. 'You will not defeat me while I hold the strength of rock and stone in my hand. This weapon was made for me. No other shall wield it or the power it holds. Choose Graanar, come with me or leave. Be the enemy of this Ice Lord and you will die.'

Tyl and Axl looked around. A group of Timmoans began to chant Gildas' name. Soon all but a few had joined in.

'Take the great chieftain Unta brothers. Take him to his homeland and honour his blood.'

'You are a curse as Clot and Unta have counselled.' One of Unta's guards looked at Gildas as the chief's body was tied to the sled.

'I know brother. I have chased death all my life, but its pace is swifter than the winds of Raajn. And now it turns and stares not just at me but all of us and these lands we are bonded to in flesh and blood.'

The sleds with the slain chieftain kin of Jesse left. Jesse's blue eyes stared at Gildas as he watched the last dozen of Clan Clotte leave.

'They will ever be the Gol enemy as they were even in the days of our grandfathers' spoke Axl.

'Ay Axl but they have good reason to hate Gol blood.'

'Bury the dead and then we ride until we reach the passage south. Do not stop along the way enough time has been lost' Tyl shouted to the remaining men.

'Go ahead Gildas, the sooner you are out of these lands the better.' Gildas nodded at Tyl as they clasped arms. Tyl noticed the tattoo on his sword hand.

'Ay the blade burns me.' Gildas looked at the patterns seared into his flesh. Blood dripped from the gash on his face and chin where Unta's blade had grazed it. Kado handed him a leather clothe from Sa's pack. The blood flow slowed as Gildas tightened it behind his head. Gildas mounted the sled again sending the dogs off into their frenzied barking as they heralded their next run on the ice.

Four days had passed since the battle with Unta during which Gildas had barely spoken. The mountains soon rose before them again. This time though, instead of the granite palely breaking through under layers of snow as it had been at the Shadaraq pass, it now bared its sleek blackness towards the sky dominating everything around it. The obsidian rock's gleam was matched by the ocean that marked the end of the great black mountain ranges.

As the entourage neared the mountains, it looked like they were going directly into the waves until a narrow path came into view at the very end of the cliffs. The path was a ledge of rock that extended all the way along the width of the mountains with only a sheer vertical cliff above and below it. The waves roared into it, spilling foam over the path. Kado could not see the end of the ledge it stretched so far ahead.

'Take what we can carry on our backs Prince, the Matavian can take something as well. Tyl we will keep going.'

'Van will be waiting at the caves. We will not be far behind.'

Gildas placed coils of rope over his shoulders along with his pack and flasks. He took off his hood and thick coat.

'When we reach the top of the stairs, we will loop the rope around ourselves and through the iron hooks along the cliff.' He undid Faad's bonds 'You will need your hands otherwise the sea will take you.'

'Gildas you will freeze without more protection.'

Gildas grinned slightly 'A surprise for you Prince.'

The path was treacherous as the water washed onto the ledge then froze to ice. Kado's feet skidded so much that in the end his steps became miniscule to avoid slipping. Kado saw his knuckles were bone white as they gripped the hooks. He stopped briefly to check on Faad. In the distance came Tyl and the long line of Graanar. The sleds and dogs had been sent back to the Icelands. They were no longer any use here. The rope tugged slightly as Gildas got further ahead.

'Hold Gildas, we are not as sure footed as you.'

Gildas stopped. Nekoda barked at Kado to hurry. Suddenly a wave crashed into the rock cutting off the barking dog.

'Hang on!' Gildas shouted as the foam burst up towards them dousing them in the frigid water. 'Hurry Prince we have another league to go' called Gildas.

Kado's fingers were like rusted cogs as they froze in position. Slowly trying to dislodge them, flesh peeled off as the ice glued it to the iron hooks. Wave after wave crashed as they inched along the path. Looking ahead he saw Gildas and Nekoda disappear into a fog. The waves crashed again but slowly Kado noticed the spray felt warmer.

'We are nearing the edge where the southern lands begin Prince.' Kado looked at Faad surprised to hear him speak. He saw the soldier's fingers were bleeding like his own.

Gildas slapped Kado on his back as he sat on a rock to rest. The path had led them into lush forests of ferns and massive cedar trees. The last half league of the path had been shrouded in a blinding fog which suddenly opened out to grotto of green. Kado peeled off his furs as he felt the heat of the rainforest re-enter his body. He had thought he would never know warmth again.

'Here this will help. You will need to bind them as well. The heat will rot the flesh.' Gildas handed Kado some leaves crushed into a paste and a casket of milk brew.

'Drink or it will turn.' Kado swigged and gagged but drank more.

Gildas went off with Tyl and Axl to greet Van, leaving Kado with Faad. The Vallyx lay hidden in a valley not far away which was covered completely in a canopy of tangled vines and ferns.

Kado tore some cloth to bind his fingers.

'Here' Kado offered some of the cloth to Faad.

A monkey suddenly scaled down the trees not noticing the two men or Nekoda sitting on the rock beneath. Faad took a knife from his trouser leg and flicked it with lightning speed at the monkey. It dropped as the blade went straight into its heart. Kado jumped at the quickness of the Matavian.

'Settle easterner. You would be dead by now if I wanted to kill you. I thought roasted monkey makes for better eating than more fish.'

'We rest here tonight. Then we begin the trek along the base of the mountains' spoke Gildas as he returned from meeting with Van.

'I need to speak with you about something Gildas.' Kado pulled Gildas away from Faad so that the Captain could not here them.

'Ay Axl has told me. We cannot linger in negotiations Prince. Enough time has been lost.'

'There may be a chance I can rally the dregs of the Drax people as an ally. Lord Jiang has formed a loose cohort and seeks others to join him.'

'Is this Lord a friend or enemy of your father?'

Kado hesitated before answering. Gildas eyed him closely already guessing the answer.

'No but Jiang would know that to have the heir to Ko in his midst would bring those still loyal to the empire under his rule.'

'You waste your time Prince on political manoeuvres. You will either need to win them quickly or it will not be enough before the scourge of the Matavian wipe your kin out.'

'If we manage to take Ange and Sa back and even if we don't, we can't go back to your icelands. It is too brutal to live there and you will not be welcome again. We can find the hidden cache of my ancestors deep beneath the feet of the mountain. There will be protection and weapons, until we are ready to fight.'

'Ay Prince. But not now. We need to find the girl and at least get that stone away from the shadow which stalks us all and kill Ranik.'

Gildas helped himself to fish on the fire. They watched Faad squeeze the raw blood from the monkey's heart into his mouth. He and Kado both grimaced at the gruesome meal as Faad sucked the blood on his fingers.

'They can help us' continued Kado.

'It will be of no use if we are too late to save the desert dweller from the shadow. Besides, I want Ranik dead.'

'You are too late clansman. The demon grows stronger the more it consumes the land. The demon will have eaten it and the girl by the time you get there. You will not defeat it and only walk to its lair to be devoured yourselves' interrupted Faad.

'Ay that may be so but Ranik will bleed just the same.' Gildas stood 'I will keep watch tonight.'

Kado looked up and saw the stars and sky clearly for the first time since they had entered the lands of Gildas. However instead of feeling comfort at such a beautiful spectacle his heart grew heavy as he thought of Sa and his homeland. All gone and now it seemed it was his turn to dance with the edge of death as well. This time death's spectre would be real when it took hold of him not just the visions of a mind clouded by opium and cowardice. But now amongst the shadows Kado felt the surge of desire to be the ruler Ko had always asked of him. He did not feel fear at the thought of himself sitting on the throne of the dragon. But how would he take it and for how long would the dragon's breath bless him, he wondered. It was hollow in so many ways to seek out the destiny his ancestors had followed for a thousand generations at a time when the very dirt they ruled upon would be swallowed by an enemy not of their making.

21

Keepers of Sorrow

Ange shivered as she rolled over on the cobbled stones of her prison. She rocked herself to keep her mind off the hunger that grew every hour she did not eat. As she licked her lips her tongue ripped the scabs off them. She tasted the salty blood in her mouth. She felt along the wall where a trickle of water ran down through a crack. She placed her mouth on it and managed to moisten her lips. The blackness smothered her. She had not seen daylight since their arrival back at the palace. She began to take gulps of air as she felt everything closing in around her.

'Please come soon Sa.'

'Give it to me' came the low growl. The red eyes appeared again.

'No!' she screamed back

'You will die here clayborn. You will become a pile of bones in a forgotten place eaten by the dark and fowl worms of the dirt which birthed your flesh.'

Ange began to cry as the words pierced her mind and made an image of mother lying dead in her village when the plague had come. Falling on her side she started to weep.

'You will kill me anyway if I give it to you.'

'Perhaps not.'

'You cannot have it.'

A menacing laugh bounced all through the darkness that she lay in. Its malice vibrated through the stone bricks.

'She does not care for you. Didn't the custodian tell you what her precious gift was for?'

Ange did not answer but she knew the shadow could sense her doubts about Ascendant.

'It was for the god they now battle inside your gem. It is to restore their realm, not save yours. Why would she leave you here at the mercy of her enemy if it were meant for the clay born? She lied to you.'

The insidious whisper lingered in the stale damp air.

Ange sobbed bitterly at these words for she had begun wonder herself. She had seen the battles inside the custodian realm.

'No! Norbu made it for a reason and kept it here to be safe. Now I am its owner.'

'Give it to me. The gods play with you. I can be merciful.'

Ange did not answer for a long time. The silence became thicker like the darkness.

'No, you cannot have it. I am its bearer now.'

A vicious snarl met her and suddenly she was thrown against the wall. Screaming with pain she fell to the floor. She lay perfectly still for what seemed an eternity waiting but the voice and eyes did not return. She licked some water off the wall and then curled up in her coat to hide herself from the darkness that surrounded her. The prism hung around her neck heavy and cold. It was as if the darkness of her cell drank the power from it without touching it. She brought Tessi's, Sa's, Nekoda's and Bensah's faces to mind blanking out everything else hoping that this would end soon. Please come soon Sa, she whispered.

The walls of the tunnel were covered in slime making the flames of the torch glisten on the walls. Tessi crept along, her heart pounding so hard she thought someone might hear it. She had been to all the other passages and had not been able to find Ange. So many hidden things; dark and evil like all that dwelt within the palace walls. She thought of Hanni again. It still hurt the most that she of all people had led the queen to them. The latch came under her fingers. She turned it and looked inside. The chamber was windowless and empty. Some barrels stood in the corner but nothing else. Swallowing hard from the fear of the demon coming back Tessi continued. A vile breeze came along the tunnel making her choke as it brushed past her. She could smell death coming from ahead. Another door came into view. She did not want to look but knew she must. What if it was Ange? The stench grew so much that in the end she dry-retched. Opening the door, the smell of decay crawled over her skin. A body hung on the wall. She passed her flame across the shadowed figure. It was not Ange she exhaled. Turning back into the passageway, the torchlight rested upon a door that sig-nalled the end of the tunnel. The air was frigid. She could also hear the waves of the ocean outside. The door opened into utter darkness. Tessi could not see how large the cell was. Her torch light was swallowed into the emptiness.

'Ange' she whispered.

Nothing. She moved the torch around, but its dim light barely reached into the far ends of the chamber. Stepping inside, fear blooming in her chest at what she may find. The door slowly closed behind her and just as the latch slipped into place her corona of light showed Ange standing in a corner with blackness surrounding her. The demon had her trapped in its arms with its talons closed over her face and mouth.

Tessi dropped the torch as her legs turned to water and stomach lurched. The shadow let Ange go. She ran straight to Tessi and hugged her.

Tessi spasmed as the demon reached inside her. Ange hung onto her to stop Tessi falling.

'See what you have done. This agony would be over for all if you had given me what I seek.'

'Oh Tessi, please believe me, I cannot.'

Ange watched Tessi convulse on the floor of the chamber as the demon chewed on the fear and sorrow in her sister's heart.

'If you kill the people, I love I will not give it to you' hissed Ange.

'Her children cry for their mother. She may have them back when their blood gives me the tears of the ascendant.'

Tessi stopped convulsing as Voloc let go of her.

'Oh, Tessi, please believe me I cannot let the beast have it for it will kill us anyway.'

Tessi lay unconscious as Ange held her. The glow of Voloc's eyes faded away relieving them of torment for the moment. Ange dragged Tessi toward the wall and placed her head in her lap. She felt the prism around her neck and touched it.

Instantly she lay stranded in emptiness. A huge chasm of dark surrounded her. She was moving with something. She was watching from inside.

Voloc stepped into the fear and chaos that lay in the hearts of the clayborn and began to search again for the custodians. Each time, it felt their nearness. The chain that once bound it to its gaolers dangled inside the pit that held its heart. It saw a spec of light in the distance. Drawing closer, it saw Belmaris. This time instead of the incendiary pain it once felt at the great star's fire, only a prick pierced the shadow warming the broken chain that lay inside. Voloc kept moving towards the flames and soon became close enough to touch the great beacon. It reached in and plucked a piece out and ate it. The chain within burst into flame and with it came the scorching fire that made shadow into ash. The demon exploded into a brilliant flare of heat in the face of Belmaris. The great star thrust the demon into the depths of the void. Awaking, Voloc let the darkness cool the fire in its depths. Voloc's hissing turned to laughter as it lay letting the void knit it together again.

'I am wounded but not destroyed. Soon ancient enemy the battle will be over. Voloc will become the devourer of light. I will rule Caemeris and destroy these usurpers and their clayborn progeny. They light of their memories has led me to their destruction and now I will wait to watch Descendant destroy its brethren and its throne. The way is opened and shall not be closed.'

Ange watched how Voloc's strength surged from the flame of the sun. The prism became cold in her palm. She could see inside the shadow and the realm of light where the custodians had been bound. It wanted to devour the whole world and sun. It could with the prism. It looked at her suddenly but did not seem to care. Its desire lay in ancient memories from its birth. It simply existed to destroy. 'How can I defeat you?' Ange dared to ask. There was silence as the shadow thickened reforming after the flames of the sun had destroyed it. Light is your enemy Ange thought.

'How did you come here?' Ange gripped the prism tighter as she peered into the seeping memories of Voloc. She saw the realm of the custodians; they were there now but in Voloc's memory it was as it had been when light first breached the void. It was magnificent, brighter than any blue sky she had seen. It burned her as she stared. She felt the pain of Voloc. The breach caused the destruction of its purity and split it open so that the shadow haemorrhaged in and light tore the void to shreds. It began in the mists of time far beyond anything Ange could understand. Then she saw the spec inside Norbu's hand. The great forger of rock and stone thrust it out into a vast emptiness of red sand. It was not her homelands but another place. It must be the lands to the south. It was where the plague came from and further. Here is how I came to your world clay born. Your blood called me where it lay mixed with the light and shadow of the jewel of Norbu. The tears of ascendant captured caemeris and trapped it inside the jewel you cling to. Its water mixed with the blood of the clayborn. Now their destinies are chained together. With the bond broken I can destroy you all. Ange realised the gate in the south needed to remain open and she needed to bring the custodians of caemeris back here to destroy Voloc. Its strength grew because its shadow had nothing now to thwart it. Then the darkness reformed. Ange sat with Voloc in an ocean of emptiness. It peered deep into the well of its solitude. For a fleeting moment Ange saw something else watching. It was beyond the void. For the briefest of moments Ange thought she saw a pale outline of a face looking toward them. It held something and thrust it. The burst of light came once more as Voloc relived the first breach of light. Does something else lay beyond Voloc and the realm of light Ange wondered.

'I see you watching Keeper of the Tears.'

Ange let go of the prism. She woke in the dungeon. There was no sign of Voloc. She knew now that she must go with Voloc to keep the bonds between light and shadow together. The gate had to remain open until she could find Norbu and bring them back. But how?

Ange lay with Tessi on the floor together shivering waiting for Voloc to return. The click of the latch letting go on the door broke the silence. Ange moved to pick up the torch which barely had any flame or lint left. No one was there only the empty dark tunnel that led to their prison.

She roused Tessi who sat up.

'Come Tessi. At least let us see the sun and fresh air. I have had no food or water for days.'

'No Ange what if it comes back or the King sees us.'

'If they want us dead sister, they will kill us. For the moment we are free so let us run.'

The girls fled the chamber into the tunnel all the way up to the passageway that led from the central courtyard.

'I know where we can hide but we will go to the kitchens first.' Tessi waved Ange forward to the stairs.

Ange remained hidden in the stairwell that led to the galley. Tessi went in and began to fill her apron with breads and fruit and some cured ham that had been cut off the bone. She heard the cooks and house cleaners laughing in the big pantry room where they were peeling the vegetables for the evening meal.

'This way Ange, there is a place to hide in the gardens. No one will see us.'

In the grotto Tessi looked at Ange in the dappled shade. It had been almost a full moon since the queen had taken them prisoner. Ange's hollow cheeks and thin frail body showed her captivity through the dirty calico tunic she wore.

Ange gobbled a crust of bread and them ham and then lay down in a patch of sunlight.

'I cannot give it away to anyone Tessi.'

'Can I see it?'

Ange took off the prism.

'Hold my hands.'

The girls lay on their stomachs holding the clear stone between them.

Tessi peered into the clear crystal and at first nothing happened but then slowly she felt herself being pulled. Suddenly a tornado surrounded her with voices calling on it. Her sight was blinded by flashes of light followed by swirling clouds coloured like the rainbows after a storm. She walked through the mist treading warily as she could not see what she stood on. Suddenly a large black shape appeared from out of nowhere and began to run towards her. Its snarling was so vicious it made her heart freeze. Then Ange came running behind it screaming telling her to run. The shadow just kept coming. Ange heard the beast's heavy grunts beside her as she sped passed to reach Tessi. Ange grabbed Tessi's hand and pulled over the edge of the mist into a massive chasm. The beast leapt barely missing Tessi's legs. Tessi screamed as she began to fall. She woke in the grotto with late afternoon sunlight shining into her eyes. Ange was peering over her.

'Oh, Ange the demon lives there as well.'

'It goes there searching for the gods.'

'It came toward me; it was a beast more ferocious than the crocodiles of the Mighty Choasa.'

Ange gave Tessi some water as she sat back to think.

'What is that place?'

'It is the world of the god who gave me this jewel. They speak of a realm called Caemeris, the first star.'

Tessi cupped Ange's face in her hands. Tears were spilling down her cheeks as she looked deeply into her eyes 'Oh sister, at least we are together for our last days alive. We will die here Ange. There is no escape if the beast lives in the jewel as well.'

Ange wiped the tears off Tessi's face.

'I know what I need to do now Tessi. I have seen into its memories and heart Tessi. Neither the custodians nor the shadow sees us, they are blind except to their own vision.' Ange dabbed Tessi's face with her sleeve. 'Do you know what they did with my things after they put me in the dungeon?'

'I think they would be in the guard's tower with the key master. The guards are permitted to keep weapons they win during battle and raids so they can use them or barter them.'

Tessi was confused by Ange's question.

'I need my dagger sister. It was a special gift from the Keep of one of the gods. Can you find it and bring it to me?'

'Why it will not harm the beast. Ange please stay hidden here and I will bring you food and water. At least the sun can warm you.'

'Yes, food and water but it is important you bring my dagger and my leather vest and sack as well.'

Ange took two more bites of the bread and then rolled the rest up in the muslin cloth. She put it inside a pouch in her dress. Looking up at Tessi she saw her eyes grow large and then she heard a stern voice.

'Take her to her chamber and the other to the dungeons' ordered Hanni.

One of the guards snatched Ange. Tessi screamed as Hanni and the other guard took her towards the inside of the palace.

Ange sat in the darkness again and picked a bit of curst off and put the rest away. She fingered the prism and knew what she had to do.

'Hurry Sa-Tuc, Gildas and Kado. I do not know how much longer Tessi has to live.'

Ranik sat at the feast seething at everyone who sat before him. The rage had been with him since leaving Esteron City with the news of the escape of the Aeserean's. The generals slopped beer and wine down their fronts as they ate. They held whole legs of pork and goat and gnawed on the bones like packs of wild animals. Ranik looked at Indrad, the general who had led the invasion. Ranik's mind churned as he thought 'Not one of them had managed to bring any of the Royal family back as prisoners. He should flog them all until their bones gleam through their hides.'

Ranik flung an iron goblet at Indrad so disgusted was he at him. It struck the soldier straight in the head. The massive man stood looking around trying to see who did it with a long thin dagger at the ready. He realised where it came from and sat down nodding to his king.

The Queen tensed her grip on the arm of the chair seeing the rage grow in her husband.

'Tias' she warned.

'Hush witch. And get those brats back to the midwife. It is no place for them here at this hour.' She had Noab and Angette sitting in bassinettes near her. She rose and picked up Angette and motioned for one of the serving girls to take Noab.

Ranik walked towards Indrad.

'You slovenly dogs. All of you. You eat my food, take my shelter, drink my wine and feast before me and yet not one of you brought me the bounty I asked for. I wanted the Queen's head before me and her snivelling brothers here to watch me slice it off.'

He picked up a jug and slammed it down on Indrad's head. Blood poured out as the jagged edge tore into his scalp. Ranik brought it down again and again until the general's face was pulverised to the point of not being recognisable.

'I want the Queen of the western lands here before me to make her submit her loyalty to me!'

The hall quietened as Ranik's tirade broke through the drunken revelry. Saliva dribbled down his chin and dripped onto Indrad's smashed head. He looked at it and kicked the slumped body into the stinking mess of sawdust, ale, and blood on the floor.

'Now!' he screamed. Within minutes the hall had cleared

leaving Ranik with a few servants. He sat down and helped himself to another goblet of wine. He had not felt the demon's presence since returning and felt relieved for it. More and more he could feel himself fading into the ever-lightless heart of the creature and losing his own will and strength. His kingdom knew it as well. The generals followed their own war paths without his consent. Nothing had been heard from Faad either. Perhaps the Icelands proved too much even for the captain. He heard a gurgling noise as Indrad began to rouse. Ranik got up and plunged his sword into the soldier's chest.

'Clean this up.'

He took a jug of wine and walked towards the stairs that lead to his chambers. He thought of the queen with the babies. Insane scheming witch! Why was she with them so much? He appeared from the stairwell to see her standing at the window that overlooked the bay with one of the babies still in her arms.

'Giandra what are you doing here? I told you to take the babies to the midwives. Where is the concubine?'

The Queen looked at her husband and wanted to plunge a knife into his chest.

'I am settling the children husband.'

'Give him to me.'

'No, you are drunk, and you may drop him.'

'Give my son to me!' Ranik roared.

Noab started to cry.

'See look what you have done. There little one.' Giandra soothed Noab.

She kissed his forehead and turned her back to Ranik to look out the window.

'Midwife, take Tias to his cradle.'

Hanni ran in flustered when she heard Ranik.

'Now, I order you!'

Hanni curtsied. She went to take Noab, but the Queen would not let go.

'My lady. Please.'

'He is mine Tias. I will put him to bed.'

'He is not yours you barren witch. Put my son down and go back to your chamber to whither into old age and fevered dreams. I should have you thrown in the tower to rot.'

'And what would you do for gold to feed your army and fat belly.'

'I have no need of your gold now Giandra. I have conquered my enemies' lands and their wealth lies in the coffers of Matavia.'

Tias screamed again as Hanni went to take him as the queen's nail dug into his arms. This time it was a high-pitched squeal of pain.

Ranik stormed over to the Queen and wrenched the boy out of her arms and flung him at Hanni. The Queen slashed at Ranik, but he hit her first. She fell to the floor bleeding. The blackness in her eyes matched his as they both fought the urge to see each other dead.

Tessi came running up the stairs as soon as she heard the shrill scream of Noab.

'Hanni what happened?' she stopped suddenly when she saw the King and Queen. Ranik turned and looked at her.

'Why are you dressed like this? You are my concubine, not some serving maid.'

Tessi did not look at him.

'Did you order this?' He looked at his wife on the floor. Noab let out a great howl in the room.

'Get that brat to sleep.'

'Hanni I will help you. My Lord I am sorry.'

'Clean yourself and wait for me.' Tessi gulped with fear.

The Queen got up and sat on a sofa. Blood poured down her lip and the bruise around her eye was already beginning to form.

'You are dying Tias. Look at you. You look a hundred summers old. All the heirs in these walls will not save you from the demon's appetite. The shadow seeks to devour all that it sees. By the time you decide to kill me, you will be too weak to lift the blade to do it.'

She got up and walked past him.

He threw the jug at the wall in anger and hatred at his wife but also, he knew she spoke the truth. Walking into his chamber he saw Tessi pouring hot water into the bath.

'I am not clean. I have prepared some tea for you while I bathe.' He grunted and lay down on the bed.

'Hurry and clean yourself, wretch.' He leered at her and grew stiffer watching her. Her skin was like velvet, soothing not like the Queen. Her skin was like marble stone and as cold to touch he half whispered to himself. 'As cold as that demon that haunts my steps.' He whispered as he closed his eyes.

Tessi could hardly breathe and her stomach lurched with revulsion at the thought of what was to come.

Breathing deeply to calm her voice she spoke 'My Lord, may I ask a favour?'

'What?'

'I would like to see my sister and take her some food and water. She lies deep within the dungeons.'

'The demon wants her. She is no concern of yours.'

'I know my Lord, but just once to see her.'

Ranik nodded 'Hurry up.'

Tessi pulled some herbs out of a sack hidden behind chair. She quietly placed it back on the floor behind the curtain. She had managed to find Ange's dagger and satchel and some galden weed in the galley. She remembered Hanni telling her it was good for sleeping, makes you go so deep into your dreams you will not remember the nightmares of the daylight.

Tessi crushed the leaves some into a cup of tea. She walked quietly over to the King as he lay in his nightshirt.

'Here my Lord. It will relax us both.' Tessi pretended to sip the drink and then offered the rest to Ranik.

He grunted as he took the cup and gulped it down. Tessi waited.

22

Bay of Tears

The Graan stood on the edge of the plateau surrounding the Bay of Tears. Kado had seen the falcons fly overhead two days before when they had crossed Vale of the Hunted alerting the city to their arrival. In the distance as the sun set the white towers of the palace dulled to grey as a thunderstorm quickened around the bay. Beneath the shadow of the storm lay a greater one as Matavian soldiers began to march towards them ready to battle the Icemen of the north. Kado gripped his sword tightly not wanting to fight this battle knowing they would be defeated. The glimmer of hope that Sa still lived remained in his mind and kept him moving with Gildas.

'How big is the outpost Captain?' Gildas asked Faad.

'A few hundred' he replied.

'Tyl collect a few who need some practice.'

'It is not that simple clansman. It may only be a few hundred, but they are the deadliest forces we have. They are only used at utmost need or for special orders of the King. For our few hundred your thousand will be slaughtered.'

'And at the palace how many remain on guard?' Gildas

341

continued ignoring Faad's warning.

'A garrison of five hundred.'

'Well Graanar do you still think we need practice.' Gildas looked at Axl and Tyl.

'I'll gather a few' replied Tyl.

'Take the dog! He is keen for a feed.'

Gildas took the muzzle off Nekoda and gave the leash to Tyl. The dog strained to run as Tyl left.

'Come Prince, we will go ahead with the Captain towards the city and the rest will follow. They will see the many and we can be like the rats of the Enan forest, silent thieves in the night. Faad will have his own victory and the Graanar shall have their fill of spilled Matavian blood.'

'You are no different to Ranik and this creature that commands his mind Gildas. Your thirst for battle is as insatiable.' Grimaced Kado at the thought of another bloody fight.

'Ay Prince, I am as cursed as they are, for in our quest for destruction we bring our own.'

'Graanar towards the city. Make haste, the rains want to wash us before we bathe in the stinking blood of the Matavian scum below.'

An almighty roar spread across the plains as the Matavians and Graan met. Thunder applauded in ear splitting peals followed by lightning bolts spearing into the earth setting the trees ablaze. Gildas ran at full speed with Axl alongside. He bared his teeth in a snarl as he sliced through the first lines of soldiers. His blade glistened as the rain began to fire down like rocks expelled by the turbulent skies. Kado could see Faad getting ahead of he and Gildas.

'Get him Prince, I will follow.'

Kado followed Faad who had gone down into a deep gully to trek towards the city walls. It was thickly covered with shrubs allowing him to remain hidden from the battle around him. Kado threw his dagger at him catching him in the shoulder as he went to get away. Stumbling he collected a rock to attack Kado but Kado high kicked it out of the way and tackled Faad to the ground.

'You will lead us to where this demon sleeps Faad or I will slit your throat now.' Kado lay on top of him binding his hands. 'I knew you would betray us.'

Faad spat at Kado 'We are all dead prince.'

Gildas came crashing through and saw them both on the ground. Grabbing Faad he shoved him forward.

Soon the putrid stench of the sewer met them as they made their way into thicker bushes. Kado saw a stream of sewerage running from a culvert dug under the wall of the city. He gagged as he entered the tunnel following Faad and Gildas.

'I will rub Ranik's nose in his own shit' swore Gildas had put a piece of his shirt over his face to block some of the smell.

As they moved further in towards the centre of the palace the stench of the sewer was replaced by the fetid smell of rotten flesh. Kado meditated silently hoping it was not Sa or Ange as well as to stop himself from heaving everywhere. Gildas smashed open door after door only to reveal horrific scenes of brutality. Gildas had run his sword through one man that lay alive on a rack, emaciated and barely recognisable for the wounds on him. His feet were rotting away with rats chewing on him.

'Butchers!' Kado hissed. 'Gildas this is their slaughterhouse for where they make their trinkets from the skins of their victims.'

'Are there any more tunnels?' Gildas grabbed Faad by the throat.

'Only the last one. We need to go back this way. This leads under the kitchen and bathes. Ranik is often down there so I think that must be where the creature dwells, away from the light. If your companions are alive, they will be there.'

Gildas and Kado pushed Faad to continue but he did not move.

'I will go no further. Cut my bonds, so I may leave. I have fulfilled my part of the bargain.'

'So, you can go and warn Ranik. For all we know it may be a trap.'

Gildas pushed Faad to keep walking but the captain refused to move.

'I will not walk to the creature's lair. I have felt its icy fingers in my heart and head.'

'Ay and I have felt its claws and teeth in my flesh. Move you stinking chunt bastid.'

Kado took a torch from the wall and led the way into the largest of the tunnels. It was completely silent. The sounds of the battle above did not penetrate the layers of rock above them. They came to the door at the very end of the passage. Gildas heaved his axe, splintering the wood and latch. Kado pushed through and saw Ange and another girl lying on the ground. The other girl was giving Ange a drink. Ange lifted her head and saw Gildas and Kado.

'I knew you would come.' Then she lay back down.

Tessi stood.

'Are you the one Ange spoke of? Please take us away from here. I am her sister.'

Gildas went to them. Tessi cringed at the size of him as he knelt. He gently picked Ange up feeling how light she. He saw how thin her face had become.

'Have you seen another? She is called Sa' asked Kado.

'Yes, but she is not here. She left with the creatures to find you.'

Kado's heart leapt as he heard that Sa was alive. Gildas handed Ange to Kado.

'Take them and leave. Ranik awaits my blade.'

'No, I have to get my children. They are with the Queen' pleaded Tessi.

'Kado take the girl! Get the stone as far as away as possible as you can' commanded Gildas.

Kado picked up Ange. She looked up at him. In her hands she held her dagger and satchel. She smiled at Kado and then went limp in his arms. Panicking he shook her, but she roused again.

'Ange, I thought you had died.'

'I am alive Kado and so is Sa. She said she would find you and bring you back.'

'Here Prince this is the way we came. Go back and find Axl and Tyl.'

Pulling him close he whispered 'We will meet at the Vale of the Hunted at the large oak. Girl come with me!' calling to Tessi.

Kado ran with Ange his heart pounding both with fear and hope that he would see Sa again.

'Now Faad where is Ranik?' Gildas had his sword to his throat

'This way.'

Soon they entered onto the ramp that led to the courtyard. Shouts and the sound of a thousand arrows being launched echoed around the cobbled stones and marble walls. Faad led them into the main hall of the palace.

'No, cried Tessi, I want to get my children.'

'We will get them girl, but I must kill Ranik first.'

'Ranik will be in the tower. It is where the royal family take refuge if the city is under siege. The children will be there as well concubine' spoke Faad.

Faad's jaw clenched as he sensed the end was near for the maniacal rule of Ranik. His heart exploded with lust and ambition to be rid of the tyrant. Gildas and Tessi saw the fever in the captain's eyes.

The inner chambers of the palace were empty with only intermittent shouts and cannon blasts coming from the battle outside breaking the silence. Gildas could hear the war cries of the Graanar as they fought their way closer. Entering the throne room Faad lead them to an arched oak door concealed by red drapes. He tapped on it. Inside the sound of a dozen bolts being released echoed across the chamber.

Gildas readied himself as the door opened revealing three heavily armoured guards. He lashed at them killing them instantly. A spiral staircase rose before him, without hesitating he raced up it. Tessi and Faad followed but could not keep up with his pace. They heard a massive cracking sound of wood being smashed, followed by shrieks.

Faad reached the door to the tower chamber. There were four guards lying dead on the floor. The Queen and midwife each held a child. Gildas held Ranik by his white hair with his blade at the tyrant's throat. Tessi entered breathless and snatched Noab from the Queen.

'You Matavian scum are all the same. Snivelling bits of dung that crumble to dust in the wind without your armour and blades. Where is your demon now King?' Gildas raised his sword and clove Ranik's head in two. The blood spurted up into the air and onto his face. He whipped his sword out and sliced through the neck cleanly and watched it roll onto the floor. Tessi was barely able to stand up so sickened by what she saw but she managed keep hold of Noab.

Gildas picked up the head and flung it at Faad 'Show them now who is their commander.'

As Faad caught the head of Ranik. Gildas cut his arm and let his blood drip onto the blade. The he nicked Faad's cheek. 'Remember who gave you the rule of this land. Remember the blade of Tarentess has marked you now. You are beholden to its command when the time comes.'

He wiped the sword on Ranik's body.

'Is this one yours as well girl?' asked Gildas pointing to Angette.

Tessi nodded barely able to breath. Gildas tore the girl from Hanni and started for the doorway.

Gildas thrust Tessi forward to leave but suddenly a dagger flew across the room and struck Tessi in the shoulder. She dropped Noab. Gildas turned and saw the Queen standing with blazing red eyes and almost snarling. Hanni shot forward as Noab rolled onto the ground out of Tessi's arms. She grabbed the baby and stood behind the Queen.

'No, give him to me!'

Tessi tried to get up but collapsed from the pain of the dagger in her back.

Gildas waved his sword at the Queen but her eyes flared with red.

'You cannot hide from it. Take your slaves and their jewel. Leave the child and I will not call the spirit back. I will spare the child.' She gently stroked Noab's cheek. On her thumb sat the thimble of poison.

Gildas hesitated. He put Angette in his leather strap across his battle vest and flung Tessi over his shoulder.

'Noab!' Tessi screamed watching Noab struggling in Hanni's arms to be let go but Gildas ignored. She watched the Queen smiling viciously at her. Angette's high pitched screams rang out as Gildas raced down the staircase and into the hall towards the passages from where they had entered. He grunted wanting to leave all of them and join his brothers in battle. As he ran into the tunnels again, he could feel the blood from Tessi dripping down his arm. The girl had gone quiet suddenly leaving only the baby's screams ringing in his ear.

He lay Tessi down gently. The wound was bleeding heavily. He tore some of her dress and bandaged the cut in her shoulder. He then tore a curtain off the wall and made a holster for the baby and Tessi. Tying it around himself he secured them both with the babe on his chest and Tessi on his back.

'Chunt basitd Gol warrior you've become a clan wife. You'll grow tits next.' He muttered to himself as he raced in the drains following the stench where it was strongest. Soon he found the culvert where they had entered. The rain had stopped but the clouds were blacker and lower. The melee of the battle had drawn closer to the city and palace. He could see sparks in the air where blades were clashing together. He gripped his sword and felt the energy surge into him. Everything slowed, every movement around him crystallised around him as he walked into the battle with Tessi and Angette secured to his body. He slayed Ranik's soldiers as if they were blades of wheat under sheath at harvest time. A Graanar came at him. Missing him by inches he pushed his way through killing as many as he could. The wounds inflicted by his enemy felt like the bites of gnats upon his skin.

The road towards the plateau rose before him. Axl signalled to him in the distance. The soldiers had thinned with most now fighting along the walls of the city below. He could feel the vibrations of the baby's cries on his chest, but she and the mother were unharmed.

'You will be a warrior when you grow with the stain of blood and battle on your new heart youngling.' Gildas whispered as he swept through the Matavians.

Kado, Axl and Tyl stood above him on the plateau hidden beneath a massive oak tree and its buttressed roots. Inside its trunk lay Ange. She roused when she saw Tessi and Gildas.

'We cannot rest here. We keep going to the northwest. Axl call the Graanar back and tell them to make for the passage of Yullaan in the north.'

Suddenly the air seemed to thicken around them. The battle cries below dulled as a massive clap of thunder shook the earth and trees.

'Make haste, the fortune of the Ice Mother has thinned.'

Gildas led them towards the northern edge of salt plains. Before them stretched the plateau along with a hundred Matavian soldiers ready for battle. Faad stood at the front leading the fearsome battalion. Gildas roared in frustration. He let out the cry of the Graan to call the clansmen to the valley.

'Protect the girl. Do not let them get her.' He gave Tessi and Angette to Axl. Put them somewhere safe.

The thunder came again almost knocking everyone over. Gildas took his sword and held it to the skies. A white flash of lightning came directly to it and coursed through his body. Kado stood with him while holding Ange tightly. Gildas ran towards the Matavians with Tyl and a hundred Graanar who had returned from the outpost.

A flash of lightning whipped across the plain and in the distance Kado saw something that made his heart leap. Not believing it at first another flash revealed Sa Tuc riding high on the shoulder of one of the demon's creatures. As Gildas fought with Faad, Sa ordered the creatures to attack the soldiers. Suddenly bodies were being thrown up into the air.

Kado laughed 'Look Ange, our assassin has come for us.'

Ange smiled.

'Put me down Kado. I want to fight' she spoke.

'No Ange you are too weak, and the demon may return at any moment.'

'You must save Tessi and her babies. They are all I have now.

I cannot die while I hold the stone Kado and the demon cannot steal it from me. Put me down so I can fight. Another battle awaits me, and I need to sharpen my blade.'

Kado put her down not understanding what she meant but followed the little girl as she put on her leather vest and pulled her dagger out. She winked at Kado and then turned and raced towards the battle.

'Run to one of the creatures when you are near and get them to take you from here.' She called back to him.

Gildas had seen the assassin and roared with victory but then he had seen Ange run into the melee.

'Assassin get the girl and take her.' He roared.

Sa looked down and saw Ange stabbing and fighting.

'Guardian grab the child.'

First moved towards her but stopped as an almighty roar blasted across the air. Suddenly a black shadow formed in the clouds and began to move towards the ground. The shape was like the Aracnine but drew in the light around it and seeped deep into the recesses of the eyes and hearts of all who gazed upon Voloc. The smell of ashes and fire seemed to come with it making the air unbreathable. Everything stilled as Voloc took form on Arglethium under Belmaris watch. A gaping hole lay in its chest but inside sat a small burning flame. It took two of the guardians and tore them to shreds; First screamed with the pain of it. Sa could feel the loss within herself.

'Bring me the tears of the ascendant.' Voloc's voice was thick with malice and power. Ange saw the shadow and knew her time had come.

Gildas saw the demon walking towards her and grabbed her.

He held the gift of Norbu's keep towards the shadow that towered above him.

'This is another gift of the god of this earth. Feel it shadow and see who shall rule this world.'

Voloc chuckled as he felt the sting of the blade in its talons. The flame inside its chest flared as Gildas blade swept near to it. Voloc screeched with pain. It battered Gildas sending him into the air. Ange flew out of his arm as he slammed into the earth. The demon followed him to finish the Ice Lord off. It reached forward to pick Gildas up to crush him and the sword.

'I have tasted Belmaris' fire and not been destroyed. I reign here now, and all shall be my servants. I have come to bring the calm of the void, my dominion stolen by Caemeris and its progeny the Custodians. Death is your destiny, as peace my cage.'

Ange ran towards Voloc and took out the prism. It shone brightly turning the darkness of the night into day.

'Give it to me. The void is the spawn of creation not the usurpers of the caemeris.'

Ange looked down on Gildas.

'Search for me in the south. Keep the way open. I will return. I must bring back the custodians.'

Ange closed her hand over the prism and looked deep inside as she latched onto one of Voloc's claws. Gildas, Sa, Kado and Tessi watched her collapse on the ground. Voloc's screech erupted across the battlefield and sky. The shadow transformed into the wolf and with its massive jaws gathered Ange into its mouth

Gildas attacked it with his blade full of the power of Norbu and cut the black hide. The wolf growled ferociously but did not let go of Ange and instead leapt over Gildas and disappeared.

'After them Aracnine' roared Sa but they did not move.

'First I order you to follow the demon. The Aracnine can still see where it lies.'

'Yes, it goes to the gate that lies deep in the dead heart of the desert. Its power grows as ours wanes. We will not follow until the Aracnine are restored and you have taken the bonds as ruler. The flame of Belmaris lies within the shadow now and with it the light of the Caemeris has followed. The first wars shall begin once more, the wars which created the clayborn.'

Gildas stood heaving until he felt an arrow strike his back. In blind fury he unleashed his anger on the remaining Matavians killing at least thirty of those who stood near. Gildas found himself looking into Faad's eyes. He swung his blade with lightning speed but stopped it flush to the soldier's neck. Faad stood rigid waiting for the lethal blow. He glanced across at a soldier ready to defend him, but his look told the man to stand back. He had seen Gildas' strength and victory could still lie with the Icemen.

'Why do you hesitate? Slice me through now' Faad looked directly into Gildas eyes.

'To see the demon, tear your flesh is more satisfying to me then to stain my blade with a skulking coward.'

Suddenly hordes of Matavian soldiers began to spill over the ridge from the city below. A few hundred Graan stood surrounded by a thousand of their enemy.

'So, what will it be clansman, another battle until we are all dead here on the plains and our blood baptises the Bay of Tears.

Or do we unite to kill this demon once and for all.'

'Gildas we will not defeat them here. There are too many of your men gone. We must go.' Kado spoke as he walked with Tessi and Angette.

'Captain Faad, please I want my son. The Queen still has him.' Tessi was holding Angette, tears streaming down her face from seeing Ange being taken by the wolf. Her feet squelched in the blood and gore of the battle.

'I will let you leave Graanar on the condition that when war comes, we fight our common enemy. It cannot defeat all of us. Not with that blade of yours and your allies here.' Faad looked at the Aracnine.

'Gildas, do not let any more of your people die. It is our only chance as revile as it is to be allies with these vermin to destroy this creature?' Kado looked intently Gildas but his eyes were like stone. His blade glinting with the red rays of the dawn ready to slice through Faad's neck.

'The girl's child, give him to her.'

'No, he will be our ransom. The Queen is useful clansman and she must be kept happy.'

'No! Give me my son. She will kill him, please.' Tessi collapsed in tears.

Gildas grimaced with anger not moving or saying anything. Then Tyl walked up to him and placed the blunt end of his axe on Gildas arm to force him to lower the sword.

'The Ice Bear has been with us so far Graanar. Take this offer now until we can be strong again. Ever her blessings are tainted with the curse of the ice. One boon to live for victory on another day, bought with the ice lords bones lying next to the scum of Matavia. If the curse of the ice mother brings defeat to this shadow that torments our lands, then her curse is gladly borne by this Graanar.'

Gildas looked at his clansman and then at Faad.

'By the first turn of the blue dawns of the next cycle we will gather to defeat the shadow Faad. Matavia will fight along with the clansmen and any men that wish to see their lands protected from the veil of evil that now clouds all of our eyes.'

'Up girl. If the child is dead before we return Faad, then you and the Queen will be fed to the bear herself.'

'No!' cried Tessi but Gildas picked up Angette and put her in the harness he had made. He turned towards the clansmen that were left and cried.

'Graanar!'

Their response echoed over the valley and plains to their battle master's call.

Sa and Kado gathered Tessi from the ground as she sobbed for Noab and Ange.

Nekoda began to howl as the sun rose over the plateau, looking for Ange. Blood poured down its side from where a blade had struck him.

Gildas began to run north with Sa, Kado, Tessi, Axl and Tyl following. Nekoda barked once more and then ran to join Gildas at the front.

'Hold steady men. Let them pass.' Faad slumped on his sword as Gildas left. The power the Graanar wielded was not of this world and would have easily defeated what army stood here. He saw the Queen alight from a carriage with a baby in her arms.

'Well done, Captain, you will be generously rewarded.'

'Can you still hear the demon?'

'Oh yes, and this little one's blood is strong and calls to it as well.' She nuzzled Noab into her bosom as she watched the Graan leave.

'Your time to rule for a thousand cycles lies close Giandra. Is there a way to cage the beast?'

'I shall rule with its power. I will kill the girls and keep the stone of power for me to hold it in its cage. With it and these children I will rule with not even death to defeat me. But we cannot let the way for girl to return to be opened.'

'We will lead them all to their deaths. Including the Graanar' replied Faad.

Epilogue

Vipax felt something touch its snout. The sentinel tasted the water. The foulness sickened the mighty serpent. Opening its eyes, a massive whale, half rotted and stinking lay upon the seabed. Its calf lay dead around their mother. Vipax uncurled herself to go into the ocean once again to see what poison now lay in her home. Blinking, her eyes became dulled by the decay. The world of Vipax was dying and the first created would perish along with it. Breaking the surface of the ocean she soared into the air, fangs glistening and scales changing the colour of the waves to gold and green. But the poison of Voloc had done its work. Her mind confused, she called for Lido and Norbu, but none answered. She called for Uchala; she did not answer but the scent of her blood remained. Then the memory came of the custodians, the last of their kind to be formed had entered the world. And chained to the creations of Caemeris came the shadow. The tears of the god had been reformed in a place where they were never meant to exist. Sticking out her tongue to taste the air and sea, Vipax soon knew of the malignancy of Voloc that festered in the heart of Arglethium;

growing evermore as nothing stopped the power of the gift upon which the evil fed. Norbu had brought the gift here which now beckoned the dark. The tears were an abomination created from the sundering of the descendant and its power a lethal blow to the clayborn. The world now teetered on the abyss with the death of Uchala and the custodians lost. The scales of the serpent began to glitter in the sun and as she swam the breadth of her waters, the mighty serpent ate the decay left in Voloc's wake, restoring life again. But Vipax mind, filled with the venom of the shadow, came to a distorted resolve: the stone and all who sought its power would be destroyed.

— — —

Gildas looked across the massive valley below and saw how the forest had begun to whither. He fingered his sword, each time feeling the pulse of the power it held run through his hands and arm. He walked back into the chamber that held the stone basin. Looking into the black liquid he saw his face reflected perfectly. He could see his history written on every gouged scar and chiselled wound. The girl could not be dead or the prism fully in the grasp of the demon as the world would have been obliterated by now. Ange had known something which would stop the demon from complete victory. The image of the girl defiantly walking towards the demon kept running through his mind; if a cripple can stop a behemoth of the underworld then who is Gildas Gol? A heart ferocious and lost to the bonds of human emotion felt a kinship with the bravery and determination Ange had shown in those last moments before she was taken. The desire to fight until he died blazed within him.

Except it was not his glory that he lusted for, but to see that the world was not destroyed before its time. His desire to stand with his fellow warrior equal in courage, and determination not to be defeated, coursed through every sinew and bone of his body.

The surface of the basin rippled just slightly as the reflection of his face faded and he saw a hooded figure bent over a pool. The person was drinking. On their back was holstered a sword and bow. The figure turned and looked directly at Gildas. A smile crept over the clansman's face.

'The door must remain open Keeper of Tarentess.' Ange spoke back to Gildas. 'Be ready when I return.'

'The blade of Tarentess and the legions of Arglethium await your call Desert Dweller. Battletrix maimed and small carve our path to victory over the shadow.'

A thundering crack rocked the Keep breaking the image in the basin. Gildas went out of the chamber and saw Axl and Tyl looking towards the vast tundra on the northside of the mountain. As he reached the edge, the mist cleared briefly letting the vista of their homelands open before them. In the far distance a miniscule black line snaked its way across the glacial horizon where an ice sheet had broken off.

'It is the end of our lands, Graanar' Tyl spoke forlornly, his broad shoulder slightly stooped.

'You shall be defeated Shadow. Our end has not come yet.' Gildas stood clenching his sword until his knuckles turned white.

Tyl looked at his clansman and saw that Gildas' icy blue eyes had turned the same cold grey as the metal of his sword and the walls of the Keep. The steely gaze that came from them was as unyielding as the mountain they stood within.

The story continues in
Book Three
Descendant's Throne

Appendix

THE CLAY BORN OF ARGLETHIUM

Ange Tsaed: from the village of Kensai located in the eastern deserts

Gildas Gol of the Graan: former warlord and Chieftain of the Graan Clans of the Northern Icelands

Sa-Tuc: Assassin to Emperor Ko

Kado Kodrax: Heir to the Drax Magisterium

Bensah El Bunani: Trader and family friend of Ange and Tessi

Tessi Tsaed: Sister to Ange

Nekoda: Wild dog / hyena cross breed, companion to Bensah and Ange

Angette (Mordraag) Tsaed-Ranik: Daughter of Tessi Tsaed

Noab (Tias) Tsaed-Ranik: Son of Tessi Tsaed

Lord Tias Ranik: Suzerain of the Lands of Matavia

Queen Giandra Ranik: wife of Lord Ranik, Queen of Matavia

Captain Piotr Faad: Knight Captain of the Matavia Garrison

Queen Nene Des Vries: Ruler of Aeserea

Prince Draved Des Vries: Brother of Queen Nene

Prince Dronagh Des Vries: Brother of Queen Nene

Lord Cotus Medret: First Knight and Commander of Aeserean Forces

Lord Jonas Warick: First Knight of the Cavalry

Lord Kyle Yonan: First Knight of the Cavalry

Jarrod Gol – Elder Chieftain of the Graan, brother to Gildas

Caelwyn Gol – Elder Clan Wife of the Graan, wife of Jarrod

Tyl of Timmo – Clansman of Timmo Clan

Axl of Timmo – Clansman of Timmo Clan

CAEMEXA BORN OF CAEMERIS

The Custodians

Baachelaus (Descendant): Diarch of Caemeris, spirit of the unknown, binder of yearning & fulfilment

Assumpta (Ascendant): Diarch of Caemeris, spirit of the clay born, binder of light & shadow

Norbu: Elder of Creation, Custodian of Arglethium

Lido: Water Custodian

Seraf: Fire Custodian

Aerean: Wind Custodian

Voloc: Dark Custodian, Born of Oblyquixiton

Belmaris: Sun

Magmeris: Dead sun, sister to Belmaris

THE SERVANTS

The Guardians, Aracnine: eight in number,
    jailers of Baachelaus
The Orynth: YU, EY, PO, XI, AX, VA. Friends to Norbu
Uchala: Sentinel, Spider in form
Vipax: Sentinel, Serpent in form

About the Author

Clare Rolfe is an Australian self-published author. Her first novel was the dystopian fantasy Ten Letters to Delacroix's Tomb, released in 2016. Her inspirations for writing include philosophy, the natural world and science. She dabbles in poetry and flash fiction and is a routine blogger on-line of her work. Find her on her webpage www.clrolfe.com

Voloc's Reign continues the story from *Ascendant's Tear* as the second book in the Legend of Caemeris series.

Stay in Touch
Facebook: Clare Rolfe / CL Rolfe
Twitter: @rolfe_cl